URSHURAK

URSHURAK

Created by
THE BROTHERS HILDEBRANDT
and
JERRY NICHOLS

URSHURAK
A BANTAM BOOK

Copyright © The Brothers Hildebrandt 1979.
All rights reserved.
ISBN 0-553-01166-9
PRINTING HISTORY:
First U.S. Edition: September 1979

FULL COLOR URSHURAK COVER POSTERS
WE HAVE PRODUCED A LIMITED EDITION OF FULL-COLOR
REPRODUCTIONS OF THE URSHURAK COVER (18″ × 24″). IF
YOU WOULD LIKE TO OWN THIS PRINT, JUST SEND $5.00
(PLUS $1.50 FOR POSTAGE AND HANDLING) TO:

BANTAM BOOKS, INC.
DEPT. CN-5
666 FIFTH AVENUE
NEW YORK, NEW YORK 10019

Bantam Books are published by Bantam Books, Inc. Its trademark
consisting of the words "Bantam Books" and the portrayal of a bantam,
is registered in the United States Patent and Trademark Office and in
other countries.
Marca Registrada.
Bantam Books, Inc. 666 Fifth Avenue, New York, New York 10019

Published simultaneously in the United States and Canada

PRINTED IN THE UNITED STATES OF AMERICA
0 9 8 7 6 5 4 3 2 1

Art Direction and Design by Ian Summers and Sally Bass

DEDICATION

To my wife, Diana, and my children, Mary, Laura and Gregory, for their support and encouragement from the beginning.
—Gregory Hildebrandt

To my Mother, first of all, who made me look for the elves and fairies when I was very young. And to my wife, Rita, and son, Charles, for their love and understanding.
— Timothy Hildebrandt

To my wife, Julie, for her typing, editing and Amazon philosophy. And to my children, Matt, Miles and Danny, for their reflective listening.
— Jerry Nichols

ACKNOWLEDGMENTS

We wish to thank the following people for their contributions:

Ian Summers, our agent.

Sydny Weinberg, Betty Ballantine, Nancy Wiesenfeld, and Ken Leish for editing, for their patience and understanding.

Oscar Dystel who believed in Urshurak from the beginning.

Joe Scrocco, John Enteman and Eli Schoenfield for business and legal involvement.

Bill McGuire, Dominic Tombro and Dale Trimmer for musical composition, editing and posing.

Joanna Jervis, Ron Galbraith, Peter Dominick, Mark Feldman, Bob Taylor, John Taylor, Bob Petillo, Nicholas DiGesu, and Sharon Brady for posing.

Hugh Cottingham for the title.

Rita Hildebrandt for the costumes.

Sally Bass for design and empathy.

Irving Elkin, Harry Wolf, Rick Meyerowitz, Michael Goodwin, Diane Watson and Ed Summer for their very early encouragement.

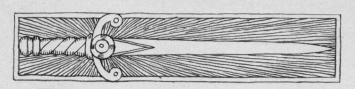

"...And lo, before the sun sets on the Day of Fulfillment, the two of the same blood shall meet~ and both shall be fulfilled.

But only one shall bear away the Crownhelm of the White Elves.

And in that hour shall be decided the fate of the land of Urshurak,..."

1

THE FOREST OF DELVINOR

On the morning of Hugh Oxhine's departure from his home high in the Bolgad Mountains of Vandor, the slanting rays of the spring sun glistened on the snowcapped peaks. He left behind him the fresh graves of his wife and children, and began his lonely descent to the foothills, traveling northeast across rolling grasslands toward the great Forest of Delvinor.

The first day passed, and the second, and the third. The tall archer pushed on across the seemingly endless expanse. On the seventh day the gentle terrain gave way to sharp inclines and deep gulleys with scattered trees dotting the landscape. He had been traveling with only the briefest of stops for food and rest, and the intense pace of the journey began to take its toll. Fatigue and hunger ate at his powerful physique. Only his burning hatred gave him strength to follow the trail left by the murderers of his beloved family.

The tracks were unlike any the Vandorian had ever seen—some half-score creatures that were neither man nor beast. The sun was nearly lost beyond the distant Bolgad Mountains when the tracks led Hugh to a long rise. He labored up to the crest and stopped, drawing a deep breath. The fabled Forest of Delvinor lay before him, dominating the entire horizon. A long corridor of towering trees extended toward him from

the main body of the forest. These were the Trocalas—the "ancient ones." A deep ravine, evening
mist rising from it, cut straight across the terrain
between the avenue of Trocalas and the crest where
the Vandorian stood. One great fallen Trocala
spanned the ravine, creating a living bridge, and
before it rose a huge stone portal. The tracks led
straight to it.

Hugh began a slow descent and paused beneath
the portal, staring up in wonder, amazed at its
massive construction and ancient origin—so evident
in the pitted, worn stone. He traversed the tree-bridge
and entered the long corridor of Trocalas. The trees
towered up, their foliage forming a canopy some
three hundred feet above. The archer followed the
tracks of his quarry, his momentary wonder replaced
by deadly intent. At last he entered the main body of
the forest.

The tall man moved slowly into the cloaked silence
of Delvinor, and the path of the creatures became
extremely difficult to follow. Hugh was acutely aware
of how easily his quarry could be concealed, and he
stopped all movement at the slightest sound that
came from the undergrowth. Even this halting ad-
vance ceased when all signs of the creatures disappeared, lost in the cushioned mosses of the forest
floor. For a moment he stood in doubt, filled with
frustrated anger. Then, off to his right, he detected a
slight movement of wind in the foliage. He followed
the rustling of the leaves and presently it brought him
to the bank of a swift-flowing river curving through
the forest. In the soft earth of the bank were sets of
deep, freshly made tracks. A surge of anger drove
Hugh at a trot along the trail. Far up ahead he could
hear the frantic cawing of crows, and he began to run,
leaping across fallen branches and the huge roots
that reached toward the water. Rocks began to appear
in the river's midst, and the water bubbled and
churned over and around them. Then, beneath the
sound of the rapids and the strident excitement of the

birds, the deep rumbling of falling water emerged. A bend in the river revealed a roaring waterfall cascading into a rocky chasm lost in clouds of mist.

And here the Vandorian at last confronted the creatures that had initiated his mission of vengeance. They were hideous brutes, man-like but huge. Their backs were hunched and they were covered with coarse fur. Long, sinewy forearms carried formidable clawed hands; their heads appeared much like those of giant rats. The brutish creatures snarled and growled horribly as they attacked their intended victims—a pair of Dwarfs and a slender youth who had been pressed back to the very edge of the precipice. In desperation the Dwarfs suddenly shifted the emphasis of their fighting to the offensive, shouting angrily and wielding their battle-axes with such ferocity that their attackers were unable to gain further advantage.

But the blond-haired lad was unable to reverse his position of extreme peril. His only weapon was a short sword, and he appeared likely to fall prey at any moment to the rat-creatures. He was kept in constant motion warding off attacks from the trio of brutes, while only the yawning chasm guarded his back.

Hugh paused for but an instant. He reached for an arrow just as the youth, whirling to ward off an attacker, stumbled, falling to one knee. A rat-beast roared with triumph and leaped forward, his jaws agape. But his lust for the kill went unfulfilled. A Vandorian arrow struck the brute with deadly force, the steel head buried in the muscle of his neck. The huge creature staggered, clawing at the arrow shaft. Then he toppled, falling a hundred feet to the swift water below. Almost in one motion, the archer drew and notched a second arrow, aimed and let fly. The arrow sang to its mark, and a second beast dropped. A third successful shot was impossible. The youth and his remaining attacker were locked in combat. Hugh dropped his bow and raced toward them, drawing his knife as he ran. But he was an instant too late. The rat-creature powered through the lad's defense, sinking his long fangs into the boy's shoulder. The youth screamed out with pain, and fell. Then the broad-shouldered Vandorian was atop the beast, wrenching the rat-like head away from the throat of the helpless boy.

The brute snarled in surprise and turned with incredible speed to attack his new foe. The antagonists struggled furiously, rolling across the mist-covered rocks but, finally, the superior size of the creature and the long toll of Hugh's journey became telling factors. The archer was pinned beneath the brute, his head forced back over the cliff's edge. The terrible jaws were only inches from his throat. Feeling the heat of the snarling creature's breath, the archer called on the last of his strength. He heaved against the smothering weight holding him down. He managed to free his right arm to drive his dagger deep into the shaggy throat. Gagging at the fetid gush of blood, Hugh shoved the dead weight of the beast away and freed his weapon.

But the sounds of combat that had rivaled the roaring water had died. The red-bearded Dwarfs stood over two slain rat-creatures, while the remainder of the murdering pack retreated hastily toward the safety of the trees. The Dwarfs ran to the side of the unconscious youth. One of them dropped to his knees, putting his ear to the lad's breast, eyes wide with fear.

"His heartbeat is very weak!" The Dwarf's voice trembled.

The other spoke directly to Hugh. "Sir! Our thanks must be of the briefest for we have to get the lad to help at once. Erbin and I cannot carry him. We need your further assistance—" He paused, for Hugh's attention was on the forest where his quarry had disappeared.

"The creatures will escape," he muttered.

"It matters not," the Dwarf instantly responded, and Erbin, cradling the youth's head, shouted, "We must hurry! His chances are poor, at best. If you don't help us, and that immediately, he's certain to die! Damn it, man! You can't waste all our effort..."

Hugh looked into the faces of the Dwarfs, one pleading, one angry. He strode to the stricken boy, stooped over him, and lifted him in his arms. "One of you carry my bow," he said, "it's back there on the bank."

"This way!" cried Erbin, heading toward the woodland. Hugh followed on the run, the limp body of the boy sagging against his chest. Behind the scurrying Dwarfs, Hugh went deeper into the great forest. At regular intervals one or the other of the youth's companions glanced back to make certain that Hugh was not falling far behind. In truth, the tall Vandorian was having considerable difficulty in keeping up the furious pace set by the Dwarfs. He was almost completely exhausted. His body was bruised and cut from his rolling struggle across the rocks. The shirt beneath his tunic was wet with his own blood. He glanced down at the lifeless face of the youth. The long, blond hair had fallen away to reveal the strangely pointed shape of the lad's ears.

"Press on, sir!" exhorted the voice of the Dwarf whose name Hugh did not yet know. The tall man had fallen considerably behind, and he struggled to catch up. His breathing was tortured, and pain now accompanied his every stride. Presently his vision began to blur and all of his surroundings to blend. Ahead, a brilliant light suddenly emerged and moved toward him. It sped forward, leaving a trail of sparks, accompanied by a rhythmic drumming of hoofbeats. The archer shook his head, attempting to clear it. He heard the shouting of the Dwarfs... and then the shouting and the hoofbeats and the drumming of his own heart, the surroundings and the brilliant light— all succumbed to complete blackness, and Hugh pitched forward, turning his body as he did, to protect the stricken boy.

Hugh recovered consciousness to the excited

Opposite: Hugh Oxhine saves the Elf Prince

voices of the Dwarfs, and to a third voice, deep and rich, but also tinged with urgency. The archer felt the coolness of the spongy forest floor against his face. He raised himself to the support of one elbow, and stared in disbelief. The Dwarfs were lifting the unconscious youth to the back of a horse-like creature of surpassing beauty. Its white coat was brilliant against the shadowed forest. As if sensing his gaze, the magnificent horned head turned to study the archer and as the great eyes of the creature met Hugh's, the Vandorian realized that an undefined personage lay concealed within the body of the animal.

Meanwhile, one of the Dwarfs had pulled himself up, settling behind the dying boy. At once, the beautiful creature whirled and galloped away, brilliant sparks showering behind, its flashing hooves propelling it without seeming to touch the earth. The Dwarf clung desperately to both the boy and their strange steed. In a matter of seconds they were gone.

"You all right, lad?" The Dwarf's voice, close beside him, startled Hugh from his trance. The ruddy-faced,

bewhiskered Erbin stooped over him. The archer rose to his feet without answering the question, but when he stood, he realized how extremely tired and weak he was, and his hunger attacked his belly with a vengeance.

"You look to be in a bad way," said Erbin. "The lad you saved is mighty important to me and I want to get to him as quick as I can. But if you want to follow, you'll be given every comfort we have to offer—no matter what the final outcome of this happens to be. Better hang on to this," and he handed over Hugh's bow. Looking impatiently up at the archer, Erbin's eyes were wide with fear for his young friend. "I can see you're hesitant," he went on, "but if you want to come, just follow this path we're standing on. It'll take you straight to Mowdra. That's where we'll be. At Mowdra."

With that, the Dwarf turned and headed full speed down the trail. The Vandorian watched until Erbin was out of sight, then turned away and began to move in the opposite direction. There was no need to involve himself further. He could no longer aid the dying boy, and his mission of vengeance had been left unfulfilled.

He had gone only a short distance when he paused, then stopped and looked back. He was unable to shed the vision of the white-faced lad, nor the sense of serene power that had come from the eyes of the horse-creature. They were some distance away by now, yet their presence remained within the silent shadows of the great forest. "Damn," he muttered. He knew his mind would allow him no peace unless he at least found out whether or not the lad lived or died. Besides, he consoled himself, the Dwarf had promised care and hospitality, and these, the archer now recognized, he needed in full measure.

He turned to follow the trail which would lead him to the place called Mowdra.

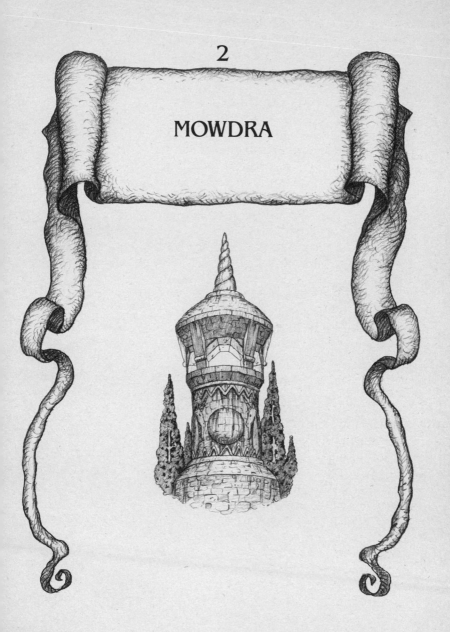

2

MOWDRA

Hugh emerged from the forest into the clearing of Mowdra. The entire area was bathed in the peace of an unearthly green glow emanating from a stone tower which dominated the clearing. Hugh paused, wary. Enchantment was in the great trees, in the quiet stream that flowed at the edge of the glade, on the bridge that beckoned one to cross over. Magic sang from every stone of the thick walls and thatched roof of the house at the center of the clearing. The soft green shimmer that came from the arches of the tower spread peace and strength over all that was Mowdra.

Eventually Hugh moved forward. He reached the house in something of a state of awe. The door swung slowly open to a spacious but empty hall. At the far end of the hall he could see an open hearth from which a fire cast friendly warmth about the room, revealing intricately carved beams and furnishings. Hugh stood just inside the doorway listening to the total silence within; it seemed he was completely alone. Then he sensed movement behind him and, turning, saw the heavy door swing shut. Simultaneously a sound came from a darkened corridor which led out of the hall fifteen paces from where he stood. Quickly and quietly he moved across.

The far end of the corridor was dimly lit, and the archer could see that a door had been opened, which he thought might be the entrance to the tower. A tall figure appeared in the doorway. He was garbed in a light-colored robe which at first seemed to merge with his long white hair and beard. He carried a glistening chalice, and from this came the same green glow that had radiated from the tower. The figure moved swiftly down the corridor. Green vapors drifted from the chalice. The old man stopped before a doorway a half dozen paces beyond the corridor entrance. He turned to look for an instant at Hugh, then entered the room. Despite the distance between them, and the brevity of the old man's passing glance, the Vandorian felt intense power implicit in that tall white figure.

The archer moved cautiously toward the partially opened door from which a gentle green glow escaped and a half-whispered murmuring could be heard. Inside, the room was drenched with light from the chalice. The old man stood with his back to the doorway, staring up at the vessel he now held aloft. He spoke an incantation, and Hugh caught the words, "May this evil be subdued by the power of love which flows now from the cup of peace."

Hugh's eyes were fixed on the old man but he was nonetheless aware of several other figures within the room. The wounded youth lay on a bed, no longer deathly still but writhing in a fevered state. A young woman sat near him, attempting to calm him, and two youths stood at the foot of the bed. The two Dwarfs crouched beside the maiden and just behind was a similarly squat figure to whom the archer accorded only a cursory glance. The wizard, for such Hugh had become convinced the old man must be, now lowered his chalice and turned toward the youth who had begun a feverish muttering, "The Death Lord...he's found out...Gorta...all is lost...all...The Quest..."

"Breathe deeply, my son." The old man bent close to the stricken youth so that the green vapors swirled around both their faces. The wizard's voice was rich with warmth and reassurance. The lad obeyed the instructions, and in a moment his eyelids drooped, then closed, and he was fast asleep.

The old man stood erect. "He will sleep peacefully, and by morning will have recovered." With these words the magical glow was set into motion, disappearing within the chalice, and at once a flame sprang alive from a candle beside the bed. The sudden change startled Hugh. For the first time he clearly saw the creature who stood beside the Dwarfs, and the archer's hand fell to his dagger. The furry creature darted behind the old man who held up his hand.

"Wait, Vandorian! This is not, as you have supposed, a miniature relative of those vile beasts you have just fought." Gently the old man reached out and brought the creature forward. "This is Oolu, a Gwarpy from Loamend, and the gentlest of all creatures." The Gwarpy peered up at the tall archer with wide eyes.

Hugh did not remove his hand from the dagger hilt, but the old man stepped beside him and placed an arm about the archer's wide shoulders. "Stay your guarded attitude, my son," he said, "and allow me to express, for my friends and myself, our extreme gratitude for your bravery and selflessness. At this moment you do not comprehend the importance of your recent acts, but for them I offer you our most abundant thanks." Hugh relaxed his stance as the old man continued, "But more of this later. May I introduce myself? I am Elgan. And these young fellows are Glenden and Ianen." He swept his hand toward the two youths who, though somewhat darker of hair and skin, bore a strong resemblance to the wounded lad. Both were good-looking and slender, the oblique shape of their eyes and pointed ears being their most distinguishing features. They nodded simultaneously to Hugh. The wizard continued, "And this is their cousin, Gwynn, not only one of the loveliest of women, but one of the bravest in all Urshurak."

The auburn-haired girl offered the archer a smile of friendship and gratitude. Like her cousins her skin was darker than that of the wounded youth, and she was indeed beautiful. Hugh acknowledged both Gwynn and her cousins, and Elgan concluded the introductions: "These stalwarts, who have already fought beside you in combat, are the twins, Erbin and Evrawk. And, of course, you have already met Oolu."

The three of them stood in line before the archer, and as each was introduced, grinned from ear to ear while voicing his pleasure at the meeting. The ruddy faces of the Dwarfs clearly expressed the gratitude they felt for Hugh's valor. The stocky Gwarpy was the tallest of the trio, yet would scarcely reach the Vandorian's chest. He surprised the archer by cheerfully remarking, "Oolu happy to meet Hugh. Oolu now runs to get Hugh some drink!" With that the furry creature chuckled, and dashed out of the room.

Elgan began to guide the archer toward the corridor saying, as they walked, "No doubt you would relish some food and refreshment, and it appears you are in need of some medical attention. I will prepare a small brew to heal your cuts and bruises, and then let us go to sit before the hearth where you can rest, and enjoy the hospitality of Mowdra."

As Hugh listened, the thought struck him that he had heard that voice in a place other than this house. Then he realized where it had been—he had heard it less than an hour before, in the presence of the horse-creature, in the forest, just after he had regained consciousness. He stared at the tall, ancient man. And the question entered his mind: "In the name of Rolmar and Dunstan, who *is* the mysterious lad I have saved? And what strange world have I entered?"

Hugh was at rest for the first time in over seven days. He and the wizard sat at a heavy oaken dining table. The fire within the hearth crackled and sputtered a few feet away. Large mugs of ale had been set out. The brew was of a nature unknown to Hugh but he drank deep and his spirits began to lift immediately, though his mind remained clear.

Elgan had secured his pipe, and puffed contentedly evidently delighting in the creation of bright purple smoke rings which drifted about them apparently immune to air drafts. Yet when he began to speak, the old wizard was sober enough. He spoke of Mowdra, which he said had been his home for several centuries. Had anyone else made this claim the archer would have been openly contemptuous, but in this enchanted place he held his silence. Elgan went on to say that the expert craftsmanship of the house had been provided by the ancestors of Erbin and Evrawk, but that he alone had created the tower. Hugh realized this claim was not a boast but a simple statement of fact to explain the special quality of the tower. As to whether the tower had been formed by laying stone on stone or by some act of wizardry was not elaborated on. But the archer envisioned Elgan as being capable of either method of creation.

Then the wizard's voice took on more serious tones, and he began to question Hugh as to the particular reasons for his entering the Forest of Delvinor. The archer's murderous outrage flooded back as he related his story: he and his wife and two children had lived away from the main body of their people because Hugh disliked the smallness and conservatism of other Vandorians.

"I blame myself," he said. "My wife always wanted to be with the others. But for my sake, she gladly lived far from our neighbors." Somber in his guilt, he stopped speaking.

Gently the old man prompted him. "What happened?"

"A week ago," Hugh replied, "I went hunting. When I came back—when I went into my home," his voice cracked, "they were all there, lying in blood from their torn throats. She, my Marya—she was on top of the two little ones. She must have died trying to protect them." Again he fell silent.

"And then?" the old, quiet voice asked.

Hugh studied his hands, remembering. When he looked up, his face was like stone, his voice matter-of-fact, "I cleaned them," he said. "She always kept the place so neat and pretty, you see. So I cleaned them. I got them clean—and then I buried them." He took a deep breath. "And then, after a time, I set out to follow the tracks of the killers. Five now are dead. Three remain. I will find them."

Elgan rose, his eyes wet with the tears Hugh had not allowed himself to shed. The old man placed his hands on Hugh's shoulders, kneading and murmuring the while. Presently the archer felt the murderous despair in his heart give place to a wash of peace that pervaded his whole being. With a great sigh, his head fell back against the chair and his body at last relaxed.

At this point, Erbin entered from the kitchen, carrying two fresh mugs of ale.

Immediately Elgan's mood shifted from one of utmost seriousness to a childlike playfulness. Such direct transformations of mood were commonplace among the members of this group—as Hugh would discover in the days ahead. For right now, he was perfectly content to go along with whatever was at hand.

"Aha, Erbin, old friend," cried the wizard, "I trust you have sampled a sufficient amount of this excellent brew to have given you the energy for your long journey from the kitchen?" The heightened glow of the Dwarf's ruddy complexion gave evidence that he had, indeed, so sampled. Elgan continued, "I would judge that such a journey would require at least a full mug of ale?"

"This time, Elgan, your judgment has been accurate by only a third," and Erbin held up three fingers.

The two of them chuckled together and seemed about to embark on an endless discussion of the merits of the "brew." This was too much for Hugh. Exhausted as he was, his curiosity would not be denied. "Is there any reason why I should not know the identity of the lad we rescued?" he asked.

"Certainly you should know," Elgan replied. "I have been at some pains to figure out precisely the right moment to tell you. However, since you ask," Elgan looked directly into Hugh's eyes, "he is Ailwon, Prince of the White Elves of Alfandel."

This was news indeed. Hugh sat up.

"I thought that all heirs to the throne of Alfandel had perished."

The old man appeared surprised. "I did not believe you would have that knowledge. That is in no way an insult to you, but I have long been aware of the ignorance that is a result of the passivity of your people."

"There are a few of my people who have traveled some distances beyond our boundaries. Ever since I was a young boy I have sought out such people. However, I do not know a great deal, and I believed much of what I did know to be mere legend."

The wizard was slowly stroking his long white beard. "I am extremely interested in what you have heard."

"Well, I have heard of the White Elves and their legendary Crownhelm. And of how many centuries ago they came to the continent, and set about to free it. I have heard of the great Lord of the North, and I heard also that some years past, the final heir to the Crownhelm had died, and that there were none left who could oppose the evil one. But I supposed much of this to be legend and myth."

"All that you have related is truth, save that for two decades it has been believed by almost everyone that there was no heir to the Crown. This is a misconception. Do you know of the Prophecy?"

"No," the archer answered.

"This evening you have played a major role in the fulfillment of the Prophecy."

Elgan paused, and then asked: "Do you know of Gorta, the witch of Zorak?"

"I have heard of her since childhood, but have always dismissed her as pure fable."

"She is as real as you, or as I," replied Elgan. "It was she who sent out the rat-creatures, or Blegons, as they are called. They were in search of the Prince, of this I'm certain. The Blegons were carrying out the destructive will of Gorta and the location of your home apparently stood in their path. These beasts have little intelligence, but possess a terrible lust for blood. The wanton slaughter of your family was the worse because it was merely incidental. Yet who knows?" Elgan shook his head sadly. "The tragedy that befell you led to your saving Ailwon's life. Still, if I might have prevented your loss, I would not have hesitated an instant. But it was not within my power. I am often a prisoner to the whims of fate, just as you are."

Hugh nodded. "You are right, of course. If only I had not insisted we live so far from others, then my wife and children would be alive this moment."

Elgan started to reply, but held his voice. He knew the turmoil in the archer's mind. He knew also of the immense value of this man, of his strength and courage, of his intelligence and kindness. He rejoiced at the knowledge that such a man would be at Ailwon's side as the quest began. And in truth Elgan had already acquired a deep affection for the Vandorian. The pain that the archer felt was thus also the wizard's, and the old man was strongly tempted to come to his rescue. Yet he knew his words would fall on deaf ears.

Then Erbin, who had all along remained silent, stepped forward. "Gentlemen. It is *my* belief that we are all in dire need of nourishment, which is not only required by the belly, but by the mind and soul as well. Behold," he called out triumphantly. He made a sweeping motion toward the corridor. "Our feast arrives! Let us celebrate the return to Mowdra, of Prince Ailwon, and the arrival of our newfound friend, Hugh Oxhine of Vandor!"

Accompanying this somewhat grandiloquent proclamation, Evrawk, and behind him Oolu, entered bearing aloft huge trays of steaming food. Rich, spicy aromas filled the hall. Heat from the cooking fires and an additional mug of ale had rendered Evrawk's nose and cheeks a shade brighter than his brother's. He began to sing:

> The food's been cooked—'twas no small feat,
> But now 'tis ready—So take thy seat!

Oolu responded with a chorus:

> So finally Oolu gets to eat!

All had joined in the feast. To eliminate all the food heaped on the platters, it seemed, would have required a small miracle. But the diners finally pushed back their chairs, allowing their legs to stretch out and their overstuffed midsections to expand.

Erbin left the table, and returned with a tray filled with mugs of fresh ale. The Dwarf staggered slightly beneath the load; his eyelids drooped and the corners of his mouth were turned up in a childish smile. While the normal effect of the rich brew was to lift the spirits without numbing the mind, its effect on Erbin accomplished the former, but failed in the latter. An after-dinner conversation began, in which the Vandorian managed to avoid participating. He

was engrossed in his own thoughts, but nevertheless
listened with one ear to what was being said, and
could detect an air of anticipation threading the
discussion, despite an apparent attempt to maintain
casualness.

When the mugs were drained of ale, so it seemed
were the diners drained of their conversation. Almost
in unison they stood, and began to clear plates from
the table.

"You are our guest, Hugh," said Elgan, "please
remain seated. I will return shortly." The wizard
gathered his dishes, and moved toward the kitchen.

The youths, Glenden and Ianen, bade the archer
good night, as did Erbin, who weaved a bit as he
headed for the corridor. Hugh felt a hand touch his
shoulder, and looked up to see Gwynn. She began to
speak, and Hugh noted, as he had during the meal,
her straightforward sincerity.

"Before I say good night, Hugh, I want to offer you
both the depth of my sympathy for your loss, and my
highest gratitude for your selfless valor. I, and my
people, will always be in your debt."

"You owe me no debt, my lady."

She nodded, and smiled. "As you wish." Hugh was
experiencing considerable discomfort. He had for
years scorned women of physical beauty, though
because of his own good looks he had attracted
many. He had always thought them to be frivolous
and lacking in purpose. Though Gwynn was a girl of
rare loveliness, she seemed also to be strong and
determined. Much to his relief, Gwynn removed her
hand from his shoulder and, bidding him good night,
left the hall. Oolu and Evrawk had also left the room,
and Hugh was once again alone.

He turned his thoughts to the coming morning. The
wizard had claimed that the one responsible for the
murders of his loved ones was the witch, Gorta. If this
was true, and he now believed it was, then he had no
choice but to seek her out and slay her. He was not
sure how to go about this, nor about his chances of

returning alive. But there was no longer anything of importance save to avenge the destruction of his family and his life's dreams.

The tall old man and the Dwarf, Evrawk, entered. Evrawk sat down opposite Hugh, while Elgan again secured his pipe from the mantel before seating himself in his customary spot at the table's end. The Dwarf also produced a pipe from a pouch.

Elgan settled down comfortably. "Now we can talk without the gnaw of hunger to impede our thoughts." He fixed his gaze on Hugh for a long instant before speaking, "Hugh, only a short time ago your acts of bravery staved off the certain enslavement of all of us... of all that is Urshurak."

Hugh was taken aback. "How could I possibly have done this?"

"The lad you saved is the heir to the Crownhelm of the White Elves. He is Prince Ailwon whom the Prophecy has foretold is the only one who can battle the oppression that will otherwise suffocate us all. The power of the Crownhelm will be the deciding factor in the ultimate clash of the opposing forces that have struggled for ten centuries to decide the final fate of the continent. There are only two who can utilize this power. Ailwon is one... and the Death Lord, Torgon, is the other. Yet there is a riddle in the Prophecy itself, for it foretells that both Elves of the same Blood will be Fulfilled." He gave a long sigh. "The time for the quest has come and our final effort must be made. If it is unsuccessful all those not allied to the Death Lord will be murdered and enslaved. Tomorrow morning we leave for we must rally all the peoples of Urshurak and unite them at the citadel of Cryslandon. There, Ailwon will receive the Crownhelm, and then lead the allied nations against Torgon."

"I have, of course, heard tales of this Torgon," said Hugh, "but I don't have much knowledge of him. Exactly who—or what—is he?... And how is it that he is such a threat to the peoples of Urshurak?"

"He is a being of great power who dwells within an

immense iron fortress that rises out of the Crater of Death at Golgorath. It is he whom Gorta, the witch—with all her powers—falls before in supplication. He is in possession of machines of war that exceed belief, and holds sway over legions of primitive barbarians. It is he who, with his own arcane powers, created the terrible gargoyles, the Vilderone, who command his vast armies. Not content with all that he has, this dark lord lusts for further power. He is possessed by such a craving for the Crownhelm that he is impregnable against the persuasions of love or reason or the offerings of friendship. It is he who has cast the shadow of fear across the lands for a thousand years, and who now—as the fulfillment of the Prophecy nears—threatens to smear the whole of Urshurak with the red of blood and the yellow bile of slavery!"

The pace of his delivery and the timber of his voice had increased as Elgan spoke, and his final words reverberated around the great chamber. The Vandorian believed the entire narrative to be true. All his life he had been vaguely aware of an atmosphere of oppression that had dampened and restricted the lives of his countrymen. "I would guess that this is connected to stories I've heard of great battles waged toward the north of the continent," said Hugh.

The wizard remained stiff-backed against his chair. But his voice resumed its normal reassuring level. "Yes. These battles have been fought periodically for centuries in the Kolgar range of mountains across the breadth of the continent. Attempts to secure peace have been made, and have failed, often tragically." Elgan's body slouched. "Tonight I feel the centuries of my age. But enough... Evrawk, kindly present the bare bones of this matter to our friend. We must all sleep before long, and I continue to ramble."

"Surely, Elgan," the Dwarf released a large puff of pipe smoke. "Sir Hugh, tomorrow the quest for the final freedom of Urshurak begins. Elgan leaves for Tal-Amon, in the eastern nation of Azmuria, where the sorcerer, Shandar—awaits him. Together they will go

to secure the ancient crown of Alfandel from its place
of hiding, transporting it then to the citadel of Cryslandon, capital city of the White Elves. Here they will
await the arrival of Prince Ailwon. The Shakín of the
Azmurians, Ali Ben Kara, will lead his armies north
toward the capital. Meanwhile Gwynn, with Glenden
and Ianen, will have headed northwest toward Penderak. Here my people await the word to begin the
trek eastward. Leaving Penderak, Gwynn will continue
to her own land of Andeluvia, where she will attempt
to persuade her pacifist uncle, King Zarin, to lend his
support to the struggle. Whether or not this is accomplished she will lead her rebel band toward
Cryslandon."

Evrawk stood, and with his thick hands clasped
behind his back, strolled to the stone apron before
the hearth. He continued: "In the morning—shortly
after dawn—Oolu, my brother, and myself will accompany Prince Ailwon as he begins his long journey. We
head south, toward the Marshes of Zorak. We must
find the witch, Gorta, and she must be destroyed. If
the fates are with us, this ugly task will be done and we
will continue southward. Beyond the Dangar Jungles,
off the southern tip of the continent, lies Zan-Dura,
home of the warrior women, the Amazons. Our intention is to enlist the aid of these fierce fighters. Without
their help we stand almost no chance for victory. But it
will not be an easy task to gain them as allies. If we
are successful we will return toward the north traveling up the great River Garnon, aboard Amazonian
warships. When we reach Cryslandon the armies will
await us, along with—hopefully—the Norsemen of
Norbruk. From Cryslandon, we will march northward,
and on the final day of the prophecy—or 'Day of
Fulfillment'—the King of Alfandel will meet the Death
Lord of Golgorath to decide the fate of our continent."
Evrawk finished, and glanced toward Elgan.

"Splendid, old friend," said the wizard. He tapped
ashes from the bowl of his curved pipe. A pause, and
then: "Hugh Oxhine... will you join Ailwon and his

companions tomorrow morning as they embark on their noble quest?"

"Yes."

Elgan nodded.

"But I go no further than Zorak," said Hugh. "Despite the connections you have made between this Death Lord and Gorta, it is she—and she alone—that I have deadly quarrel with. If you still want me along, then understand this: I will contest your Prince for the right to deal with this foul witch. I have no intention of disrupting your plans—on the contrary, I will do all in my power to see they are carried out. But when the moment of truth arrives, I feel it my absolute right to wield the avenging weapon against her." Hugh paused to allow the weight of his words to have their effect. "I am a curious man," he said, "and have many questions to ask. But I'm as practical as I am curious, and totally aware of my need for a good night's sleep before embarking on this journey. Is there anything else I need to know that can't be explained to me while en route?"

"Yes, you must know what you will face in the Marshes of Zorak. I will be as brief as is possible. And when I'm finished... we'll go to the kitchen, where I'll prepare you a herbal beverage which will induce sleep of the most restful kind. Is this agreeable?"

The Vandorian nodded affirmatively. "Fine," said Elgan. In the fire some coals fell and the flames crackled and hissed with new vigor. The wizard gave Hugh a penetrating look. "Gorta is extremely powerful, more powerful and dangerous than you can imagine. Her domain lies somewhere beneath the swamp of Zorak, and much of her environment is an evil illusion that has become reality and will remain so as long as she retains possession of her powers. Gorta and her cauldron, which is the source of her power, must be destroyed. If they are not, we cannot hope to defeat Torgon!

"Let us speak no more of these things tonight! Come, we'll go to the kitchen..." The wizard moved

toward the corridor, Hugh and Erbin right behind
him. They entered the kitchen opposite the room
where Prince Ailwon slept. Yellow candlelight crept
into the hallway from beneath Ailwon's closed door.
The Vandorian guessed that Gwynn was within.
Though it had not been directly stated, it was obvious
that she and Ailwon were lovers.

The kitchen was large, well equipped and spotless-
ly clean. Cooking utensils of all shapes and sizes
hung in a double row, almost covering an entire wall.
All kinds of roots and herbs were hung to dry. Wooden
kegs were stacked against the far end, and a variety of
large earthen jugs and wooden buckets filled with
grains half surrounded the kitchen table. In a corner
beside the butter churn, huddled within a tinderbox
was Oolu, sound asleep. A big yellow tomcat slept
between the Gwarpy's legs, while the cat's pure white
mate, equally large and equally comfortable, was
curled atop the confines of Oolu's lap.

Hugh managed a small laugh. "I hope I will be as
peaceful soon."

"You shall, I assure you," declared Evrawk, pointing
toward Elgan who was busy mixing together a variety
of herbs.

"This Gwarpy is completely unlike any creature I
have ever seen," said the archer. "He possesses some
characteristics of a human, yet is so much like an
animal."

"I have always thought of Oolu," responded the
Dwarf, "as the harmonious link between humans and
animals. He seems to be completely comfortable with
both, and has little sense of hierarchy in regard to his
world."

"How do you mean?"

"Well, he seems to place value on *all* things, and is
not apparently too concerned with the value of one
thing as opposed to another. I have never heard him
compare anything to anything else... yet he is quite
capable of special fondness for particular *types* of
things, just as most of us are." The cat in Oolu's lap

half opened her eyes to slits, raising her head to investigate the disturbers of her slumber. Having completed her survey, she re-situated herself into a motionless ball of fur, while her yellow companion and the object of the discussion slept merrily on. Evrawk continued, "Oolu has affection for all creatures. He fully understands the realities of survival. He loves rabbits, mice, and is even quite fond of rats, but this doesn't spoil a bit his friendship with these cats who—contrary to their present appearance—are relentless pursuers of them all."

"Surely this fondness for beasts," interjected Hugh, "is due to his being very close to one himself. I mean no insult, and find him quite amusing, but it seems apparent from his speech that he is much more animal than human."

"Do not be fooled by Oolu's way with words," said Elgan. He turned from the stove carrying two steaming cups which he placed on the small table before Hugh and Erbin. The wizard spoke. "Unlike myself, Oolu finds it unnecessary to produce great quantities of words." Elgan turned to look thoughtfully at the Gwarpy. Hugh Oxhine stretched, and emitted an enormous yawn. "Ah," said Elgan, "the herbs have done their work, not to mention the wear and tear of the past week. Come, let us retire." He picked up the flickering candle, and exited the kitchen. Evrawk and Hugh followed suit. The wizard opened a bedroom door off the corridor, entered and lit the bedside candle from his own. "I'm certain you'll find this quite comfortable," he said. Hugh didn't bother to examine the simply appointed room, but eyed the quilt-covered bed with hunger. "Sleep well," said Elgan, and he left.

"Yes... good night," the archer's voice was muffled by the hooded garment he was pulling over his head. He quickly stripped himself of his clothes, which were resistant to removal due to the saturation of sweat, dust and dried blood. He dropped them to the floor, and crawled into the bed that received his tired body

as would an ardent lover. There was only a momentary reflection on the evening's strange events before
Hugh slid into the dark peace of sleep.

Elgan and Evrawk walked slowly down the hallway,
and stopped before a closed door. From within came
Erbin's rhythmic snoring. "I'm amazed," said the
Dwarf, "that Glenden and Ianen can sleep through
that din. I hope I will be as fortunate." He turned to the
wizard, and his voice became serious. "So at last—tomorrow it begins.

"Yes, Evrawk," said Elgan. His voice almost a whisper.

He looked toward the door of his tower and said,
"...Elvgard—it has long lain dormant. The time has
come to bring forth the Elfin sword from the Valley of
Life." Evrawk stood staring at the wizard then turned
and entered the bedroom, closing the door. The
snoring of Erbin had stopped.

The old wizard stepped into the dimly lit ante-
chamber at the corridor's end. Facing him was the
tower door beyond which he would make final preparation for the coming morn. Elgan extinguished the
candle on the wall, and sat down on a bench situated
across from the door. He leaned back against the cool
stones, then blew out the candle he held. Elgan's
mind traversed backward twenty years: before him
was Evrawk, holding up a newborn infant. Sweat ran
from the Dwarf's brow, mingling with tears of joy that
streamed from his eyes. The babe was given to the
arms of his mother, the Queen. She spoke his name,
"Ailwon: 'Bearer of The Light.' " The sorcerer, Shandar,
touched the child, and the power of his unspoken
words transcended the walls of the darkened cottage
hidden deep in the Forests of Andeluvia.

Elgan was smiling as he sat in the darkness. "And
now he is ready," he thought, "though we almost lost
him. But we did not, and we gained a powerful ally to
accompany him on this perilous journey." The almost
tragic events of the day indicated that someone

within the allied ranks had knowledge of Ailwon's existence. Despite all the secrecy... despite all the precautions of the past two decades...could it be that the same assassin that had slain Ailwon's father and every known heir was once again at work? "We will have to be alert," he thought, "we cannot, we *must not* fail!" His mind's eye then formed a vision of the morning; of Ailwon standing straight and determined. The lad's courage and intelligence and sensitivity had been finely developed during two decades of tutoring. And of course he would be aided by the power of the sword, Elvgard, and more importantly, the Crownhelm. Elgan fervently hoped it would be enough. It must be! He envisioned the interior of his tower, and he saw himself ascending the winding stone stairs to the top.

Within the tower room there appeared a great white tree. From its base there flowed a spring and beyond the spring in the center of the tree glowed a gold and silver ark. Within the ark a sword appeared. The vision of the tree diminished and on a slab of ancient stone in the center of the tower room lay a dazzling sword.

Elgan rose from the bench and entered his tower, closing the heavy door tightly behind him.

The Taral Road ran the entire distance of Delvinor,
emerging at the northern entrance of the great forest,
then climbing into the foothills of the Kolgar Mountains. Two hundred miles away, in the house of
Mowdra, all was silent. But here on a ridge overlooking Delvinor a sound could be heard, and it began to
grow: a rhythmic pounding, vibrating across the
grassland. Beneath the crescent moon horsemen
topped a rise, armored figures mounted on giant
steeds, four abreast, a dozen of them, two dozen,
pounding the soft earth into dust. The leader held up
his arm, and they reined to a halt, their black fierce-
eyed mounts blowing, stomping their hooves.

Moonlight glinted from heavy armor and helmets.
The leader pointed toward the forest below, a mile
distant. He lifted his visor... exposing the terrible,
heavy-browed face of a gargoyle, the Vilderone—created executioners of the Death Lord. His voice was not
unlike the deep growl of a predator: "Before us is the
road which will lead us to the home of the accursed
wizard. And there we will take the Elfin brat..."

He snapped his visor shut, and dug spurs into the
massive sides of his horse. The others followed, and
the dark band galloped down toward the forest, the
drumming of hoofbeats rolling across the hills until
its sound was lost to the stillness of the night.

3

ELVGARD

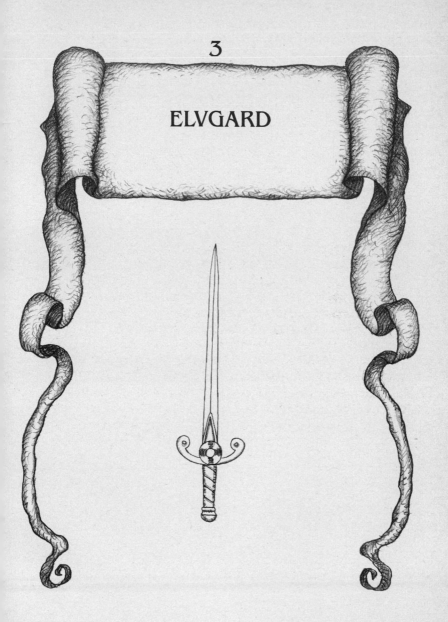

The giant trees which were the protectors of Delvinor had stood for tens of centuries. With only very few clearings, the forest of these ancient trees, the Trocalas, stretched two hundred miles from north to south, and two hundred and fifty miles from the Bolgad Mountains eastward to the River Garnon.

None of these mighty guardians were taller or more massive in girth than those surrounding the clearing of Mowdra. They stood in dark contrast to the growing light of dawn. Though night still reigned beneath the canopy of foliage, the rustlings of nocturnal beasts had ceased. A song thrush began a tentative melody; a jackdaw argued a harsh counterpoint. They were soon joined by a myriad of other birds and the forest clearing filled with song.

The woodland chorus failed to rouse Hugh Oxhine from the depths of his slumber, but the clink of metal against metal opened the archer's eyes. The room was still dark. Where was he? How long had he slept? Slowly the events of the previous days returned to his memory. As on each morning since his loss, he began to recreate his sorrow and hatred, but somehow this morning the images of tragedy were less vivid, his sense of grief less terrible. The rage he habitually called up with such ease seemed reluctant to be roused.

There were more clinking sounds from the kitchen. Hugh sat bolt upright. What meal was being prepared? Had he slept more than a night? Now footsteps echoed in the corridor, a door opened and closed. The Vandorian swung out of bed, groped for the window, and pulled back the heavy drapes. Outside the light was still dim, but he could discern the shadowy forms of Erbin and Evrawk, their arms loaded with bundles, trudging down the slope toward the stable. A squat figure that Hugh determined was the Gwarpy, Oolu, emerged to greet the Dwarfs. Sounds of low conversation and laughter drifted up toward the house; the Gwarpy began to move up the slope.

Hugh turned from the window. His clothes were not on the floor where he had dropped them the previous night. Naked and cursing softly, he was exploring beneath the bed when a gentle rap at the door interrupted his search.

"Who is it?" he asked irritably.

"It's Oolu, is who. Got things will make Hugh feel good!"

The archer opened the door partway to see the grinning Gwarpy holding a lit candle in his right hand, while his left arm cradled a neatly folded stack of clothes. He offered the candle and the cleaned clothes, and when both were accepted, reached back and produced a bucket of fresh water and towels.

Hugh muttered his thanks; the Gwarpy was grinning and his eyes, as usual, were wide and bright with delight. He was obviously fascinated by the tall man's size and stretch, never having seen a being of such height. "Hugh sure big—got big muscles!" he exclaimed, disappearing down the corridor.

The archer closed the door, smiling. Though he still felt uncomfortable in the presence of the furry creature, he now found it difficult not to feel an amused fondness for the Gwarpy. Eagerly Hugh bathed and dressed, relishing the feel of clean cloth against his body, and presently stepped out into the corridor, having carefully extinguished the candle. Oolu had returned and was seated on the floor beside the door, examining something of interest between the toes of his right foot. Near him was an earthen bowl piled with biscuits, fruit and a dried food called keku, made of grain and herbs.

"This'll fill ya, I think," the Gwarpy said, handing the bowl to the archer. "Erbin says, 'Give Hugh his food and bring him now, Oolu,' so Oolu done it."

With that, the Gwarpy jumped up and started toward the rear of the house. Hugh followed, eating rapidly, and his question to the furry creature in front of him was made less than clear by a mouthful of biscuit. "We'll be leaving soon, eh?"

"Quick soon, yep." Oolu turned right at the corridor's end, and Hugh paused to glance at the tower door.

"Old Elgan gonna be out quick soon, too," Oolu said, glancing back to confirm Hugh's sense of the wizard's presence somewhere behind the door to the mysterious stone tower.

The archer and the Gwarpy stepped outside, where Erbin could be seen leading a large chestnut stallion from the stable. He hailed the archer, "Hugh! Come see the fine animal we have for you to ride!"

Hugh and Oolu descended to where the Dwarf stood holding the reins of the handsome beast. Additionally, three heavy-coated ponies, already saddled and loaded with supplies, stood loosely tethered to a hitching rail, contentedly cropping the grass.

"I'm thinking that we neglected to inquire as to whether or not you ride," said Erbin, as the archer approached him.

"I've ridden often, but not in a number of years," Hugh replied, while his eyes expressed admiration for the chestnut. "And never a horse such as this."

Evrawk emerged from the stable, a saddle beneath one short, powerful arm. "Good morning, Hugh."

"Morning," the Vandorian replied somewhat absently, as he moved to the near side of the horse and began to stroke the muscular neck while talking to it in soothing tones. "What's he called?" he asked.

"You'll hafta ask Gwynn, or one of the lads," replied Erbin. "They brought this big fella down from Andeluvia, where he was raised. The Brown Elves provide horses for the White Elves and for the Azmurians. This fella is the type used by the Azmurians—there's not many of them left in Andeluvia."

Hugh had put the small remainder of his food down. Now he turned to Evrawk. "Let me saddle him."

"Surely," said the Dwarf, handing over the saddle. The feel of the well-worn leather was good to the archer's hands, and he saddled and bridled the animal. He stroked the horse's head while checking, to his own satisfaction, the placement of the bit in the sensitive mouth. Hugh felt the animal respond to the sureness of his handling, felt the excitement in the muscular movement beneath his hand. And felt his own restlessness. "How long before this quest is to begin?" he asked. "For myself, I am anxious to be off." Without waiting for a reply, he added, "I'd better get my weapons. I left them..."

Evrawk interrupted. "Oolu has already gone for them." The Gwarpy emerged, hurrying down the slope, belts, scabbards, long bow and quiver of arrows in his arms. He stopped before the archer, grinning as usual, and presented his burden. Hugh grunted his appreciation, and secured the weapons into position as they were handed to him. He had been told that Gwarpys hadn't the slightest inclination toward violence, but he noted that Oolu nonetheless had great curiosity about the weapons. The last buckle fastened, Hugh was ready.

But Erbin and Evrawk continued to lead bridled horses from the stable. Three slender, fawn-colored mounts joined the ponies and Hugh's big chestnut.

Now the youngsters, Ianen and Glenden, came from the house, carrying various articles for travel. They were pleasant enough lads, Hugh thought, as they exchanged greetings, but he couldn't see them

as royalty. A staccato tattoo of hoofbeats preceded the
arrival of a gray-and-white-dappled steed, led, with
difficulty, by Erbin. Oolu stepped beside the spirited
animal and spoke to it in a series of grunts and
chortles. The stallion snorted and shook his mane,
but immediately ceased his excited prancing.

"Who's to ride that lively fellow?" asked Hugh.

"I am," said a voice from behind the archer. Hugh
turned. Coming toward him was the lad he had saved,
the White Elf Prince, Ailwon. Walking beside the youth
and holding his hand was Gwynn. Ailwon was clad in
white. Hugh stared. Though the young man's features
were familiar, it was as though Hugh were seeing the
Elfin Prince for the first time.

"Good morning, Hugh," said Gwynn.

"Yes...good morning..." Hugh replied, but his eyes
never left the youth.

Gwynn glanced at Ailwon, then back at Hugh.
"Well," she said, "this is fine. One of great valor has
saved one who is to lead us all to freedom—and
together they are about to embark on this most
noble, yet most dangerous, of quests. But it appears
neither is capable of mouthing even the simplest of
greetings to the other."

Ailwon glanced at Gwynn, who had punctuated her
remarks with a gentle nudge. He smiled and looked
back to Hugh. There was warmth and sincerity in his
blue eyes. He stretched out his hand, palm forward,
then laid it firmly on the Vandorian's shoulder.

"I understand, Hugh, that you have been thanked
many times over by my friends. And now I thank you
myself for saving my life." Ailwon withdrew his hand,
looked down at the ground, then again at Hugh. "I
can only offer my deepest friendship, and the hope
that I can someday perform some great service for
you." Then the young man grinned broadly, "I'm very
happy that you will be with us as we begin our quest."

Hugh said, "I am glad, and amazed, that you have
recovered so quickly and so completely. But I must
point out that I have no concern in your quest. You

have my company and my assistance because it suits my purpose—to revenge myself and my family on that vile Witch of Zorak. I have always kept myself to myself, and now I am truly solitary. And as I explained to Gwynn, you owe me no debt." He looked to the Brown Elf and saw the sadness in her eyes as she returned his stare: Ailwon's face also showed disappointment. The archer turned abruptly and busied himself with his mount, aware that the other members of the group had ceased their chores to watch the exchange. Now they resumed their preparations.

Once again, impatience swept over Hugh. Damn, but he ached to be in the saddle and on his way! Would these people never get started? Where was the old man?...

"He's beautiful, isn't he?" Gwynn's voice came from beside the archer. He glanced at her, then realized she was speaking of the horse.

"He surely is. What name is he called? And how is it that such a creature is being given to me?"

"He is called Santor. It means 'Strong One' in the ancient tongue. I, too, wondered why he was brought, but Elgan assured us he would be needed, and I no longer debate with him on such matters." She smiled, and offered her hand to the archer. "There is the possibility that I will not see you again, but I hope it is not so." Her voice took on a pleading tone, "Please, help Ailwon. He needs your help so badly... " She turned from the Vandorian at the sound of the tower door opening.

Elgan stood at the entrance to the tower. He held a white scabbard before him with both hands.

Ailwon went up to meet Elgan and they paused, facing each other two thirds of the way up the slope. The rest of the company formed a half-circle behind the Prince, while Hugh remained beside his horse.

Now Elgan withdrew the sword from its sheath and held it up. The blade was brilliant. Suddenly Hugh realized that the glade had become quiet, the birds

Opposite: Mowdra

silent, the horses still. Into the hush the wizard's voice
fell plangent and clear, startlingly powerful for all its
quietness, and seeming to come not only from that
straight, thin figure but from the ancient forest surrounding them:

"To you, Ailwon, 'Bearer of Light,' Prince of Alfandel,
heir to the Crownhelm, to you is entrusted the power
of the sword called Elvgard, the sword of your name-
sake, the first, the mightiest—and if the power of the
light is upon us, the final weapon ever to be used by
the White Elves!" He handed the sword and the
scabbard to the Prince and his voice became almost a
whisper. "With loathing we go, because we must, to
battle, but—" and he raised his arms to the sky, "but
with joy we begin the quest to end a thousand-year
struggle and bring everlasting peace and freedom to
Urshurak!"

The clearing was suddenly flooded with a pure light
from the sun, which had at last cleared the giant
Trocalas. High above them an eagle traversed the
blue with effortless movements. The wizard dropped

his arms to embrace the Prince, and Hugh could no longer hear the gentle words of an old man taking leave of his loved ones. The archer turned toward his horse and the Dwarfs and Oolu headed toward their ponies.

He turned again at the sound of footsteps to see the Dwarfs and Oolu coming toward him. The Gwarpy grinned. "Quick soon finally come, eh, Hugh?" A wave of excitement came over the archer as he untethered his horse and swung into the saddle, moving away from the stable. Wheeling Santor around, he saw Elgan, his hand raised in a gesture of peace. Ailwon and Gwynn broke what might be their final embrace, and in an instant the Prince was up on the gray and cantering toward the stone bridge. Hugh followed, then Erbin, Evrawk, and finally Oolu. By the great trees, Ailwon stood aside to let the others pass. He waved one last time to Gwynn, then his horse reared and he disappeared into the forest.

Gwynn kissed the wizard, and ran to join Glenden and Ianen, who were already mounted. Leaping astride her waiting steed, she too cantered toward the forest, her cousins following close behind. In a moment, they, too, had disappeared. Only Elgan remained.

The old wizard looked up. The sun was climbing in a clear sky, birds chattered once again, the hum of insects was all around. His gaze descended the lengths of the towering Trocalas to the trail that extended from Mowdra's stone bridge into the shadowed woodland.

"So at last... it has begun."

4

THE QUEST

Hooves thudded upon loose earth, raising clouds of dust that trailed behind horses and riders as the allied band traveled the Taral Road, toward the southern exit of the Forest of Delvinor. The Trocalas towered on either side, their branches reaching toward one another, meeting high above to form a nurturing cover of green. Only an occasional dappling of light fell to the road below.

Hugh had given Santor full rein. The big chestnut had eagerly taken the lead, and Hugh had only to turn him southward when he reached the road. Finally the archer had to restrain the horse somewhat or the others would soon have been left far behind. As his horse began to canter, Hugh settled into the pace of a long ride. Ailwon drew up beside him, and met Hugh's quick glance, but neither spoke. From behind came the rhythmic beat of a drum, which was then joined by the sound of a flute. Hugh turned in the saddle. Oolu tapped a primitive drum, which hung from his shoulder. The Dwarf twin, Erbin, had begun playing a pleasant melody on a long, hand-carved flute, and was soon joined by Evrawk with his mandolin. All three instruments blended, the rhythm matching the cadence of the hoofbeats. There was a power in the ancient music completely out of proportion to the simplicity and fusion of harmonies of flute and mandolin and drum.

Despite the shield of protection Hugh had constructed around his emotions, he was having considerable difficulty remaining aloof from the keen excitement of this venture. He knew that as the drudgery of the journey set in, and the hardships of life in the open mounted, there would naturally occur a diminishing of enthusiasm. But even these initial feelings had been completely unexpected, and he fought against them. Hugh was unaware that the Elfin lad who rode beside him was having difficulties of his own.

When Ailwon had stood before Elgan, had been given the legendary sword of his ancestors, and had listened to those triumphant words that had been like a song of hope, his chest had filled to near bursting with courage and with the pride of youthful dedication. The trust that was apparent in the face of the wizard, and the hope that filled Gwynn's eyes before he had kissed her, had only served to inspire him further. Nothing could stop him! But before he had reached the road, a dread fear of failure had struck him as swiftly and unexpectedly as would a hidden assassin. Never in the years since learning of his destiny had he experienced such terror as this.

Ailwon's mind had formed images of the dreaded Gorta—but with no conscious effort on the young Elf's part to do so. He didn't know what the witch really looked like. No one did. Once outside the protection of Delvinor she could be anywhere, in almost any form. Her realm extended far outward from the swamps. This was evident in her past actions during the long struggle for control of the continent. How they would gain entrance to her domain he couldn't imagine. It was known only that it was somewhere beneath those vast, dark marshes. Should they find it, how would he defeat such a foe? And should he get past the witch, he must destroy the source of her power: her cauldron—for if this were not done Gorta could not be completely defeated, and could regenerate her powers. Now the worst had happened. Fear had risen within him. And he had always been taught that this was Gorta's greatest asset: the ability to arouse self-doubt in her enemies. "She is extremely dangerous," Elgan had told him, "but hardly invincible. She is a fanatic—she makes mistakes. She *can* be defeated. You must not believe in her reality, but in your own!"

Ailwon shook his head, tried to concentrate on the music that continued behind him, the music he had known since infancy. He thought of Gwynn. They had met when they were still children, before he knew of his ancestry or of the weight of responsibility that would one day be his. She, with her uncle and aunt, had come to visit Penderak. The Andeluvian King and Queen had become her guardians when she had been orphaned. The visit was an official one with the Dwarf leaders. There would be many more in the ensuing years, during which Ailwon and the beautiful Brown Elf maiden would become fast friends. They were of similar age, but she matured much faster than he. She was keen of wit, outgoing and talkative, while he was quiet and shy. She could outrun, outswim and outfight him with ease. But she never demeaned him, and he knew that she had exhibited the same superiority over boys in her own land—and still did. When Erbin and Evrawk had begun to train him in the skills of weaponry, it was Gwynn, always eager for new endeavors, who often provided the challenges to his progress, usually beyond his ability to succeed. But he had progressed in these martial skills, and was perhaps now her equal, perhaps her superior. It didn't matter to him, nor to her. What mattered was the love between them that had grown ever deeper, until they had promised themselves to one another for the rest of their lives.

Ailwon's thoughts of his lover were interrupted. A small fallow deer stood in the middle of the road. He stared for an instant at the oncoming band, then bounded into the forest. The group emerged from the main body of the forest entering the corridor of guardian Trocalas. The music had ceased. Without an exchange of words, their collective pace increased, their mounts cantering toward the light marking the exit of the shadowed corridor that surrounded them. Then they were into the open, feeling the sudden warmth of morning. The gait of the horses slowed only a fraction as they crossed the great felled tree that extended from Delvinor to the far side of the ravine. The hoofbeats were sharp upon the hard surface fibers of the Trocalas, worn smooth by centuries of crossings. Life continued its flow beneath the pounding hooves, flowed despite the layers of hundreds of years. Then they were across, each of them feeling the coolness of shadows from the ancient stone portals as they passed through, all sensing the final presence of Elgan. Again, without suggestion or comment, the pace changed, slowed to a trot, then to a fast walk. The sun climbed from the east; before them the rolling hills were brilliant with the fresh green of early spring. The vista was immense, stretching almost totally unobstructed from the east to the south, clear to the distant mountains that formed the far western horizon. Horses and riders settled into the pace of the long ride. Soon the Forest of Delvinor was far behind.

The archer took a mouthful of cold water from the metal cup, swishing it about to clean his teeth, spitting it into the campfire, creating a hiss on the heated rocks and glowing embers. Hugh was a quiet and private man and for the first time in what seemed like a long while, he felt satisfied. Though a subtle sense of lack, of unfulfillment, had marked his life, he had always enjoyed an alliance with nature that never failed to provide him with comfort. The passage of this first day of the journey led to his present contentment. The weather had been perfect, and they had covered a great deal of ground. He was certain that by morning he would be suffering some physical discomfort from the many hours in the saddle. It had been years since he had ridden, but the pure pleasure he derived from it would more than make up for some initial stiffness and aches.

He had been amazed at the accomplishments of the Dwarfs and the Gwarpy in regard to their encampment. When it had come time to begin the search for a suitable area to stay the night, Prince Ailwon had called Oolu to move from the rear to the position of leadership. The furry creature had led the band some distance off course, and Hugh had to restrain himself from questioning their direction. But suddenly they had come across not only a swift-flowing stream, but a site that contained all the necessary requirements for comfortable camping. Then the Dwarfs had taken over, organizing the setup of their encampment in the quickest time imaginable. Wood had been gathered, water carried, a fire built, the horses unpacked and cared for and hobbled, and sleeping arrangements made ready. Soon a stew was bubbling in a pot hung from a spit, and a rolled pastry was browning—the combination sending off delightful odors into the night air. And the meal had been delicious! Hugh had never eaten such excellent food prepared in the open. With the conclusion of supper, the cleanup had taken place with as much dispatch as the preparation. Yet despite the speed and efficiency, the chores were completed with the same casualness that Hugh had come to associate with this group. They had all gone to the river to wash, before returning to relax beside the fire. The Dwarfs had each produced goatskin wine flasks. When both Ailwon and Hugh had declined to share the spirits with the twins, Evrawk had been genuinely disappointed, but Erbin's sorrow appeared a bit feigned, and within moments he had refilled his cup for the third time. Some banter regarding the love lives of the brothers began, which Ailwon found amusing, and Oolu—predictably—hilarious. It seemed that the pair had been considerably popular with the lasses of Penderak. While neither were young men any more, their popularity had scarcely diminished with increased age. Evrawk, it seemed, had finally settled down to courting just two of Penderak's loveliest. But Erbin required the aid of his fingers on both hands to list off the ladies that continued to capture his fancy: Rosy, Gert, Helen, Wilda, Flora, Hester, Nita, Tillie...

"When is it that you two lads are going to settle down?" jibed Ailwon, who had observed some of their escapades.

"Well, for certain we don't want to spoil family tradition," Evrawk declared. "Papa was fifty-five when he hitched with Mama, and she was forty-three. They'd had their eyes on each other for twenty years, but they both kept getting distracted, as you might say. Dwarf women aren't supposed to bear little ones much after forty-five, but she had twelve of us in the next ten years..."

"And hardly missed a night at the tavern..." Erbin was getting well into his cups. "Had four of us right there... So to stay even with Papa, we figure we got two more years—"

"Three," corrected Evrawk.

"...Three more years 'fore we gotta make any hard choices." Erbin started to tip his wine, but stopped to consult his fingers on the accuracy of his brother's arithmetic.

The Dwarfs began inquiries as to the specifics of Oolu's relationships with female Gwarpys, but received more chuckles and chortles than concrete information. Then Ailwon excused himself, and left the campfire circle. Evrawk brought out his mandolin. As he began strumming it, his brother started to sing:

Oh... that great Glopslukin called Torgon,
'Bout whom this conclusion is foregone:
He's certain t' bellow, an' sure t' throw fits,
He'll swear, an' he'll holler through teeth that he
     grits...
But he's gonna get kicked hard right where he
     sits!
Oh... that great Glopslukin called Torgon.

Hugh found himself smiling. "You don't make him

sound nearly so fearsome as did the wizard," he said.

Evrawk stopped playing. "He's fearsome, all right. Make no mistake. We might joke a bit about him—we've been harassed so long—but he's no joke. Not a bit of one."

"Tell me more," said Hugh.

Evrawk carefully placed his mandolin against a rock. He produced his pipe, and filled it. Hugh slid off the log where he had been sitting, leaning back against it, stretching out his legs.

The Dwarf lit his pipe and emitted a puff of smoke. "Torgon's a White Elf Prince," he said. "Strange as it might seem...he's an ancestor of Ailwon's—or at least he used to be. A thousand years ago, he was an Elf."

"That sounds almost unbelievable," said Hugh, "considering what I've heard about him."

Erbin took a healthy swallow from his goatskin flask. The Dwarf's mind seemed to have sobered with the turn toward more serious conversation. "Up until ten centuries ago," he continued, "the White Elves lived in peace, didn't have a weapon among 'em all, didn't even have the city back then. There was only one large structure: a tower that rose atop a hill between the twin lakes that feed the great River Garnon..."

"The Tower of Enlightenment," interjected Evrawk. "It still stands today. Anyway...there was a King and a Queen: Alamar and Therela by name, who had twin sons, Alfheim and Corthren. During those days there was a belief that somewhere to the north was a place of great magic and power—"

"What's now called Golgorath," said Erbin.

"Right... " affirmed his twin brother, who then proceeded with the story. "Nobody knows just what happened, except that one day Alfheim and Corthern rode off to look for this place, and when they didn't come back after a moon cycle, King Alamar went to look for his sons. He was met by a lone horseman. At first King Alamar didn't recognize who it was. Then he saw that it was his son, Corthren... only he was

changed, transfigured. So the King said, 'My son, are
you well?' And he replied, 'I am no longer your son. I
am not Corthren.' And he untethered this sack that
hung from his saddle...and he shouted at the King: 'I
am Torgon!' He pulled the grisly contents out of that
sack, and held it aloft. It was the head of Alfheim, his
brother! He hurled it at his father, turned his horse,
and rode north. Well," continued Evrawk, "as you can
well imagine, this just about killed the King. But he
returned to his wife and people. He told them the tale
of horror. Within just a few days, hordes of barbarians,
Gnomes and Borgs, swept down from the north.
They'd fallen prey to the power of this Torgon. The
White Elves were helpless. Those that weren't slaughtered or taken into slavery fled southward. Torgon's
forces pursued, capturing and murdering whenever
they caught the Elves..."

Evrawk's voice trailed off. He stared into the darkness that lay beyond the fire's glow. For a moment the
only sounds were those of the running stream, and
the voices of the night.

Erbin continued, "The Queen had been killed in the
first attack. One son had been murdered by the
other... and the murdering son, through the evil
power at Golgorath, had become a blood-lusting
tyrant. The King was a man of peace. He didn't know
how to deal with this type of thing. All he could
foresee was slavery and death..."

"Then the sorcerer Shandar came to him, and the
two of them left. They were gone for three moon
cycles."

"The White Elves," Evrawk went on, "had been
driven all the way down to the Jungles of Dangar.
They were in hiding there, when their King and
Shandar appeared before them. The King had
changed. He wore the Crownhelm, and carried the
great sword, Elvgard. And Shandar told them a
Prophecy—that there would be no peace for a thousand years...and there would be *none*, none at all if
they were to submit to tyranny... Hateful as it was to

them, they must fight... and their children must...
and their children's children... for a thousand years
they must fight! Till the Day of Fulfillment and freedom!"

"And so," said Erbin, "the White Elves fought back.
Led by their King, and the power of the Crownhelm
and sword, they drove the barbarians northward.
They looked for allies, and gained the support of the
Azmurians, and of the Dwarfs of Penderak. Finally, on
the Plains of Kiberuk, the allied forces engaged the
Death Lord's armies in a great battle which resulted in
something of a draw. The allies withdrew to the south,
Torgon's forces to the north."

"It was then," continued Evrawk, "that the White
Elves built Cryslandon around the Tower of Enlightenment. And Torgon started building his fortress at
Golgorath. For almost a thousand years the allies
have staved off attacks from the north... and some
from the south, from the witch. All the while seeking a
peace..."

Erbin picked up the tale, "Two decades ago the last
White Elf King, Ailwon's father, was killed, as were all
the other heirs to the Crownhelm. It's thought that it
might have been a traitorous White Elf that did the
murdering... and it looks as though the bastard's at
work again."

"Then," said Evrawk, "Elgan, Erbin, Oolu and me
took Ailwon's mother to Andeluvia, into hiding... And
it was then that she discovered she was carrying life.
Ailwon was born, but not long afterwards his mother
died. So, we—the four of us, and sometimes Shandar—raised the lad, moving him around between
Andeluvia, Penderak and Mowdra, to make sure that
the traitor wouldn't find out about him. But it looks as
though we weren't quite sneaky enough." The Dwarf
paused for a moment.

"Oh, yes," he continued, as he remembered what
he had wanted to relate, "Shandar had hidden the
Crownhelm in a place known only to the wizard and
sorceror these past twenty years."

Hugh had been listening intently. He shifted his position, before asking: "Without a King or Queen, who has led the White Elf nation?"

"You've never heard of Deciedon?" asked Erbin.

"No," replied Hugh.

"He's as big a hero to the White Elves as your own Rolmar and Dunstan were to the Vandorians. He was the youngest general ever to lead the Lejentors: the White Elf cavalry..."

"And," said Evrawk, "he was a good friend of Ailwon's parents. He was the only one the White Elves ever considered to have lead 'em, after the King and the heirs—the Sevenas as they're called—were killed. And he's ruled just like a king..."

"He's been holding off those bastard barbarians of Torgon's for twenty years!" exclaimed Erbin excitedly. "Gawl! He's the best damned swordsman on the continent... and he's brave as they come... Damned nice, too. I saw him less than a moon cycle ago and had a couple of brews with him," the little man added with a laugh, taking a healthy swallow of wine.

"It's a good thing Deciedon's up there in Cryslandon," added Evrawk. "It's for sure that Torgon's rallying all his forces, now that he probably knows about Ailwon... If he attacks, it'll be the White Elf citadel that he'll go after first."

"Have to get Ailwon up there quick soon, yep," declared Oolu. The Gwarpy stood up, stretched and yawned. "Ol' Oolu's gonna sleep now real good... Gonna early git awake, yep." He turned, and walked off to a tall clump of grasses, curling up, falling asleep almost instantly.

Hugh ran his hands across his face, and through his beard. He stood. "I can take care of the fire before I bed down," he offered. Then, without waiting for a reply, he asked, "Where did the Prince go?"

"I believe he wanted to do a little solitary thinking," said Evrawk. "I'll tend to the campfire...I'm a bit shy of being ready for sleep."

Hugh nodded. "Good night then," he said, and went

toward his sleeping place, which was situated on an incline beneath the branches of a cluster of fir trees. Erbin followed him.

Evrawk said good night to the archer, then turned his attention to the fire. When he had finished with it, he went to find Ailwon. One of the horses whinnied; the spirited gray, he thought. Evrawk stood still for a moment, but could detect no unusual sounds, and he continued on. He found the Elfin lad further up the slope, seated on a huge rock.

"Sorry to intrude on your thoughts, lad... but you asked me to let you know when I was heading for sleep."

Ailwon kept his eyes to the sky. "Yes... Thank you, Evrawk," he replied, "I was thinking about Gwynn. I've never worried about her before, even though she's engaged in battle many times in the past two years. It seems odd to me: I've never been tested in situations of crisis—at least not until yesterday. While many others have performed so nobly in the past; Gwynn, Deciedon, you, Evrawk..." he smiled, "your brother and... many others. And yet the task has fallen to *me*. The fate of all Urshurak rests on *my* shoulders..."

"The hope and trust is well placed, lad. Don't lose faith in the Prophecy... nor in yourself."

"The Prophecy does not guarantee success for us, Evrawk."

"Let me tell you this..." The timbre in Evrawk's voice caused Ailwon to turn toward him: "From the first moment—the first instant—that I pulled you from out of your mama, I knew that you were the one to lead us. It was you, and nobody else. You would be the one to face the stinking devils that want to put us all into chains... And it would be you that would be the one to unite all the people of Urshurak to fight for their freedom!" Evrawk looked at him. "Of course I knew that according to your blood, you're supposed to be the one... But what I knew then, and what I'm twenty times more sure of now... well, I'll be damned if that didn't have lots more basis than bloodlines and prophecies."

The moonlight escaped momentarily through moving clouds, and Ailwon could see the grit and determination in the Dwarf's face. The warmth, the wisdom, the fierce passion for freedom; all that was Evrawk shone from his face in that brief moment.

The Elfin lad slid from the rock, dropping lightly to the ground. He laid his arm across the older man's shoulders, and, in silence, they descended toward their campsite.

The stillness of night that surrounded the empty house of Mowdra was abruptly interrupted. The front door burst inward. Hulking forms of armored Vilderones shouldered their way into the hall, steel visors covering the brutish features, fierce weapons clenched in the huge fists. Flaming torches were held aloft. "Search every room!" growled the leader. Their steel-hobbed boots created a din in the corridor, and bit gouges into the hardwood floor. Doors were kicked in as they proceeded toward the rear of the house.

"Search that last room! I'll search the tower!"

"Yes, Rogmun."

The Vilderone leader kicked at the great tower door. It did not budge. Again! The door remained firmly closed. The gargoyle drew his heavy broadsword. He raised it, taking aim at the area where he guessed the inside latch would be. But before he could strike, the door slowly, silently, swung inward. Rogmun blinked, then, without lowering his weapon, he charged into the dark room. Silence. The Vilderone swept his torch about the room, disclosing the tools of the wizard: books, stacked and scattered, closed and opened. Scrolls, vials, cups, bowls, pots... A ponderous table hewn from wood of a Trocala... but no signs of life.

Rogmun lifted his heavy visor. His fierce eyes fixed on the stone steps that ascended into darkness. He advanced toward the stairwell, the echo of his heavy footsteps carried to the unseen upper reaches of the tower, reverberated, then descended, the echo fading...but not disappearing, transforming to a distant ringing that had in it a quality of voices. The Vilderone stopped still, one foot on the first stone step. He looked behind, then back up into the shadowed stairwell. He gasped; his huge torso jerked involuntarily. Just below the point where the stairs curved from sight stood a tall silent figure, half in shadow, staring down at Rogmun: the ghostly form appeared to be ancient, its white hair and beard were long and flowing.

A voice came from behind the Vilderone leader: "We can find no one. Did you search the tower, Rogmun?... Rogmun?..." Rogmun turned. His lieutenant repeated the question: "Did you search the tower?"

Rogmun looked back. The stairwell was empty.

"Yes! I searched...There is no one here!" He turned, and strode toward the door, then stopped and flung his torch into a stack of scrolls. "Burn it!" he shouted, "Burn this accursed place!"

Within moments the interior of Elgan's house was ablaze, and by the time the last Vilderone was

mounted, the entire structure was being devoured by
flames, as was the stable. The clearing was alive with
light, and with the roaring and crackling of yellow-
white heat. The Vilderone horses snorted and reared,
their eyes wild with fear. "We go straight to the great
River Garnon...to the meeting place with the traitorous one!" Rogmun shouted above the noise of the
burning buildings. He turned back to stare at the
house, the ringing voices in his mind still alive. He
shook his head, wheeled his horse, galloped toward
the bridge. The Vilderone steeds raced from Mowdra.
Behind, the roaring blaze reached its zenith, sending
heat and sparks high into the air. Suddenly the
tongues of flame were reversed, the energies of heat
withdrew, returned to their sources. The fire died
completely, leaving the buildings unscathed in the
moonlight. The quiet and the coolness of night
returned to Mowdra.

5

NORBRUK

T ark-Volmar trudged across the hard turf which was still frozen from winter, the hardy grasses more brown than green. He had sailed north to this point from his coastal village of Kozmor on the southern curve of Norbruk. The sailing party had consisted of just two ships. He with a score of men had been in one, and his wife, Asar, had been in the smaller ship with a dozen of their people. Tark-Volmar had been against his wife's accompanying him, but she had insisted. She had also refused to remain with the others when they reached their point of landing, and had climbed behind him up the rocky cliff, the waves of the frigid sea crashing below them. Upon reaching the top, Asar had stayed a few paces behind her husband, for she knew him to be in a dark mood. Despite his boisterous temper, she didn't fear him, and well knew the humor and gentleness beneath his bluster. But she knew also his passionate distaste for the meeting which motivated their voyage. An argument with her would do nothing to aid the situation.

They had almost reached the fjord: the "Cruska," It was called, the "Division." It was, by far, the longest arm of the ocean, and was roughly the divisor between the Frocald Sea and the Sea of Balta, the combination of which bordered Norbruk. The Cruska was also the dividing line between the clan of Hel-

strum and the clan of Skelf. It had been agreed by
Tark-Volmar, leader of the Helstrums, and by the Skelf
chieftain, Kolak the Black, to meet on opposite sides
of the fjord to insure that this encounter not end in
battle.

Tark-Volmar and Asar arrived at the place of meeting. No one waited on the opposite of the narrow inlet.
"Typical of the bastard," Tark-Volmar muttered. The
Skelf clan leader, Kolak the Black, was as tall and as
burly as Tark-Volmar himself. And like himself, Kolak
was tempestuous and stubborn. Though they had
been at odds for their entire lives, carrying on the
feuds of their ancestors, Tark-Volmar had always held
his counterpart in grudging respect. But no longer!
Not since his adversary had begun courting favor with
the Death Lord of Golgorath. The Helstrums and the
Skelfs had skirmished for five hundred years, but had
always contained their differences to within the
boundaries of their own country and among their
own race. But during the past few years the Skelfs had
accepted arms from Torgon in increasing amounts,
and in the past year had openly acted on the Death
Lord's behalf. On a half dozen occasions, Skelf sailing
vessels, manned by Norse sailors and assisted by
Torgon's barbaric warriors, had attacked Helstrum
fishing boats. These acts of aggression had resulted
in a number of deaths among Tark-Volmar's people,
and, worse than this, had caused a large number of
Norsepeople to be added to the growing number of
the Death Lord's slaves. Norsepeople as slaves! This
could not be tolerated! There was no longer a doubt
that Norbruk was among the nations that the Death
Lord intended to conquer, annihilating the inhabitants or throwing them into slavery as he triumphed
over them.

Thus Tark-Volmar had reluctantly sent word to the
Skelf chieftain to meet on this day at the Cruska. This
was Volmar's last, desperate attempt to unify the
Norsepeople against the threat of alien conquest. If
this failed and he had little hope that it would not,

there would be few alternatives other than to seek
support from other nations. This would mean an
alliance with the Azmurians. He shuddered at the
thought. The Norsepeople and the Azmurians had
been bitter enemies since ancient times. But the
threat of Torgon had somewhat eased the tensions
between them during the last two centuries. Tark-Volmar himself had been at the Azmurian capital, Tal-
Amon, when he was a boy. He had accompanied his
father. This had been almost forty years ago, and
there had been no personal exchange between either
nation since. There was still no love wasted between
them, yet the Azmurians were Volmar's first choice if it
was necessary to seek allies. Despite the vast difference in terrain and climate, the southern portions
of Norbruk and the city of Tal-Amon were not extremely far apart in terms of traveling time. This—due
to the excellence of the Norsemen as sailors, and to
the inland waterways of Azmuria—had prompted
some trading during the past years of the uneasy
truce. More important than traveling distance was the
Norse acknowledgment of the Azmurians as expert

fighters, masters with the sword and bow and arrow.
As distasteful as it might be, Tark-Volmar was fully
prepared to leave immediately for Tal-Amon, in the
event that this meeting ended in failure. He allowed
himself an inner smile at the prospect of again
meeting the Azmurian leader, Ali Ben Kara.

Volmar glanced back at his wife. She was calmly
watching the sea, her gaze concentrated on the spot
where Kolak the Black would first appear. Tark-Volmar
swore beneath his breath. He had accurately predicted that the Skelf chieftain would try to keep him
waiting, and thus he had deliberately delayed his
arrival by almost a half-day. And still he had to wait.
He paced along the edge of the cliff, cursing with
almost every step. A gust of wind blew his heavy fur
cape sideways, and he glanced toward the sky. High
above, great masses of clouds were being driven
toward the Balta Sea. The unusual wind direction
would work against him, should he have to sail to the
south, but this concerned him little. The hardships of
their environment had rendered the Norsepeople
fully capable of coping with almost any normal life
situation that confronted them.

"He comes," said Asar.

Three sailing vessels had appeared from behind an
outcropping of a cliff, and were veering toward the
natural harbor. All three boats were adorned with
frowning dragon heads atop the towering prows.
Within minutes forty Norsemen were climbing up the
rocks. Tark-Volmar watched as they gained the top,
and came forward. Kolak the Black, so named for his
thick black hair and huge beard, had apparently
acquired some extravagant tastes since Volmar had
last seen him. His cape was made of woven cloth,
rather than from animal skins and fur, its edges were
brocaded with golden thread. There was gold in his
helmet, his sword handle and scabbard, and in the
clasp that held his cape. He stood facing Tark-Volmar
across the fjord, his feet spread wide, his thumbs
hooked in the wide weapon-belt.

"Let's get on with it," Kolak's voice boomed across the divide. "I'm not eager to waste more time than necessary."

Tark-Volmar's teeth were clenched; his mighty shoulders heaved as he sighed. "This meeting's got no more appeal to me than to you," he began, "but there's no time left for us to fight among ourselves. Neither I nor my people can overlook your alliance with Torgon, so he could kill us or make us slaves... But we *can* set that quarrel aside—for a time. We've killed each other, and taken prisoners before, so your treachery can be put aside...maybe even forgotten, if we can straighten out our differences."

Kolak threw back his head, and his laughter roared above both the wind and Tark-Volmar's voice. Volmar felt the heat rising from his neck, felt the light touch of Asar's hand on his back. He gritted his teeth once more, heaved another sigh, and began again:

"We're all Norsepeople. We've got lots more things of common nature than we do differences. It's time—long past time—to unite our people. We've got to face this bastard Death Lord together. You can't gain by joining with him...He'll destroy you along with every-body else after he uses you. You'll be a damned slave too. Even now, you swear allegiance to him..." Kolak was nonchalantly gazing at the sky. His men behind him joked, and laughed in low voices. Tark-Volmar's face was beet-red, growing redder by the minute.

"Damn it, man!" he bellowed across the chasm. "The bastard is already your master. The Norsepeople have never known masters... We are all equal—*all* of us!" The final words were shouted with such force that their echos descended the walls of the fjord.

Tark-Volmar had finished. Kolak had been unable to ignore his last sentence. He glared across the Cruska. "You live in the past, Volmar," he shouted. "You are too stupid to understand the power of the Death Lord. You haven't seen his giant machines, his fortress. You don't know a thing about the power of Torgon! He will control all of Urshurak!...and I will be

given all of Norbruk!" He started to turn away but
looked back toward Tark-Volmar, and he began to
laugh: "You'll never get smart, Volmar...not when you
need a woman to give you courage." He turned his
back to them, roaring with laughter. His men were
laughing too as they walked away.

Asar spat toward them, and cursed. Tark-Volmar
was livid. He watched the Skelf chieftain swagger
away, the gold-brocaded cape flowing behind him, his
brawny arms about the shoulders of two of his
lieutenants, his helmeted head thrown back, black
hair flying out from beneath the helmet. Then Tark-
Volmar remembered: Beneath the helmet that he was
loath to remove within anyone's sight, the top of
Kolak the Black's head had grown as smooth and
shiny as an eagle's egg. Volmar grinned, and shouted
after the departing group:

"When I next see you, have your weapons ready...
Kolak the Bald!" Kolak stopped dead in his tracks,
wheeled about, rushing back toward the edge of the
Cruska, shouting and cursing.

But Tark-Volmar and Asar had turned away, and
were headed back toward their boats. Volmar's arm
was around his wife. They both snickered like amused
children, while the bellowing of Kolak the Bald grew
more distant.

6

ELGAN

Elgan walked slowly through the forest. At this time in the plan there was no need for haste. Even if every aspect of Ailwon's mission were carried out in the minimum amount of time, the wizard would still be able to reach Tal-Amon, go on to Evshimin, and arrive at Cryslandon several days before the Elfin Prince. Elgan would use a much swifter mode of travel when he reached the desert, but for now walking suited him fine.

During the previous four days of his journey the nature of Delvinor's terrain had gradually changed. The sharp contrasts of elevation that spawned chasms, ravines and waterfalls in the land surrounding Mowdra was no longer evident. From the towering peaks in the Bolgad Mountains, the land running eastward to the River Garnon had begun to decline, and had been reduced to a series of gentle moss- and ivy-covered slopes. The woods here were especially dark and damp. Heavy undergrowth surrounded the giant Trocalas, and the leaves of the smaller trees, the dense growth of ferns, the sprawling ivy and the earth itself clung jealously to the wetness bequeathed them by the rains of the past days.

The wizard's feet and the bottom of his robe were soaking wet within moments of resuming his journey each morning, and remained so until nightfall when he sat beside his campfire. Elgan gave no thought to this; nor, if he had, would he have considered it a matter of discomfort or inconvenience. Such had not always been the case. Long years ago, centuries ago, he'd been at definite odds with the surroundings of nature. He had reflected a good deal on this, and on related matters, since first setting out on this cool morning.

The passage of many years had scarcely dimmed his memory of himself as the wealthy magician and trusted advisor to the early kings and barons of Vandor. He had then been known as Tamen of Vandor. Magician. Philosopher. Advisor supreme. He was the most influential of men. All sought his advice, and the blessing of his magics: kings, barons, the wealthiest of merchants. He was not available to commoners, except during special ceremonies when he would appear before the masses to enthrall them with wonders.

And he proclaimed the same philosophy to all: he assured them of the validity of their beliefs. Vandorians were above the stupidities of the other races. They were superior. Vandorian men were, of course, superior to women, and adults to children. But as a people, there could be no wavering from the course that had served them so well. Was it not true that there was hardship and deprivation in many of the lands beyond the Bolgad Mountains? But not in Vandor. Of course, hard work was an absolute necessity to insure prosperity, and they must be obedient (how else would royalty and the wealthy maintain power?). Hard work, obedience to authority, the acquisition of goods, sacrifices to make possible their acquisitions, neatness, cleanliness, good manners, adherence to traditions: these were the ingredients that must guide the lives of Vandorians. So had decreed Tamen, Grand Wizard.

Elgan paused in his thoughts to chuckle. There always seemed to him to be some irony in the idea that both he and Torgon had changed their names after embracing the changes of their natures. The

wizard looked up. Above him a bird indulged himself
in a free-spirited call. Elgan stopped walking, and
returned the call. The bird cocked his head, observing
the old man for a moment. Then, hopping down the
branch, he stopped directly above the wizard and
resumed his song. The old man politely voiced his
pleasure at meeting so fine a fellow, and recom-
menced both his walking and the review of his
memories: as Tamen, he had never quite believed all
he had preached to the Vandorians, but never, in that
time, confronted himself with these doubts. To do so
would have constituted a grave threat to the illusions
he believed were essential to his survival: his material
wealth, his title, his identity as a sage of great wisdom.
These constituted his power. He guarded them as
jealously as did any in Vandor. And he employed the
same tactics as the rest. He suppressed all his feelings of sadness and anger, of loneliness, denied the
feelings of emptiness that were the result of his
self-imposed enslavement. Finally he was struck by
the realization that he was growing old, and the fear
of death attacked him with all its awesome force. The
Grand Wizard came near to panic, though he covered
his fears beneath his usual guise of stoic wisdom.

Then word had come of the approach of a wan-
derer: a black man, a sorcerer, it was said, and a
prophet. When he arrived before the gates of Romak,
the central city of Vandor, a group of the elite had
gathered atop the protective wall. Tamen was their
spokesman, and shouted down questions to the
ragged prophet. And the old man told the wealthy
and important Vandorians that his name was Shandar. He had wandered among the peoples of Urshurak for years, foretelling the change that was to
come among them: of a force that would soon bring
them a choice to be made between a return to the old
ways that could free them from the bonds of hatred
and disunity, or a continuation of their present course
that was certain to bring them beneath the iron rule
of slavery. Tamen and the others had mocked this

madman, and prepared to send him away. But before doing so, they had questioned him as to where he had come from. Shandar had answered that he lived among the Azmurians in the Azante Desert. But first he had come from the earth, and from the earth had entered a tree, and from the tree had become a mammal, and from the beast he had come to his present form. Such were the powers of change, he had said. The Vandorians had howled with laughter, and had sent him away.

Within an hour of the visit and expulsion of the sorcerer, Tamen had become ill. Each day his health had declined, and soon the Grand Wizard of Vandor lay dying. He felt the life forces slipping from his body, and pangs of anger and despair and sorrow rose in him at the waste of his life. He cried out to the darkness, and began to weep. Then a calm that was not death had settled over him. And he had felt the enormous powers that had been held in bondage these long years, felt them spread outward from the core of his being, and he had stood up and walked away from his deathbed. He had left the house and had gone away from Vandor, joyously leaving behind his title, his position, his security, his caution and his wealth. Across the Bolgad Mountains he went on foot, through the Pass of Camen, and then northward across the rolling grasslands. Drawn forward by unrelenting forces, he followed an unmarked path that would not be traveled for a thousand years until the coming of the Vandorian, Hugh Oxhine.

On he walked, he with no name, neither eating nor sleeping. Finally he had come to the Forest of Delvinor, and the joy of his destiny rushed outward to meet him. He had entered among the giant Trocalas, enthralled as a child would be by the wonders of the forest, seeing through the eyes of innocence the glory of growing things, feeling the thrust of life beneath his feet. At last he came to the clearing which would be called Mowdra. In the center the sorcerer, Shandar, sat silently on the ground... waiting. And he with no name had spoken. "I am Elgan," he had said, "which means 'Oneness.' " Shandar had come forward, and they had embraced, and tears of joy flowed from the one who had been reborn as Elgan.

The living memory of this encounter now produced tears of joy in the wizard as he walked, and they refreshed him. This had been the purpose of the deliberate pace of his journey eastward, and the intentional recalling of his past. During the days and months leading to the actual inception of the quest, he had felt an increasing drain on his powers and energies. He had been greatly in need of rejuvenation. The struggle had been so very long. And always the knowledge had been with him that no matter how intense the efforts at peace, the final destiny of Urshurak would be decided, in part, by hateful warfare. Through the centuries, the collective voice of the murdered cried out, not for justice and not for revenge, but for meaning. Within the wizard there was absolute loathing of the battle that must come, but there was a great relief that at long last the Fulfillment drew near. And Elgan could feel the spirit of the quest that was alive across the land, that would unite the people in the common cause of freedom.

The voice of a river intruded upon his thoughts. He stilled his mind to better experience its song and the fragrance of its life. The river came into view, and Elgan went to it, refreshing himself with its substance. Many creatures watched from hiding as the old wizard drank and washed himself. He became aware of their presence, and called them to join him. The creatures then came from their places of hiding, and approached the river to share its bounty with the ancient being.

7

THE STORM

T hat, I'd suppose, is the Pass of Camen." Erbin pointed toward the mountains on his right. The small band had not strayed far from the river since finding it the night before. Erbin's supposition aroused no response from the archer who rode beside him. But the Dwarf was undeterred: "If that's true, then that's where the Vandorian heroes Rolmar and Dunstan gained fame among their people, eh?"

Still no answer. Yet Erbin was unflinching in his pursuit of knowledge. His eyes remained riveted on the historic mountain pass, his mind alive with fantasies of battles. "Perhaps," he persisted, "you'll give me an account of some of the heroics that went on there. Anytime you might feel up to it, Hugh..."

"Perhaps," replied Hugh.

The Dwarf smiled and nodded. Erbin's optimism was almost irrepressible, and he viewed even so vague a response as this to be a near-solemn promise.

Hugh was scowling. Before he had drifted off to sleep the previous night, he'd been struck by a sudden fear. He was growing too close to these people. Feelings of attachment had been gradually building ever since he had first become involved, especially toward the Dwarfs and the Gwarpy. He must not lose sight of *his* quest. Friendship with these people could only serve to complicate his life, could only distract him from his purpose. When he had awakened that morning, he'd determined to permit no further breakdowns in the fortifications that guarded his emotions. He had thus avoided conversation as much as possible. This had been no easy chore. His companions, especially Oolu and Erbin, seemed totally dedicated to friendliness.

Before long, the running water turned southeast, and the small band was again riding across rolling grassland. The clouds that had engaged the moon in a running battle for the entire night found no quarrel with the bright sun. This day was as clear as the previous had been. The terrain began to descend, gradually at first, then more steeply. Large gray rocks appeared along both edges of the river, spreading to the surrounding land, discouraging the various forms of life. After a time only the hardiest scrub brush poked from beneath the accumulated rocks and shale, and as the descent continued even the brush disappeared. By midday a lifeless wasteland spread before the band. Only the river disrupted the desolation, and it was so shallow and sluggish that it appeared not to be flowing at all. Waves of heat created a shimmering, distorted view as the horses slowly picked their way over the hard, uneven surface. The sun boiled down, the heat became oppressive. After some initial cursing and complaining in regard to the surroundings, conversation between the horsemen died completely. Feelings of apprehension grew among them.

Sleeves were rolled up, weapon belts hung from saddles to enable the men to loosen their garments. Still their shirts and tunics and their pants became soaked with perspiration. Beads of sweat ran from their foreheads, yet fear of the torrid sun kept them from removing their hoods. Finally, the unyielding monotony of the rocky terrain was replaced on the distant horizon by myriad colors. The band urged their mounts forward.

As they drew nearer they could see how startling was the demarcation between the wretched terrain they were leaving and that which they were about to enter. Before them was a sea of wildflowers, comprising the most incredible array of brilliant colors they had ever seen. Though Ailwon's gray stallion balked before entering, they were soon trotting over the immense field. A profusion of color lay all about them. Daisies; blue columbine; pink bitterroot; wild flowers; a variety of sizes of bluebells; countless goldenrod, stained red at their centers; larkspurs, some over seven feet high, and even they dwarfed by the giant sunflowers. The perfume from such abundance was extremely potent, and the further the small band rode, the more overpowering became the sweet odors. The heat of the day had barely diminished, the air was humid. An air of lethargy had begun to affect both horses and riders. Their movements became slow and sluggish. The heavy air vibrated with a barely audible droning sound that seemed to emanate from below the ground. Oolu yawned, as did Erbin. Hugh shook his head, fighting to clear his brain of an increasing thickness, but felt his desire to combat it slowly diminish. Evrawk slumped forward in his saddle, and though he appeared to be sleeping, he began to hum a pleasant tune. Erbin's pony had wandered sideways, gently colliding with Oolu's long-haired little steed. With that, both animals ceased their forward motion and stood still with heads drooped, slowly swishing their tails. Neither of their masters had an inclination to urge their mounts on, and leaned against one another, the right arm of the Dwarf around the furry shoulder of the Gwarpy. Oolu was snoring, while Erbin's smile and the droop of his eyelids made him look as though he'd consumed a half-score cups of brew.

Ailwon made a great effort of will to ward off the oppressive atmosphere. He had a tremendous urge to dismount, to lie down among the gorgeous flowers and sleep. He fought against such urges, and turned toward the others. Only the archer's horse was still in motion, but the tall man was swaying in the saddle, his eyes glazed and dull. Ailwon shouted at him—only the shout seemed to barely exceed a whisper: "Hugh, we must escape this place! There is treachery about here!"

Hugh's voice was slurred as he returned the whisper: "You're wrong. We don't have to leave. Why should we? This is the most beautiful place I've ever been in... Let's stay here... Let's lie down and rest..."

Ailwon tried to protest, formed the words in his mind, but when he attempted to speak them no sound came forth. His whole body felt numbed. His horse came to a halt, and the Elfin lad slid from the saddle, would have fallen to the ground had he not caught hold of the pommel. He stared down at the flowers that seemed to both blend together and to stand out singularly in the most vivid of realities.

Hugh rode slowly past, looking down at Ailwon, smiling as if intoxicated. The archer's horse plodded forward, leaving the others behind. Hugh stared ahead at the endless montage of colors. "Maybe I'd better stop and rest..." he thought. "...Yes, I'd better sleep..." The sky before him began to darken, and he thought at first that he was falling asleep atop his horse. The low droning had stopped; there was no sound at all, there was absolute calm. Hugh felt a slight breeze on his face, and there was coolness in it and moisture. The distant sky was changing rapidly, only a slender streak of light fringed the horizon. The wind was increasing. The clouds churned, grew more dense, blocking the sunlight until it appeared as though night was near to falling. The turmoil of moisture charged the atmosphere, lightning flashed from cloud to earth and returned, its energy echoing in the slow roll of thunder. The power of the oncoming storm was preluded in the force of the wind, that drove premature droplets of water before it. Hugh was fortified almost instantly by the living force in the sudden change of environment, as was his steed. Santor whinnied, and reared as a second streak of

light forked east to west against the darkness, followed by crashing thunder much closer than the first.
Hugh calmed the big stallion, regaining control just
as the rain began to fall.

He heard voices behind him, and turned. The
others had emerged from the spell of lethargy, and
they too fought to steady their mounts, amidst
flashes of lightning and claps of thunder that had
increased in frequency and seemed to come from all
around. Santor reared again, almost unseating the
archer. An incredible ball of light had rolled right
beneath the horse, exploding among the other
members of the band. The horses were wild with
fright; Erbin was tossed from the saddle, but held to
his reins, managing to keep his pony from running
off. Another lightning ball seemed to come from
nowhere, blazing past not twenty paces away.

"This *must* be the work of the witch!" shouted
Evrawk.

Ailwon rode closer to the Vandorian, fighting his
panicked gray. "Hugh!" yelled the Prince, above the
noise of the thunderstorm, "we had better seek
shelter. Evrawk is right...There is witchcraft at work
here!"

The Vandorian turned back toward the south. His
face was pelted by rain, his clothing was saturated
and stuck to the hard muscles of his frame, the wind
whipped against the wetness on his body. The sea of
wildflowers bent and threshed, yielding in the violent
air. His horse had calmed, and stood unflinching,
waiting for his master's command. The archer turned
to the others. The ponies had moved close for protection, Ailwon's mount still dancing nervously. Hugh
had never seen such a bedraggled and woebegone
group. Suddenly Hugh roared with laughter: "Come,
lads!" he called. "This magnificence is surely no work
of evil!"

The rest stared at the archer. He laughed again at
them, at himself, at the storm that raged about him.
His hair was plastered down, wet curls lay on his

forehead, his beard dripped. But his eyes were alive
with passion. None in the group had seen more than
a hint of this part of the tall archer before.

"Well," he called to them, "if you all wish to run for
cover then so be it. I intend to ride south...*now!* If this
is the work of the Witch of Zorak, then I find *her* more
stupid than clever." He pointed toward them. *"Think!"*
he cried, "a moment before we were trapped beneath
a spell of lethargy...then this storm..."

His voice was lost to a tremendous clap of thunder.
Santor snorted, jerking up his head. The archer
steadied his horse and guided him back around to
the south. He stood straight up in the stirrups,
shouting into the wind, the strength of his voice
carrying to those behind him:

"Whether you be the work of nature, or of that foul
wretch of the swamp...*damn* you—I'll test your
powers!" Hugh dropped to the saddle, snapping his
heels against the stallion's flanks in the same movement. Santor bolted forward, opening a path through
the wildly swaying flowers. The Vandorian's shoulders
were squared as he leaned forward into the face of
the storm.

Hugh's companions stared after him. They looked
at one another, their faces briefly illumined by lightning. Then Aliwon urged his steed forward; Oolu and
the Dwarfs followed in unison. They strove to catch up
to the horse and rider who galloped before them
toward the dark horizon and the Marshes of Zorak.

8

PENDERAK

The City of the Dwarfs was rooted directly in the granite escarpments of the Kolgar Mountains. Many of its buildings were scarcely distinguishable from the rugged cliffs, and the spires and pinnacles that rose from scattered turrets and towers mingled with the tall, slender firs that surrounded the city. The craftmanship of the Dwarfs had captured the strength and vitality of the environment.

Night had overtaken Gwynn and her cousins, Ianen and Glenden, before they could reach Penderak on the sixth day of the quest. But by night they had encountered no difficulty in locating the City of the Dwarfs. The life of that community sprang out from the darkened countryside so vividly it was almost startling. Torches burned in every wall turret, the windows were alive with light from candles and hearths, campfires dotted the hills beyond, and lights could even be seen in the lofty windows of distant towers that guarded the rear of the city. Such warmth was a welcome sight to the trio, who were weary with travel.

Gwynn led the way down a winding path toward the stone bridge which arched across a natural moat. They were challenged at the entranceway, but when Gwynn was recognized a jubilant call went from guard to guard, then inward to the city, announcing the arrival of the Brown Elf heroine. The winding city

streets were thronged with boisterous Dwarfs, who moved freely through the narrow streets and open squares, going in and out of open houses and shops. Any such gathering of Dwarfs was certain to promote an abundance of hearty laughter, passionate discussion and robust debate. And it appeared to Gwynn as though nearly the entire nation had gathered within and around the city.

Gwynn had spent a good deal of time in Penderak. She knew the spirit of its people, knew how they delighted in communal gatherings, where both emotions and beer ran freely. She knew, also, that no one here, save Erbin and Evrawk's parents, knew the reasons behind the call they'd received to gather at the city. However, Esrund, the twins' father, had been chief spokesman among the Dwarf leaders for over four decades. Thus, when he had sent out the call to gather, the Dwarf nation responded. They had begun arriving four days before, and were waiting for word as to the meaning of the gathering. But even knowledge of the dangers that lay before them would not have diminished the celebration taking place, now into its fourth night.

Gwynn and her cousins dismounted and tethered their horses, making their way through the crowds on foot. Neither Glenden or Ianen had been to the Dwarf nation before. The spontaneous display of communal spirit was foreign to them... and totally delightful. The knowledge that their cousin, Gwynn, had spent a goodly amount of time within this environment gave them some understanding of her personality. As she had matured Gwynn had exhibited ever-increasing displays of powerful emotions, so out of character for most Andeluvians. The lads marveled at the easy, enthusiastic affection Gwynn displayed as she exchanged heartfelt greetings with individuals within the free-flowing crowd.

A particularly robust voice boomed out a greeting to her. She searched for its source, and upon finding it called out with delight: "Nolan!...And Wilda!"

A black-bearded Dwarf, with an equally black patch covering his left eye, maneuvered through the crowd toward her. With him was a red-haired Dwarf woman, who clutched an enormous mug of beer. Gwynn and the Dwarfs met midway beneath a tunneled arch, and all three embraced. Gwynn introduced the Dwarfs to her cousins. Nolan and Wilda were both members of Penderak's governing council, and were great friends of Erbin and Evrawk. Wilda's eyes lit especially bright at the mention of Erbin's name. Gwynn told them that she needed to find Esrund as quickly as possible for she had brought a message of the greatest urgency.

"Sure," said Wilda. "He and Maude have been telling everybody, 'Watch out for that long-legged Elfin lass,'...Been saying that for two days!"

Gwynn grimaced. "We were due this morning," she said. "We ran into a fierce storm on the way up."

"Well, let's lollygag no longer!" cried Nolan, his good eye wide open. "They're over at the Tavern-Meet right now!"

"As usual!" Wilda shouted above the street sounds.

"As usual!" agreed Nolan, and they surged through the crowd. The Brown Elves followed as closely as possible until the five of them reached an opening in the free-flowing arrangement of buildings that constituted the city. It was generally referred to as 'The Square,' though in fact, the buildings that faced it were arranged in a circular pattern. The Square was the principal gathering place for the city's inhabitants. At its center stood Tavern-Meet which was at once an inn, a tavern, an eatery, a dance hall, and a town hall where the Dwarfs debated issues concerning the affairs of Penderak. The most serious of debates and the most ribald of parties took place within this structure, often with the former directly preceding the latter. The essence of Tavern-Meet was carved deep into a massive wooden beam above the door: "LIBERTY—SOLIDARITY—TOMFOOLERY."

It seemed that a large collection of Dwarfs was enacting this message to its fullest: a chaotic co-min-

Opposite: Gwynn at Penderak

gling of lively music and loud voices rose from the below-ground-level hall, spilling into The Square. Following their escorts, Gwynn and her cousins passed through the open main entrance, turned to the left, descending a half-turn of wooden steps to the tavern below. The huge room was filled with Dwarfs, and with pipe smoke that drifted upward to form a bluish haze about the ceiling and the first-floor sleeping rooms. A group of musicians set the festive mood as horns, fiddles and flutes, backed by drums, brought the emotions of the people to a fever pitch. Scores of dancers swung about with arms locked, their solid shoes pounding the rhythm on the wooden floor, their beet-red faces expressing the delight of a Penderak folk dance. Barely subdued by the sounds of the musicians were the voices of the other patrons, most of whom were engaged in combinations of discussion, debate, game playing, drinking and eating. A long table held steaming food, promoting a constant coming and going of hungry Dwarfs. Rich smells of cooked meats and cooked cabbage, sage, hot peppers and hot pastries vied with the aromatic odors of a half-hundred burning pipes. And, seated at a huge round table, cheered on by a score of their neighbors, Esrund of the house of Uxmun and his wife Maude had locked hands in a contest of arm-wrestling, to decide for the umpteenth time who was the stronger of the sexes. Esrund was nearly as thick as he was tall, and despite his advanced years there were still none in Penderak to approach him as an arm-wrestler, save his son, Evrawk... and his wife of fifty years. Neither he nor she, it seemed, had been able to gain an advantage during a full five minutes of struggling. Suddenly Esrund looked up, and cried out: "Gwynn, my lass!"

Maude looked up, saw the beautiful Elfin maid standing across from her, and at the same instant her knuckles were slammed against the wooden table.

"Why, you thieving..." she hollered. But old Esrund was headed around the table toward Gwynn, and

Maude scrambled to the short side, beating her husband by a second, grabbing the slender young woman in a bear hug.

"Where've you been, dearie?" shouted Maude. "We was worried to death!" She stared up at the smiling Elfin maid; her solid round arms pinned Gwynn's arms to her sides.

Gwynn freed herself, and swept her hand across the room. The music continued to blare, the dancers still stomped about. "It's apparent to me...the worry's so thick here it could be sliced with nothing by the sharpest cleaver." Hoots and hollers came from the gathered crowd. It was Esrund now who grabbed Gwynn, leading her toward a chair. "We were scared silly, lass...This's all just coverin' up," he said.

Gwynn was pushed gently into a chair. "Let's quaff a few beers," continued Esrund, "and you can tell us all the news." Ianen and Glenden were similarly placed in chairs, foaming mugs of ale placed before them. Gwynn stood up. She put her hands on a shoulder of both Esrund and Maude. "You know how highly I regard your hospitality," she said. "But..."she hesitated, "we must tell your people..." she paused, and then: "It has begun."

The white-haired couple looked toward one another, then back up to Gwynn. "We knew, of course, this must be true," said the Dwarf woman, "But—"

"But," interrupted Esrund, staring at the floor, "it seems that after all these years...the time can't finally have come..." He looked up. "Well, let's get on with it!" The Dwarf patriarch climbed atop a chair. "Listen, my friends!" he shouted. The music and the dancing ceased. "There's to be an announcement that'll curl your ears! Go out into the streets and the hills! Gather in everybody! We'll meet back at The Square!"

Indeed, everyone that could fit within the city had crammed inside its walls. With the knowledge that the announcement was to be made from The Square, it was natural that as many had gathered around that area as was comfortable. But, somehow, the entire arrangement had been structured with a minimum of pushing and shoving. And true to custom, those who could not hear the actual proclamation would have the gist of the message passed back to them by extemporaneous orators.

The houses and shops were quickly deserted, their lights extinguished. The Square was illuminated with burning torches, yellow-orange light played on the people and on the leaded windowpanes of the surrounding buildings. Dwarf men, women and children stood in The Square, sat on steps and atop arches and cross-beams, perched on stoops, gables and rooftops. All faced the doorway of Tavern-Meet, where Gwynn, Esrund and Maude, Nolan, Wilda and a handful of other Dwarf leaders were standing. Ianen and Glenden stood in The Square within the crowd, finding a secret excitement in mingling with the Dwarf populace. They were quickly asked to squat down so as not to block the view. Only a low murmur traveled through the throng, and this died at once as Esrund began to speak:

"My friends...Most of you know that this lass beside me is Gwynn of Andeluvia. And for certain you know of how she raised a small group of Andeluvians, and how they've fought off the barbarians for nearly two years...Well, now this brave lass has something to tell us all, that—like I said before—will curl your ears...."

Gwynn looked around at the expectant faces, and began to speak:

"When I was a small girl I made my first visit here, and I've returned whenever it was possible. Loving Penderak and its people has been the easiest thing I've ever done. So my heart swells to near bursting with the news I bring, for it is news of life and hope... Yet I can scarcely bear to tell it, for it also carries with it the bloody threat of warfare." Her words were passed through the streets almost as an echo. "You know of the Prophecy, and know that the time of the Fulfillment draws near. You believe that there is none with a claim to the power of Crownhelm, and thus, none to

stand against Torgon with any thought of success...
And you believe that the time inches forward when
you and those you love will be slaughtered, or thrown
into slavery. I marvel at your courage, in the face of
these beliefs...But, there *is* an heir! There *is* a Sevena!" A murmur spread through the crowd. "After
King Aradel and the remaining Sevenas had been
murdered, a child was born to Queen Lurona, born in
secrecy... in Andeluvia!" A cheer went up from the
crowd in The Square, and then another further back,
and another. "He is the Prince Ailwon... soon to be
crowned at Cryslandon." Her voice had dropped. "I
ask you to join us there... for afterward we march
against the Death Lord. In dark Golgorath we will
decide the final fate of Urshurak...." Gwynn's voice
was barely more than a whisper. Then she looked
around at the people, and shouted: "And when we
return from Golgorath... we will gather again at
Cryslandon... *And where we will all hold the
damnedest celebration ever seen on the continent!*"

The crowd cheered lustily. Gwynn stepped back,
and Esrund shouted above the cheers: "Even now, our
sons, Erbin and Evrawk," his arm went around Maude,
"accompany the White Elf Prince southward. They will
destroy the witch, Gorta...They will go on to Zan-Dura
and make allies of the Amazon women, and then
return to Cryslandon. Tomorrow we start toward the
Elfin citadel. There we will be unified: the White Elves
of Alfandel, the Brown Elves of Andeluvia, the people
of Azmuria, the Norsepeople of Norbruk, the Amazons
of Zan-Dura... *and the Dwarfs of Penderak!*" The
people roared. Esrund started to exhort them further,
but it was needless. The collective cheering disappeared, replaced with a number of individual shouts
and with jubilant laughter. The energy of intense
listening and joyous response was transferred to
action, as the crowd began to disperse, intent upon
making preparation for the beginning of the single
most important event of their lives.

Gwynn watched them, and heaved a deep sigh. Next she must confront her pacifist uncle, King Zarin. Maude touched her arm. "You can put up with me and Esrund at our house," the Dwarf woman said, "and of course the lads are welcome too."

Gwynn smiled. "Thanks for your kindness," she replied, "I think that Glenden and Ianen would enjoy that immensely, as normally I would. But I feel the need for a night by myself, and so I'll take a room at the inn. I hope you understand..."

"Of course, dearie." The Dwarf woman gave Gwynn a hug, and said good night. "Come on, Esrund, we better get on with it."

The old Dwarf leader's eyes were shining, and he was smiling as he passed Gwynn. "Got to get out my armor," he said to the young woman. She bent down, kissed him on the forehead, then watched as he and Maude took her cousins in tow.

"Come on, Gwynn," said Wilda, who, with Nolan, had remained standing nearby, "We'll see that you get a room in the inn."

"Sure," chimed in Nolan, itching behind his patch, "we can do that easy...."

"No females on this journey that Erbin's gone on, eh?" the Dwarf woman asked Gwynn.

"No," Gwynn replied.

Wilda shook her head. "Bet he's really downing the spirits." She took a healthy swallow from the ever-present mug. "Those Amazon ladies will have to watch themselves." She took Nolan by the arm, and strolled through the scattered crowd. Gwynn laughed as she followed the Dwarf pair toward the entrance of Tavern-Meet.

9

ONWARD

G wynn awoke with a start. Sounds of activity entered her room from The Square below, and sunlight crept through the half-open shutters. She jumped out of bed. She'd had no intention of sleeping past daybreak. Using the pitcher of water and bowl beside her bed, she quickly washed, and was fully dressed and combed within five minutes. She had allowed herself to be talked into a before-bed drink with Wilda and Nolan. But the lone drink had been miraculously transformed into an even half dozen, and her bedtime had been set back three hours. She gathered her weapons and bedroll under one arm, and turned toward the door. She paused with her hand on the latch, smiled and thought that she would always trade an extra hour's sleep and an early rising for companionship such as she had experienced last night.

Footsteps, then voices, came from the hallway just outside her room, and Gwynn opened the door. Her youthful cousins were coming toward her. "Good morning, my lovely cousin!" called Glenden, who was in the lead, and wore a far broader smile than he had ever before revealed to her.

"...Your *lovely* cousin?" she inquired. "What's got into you?"

"Why should you be surprised, Gwynn?" the Elfin lad asked, his eyes open with astonishment. He spread his arms wide. "It is a glorious morning!" he exclaimed. "Today begins the quest for Fulfillment for the people of Penderak! As both Uncle Esrund and Auntie Maude have declared, today is—"

"*Uncle* Esrund and *Auntie* Maude—now the picture becomes clearer. Those two old charmers had you up half the night, I'll wager. I gave way to a similar spell..." Gwynn tilted her head. "But what of your brother who supports that wall behind him? He seems decidedly less enthused about the state of today's affairs."

Ianen was slumped against the wooden wall, rubbing his forehead with slow, circular motions. "We drank beer!" said Glenden proudly, "Ianen liked it better than I."

"It felt so wonderful, last night..." the boy moaned.

Gwynn nodded. She well knew the old Dwarf couple's love for both ale and company to share it with. "I can understand how you've embraced this bright morning with less ardor than your brother," she said to him, and began guiding him toward the front of

Tavern-Meet. "Just wait until we begin riding..." she warned. Ianen moaned again.

The clear call of a trumpet sounded outside, from off in the distance. As Gwynn opened the entrance door a second trumpet answered from close by. The Square was now largely deserted, and the Brown Elves crossed it toward the main road out of the city. Along the road, they were struck by the incredible array of activity, set into motion by the mobilization of the people's army of Penderak. Taking place before them was what appeared to be a completely disorganized effort to group together a combination of Dwarfs, riding animals, beasts of burden, wagons and poultry. Should this objective ever be accomplished the combined numbers would reach into the thousands. Men and women came from every direction, on foot and mounted on ponies, mules and donkeys, with a few even astride cows. Others shouted directions to humpbacked oxen that pulled wooden carts. A herd of bleating goats along with honking geese and clucking chickens contributed to the noise and confusion.

Some of the animals had been intentionally brought as food sources, while several others had simply followed the crowd. To complete the disarray, every Dwarf child in the city had added his or her diminutive presence, and together were having the time of their lives darting, chasing in and out, dodging between the carts, animals and grown-ups.

"Look!" shouted Glenden, "it's Uncle Esrund!"

The old Dwarf leader was headed in their direction through the crowd—sturdily clanking toward them, his thick torso covered by armor which had survived the wear and tear of generations of Uxmuns for almost 800 years. The ancient covering was battered, scratched and dented, and its design was outdated by some five centuries. Its elements of chain mail, breastplate, backplate and shoulder guards were held together loosely by worn connectors. Added to this was the Uxmun broadsword, the vintage of which roughly approximated the Uxmun armor, and was encased in a scabbard that swung freely from his shoulder belt. Only Esrund's genius as a craftsman had made possible another wearing of the protective garb, and its total effect would have been roughly the same if he had tied a number of cooking utensils to his body. But the pride of ancestry and longevity shone from the old man's face. There was not a Dwarf in Penderak who would consider Esrund's appearance to be anything but splendidly heroic.

Maude was beside her husband, while Nolan and Wilda were close behind. "I can't yet believe that it's begun," said Esrund as he greeted Gwynn. "Looks well on the way," he added, surveying with pride the scene of gigantic disorder behind them.

"I see that the Uxmun armor will serve you well again," Gwynn said.

"Yes," Esrund nodded, "for the last time. I fixed it up a bit..."

"We helped him!" Glenden exclaimed. Gwynn glanced sideways at the lad. Could this be the same withdrawn youth who had arrived with her just last night?

"...And helped him into it," added Maude. "He grew out a bit since he last wore it," she cackled.

Esrund glared at his wife. "A fine thing, me goin' off to battle, and you talkin' like that."

"And I'd be right there, too, if it weren't for this damned stiff hip, and twenty-three grandchildren.... It's not like I won't be doing any—" She stopped, looking down at her chubby, wrinkled hands which were clasped tightly before her. "You'd best be going...." she said. Beneath the banter, her concern was tight-held.

"I suppose...." he replied, reaching over to kiss her on the cheek. She didn't raise her head, and Esrund turned toward Gwynn and her cousins.

"...See you lads in Cryslandon," he said, shaking hands with the youths. "Sure, Uncle Esrund," they replied in unison. Gwynn gave the old man a strong hug. "Watch yourself, when you're in that rocky country," he said to her. "Maybe you'd best come back down through here...."

"No," said Gwynn. "That would consume far too much time...I'll be careful," she said, "but I'm thankful for your caring."

Esrund nodded, and turned to go. Maude went to him and they embraced for a long moment. He was beaming as he walked away. Maude approached Gwynn, tears rolling down her full cheeks. "Watch that old man for me," she said, as she and the young woman embraced. Then she too was gone, lost within the turmoil which continued in the street. Gwynn said her good-byes to Nolan and Wilda. The Dwarf pair then hurried off. Gwynn led Glenden and Ianen toward the stable, where she had seen to their horses' needs, and where she, Nolan and Wilda had shared their first before-bed drink.

When the Brown Elf trio returned to the main city road, the march from Penderak was ready to begin. Order had, in some incomprehensible manner, been established from the chaos that had prevailed when they'd left to retrieve their mounts. The army of the Dwarfs waited expectantly. Not a one of their number wore anything that approached complete military garb. There were no divisions among their ranks: no regiments, no legions, no battalions. Not a one of them stood taller than four feet, and the weapons they carried were more often crafted for usage at home rather than on the battlefield. A few carried crossbows, but more had slingshots stuck in their belts. Some were armed with broadswords and dirks, but many more shouldered scythes and pitchforks and sickles. Several of them carried ancient battle-axes, but more had brought hatchets, hoes, picks and shovels. There were a few long pikes noticeable in the throng, and some carried clubs and quarterstaffs. If there was formality at all in this crude army, it was spread among the small groups scattered throughout that would provide music to accompany the march.

The Dwarf leaders were grouped at the arched entranceway of the walled city. Gwynn and her young cousins watched as old Esrund climbed a curve of stone steps until he reached a ledge that ran above the arch. He faced the massed Dwarfs, and began to speak, his voice soft, sounding out of character, yet carrying to the final line of the ranks.

"Many of our people," he said, "are waiting for us... and while they wait they are starving, they're beaten, they're shackled with irons and bound with chains. They labor beneath the weight of oppression: brutally forced to carry on work which slowly suffocates the land. They are brothers and sisters of our own blood. They are waiting for us in Golgorath... and there are others who wait, others who labor side by side with the Dwarfs. There are White Elves, and Brown Elves. There are Azmurians and Norsepeople. They too are our brothers and sisters!" Esrund's voice had lifted, "They too wait for us in dark Golgorath!" The sun was reflected magnificently off the Uxmun armor. The old man's voice rent the still, morning air: *I hear the voices of the slaves of the Death Lord! They cry out as one voice: 'Free us! Free us!' My people! Our brothers and sisters are waiting for us! Let us go to them! Forward to Cryslandon!*

A thunderous roar went up from the crowd. Esrund descended the steps, and mounted his pony. A single trumpet pealed and the people's army of Penderak started forward to the music of bagpipes, flutes, pan pipes, horns and the beat of fourscore drums which set the pace. The people who would remain behind, who lined the street, cheered lustily as row after row of Dwarfs, animals, carts and wagons passed beneath the tunneled portals.

Gwynn's spine was tingling. "Let's go," she said, to her cousins. They mounted their horses and began at a fast walk, exiting through the rear of the City of Dwarfs, into the hills, passing between silent campsites. They would soon lose sight of the city. Gwynn pulled her mare to a halt, and looked back.

The Army of Penderak had started up a rise beyond the city walls. The brilliant sun picked out the myriad colors of the stream of Dwarfs and animals against the brown of the Kolgar Mountains. The nasal rhythm of bagpipes drifted back as did the pounding cadence of drums. The Dwarfs were singing. Gwynn could not determine the words of their song, but the tenor of their voices carried forth the clear message of freedom...

10

THE WITCH OF ZORAK

From the Forest of Delvinor the land gradually sloped down to the marshes in the south. Patches of low-lying fog accompanied the initial appearance of the wetlands, and surrounded the dark evergreen trees that stood in tight groups atop small ground swells. The soft grasses of the rolling hills were replaced by the tough, reedy growth of the marshland. Tall rushes and cattails began to appear. Wand-like carnivorous plants formed fringes around shallow lakes, swaying seductively to attract their flying prey.

Into this environment had ridden Ailwon and Hugh, the Dwarf twins and Oolu. Their horses had balked, and entered reluctantly only after sharp commands from their riders. The horsemen were aware that on all sides of them were unseen creatures watching their progress toward the lair of the Witch of Zorak, and they could detect subtle movements in the shadows of the small groupings of trees. No one in the party was in the mood for conversation, save Oolu. The Gwarpy began a question-and-answer session, asking questions of himself and his pony, providing the answers for both: "It's damp an' cool sure, ain't it, Carrot, ain't it, Oolu?" asked the questioner. And the answerer replied: "It are sure. Not like Loamend at all, it ain't. 'Snot near so sunny here. Nor's there hills'er flowers'er not one Bobabo tree." Off to

the right a long dark-green reptile poured off a log
into the shallow water, disappearing in a tangled
thicket of alders. "But then again, Carrot..." reminded the questioner, "then again, Oolu, nothin' up there
in Loamend is like *that!* So there's things here that
ain't there didja know?" But the answerer was well
aware of this truth: "Course sure we already know
that, yep." Both questioner and answerer looked
searchingly at the surrounding marshland for the
half-hundredth time. They massaged their growling
belly, and there was no question nor necessity for an
answer to the Gwarpy's complaint: "No berries, no
nuts, no root plants. Sure lots hungrier down here'n
up there, yep." And he joined the rest in silence until
they arrived before the great stretch of swamp that
was known as Zorak. They had come up a gradual rise
in the wetland, so that the impact of their first
sighting of the swampland was considerable, and
gave impetus to the general sense of apprehension.

They pulled to a halt. Zorak lay below them, a vast
expanse of stagnant water and mist. Out of this grew
twisted trees with fan-shaped trunks and moss-covered branches that reached outward like grasping
tentacles. There were rot-holes formed about the
base of most of the trees, which produced foul odors
and which spawned profusions of primitive, fleshy
water plants. From where the small band sat their
horses they could hear sounds of creatures moving
through the murky waters. "I have seen this before,"
breathed Ailwon "I've never been within a thousand
miles of these swamps, yet I know this place."

Hugh turned toward Ailwon, and through the mist
he thought he could discern the ancient features of
Elgan overlayed upon the youthful features of the boy.

The young man dismounted. The gray horse snorted nervously, and Ailwon stroked its muscular neck.
He pointed to the marshes. "There are no words to
convey the ominous power of this sight. And this is
merely the surface of the danger that confronts us."
He looked up to the broad-shouldered Vandorian.

Hugh looked toward the dark scene below, but he did not see it. His mind was filled with visions of his youth, of his slow withdrawal from his people and eventually from his own parents. He envisioned his marriage, the births of his children, the move into the wilderness, the slaughter of his family, his desperate chase to find their killers, the enchanted forest, the fight to save Ailwon. In an instant flashed the pictures of Mowdra, of Elgan, of Gwynn, of his ride into the face of the storm... Hugh looked down at Ailwon, and turned toward Erbin and Evrawk, who were watching him intently, and toward Oolu.

They dismounted, leading their steeds to the edge of a grove of trees where the ground was reasonably dry, but where the horses had access to water and grasses. They entered the swamp, or rather, it seemed that the swamp somehow enveloped them, and they soon found themselves completely within its midst. The stench was potent. The air was humid and oppressive, yet each of them felt chilled. Things slithered near their ankles as they waded through the black waters. Their every sense was alert, their hands held weapons.

High above them, hidden by overgrown vines, was a winged creature with great yellow eyes, its reptilian body half covered with hair. It sat watching their every movement, then flew silently off into the depths of the swamp.

The mists grew thicker as the allied band moved deeper into the swamp. Enveloped by the gray vapor, their senses became dulled, and they could see only an armspan in front of them. Soon each member of the group walked alone.

Ailwon inched forward deliberately, moving further and further from his comrades. All was silent in the gray darkness of the mists; then the distant sound of a gently strumming mandolin came to him, and he heard the clear sweet voice of a woman singing a wordless song. Entranced, Ailwon followed it forward.

© HILDEBRANDT

Slowly, the mists separated, and before the Elf loomed a monstrous tree, that seemed to stare down at him with great dead eyes. Enchanted by the voice, Ailwon approached the mouth-like cavern at the base of the tree. Elvgard grew heavy and fell from his hands. The song grew clearer, the voice more familiar, as he entered the tree, drawing him ever downward through a maze of dark passages. He felt his way along the tunnel cautiously, until he saw a faint glimmer of light that gradually grew brighter as he approached, becoming the bright yellow-orange of firelight.

He emerged into a clearing in a beautiful forest. The trees surrounding it were heavy with foliage that reached across the clearing, allowing the view of only a small circle of star-flecked night sky. The night air was cool and still, save for the happy chirping of crickets and the haunting voice of the woman. She sat before a burning campfire, her back toward Ailwon. The firelight picked out the edges of her long auburn hair. Even before she stopped singing and turned toward him, he knew it must be she: Gwynn! She smiled, her green eyes laughed at his look of astonishment. He shook his head again, the thickness in his mind fighting any clarity of thought.

"Poor darling," she said to him, and her voice was flavored with amusement, "don't try to figure it out... not now. Come sit beside me." He slowly walked forward to stand above her, staring at her with disbelief. She was garbed in her riding clothes, exactly as when he had left her. She laid aside the mandolin, lounged back against a fallen log, and as she looked up at him he was forced to realize that indeed it was Gwynn. Her hair fell softly about the perfect symmetry of her smoothly tanned face. Her lips were turned slightly up at the corners in a playful smile. She drew up her long, supple legs, and clasped her hands about them.

"Ailwon," she laughed at him, "are you just going to stand there and stare at me, or will you come sit beside your lover?" She offered her hand, and when he took it she drew him down beside her.

"I'm sorry, Gwynn," he had difficulty forming the words. "It's just...it's just that I can't understand how you—" He frowned, and tried to remember: "The others, what happened to—"

"I'll explain everything in just a while," she interrupted, "but for now just tell me one thing, my love; there is one thing that is vitally important to our success. I must know where the Crownhelm is hidden...!"

Ailwon tried to understand. "Crownhelm? Why must you know where it is? It will be taken to Cryslandon only a short time from now... I don't—"

She laughed, and leaned her legs against his. "This is not my doing, it is Elgan's—you do remember Elgan?" she joked. "He reminded me that if anything should possibly happen to him and Shandar then no one would know of the Crownhelm's whereabouts except you...and you would be far away." She stroked his cheek with her slender fingers. "It's really just a simple matter, my love..."

Ailwon felt an increase in his confusion. "You know, of course, that you're trusted by everyone, and you know my trust in you..." he said to her. "But, I have been sworn to secrecy. Not even Erbin or Evrawk knows the place of the Crown, nor does trusted Oolu. Even I wasn't told until—"

Gwynn's hand had moved from the lad's cheek to his lips, gently closing them. She ran the fingers of her other hand into the thickness of his blond hair, turning his face toward hers. Her eyelids drooped seductively, her lips were parted. She moved against him, kissing him deeply, forcing his mouth open with hers. He was gently pushed to his back; the grass was moist and cool against his body. He was breathing heavily beneath Gwynn's kisses; her hand reached beneath his shirt, massaging his chest. "Ailwon... Ailwon... you must tell me... Where is the Crownhelm?" she breathed, "where is the Crownhelm?"

Ailwon's chest heaved rhythmically, his body was afire. Yet his passion was jabbed with a pinprick of doubt each time she repeated her question, and with each question there was a subtle increase to the edge of anger that had begun to creep into her voice. The soft curves of Gwynn's body writhed against the Elfin Prince, and her kisses were unceasing, but Ailwon could feel that the warmth of her passion had disappeared, had become cold with hatred. He grasped her shoulders, pushing her back from him. As he stared at her, his mind cleared. Her beauty was that of Gwynn, but behind the beauty was cruelty, and the green of her eyes was filled with a liquid energy of fanatic hate.

"You are Gorta!" Ailwon shouted. She shrieked her hatred, and lunged toward him, her lips drawn back from her white teeth. *"Yar zaggon por yar vaggot! Zamut tar Gorta!!* You bastard Elf! You dare rebuff Gorta!!" She struck him across the face. He had risen only to his knees, and the power of the blow knocked him backward. The witch in the form of his lover attacked again, kicking at him; her foot catching him solidly in the ribs. Ailwon rolled to escape the onslaught, but she was after him, another blow from her foot landed just below his kidney, she struck hard against his cheek with her fist. She was livid with rage, screaming her hate for him and all with whom he was allied: *"Zaton Yar Zabbath!* Impotent runt! Now you and your allies will have to deal with me and all the powers of darkness!!"

Ailwon's face was covered with blood, his ribs felt as though they were cracked. He managed to twist away from a fierce kick, and reaching out quickly he caught her ankle, spilling her to the ground. But she sprang to her feet with the quick agility of Gwynn of Andeluvia. The indignity had served only to increase her rage. Nearly insane with hatred she attacked again. She screamed out a command in this language of the underworld: *"Yar Zaggon por Vaggot!! Ramaelgadon!"* And as if he were trapped in a horrible nightmare Ailwon watched as her face began to transfigure. Then he was struck across the forehead, and he fell backward, lapsing into semi-consciousness.

"This seems to be an impossible chore," Hugh commented tersely.

Erbin scratched beneath his hood. "That it does, lad," he agreed, "but we've got to—"

A cry of surprise and distress a half-hundred yards away cut short the Dwarf's sentence.

"It's Oolu!" exclaimed Evrawk, and the three began running toward the direction of the cry. They splashed through the waters, Erbin falling once, rising completely drenched, running again. Suddenly, the monstrous tree loomed before them; the cavernous mouth, gaping at its base, was lit by an unearthly glow. Oolu was gripped with terror, but he saw that the light was Elvgard. He rushed to the mouth of the tree and picked up the Elfin sword.

Hugh, Erbin and Evrawk burst from the swamp. "Look! Look! Elvgard!" shouted Oolu. The Gwarpy was frantic; he was nearly sobbing.

"This is the entranceway!" shouted Hugh as he leapt into the mouth of the tree. Oolu ran after him clutching Elvgard. Erbin and Evrawk followed, battle-axes clenched in their fists.

"Curse you!" screamed Erbin. "You'll not take him from us! Bitch!"

Ailwon hovered between consciousness and coma. Then his hair was grabbed, and his head yanked up causing an abrupt return to awareness. The soft grass of the clearing had disappeared, leaving behind large rings of stones to form the floor beneath him. Gone too was the green foliage of the trees. In its place was a vaulted ceiling of stone. Ailwon looked around an enormous subterranean hall. Surrounding him were a hundred or more of the hulking rat-creatures, the Blegons. Directly before him was an enormous cauldron in the shape of a demon's head from which issued a column of smoke and a sulphurous glow. This was the source of all of the powers of the Witch of Zorak, and beyond it, seated on a carved throne, sat Gorta herself.

As Ailwon's eyes met hers she descended the steps of her throne, walking slowly toward the youth. Every eye of her adoring Blegons was on her. She was tall, much taller than she had been as Gwynn, and she was slender. Her lithe body was barely covered by animal skins. Her hair, parted at the center and flowing over her shoulders, was pitch black. A pair of horns crowned her brow. Her white face was beautiful, save for the cold hatred apparent in it.

Ailwon looked up as the witch stood before him entranced by the power of her dark eyes. She stared down at him with contempt. "So *you* are to save the people of Urshurak?" She sneered. "This beaten whelp is the Sevena to the fabled Crownhelm of the White Elves!" She motioned toward the flaming cauldron. "Bring him," she commanded.

The Elfin lad was jerked to his feet by two of the hideous brutes and half dragged up to the cauldron.

He was pushed to his knees. His head was jerked up again by his hair. He was forced to stare directly into the face of the demon. Gorta's voice came from behind:

"*Ramaelgadon! Torgon tar Gorta!*" screamed the witch.

Ailwon could hear increased activity within the cauldron. Sparks shot toward the ceiling within the column of smoke and the glaring eyes of the demon cauldron came alive. The helpless youth felt their power begin to draw his mind toward them. He tried to close his eyes but could not.

Gorta's enraged voice came from close behind him: "Where is the Crownhelm? I demand to know!"

Sweat poured from Ailwon's brow, running across the caked blood. He struggled furiously to repress the thoughts that began to form as a vision in his mind, but he was helpless...the burning eyes of the demon cauldron penetrated his mind. "No!" he cried. "No!" The eyes of the cauldron flared and cut ever deeper into the Elf's resistance. A great terror overcame Ailwon as the image of a giant figure on an iron throne took shape. He knew it was Torgon, the Death Lord of Golgorath. Ailwon fought, but could no longer resist the powers of darkness. Torgon lifted his iron fist and pointed at Ailwon. Into the Elf Prince's mind came a vision of a beautiful valley with a giant white tree at its center. From the base of the tree there flowed a stream. The sound of the rippling water grew louder and clearer. The water seemed to form a voice and a word formed within the sound of the flowing water. "Evshimin" it seemed to say. Another word was formed... "Crownhelm."

A scream broke the spell. One of the Blegons that held Ailwon fell to the floor. A whistling arrow had found its mark in the muscled hump of the creature's back.

Another arrow struck the other Blegon holding Ailwon, who leaped to his feet amid the confused grunts and growls of Blegons and the hate-filled curses of the witch. Hugh, Erbin, Evrawk and Oolu had come out of the same tunnel as had Ailwon. The sight of them gave rise to an exultant feeling in the Elfin lad. Beneath a blistering verbal attack from the witch, the Blegons had recovered from their surprise and most of them had begun swarming toward the small allied band. Several of their number were dropped immediately by the rapid fire of Hugh Oxhine's bow.

Erbin shouted, "Ailwon! I have it!" He was holding aloft the sword of the White Elves, but between the Dwarf and the Prince was a swarm of snarling rat-beasts, and Ailwon himself was being attacked.

Erbin and Evrawk had begun to cut a swath through the enemy to allow the delivery of Elvgard into the hands of Prince Ailwon. The broadsword of the Vandorian and the battle-axe of the Dwarf rose and fell in fierce, rhythmic strokes. Bloodied clots of fur flew far and wide, dying screams filled the air, and the shrill hatred of Gorta rose above the entire din. Then Erbin was knocked to the floor, the force of the blow from the heavy Blegon causing Elvgard to sail from the little man's hand. The sword hit the floor, spin-ning, glistening with the light of the cauldron that sparked and hissed. A group of rat-beasts pursued the spinning sword. But somehow from out of their midst came the fleet Gwarpy, Oolu. He scooped up the mystical blade, turned and began dodging and dart-ing through a tangle of the beasts, who grabbed and grasped for him, but with no success.

"Oolu got it!" the Gwarpy yelled as he dodged and weaved his way toward Ailwon. In another instant Ailwon had the sword securely within his grasp and was headed toward the cauldron of Gorta, Blegons falling away from the deadly enchantment of the brilliantly shimmering sword.

The rat-beasts had fallen prey to confusion and fear. Even Gorta's screams could no longer rally them. Only she stood between the White Elf youth and her final source of power. Ailwon reached to push her aside. But she screamed out; there was a blinding

flash of light. Terrible roars filled the cavern. Ailwon
blinked open his eyes. Gorta had disappeared. In her
place was an awesome beast, some three heights of a
man tall. It stood upright on two hooved feet that
extended from huge, fur-covered legs and thighs. Its
tail was long and powerful and lashed wickedly in
concert with its hooves that clashed upon the stone
floor. The beast stared down from its lofty height, its
horrible feminine face exuding hate, its fangs protruding. Long, stringy hair fell from its head, across
its breasts and downward. Its clawed hands extended
from fur-covered arms. Its ear-shattering roars
seemed to be imbued with demonic laughter.

Ailwon stared up, transfixed. The beast seemed to
grow in height, to rise above him until he could
scarcely see its enormous head. Then Elgan's voice
came to him above the roars of the demon: "You must
not believe in her reality—but in your own!" The Prince
looked down at the sword he clutched and the power
of it ran through him like a current. He cried out in
defiance, and attacked. Elvgard flashed in the air,
then drove deep into the belly of the monster. The
beast screamed in rage and Ailwon pulled his sword
free, leaping toward the cauldron. "You bitch, mur-
derer!" screamed Hugh Oxhine as he let fly an arrow
that found its mark in the monster's heart. Ailwon
raised Elvgard above his head with both hands, then
hesitated, turning back toward his companions. "Get
out! GET OUT!" he screamed.

Oolu scrambled into the tunnel, followed by Erbin.
Hugh was frozen in his tracks, his disbelieving eyes
staring at Ailwon's form silhouetted against the brilliant yellow flame. Evrawk pushed the archer into the
tunnel just as Elvgard struck the burning cauldron of
the Witch of Zorak. A column of flame and a bolt of
light leaped upward from the cauldron and there was
a flare of brilliant white light as the cauldron exploded in a shower of sparks. Ailwon was knocked to the
floor. He leaped to his feet, retrieving his sword. On
the floor beside the erupting cauldron lay Gorta,

blood gushing from her death wounds. The perfect features of her white face were contorted in the pain of defeat.

With a roar like thunder the cavern ceiling collapsed, and the waters of the swamp poured through. The youth fled into the tunnel, great waves of roaring water rushing behind him. Around a bend the tunnel was illumined by light streaming in from its exit. Before him were his companions, shouting words of encouragement to aid his flight from the thundering waters. But Ailwon needed no exhortations. Even Gwynn of Andeluvia could not have outrun him in *this* race. Then they were all into the open air. The swamp waters had almost disappeared, filling the underworld below. The twisted trees of Zorak had vanished, perhaps had never been there. In their stead were beautiful green willows. With the disappearance of the swamp, the thick fog and humidity had lifted, the sky was clear, early evening was bright with stars and with moonlight.

The members of the group looked toward one
another. They were all dripping wet and covered with
muck, their faces and hands cut and smeared with
blood. The White Elf Prince began to laugh. Oolu
started chuckling, and soon Erbin and Evrawk were
roaring with laughter. Strangely, Hugh did not feel the
elation of his comrades.

The death of Gorta had been *his* goal, and Hugh's
mind was now flooded with thoughts of his wife and
children.

Ailwon spoke, "Has the revenge which you sought
brought any peace to your heart? Or is there the
feeling that all is not yet complete? Not until all the
people of Urshurak are set free will any *one* be at
peace. Hugh, will you go with us further?"

The archer stood for a long time lost in his
thoughts. Then turning quickly, he mounted Santor.
"Let us continue southward."

Ailwon responded with joy, "Then it's on to Zan-
Dura."

They all mounted their steeds and Oolu's chuckle
drifted back to the grove of willows which had once
been the lair of the Witch of Zorak.

Opposite: Gorta the Witch

11

TAL-AMON

With a joyous sense of release, Elgan ascended into the freedom of the upper air, one with the great flying beast whose form he had taken. Eastward he soared, over the Gendi Mountains that lay golden brown beneath the sun, across the canyon of Nenturi, carved through mountain rock by the Kafzida River. On he coursed above the shimmering waters that wound through the red-sand of the Azante Desert. At the port of Abu-Sambar the waters of the Kafzida forked eastward from the Great Garnon, giving life to the ancient city of Tal-Amon, capital of Azmuria, and then continued its flow to the Bay of Abaqui where it emptied into the Frocald Sea. The shadows of the great dunes of the Azante began to extend further eastward as the sun descended. Now groupings of pointed rocks reached up from the sand, and small communities of tents began to appear. As the western sun neared the completion of its ritual, as the shadows below crawled further toward the coming night, a full moon appeared just above the horizon, and below it was the city of the Azmurians: Tal-Amon.

The great flying beast began its descent, gliding toward the city, toward the stone geometry of shapes; low, convex, pyramidal dwellings, studded with the towers of Tal-Amon. At the center, rising high above the rest, was the Tower of Akarif, the elongated lines of

its eternal design pointing into the pause between
the powers of the failing day and the oncoming night.
The great beast drifted down against the cool rush of
evening air, toward the arched openings of the Tower
of Akarif that appeared golden-white against the
deep blue of the eastern sky.

Elgan stood looking inward, watching a solitary
figure at the center of the upper room of Akarif. The
sorcerer, Shandar, sat cross-legged, perfectly still.
Beneath the peaceful figure and spreading outward,
its diameter covering half the floor, was the Circle of
the Cosmos, its carefully designed ceramics depict-
ing the ordered whole of the universe. The object of
Shandar's gaze was within a tiled square at the core
of this cosmic circle. As Elgan entered the tower
room, his shadow fell across the Circle. The sorcerer
looked up. Their eyes met, and Shandar stood.
He turned toward Elgan. Within the oblique shape
of Shandar's eyes there was no indication of surprise
at seeing the wizard standing there. The sorcerer
spoke, sounding much as if he and Elgan had previously been together only moments before. "The
White Elf Prince has been successful. Gorta, the Witch
of Zorak, is no more."
The words were spoken calmly and quietly, yet their
significance was such that Elgan felt long centuries of
concern drawn from him in a single instant. He stared
down at the floor, his legs felt weak. When he looked
up, Shandar was watching him, his left hand raised,
the palm toward Elgan. The two ancient beings
moved toward one another slowly. Elgan returned
Shandar's sign of peace, he felt the sorcerer's serenity
within him. As always Shandar appeared to Elgan
exactly as he had on the day they first met in the
clearing of Mowdra almost a thousand years before,
and yet, as always, Shandar appeared to have
changed since their last meeting, seeming to be
forever in a state of becoming, seeming always to be
moving forward toward that which was greater than

his present form, while never abandoning the matter which had given him eternal birth.

They came together, their upraised hands inches apart in a transference of the energies of their complete love and acceptance. Without moving his right hand Elgan placed his left on the bony shoulder of the sorcerer. Shandar reached out, touching the lined face of his friend, and then they embraced. Elgan felt a twinge of concern. Though the long, sinewy muscles of Shandar's body remained firm, worn solid by countless journeys through the wilderness, it was apparent to Elgan that the old man was thinner than ever.

They stepped apart to observe one another. "Do you feel the same relief as I that Ailwon has overcome his first challenge?" Elgan asked.

"Relief... and sorrow. I feel sadness that Gorta forever turned her powers, her potential inward, failing always to experience joy, moving relentlessly toward her own destruction. I have something to show you," he said, and his dark bare feet carried him silently back to the cosmic circle. Elgan followed. "Before, this space depicted the power of the fires of Gorta," Shandar said, pointing to one of the inlaid tiles of the Circle. The space was now totally black, and though the surface was of ceramic it appeared to the eye to have no surface at all but instead an endless depth. "The composition began to change just before Ailwon overcame the witch's power. What we see is the void, the energy of nothingness that will exist so long as Torgon is possessed of it, and it of him. Let us hope that we all can remain strong in opposition to such power."

"We have chosen this path," said Elgan. "There is little else but to remain steadfast. In addition, Ailwon has gained an ally to accompany him on the quest. I'm certain that this man—a Vandorian—had much to do with the success at Zorak. His name is Hugh Oxhine. I'll acquaint you with him after we've embarked."

© HILDEBRANDT

Shandar smiled. "I thought that I could sense a power that exceeded the aggregate of the Prince, the stalwart Dwarfs and my friend Oolu." He sighed. "But I do not always trust my perceptions any longer...I'm happy to learn that my senses were somewhat accurate."

Elgan laid his hand on Shandar's arm. "If it is indeed true that anguish seeks companionship of its own type, then you'll be pleased to learn that I too have recently suffered from acute attacks of a seemingly endless accumulation of age."

The sorcerer nodded knowingly. "Let us go down now. The Azmurians are ready to march tomorrow, and we may have gained still another powerful ally... if he and Ben Kara have not pummeled each other senseless by now. Tark-Volmar, the Norsepeople's leader, has traveled from Norbruk to seal an alliance against the Death Lord, and also against those among his own race who have gone over to Torgon." Shandar's eyes brightened with amusement. "He's a blustery sort, this Volmar... and, as you know, beneath all that culture and eloquence, our own Shakín, Ali Ben Kara, nurtures a solid streak of cussedness. They've been verbally battering each other for a day and a half, over who would be in charge of this joint venture, should it ever come about... " He moved toward the doorway. "I'm surprised that we haven't been able to hear the Norsemen even at this lofty height."

The two ancient beings made the long descent from the Tower of Akarif. As they neared ground level a bellowing voice thundered to the battle cry of the Norsepeople. Shandar and Elgan increased their pace down the stone steps. There were no further outbursts, but the wheezes and grunts of two men struggling came from The Square which separated Akarif from the home of the Shakín. The wizard and the sorcerer reached the bottom of the tower just as a cry of surprise came from outside, immediately followed by a loud splash. Shandar and Elgan stepped into the open courtyard. Within the sandstone walls was a profusion of vegetation surrounding a large, exquisitely tiled pool, and at its far end stood the huge Norseman, Tark-Volmar, laughing so hard that he could barely breathe. Ali Ben Kara floundered within the pool, treading water but still managing to sputter a continuous stream of curses. Shandar began to chuckle. Never had he seen the Shakín of the Azmurians appear so undignified.

Ben Kara swam to the side of the pool, climbed out and started toward Tark-Volmar, water running from his short robe and his muscular black body. Elgan and Shandar hurried to reach the Norseman before the furious Azmurian. Ben Kara raised his clenched fist in a threatening gesture. Tark-Volmar was still doubled over with laughter.

"You overstuffed, red-faced buffoon," shouted Ben Kara, "it appears that you need a cooling of some of the heat generated from your idiot laughter! Come! Let us see who ends up in the water this time! I'll be prepared for your barbaric tricks now..." Shandar let slip a snicker, and the Shakín glared at his ancient mentor.

Tark-Volmar finally managed to gain some control over his thunderous laughter. "Enough, enough," he gasped, holding up a beefy hand to ward off the anger of the Shakín. Ali Ben Kara cursed again through gritted teeth, and marched into the pavilion that framed his living quarters, passing beneath the enormous black visages carved from the building front. The solemn countenances of the carvings contrasted with the dripping wet Azmurian leader and the near hysterical Norseman.

By the time Ali Ben Kara returned from his quarters dried and in fresh clothing, Tark-Volmar had finally subdued his laughter. The Shakín and the Norbruk chieftain resumed their business, seated at the long black-marble table within the pavilion. Ali Ben Kara began to inform Shandar and Elgan of the grudgingly reached agreements between himself and Volmar.

After Volmar had expressed a desire for an alliance between his people and the Azmurians, Ben Kara had given him the rough details of the quest that had begun. The Norseman had at first balked at joining such a campaign. He had only limited knowledge of the other nations of the continent. He knew that the White Elves had somehow staved off intermittent raids of the powerful forces of the Death Lord, but he distrusted heirs to magical crowns and swords, or things of that nature. And as for the rest of the allied nations, Brown Elves led by a girl? Dwarfs no taller than his belt buckle? A nation of Amazon women? He could hardly imagine fighting side by side with such a crew. But Ben Kara had been insistent that the Norsepeople join in the total effort if there was to be any alliance at all. Finally Volmar had named the conditions for his joining the quest, and had sworn Ben Kara to secrecy as to the nature of these conditions.

"I don't understand this necessity for secrecy," said Ben Kara, who had recovered his usual aplomb, and lounged gracefully in his ebony chair.

"You don't have to understand," growled Volmar.
"All you have to do is keep your mouth shut... or else
lose the support of ten thousand of the best damned
fighters on the continent!" The Norseman was
stripped nearly bare to the waist, and still perspiration ran freely.

"By thunder!" he exclaimed, "it's hot in this accursed land!" He slammed his fist against the table.
"Let's get on with this! I hunger to squash the life of
those bastards who've made free Norsepeople into
wretched slaves!"

Elgan sighed, "It seems," he said, "that I'm forever
in a position where it is necessary for me to restrain
people bent on action." He stroked the entire length
of his white beard before continuing: "If we're to be
successful in our quest, then we—all of us—must
dismiss the hatred that often threatens to engulf us.
Let our anger fight this tyranny... but not our hate.
Hatred is an emotion—like others—which teeters upon
the edge of its opposite... Thus hate is more easily
overcome by love than by additional hate."

Tark-Volmar was incredulous. "Are you saying I'm to
love this bastard, Torgon?" he bellowed. "I'd love to
smash his ugly skull.... That's what I'd love!" The
Norseman almost smiled, rather pleased with his
retort to the wizard, who he thought to be a queer old
fellow.

"Why do you hate him?" asked Elgan.

"Why do you ask such foolish questions?"

Elgan slumped in his chair. He was clearly tired of
these battles, knowing that no matter how he might
put forth his views no one would change until they
were completely prepared to do so. But at that point
Shandar interceded for his old friend. He sat down
next to the Norseman, fixing his gentle gaze on the
huge man, who had clearly become agitated.

"All living things, Tark-Volmar, live in the way dictated by their needs. Thus the bear is no more evil than
the dove. If there has been evil in Torgon's actions it
lies in a decision made long ago—or perhaps in the

lack of his decision—to allow the energies of Golgorath to dictate his actions. Now he simply follows
his hungers. They are hungers for absolute power,
and the outgrowths are murder and destruction,
slavery and suffocation. The Death Lord must be
overcome... but the fires that burn in us should be
those of love, not of hate."

Volmar was disarmed by the serene power that
flowed from the ancient man. But he had enough in
his reserve of irritation to slam his fist once more, and
demand to know of Shandar: "You speak of the evil of
not making decisions... yet you justify this whole
bloody venture on some kwarkanilly prophecy?"

"We *have* made our decision. We have *chosen* to
follow the Prophecy. We will ultimately decide our own
fate...yet our goodness alone will not determine the
outcome, nor will the evil actions of Torgon dictate
the final results. Our tools are our determination, our
acceptance of one another, and our faith...."

"All right... all right..." muttered Tark-Volmar, "I'll
think about these things. But let's get *started!* I'll go
with you and your armies to the Elf city. My men will
sail back to our homeland to send our warriors to
Cryslandon. I intend to judge this boy Prince before I
send men into battle behind him."

"You may accompany my armies if you wish,"
replied the Azmurian Shakín, "but I will not be with
you...I'm going to the port of Abusambar to await the
arrival of Prince Ailwon when the Amazon fleet
reaches that point."

"And why didn't you tell me this?" shouted the
Norseman. "You won't meet the White Elf squirt before
I do!" His huge fist punished the black marble for a
third time. "By thunder, I'm going with you!"

Ben Kara shrugged in casual agreement, but in-
wardly grimaced. Tark-Volmar suddenly turned. Elgan
and Shandar were nowhere in sight.

"Where did those two go to?" he asked in amazement.

12

ANDELUVIA

A gentle rain tapped on the windows of King Zarin's hall as he slouched forward on his wooden throne, his chin cupped in his hand. He had chosen to meet with his niece, Gwynn, in the royal hall, realizing that he'd need every advantage to bolster his authority in the coming verbal combat with his strong-willed niece. He was determined not to give in to her petitions for Andeluvia's support in the campaign against the Death Lord, despite her revelation that a successor to the Crownhelm would lead this quest. Never would he give his blessings to an action that raised a weapon against *any* foe, no matter how great a tyrant. Nor would he allow Gwynn to indulge herself for another moment in this adventure. She had resisted all his previous appeals to cease her activities with the band of rebels she'd gathered to protect Andeluvia's borders. But no more! He would be adamant. Still, he dreaded the upcoming debate. What, he thought, had gone wrong? Gwynn had inherited all the beauty and stature of Zarin's gentle sister. She had been thoroughly educated in the Andeluvian tradition of pacifism by her parents and then by Zarin himself after the deaths of his sister and her husband. His own wife, Queen Wanel, had spent hours teaching her niece the proper ways to behave. But, from the beginning, Gwynn had been headstrong. Soon after

Opposite: Shandar and Elga

the loss of her mother and father she had begun to
engage in athletic competitions, at first with boys her
own age and then with older Brown Elf youths. Before
long there were few who could match her speed,
strength or agility. Both Zarin and Wanel were dis-
mayed at her behavior, but felt sure it was only a
phase that she would outgrow. Too late they came to
realize the complete fallacy in their thinking.

Zarin sighed, and glanced about the dimly lit hall.
There was a quiet simplicity about the place with its
stone walls and floor, its unadorned wooden beams.
The King pushed himself to a standing position, and
began slowly pacing down the worn, once brightly
colored carpet that served as a runner between the
wooden throne and the double entrance doors. His
head was bowed, he stared absently at the pattern of
flowers running through the carpet. He stopped before the doors, turned and started back, then
changed direction and strolled toward the wall a
score of paces to his right. There were a full dozen
windows on this side of the room, tall and slender
with arched tops. All of them had been covered with
heavy tapestries that had previously hung on the
opposite wall. Zarin was far from being an old man,
but his eyes were extremely sensitive to bright sunlight, and the tapestries had guarded the throne
room against more than the most muted of lights for
over five years. The King pulled back one of the
drapes, squinting into the gray morning. The rain
had stopped. He looked beyond the courtyard,
toward the long rows of fruit trees, alive with blossoms. A broad road ran upward through the or-
chards. It once carried a good many travelers in and
out of the valley at the heart of Andeluvia. A solitary
wooden cart was moving slowly in the mud. The horse
and driver struggled to pull its burden through the
quagmire. In the brightly blossomed tree branches
above, songbirds indulged themselves in a constant
outpouring of chirps and trills. But the King's eyes
were locked on the slow struggle that went on in the

muddied road, and his ears were immune to the
songs released to the spring air. He dropped the
curtain and turned at the sound of soft footsteps in
the side entranceway. His wife, Wanel, entered the
throne room.

"Good morning, dear," she said, trying to appear
cheerful. The Queen feared discord as much as her
husband, and the prospects of fierce debate between
those she loved was especially frightening. She knew
how determined Zarin was to resist any pressures to
any further entanglement of even a single Brown Elf
in the conflict between the allies and the Death Lord.
The excited announcements by Gwynn, Glenden and
Ianen in regard to the existence of a Sevena to the
Crownhelm of Alfandel had had no favorable effect on
the King. Indeed the uncharacteristic behavior of his
sons had been further motivation for an adamant
stand against involvement. He was furious—furor was
typically disguised as disappointment—when he
learned that Gwynn had known all along of the
proposed meeting with this 'Prince Ailwon' at the

home of the wizard. He would never have allowed his young sons to attend such a meeting, even though they had begged permission to accompany their cousin when she delivered horses to Delvinor.

It seemed that Zarin had not even heard his wife's gentle greeting. He returned to his throne and slumped down. "Where is Elsep?" he muttered, more to himself than to Wanel. She'd seated herself beside him.

"I saw him a few moments ago," she said, in reference to the King's young advisor. "He said he'd be here shortly."

"Good," said Zarin, nodding with satisfaction, "I'll need his support... He's been such a comfort to us in these troubled times, hasn't he, Wanel?"

"Yes," she replied without any real conviction. Though she kept them to herself, she had strong reservations in regard to the influence that Elsep had on her husband. With the demise of the longtime advisor who had previously served the royal family, Zarin had felt an immediate need to fill this position, and had spent little time or thought in finding someone suitable. Elsep, who was a peer of Gwynn's, had become the King's advisor more on his ability to please the King than to advise. He was short of stature, though muscular of build; his physical movements were awkward, as were his speech mannerisms. He'd attempted to cover his clumsiness with false charm, with fluctuating bravado and humility, and with attempts to impress by the calculated selections of his garb.

The King and Queen conversed no further. Zarin fidgeted nervously. Then the double doors opened and Gwynn, followed by the young Princes, approached Zarin and Wanel. The King sighed. A round of small talk began in regard to the weather, the women and the young lads agreeing that it was a beautiful day. King Zarin made note of the terrible condition of the road which had resulted from the spring. This skirting of the inevitable conflict was

bound to be short-lived, and Gwynn made rudely
certain of this by speaking above the level of the
King's voice:

"Excuse me, Sire," she began, "but time is a factor.... We are prepared to leave. We have been at work
since long before dawn. Those who have already
fought beside me are ready to ride, and word has
gone into the countryside so that those who choose
to unite behind the Sevena may join us at Cryslandon.
We need only the blessings of our King and Queen."
She looked toward Wanel, who smiled slightly but
quickly dropped her eyes when she felt her husband's
glare. Zarin stood, his brows knit tightly in a troubled
frown.

"You mean you have been out among the people? I
thought you had been asleep all this time.... " he
said, with a hard look toward his sons.

"We did sleep for three hours. If you're not willing to
sanction our quest—as I suspect you aren't—may we
discuss your objections without further delay?"
Gwynn had determined to avoid any subject which
diverted them from the central conflict she antici-
pated.

The King was muttering about waiting when an
entrance door opened. "Here he is now," said the
relieved monarch. Elsep strode briskly toward them,
his face set in a confident smile that disappeared for
an instant when his foot caught in a wrinkle of the
carpet, causing him to abruptly break his stride. He
was embarrassed, but smiled as he regained the
artificial gait, both of which had been manufactured
chiefly to impress Gwynn, who wasn't paying particular attention to either, but who hadn't failed to notice
the farcical near-trip.

"Ah! My Lady Gwynn," Elsep cried, "you are lovelier
than ever!" He bowed low to her.

"We're too unfamiliar," she said, smiling politely,
"and at the same time familiar enough, for you to
exclude both the 'My' and the 'Lady' from your greetings to me. But I thank you for the compliment." She

eyed his carefully combed hair, the decorative medallions that hung about his neck, and the gaudy tunic. "And you too, Elsep," she added, "are lovelier than ever."

Elsep's face colored slightly, and he had difficulty maintaining his smile. But he decided the remark must have been more straightforward than derisive, and he was able to recover his stance of confidence. Gwynn turned back to her uncle. "May we get to the heart of our problem, Sire?"

Zarin sighed again, and began pacing before the group, his hands clasped behind him, his head bowed. "All right. You wish me to sanction this venture, to encourage my children, my niece, my people to go off to war, to kill or be killed...." He stopped his pacing and looked at Gwynn. "You must surely know that I cannot do this...nor can I permit you to do this."

"You mean you *will* not do these things?"

"I mean I *cannot.* My father detested warfare, and my grandfather, and my great-grandfather... For a thousand years the Andeluvians have refused to engage in warfare...as did your own father."

"As does his daughter," replied Gwynn, and her voice remained level, discharging only feelings of good will toward her uncle. "But I am not my father, nor are you yours, nor are you your grandfather or any of our ancestors. You have the ability, the right, the obligation—considering these circumstances—to make your own choice... not one dictated by the past."

"What the King means—" began Elsep.

"I understand what the King means," Gwynn said, with a quick glance toward the short man behind her. She again addressed herself to Zarin. "There is little time left. The days of the Prophecy that remain are few. I know you don't fully believe in such things and I wish that Elgan or the sorcerer, Shandar, could be here to say these things to you. But they cannot, so it has been left to me." She moved closer to the throne where the King had reseated himself. Gwynn felt

Elsep's eyes follow her movements, but she pushed
this awareness to the back of her mind as she began
to warm to her task. The power in her voice noticeably
increased as she spoke to persuade Zarin of the
rightness of her convictions: "You have spoken of the
tradition of Andeluvian leaders to support the cause
of peace. There has always been a great respect
among the other nations for this noble tradition. The
Brown Elves have always spoken out, and acted to
bring a healing force to the land, and have been a
great inspiration to the other nations. When distrust
and despair have become overwhelming, when the
light of freedom had dwindled to a mere spark, the
steadfast example of Andeluvia has oftimes kept alive
the faith that someday the nations of Urshurak would
unite to overcome the forces of oppression. Sire, I
would never consider asking you to *bear arms*
against this foe. But come with us! Give us your
support! ...Or at least your blessings. Let those who
wish to unite beneath the banner of freedom do so.
Allow them the choice! Our people are such that they
will not act without sanction from you...."

"I find it hard to believe that you're asking us to
support some wild-eyed Prince of the White Elves,"
said Elsep, who had moved beside Gwynn. "Were it
not for the White Elves this predicament would not
exist. As I understand, the Death Lord was once an
heir to this fabled Crownhelm, that you seem to put
so much stock in. If such a dire situation is an
actuality, then it is the White Elves that are at fault. It is
their responsibility...and theirs alone."

Gwynn checked her rising temper with some difficulty. She turned back to her uncle to answer the
charge: "It's hard for me to believe that you don't see
the absolute seriousness of the situation. Even if you
doubt the reports of the terrible war machines of
Torgon, even if you disbelieve the Prophecy that tells
us that the day draws near when either freedom
or slavery will be established forever...even these
doubts must surely weaken in the face of the known

facts. For over three hundred years the Brown Elves have been the prime object of the barbarian raids to secure slaves. So many of our people have been carried off that the entire northern half lies deserted, homes empty or destroyed, the fields fallow. And those who have yet to feel their limbs shackled by chains tremble with fear that such a fate might yet befall them. Andeluvia lies in a state of immobility, depressed by its own passivity. Surely you cannot fail to see this...." And half turning to Elsep she continued, "As for your charge that the White Elves should not be supported because one of their own race succumbed to some destructive force almost a thousand years ago... let me answer with a question: If your horse had bucked you off into quicksand, and her colt is prepared to pull you out, do you then thumb your nose at the colt... as you slowly submerge?" She gave Elsep a hard stare. He opened his mouth to speak, but thought better of it, and began to study some point of interest on the floor.

Gwynn took a deep breath, and turned back to Zarin. With that, Ianen and Glenden came to her rescue. They began to barrage their father and mother with profundities they'd carried back from the House of Uxmun: the problem could not be resolved, they said excitedly, by pretending that it didn't exist. Wouldn't the decision to not act at all, they questioned, be an act of violence in itself? Wouldn't the results of such inaction be violence a hundredfold greater than any that would take place during the final battle at Golgorath?

The King held his head with both hands.

"Let us go," pleaded Ianen, "we will not fight. But let us join in this quest. We have met the Sevena. Let us go to Cryslandon to aid him in any way that we can. The allied nations are doomed without the unity of all who love freedom..."

"Please, Father..." joined in Glenden, "no nation alone can hope to match the terrible power of the Death Lord. Only in the unity of all of us can we avert slavery and destruction!"

Zarin was dumbfounded. Surely these were not his sons speaking out so passionately!

Gwynn continued to stare directly at the King. She had not missed a word of the spirited arguments put forth by her young cousins, and she was completely delighted with their newfound sense of openness and adventure.

But all their pleas had failed to allay the King's fears. "I cannot allow this insanity to continue!" he cried. "I never dreamed a single night's stay among those rowdies in Penderak could have such disastrous effects... " He glared at Gwynn. "You'd think I would have learned by now... "

She saw the deep hurt and the fear, and she went to him, kneeling beside him, taking his hand in hers. "My uncle, we have been attempting to convince you with logic of things that cannot be logically explained. Our hearts burn with the fires of optimism, while it appears that yours is heavy with sorrow and hopelessness. I've been trying to convince you how wrong it is to feel this despair... " Zarin's lips were taut. He swallowed tears that threatened to weaken his position. Gwynn squeezed his hand gently. "I will press you no more," she said. "I'm going now. I will not be deterred from the pursuit of the quest... But I will make no more attempts to change your views or gain your blessings." From the corner of her eye she could detect the pain of disappointment on the young faces of her cousins.

Ianen stepped forward. "Wait, Gwynn," he said, looking with compassion at his parents. "Glenden and I are going to Cryslandon."

"We will bear no weapons," Glenden added. "This we promise you. We go only to aid the wounded and bury the dead."

Ianen continued. "We are deeply sorrowed by the pain you and mother feel, but our minds are made up."

Zarin slumped slowly in his wooden throne. "My sons... my sons..." Wanel placed her hand on her husband's arm as he struggled to contain his tears. Zarin spoke. "If you go, I must tell you this. Deciedon, governor of Cryslandon, was here two days ago. He told me he had uncovered and captured the traitor. He would not reveal his identity, declaring this knowledge was for the Sevena alone."

"Then it is as we suspected," Gwynn cried, looking at her cousins. "Ailwon is known to the traitor! We must leave for Cryslandon immediately!"

Zarin stood. "Wait. I cannot encourage my people to join... this quest... but I cannot allow you to leave without giving you my blessing. But you must promise me that you will take the Retnor Pass through the mountains. Deciedon's concern for your safety is such that he will have a detachment of White Elf Lejentors there to escort you to Cryslandon. Promise me you will do this."

Gwynn stepped to the throne and embraced her uncle. "I promise."

Glenden and Ianen whooped and, talking excitedly to each other, left the hall to make some final preparations. Gwynn once again embraced her guardians and turned to leave, but Elsep, in a typically ill-timed attempt to impress the King, again stopped her, grasping her shoulder with his strong fingers. "I cannot understand," he began, through a smile so forced as to appear painful, "I cannot comprehend how a woman so beautiful as yourself finds it necessary to go riding off at the head of a band of rebels to face almost certain death."

Gwynn nodded, "I know you don't understand this, Elsep," she said, "nor do you understand that neither my sex nor my appearance has anything to do with any of it." She smiled and said through her teeth, "And, Elsep, remove your hand from my shoulder... If you should ever touch me again without my permission I'll strangle you with those pretty chains you wear around your neck!"

The King's advisor released her as quickly as if she'd stuck his hand with a dagger, and Gwynn strode from the hall. Elsep looked toward the King helpless-

ly, and started to speak. But Zarin stopped him with a
wave of his hand. "Not now, Elsep... I wish to be left
alone." The King's advisor turned awkwardly, and left
the throne room, nervously fingering the medallions.
Queen Wanel rose from her throne. She didn't speak
to her husband, but touched him gently as she
passed him on her way to the side entrance.

Zarin sat motionless save for his hands which
slowly rubbed the arms of his chair, his fingers
working steadily but without feeling the wood. He
stared down at the long stretch of faded red carpet. A
vision began to form wherein his two sons and Gwynn
lay upon the carpet, the red of their blood running
from them, fading in color as it blended with the
flowers woven in the fabric.

13

THE AMAZONS
OF ZAN-DURA

Gorta the witch was dead. The queen of the underworld had spread havoc across Urshurak for centuries. But she, who had seemed unconquerable, had been slain by the youth, Ailwon... and now she was no more.

Ailwon had left behind the illusion of her stronghold, and led his small band south toward the sea. From Zorak they crossed the gray wasteland of the Croalic Moors. Then before them, rising into the mountains, was the endless green of the Dangar Jungle. The jungle foliage in the mountains was not an obstacle; but once they began to descend this condition would change radically. It would then become necessary to find one of the southwesterly flowing outlets of the River Garnon, which would cut a path for the group through the lowland jungle and bring them close to the sea, hopefully not far from the homeland of the Amazons. Thus it was decided that the Gwarpy, Oolu, should guide them, for, of the races of speaking creatures of Urshurak, it was the Gwarpys who had clung most tenaciously to their instincts. If any of them could find their way through this immense tropical wilderness it would be Oolu.

They were able to traverse the mountains most of the way on horseback, but were aware that the beasts might possibly have to be abandoned when they reached the denser portions of forest. Soon they came across a narrow, slow-running river, which carried them into the darkest tracts of the Dangar Jungle.

The forest became thicker and more impenetrable by the hour, and it was easy to understand the centuries of isolation of the Amazon women, since their complete withdrawal to the crater island of Zan-Dura. Ailwon and his companions were forced to the very edge of the river, where the banks were naked of foliage. There they were able to lead their mounts, though this made their progress especially slow. But each was reluctant to leave his particular horse to the fates of the jungle, and each hoped to have his mount beneath him when the moment came for the ride from Cryslandon to Golgorath.

With each mile of penetration southward the jungle spoke louder of its distaste for intrusion. It was so twisted and matted with trees and undergrowth, and so entangled with vines, as to present an almost impassable barrier. The river was too shallow to be navigable by more than the smallest boats, and where patches of sunlight fell on the sloped banks there were sure to be a number of languid, wickedly grinning alligators which proved themselves to be continual menaces. All around the small group were a seemingly endless number of monkeys—small, gray, long-tailed creatures that chattered fiercely from the trees—and lending their harsh, repellent voices to the dissonance were a variety of large-beaked, brilliantly colored birds. Several times the group saw giant sloths—larger than bears—standing erect within the forest, feeding on the trees. And once they were startled by a huge animal with armor-like hide, that sluggishly emerged with a loud thrashing, but when confronted by the five strange creatures, it turned awkwardly, and shuffled back to safety.

After following the river for six days the allied band found themselves completely out of food. There was practically nothing edible at the water's edge, save the small jungle animals. Hugh was almost out of arrows, and neither Ailwon nor Oolu was inclined to partake in the eating of flesh even if it were available.

On the seventh day the river began to subdivide; finally its main stream disappeared underground. Thereafter the forest started to thin, and fruit-bearing trees came into sight. Soon they were able to ride their horses, and just as night fell on that same seventh day they heard the crashing waves of the Sea of Kresna.

Ailwon, Hugh, the twins and Oolu emerged from the jungle into the almost pitch-black of a clouded night. None of the five had ever before seen an ocean, and as they stood on the sandy beach it was apparent that it would be morning before the expected view would be forthcoming. The dark of the sea was scarcely distinguishable from the dark of the sky, and they contented themselves with listening to the rhythm of the rolling waves breaking against reefs, and with the smell and feel of the fresh cool air that blew in from the great body of water.

They tended their horses, and went to the water's edge to wash. Having freed themselves of the oppression of the jungle it was extremely tempting to plunge into the water; but they'd been warned of the dangers of the great sea, and instead fell to their tasks of setting up camp, the chores having become so routine that they were performed without thought. They dined on gathered fruit and nuts, then settled back around the campfire. But having, at last, completed the long southern journey, there now occurred a general letdown, which served as a damper on the usual evening conversation.

Evrawk in particular was silent, suffering one of his occasional sullen moods. Erbin began to bemoan the fact that the wine that filled his goatskin flask at the journey's beginning had long since been replaced by water. Oolu suffered no mental depressions, but the Gwarpy had shouldered the burden of leadership for many days and within a matter of moments after the meal's completion he curled up and fell sound asleep. The usually quiet Hugh was the most vocal of the five, asking Ailwon a number of questions in regard to the Amazons of Zan-Dura.

The young White Elf Prince answered as best he could, but explained that there was only minimal information known about the warrior women, since not one of the allies had traversed the jungles to make contact with them save for the sorcerer, Shandar, and that ten centuries before when the civilization of Zan-Dura was still very young. It was, of course, known that the Amazons had little trust for those outside their own race.

Ailwon sensed a deep unease in the archer to whom the thought of an all-female society—and of female warriors, at that—was completely alien. Still, there was not much information or reassurance the Prince could give. Hugh would just have to get used to the idea himself. With this thought Ailwon bade the others good night, and settled into his bedroll. He hoped to gain a good night's sleep to better prepare himself for his next challenge: that of finding and gaining entrance to the nation of the Amazons. Hugh soon followed his example. Then Erbin stretched out, clasping his hands behind his head. He stared up, reflecting on old friends and ribald evenings in the City of the Dwarfs. Only Evrawk remained sitting. He peered into the black depth of sky and sea, listening to the water. Moments passed, and then an hour. Still Evrawk sat motionless. The great sea murmured and sighed in the darkness, speaking to the Dwarf of implacable power, of teeming life, of living gardens on its floors, of mighty cliffs and escarpments of coral, built through patient eons of time. All this and more Evrawk learned as he sat like a stone in the sea-mists. Of facts he gained nothing, but he listened to the sea, and smelled it, and felt it, and it spoke to him of its essence. With a gentle hiss the waters were drawn to the hidden moon and the tide rolled outward. With it went the dregs of Evrawk's dark mood. He was smiling as he lay down, asleep as his head touched sand.

The wet chill of dawn awakened the party. Erbin

raised himself on his elbows, rubbing his eyes, looking expectantly toward the ocean. But the night
refused to completely relinquish its dark cloak, leaving behind a thick fog scarcely distinguishable from
the water. The water scarcely moved, hardly breaking
against reefs that loomed like hulking shrouds within
the gray mist.

Erbin stood up. "Sure's a lovely view of the sea we
got here this morning... " he said, his voice hoarse
from his night's sleep, "and look there!" he cried with
mock excitement. "Zan-Dura...the home of the Amazon women! Must be ten miles long and a mile
high!...Look at it glitter! It must be pure gold!" He was
shading his eyes, and squinting into the fog, through
which he could actually determine nothing beyond
fifty yards. But the little man was undeterred by such
meager obstacles to his imagination and sense of
humor: "Hey, lads," he cried, "I can see one of them
Amazon ladies now!...She's waving at us...no, just at
me, I think... Gawl! She must be twoscore feet
high!..." He began to laugh, before giving way to a fit
of coughing. His brother was chuckling and Oolu
cackled loudly as he sat on the sand, picking at an
insect that had spent the night within his fur. "Erbin's
sure funny fer a fella... " said the Gwarpy.

Behind the group the forest was quite still; only an
occasional chattering came from deep within. But
when the five walked toward the water, they discovered a good deal of activity taking place that had
been disguised by the quiet dawn. A number of small
lizards moved across the yellow sand in search of
food, and land crabs emerged from their holes to
scurry over the beach. Sandpipers skittered about,
their heads darting down; while offshore multitudes
of birds fed on the reefs, the sides of which were
covered with bright-colored starfish and brownish
sea anemones that clung to the rocks, awaiting the
flood tide.

A discussion began as to their next move. All during
this talk Oolu was peering into the fog. Finally he
began to chuckle excitedly, and started jumping up

and down. "You think yer just jokes, Erbin!" The
Gwarpy laughed, "But I kin see it! I kin see it!" The
others squinted and peered but could see nothing.
Oolu, however, scurried back to the edge of the forest,
and within a moment had scaled a tree, was perched
at its top and called out through a mouthful of the
fruit he had plucked on the way up: "Yep! Yep! It's there
fer sure! Straight out from us! Mebbe five miles!
Zan-Dura!"

The incredible eyesight of the Gwarpys was well
known, and none of his companions doubted Oolu
for an instant. Now it became necessary to take
action. A raft must be built, which would carry them to
the Amazon ocean city. First the horses would have to
be taken care of. A spring was found, the source for a
tiny stream that trickled toward the ocean. There was
ample vegetation here, and a makeshift corral was
quickly constructed from tree limbs tethered together with vines. The horses were put inside, and it
was hoped that there were no large predators about.
Then the group's attention was turned toward the
next task, and this presented a problem. Of what were
they to construct their raft in order for it to be
seaworthy? The tree trunks here were impractically
large, and the branches, while serving well for a
corral, were far too erratically shaped for a raft. Oolu
again provided the answer: he pointed to a spot far
down the beach, where the ocean waters had intruded inward to form a lagoon, mingling the life from the
sea with that of the land. Lining the sides of the water
was a profusion of leaning, but straight-limbed, palm
trees. Erbin was certain that they would be perfect for
the construction of the raft, and it was likely that they
could find raw materials from which they could
fashion some type of paddles. Erbin went even further: it would be far easier, he exclaimed, to launch
their craft from out of the lagoon, than from other
parts of the beach where it would take some degree of
skill to navigate between the many reefs. Ailwon
thought well of these points and suggested that Erbin
and Oolu explore the possibilities while the rest of

them broke camp. The two responded with characteristic enthusiasm, and hurried off toward the veiled lagoon.

Daybreak had come but was unable to penetrate the dense fog. Ailwon, Hugh and Evrawk bent to the task of gathering their bedrolls and weapons, and then saddleries which they put into a dry place near the horses. There was considerable satisfaction among them that they had arrived at a point that would require no further travel to reach the Amazon land. Ailwon heaved a sigh. "Well," he said, "if Oolu's judgment of the distance we must navigate is as accurate as his sense of direction and as keen as his eyesight, then we'll—"

"Stop!" exclaimed Hugh, holding up his hand. He stood frozen, listening, his head bent toward the sea. "Do you hear it?"

"I hear something... or feel something... " said Ailwon.

The sound—which was almost a vibration—was faint, but growing stronger. It gained in volume and presently it seemed almost like singing. A number of feeding birds fluttered up from a rocky reef, then another flock flew up in fright, followed by another. For several seconds the air was filled with the beating of wings, which was replaced by the strange sound which had grown in volume as it evidently came closer.

With the first instant of the flight of the birds Hugh had pulled his long sword, and Evrawk had reached for his battle-axe. Ailwon now stepped forward to the edge of the sea, his hand on the hilt of his weapon.

"Careful, lad," cautioned Evrawk. The three of them stood still, listening, waiting. The sound grew louder. Small waves rushed in, splashing across Ailwon's feet and ankles. He felt as though some vibrant power was preceding the growing sound, felt power rush across his body in waves. He heard shouting coming from far down the beach as Erbin and Oolu ran toward their companions. A wave almost waist-high rushed in, crashing across the Elfin lad, nearly knocking him

over. The sound was so close it seemed to Ailwon to
be coming from within himself. Suddenly, appearing
through the fog's thickness, moving toward him, was
a bright crimson light. Ailwon stumbled backward,
jerking Elvgard from its sheath. He heard, from
behind, a Vandorian curse of surprise... Then—as
suddenly as it had appeared—the glow was gone, the
singing tone died completely. The ocean waters protested mildly, then returned to their former calm.

Ailwon had retreated to where Hugh and Evrawk
had been joined by Erbin and Oolu. The Gwarpy
peered out from behind the tall archer.

"What was—what is that damned thing?" questioned Erbin, more to himself than any of the others.
A shrouded, hulking form lay silently beyond the
string of reefs that protected the shore. Sounds of
movement came from atop or within the dark form,
then the soft splash of an object striking the ocean
surface. Seconds later the companions could hear
the sound of oars being pulled through the water.

"I believe," said Ailwon, "we are about to be visited
by the women of Zan-Dura."

From out of the mist came the Amazons, coming
swiftly in a long slender boat, rowed forward by a
dozen of their number, with another ten in the bow
and ten more at the stern. They were helmeted and
heavily armed. The small allied band drew deep
breaths, and waited. The vessel came close. The
women in the bow of the boat stood, leaped lightly
over the sides—five from one side, five from the
other—then ran splashing toward shore, holding
shields and long spears. They were followed by the
group of warriors in the boat's stern, who exited like
the first group, but who held swords rather than
spears. Then the oarswomen were in the water, pulling the boat aground. The warriors formed a double
line along the beachfront, the spearswomen stood to
the front, while the swordswomen lined right up
behind them. The other women had replaced their
oars with swords, and they split ranks to flank the

allied band on either side. There was a long moment
of silence.

The women were tall, strong and lithely built. Their
garb was uniform, in keeping with their discipline as
warriors, and it was sparse in reaction to the tropical
heat. They were deeply tanned, with long dark hair
flowing from below their helmets. Their features were
distinct and finely chiseled with deep-set dark eyes,
well-defined mouths and strongly set jaws. The
woman standing at the farthest end of the flanking
line stepped forward. Her voice was firm and authori-
tative. There was no hint of friendliness in her tone:

"You must consider yourselves prisoners of Zan-
Dura. Drop your weapons... all of them. I strongly
advise you to carry out my commands without resistance."

Ailwon was the first to discard his weapon, followed
by the Dwarfs. Oolu simply stood grinning at the
women, holding out his empty hands, and running
his hands through his fur to indicate that he had
nothing hidden. Hugh had not relinquished his arms.
Ailwon turned to him, silently requesting his cooper-

ation. Reluctantly, and with disgust, the Vandorian tossed his bow and arrows to the sand and then his weapon belt.

"We've come in friendship," Ailwon stated. "We are in need of the services of your people."

"We shall find out the truth of your intentions," said the woman. She turned to her sister warriors. "Bind them and take them aboard." Half of the rank of swordswomen turned and walked to their boat, quickly returning, carrying metal shackles. This was too much for Hugh.

"No!" he shouted. "I'll be damned if I'm to let any woman shackle me like some damned slave!"

"Hugh... don't!..." warned Ailwon.

"You shut up!" the Vandorian returned, pointing his finger at the youth. "I've had enough of your advice."

The Amazons had closed around the tall archer. His weapons had been secured. Hugh's face was red with anger. He turned toward the leader of the women. "I've been taught since childhood never to strike a woman... but any that tries to shackle me will find that I'm a man who is fast learning to break rules!"

"Fortunately for us," replied the Amazon commander, "we have no like injunctions about striking men. Take him!"

Hugh was struck at the base of the skull by the butt of an Amazon spear, and he was unconscious before he hit the sand.

"Bring chains," said the Amazon leader, standing over the fallen archer. "Secure this big one well." She turned to Ailwon, whose hands had been shackled behind him. "You go before our Queen."

There was a great black funnel... At the very end of it, barely visible, was consciousness, and the throbbing mind moved toward it. A high-pitched tone that grew louder as the mind rushed now toward the bright opening...

Hugh moaned as he came awake. The first thing he saw was the fuzzy face and the flat, wide teeth of Oolu.

"Hey, Hugh," cried the Gwarpy, "you finally get awoke!"

The Vandorian reshut his eyes. "I'm not too sure of that," he muttered.

"Sure. Yer awake. Yer talkin' ta ol' Oolu."

The archer started to sit up, but could not. He cursed. His wrists were shackled up with chains that encircled his waist; a stout pole was run behind his back, secured within the crooks of his elbows. His feet were chained, with just enough space between them so that he would be able to walk. He cursed again. Then he became aware of a rocking motion and heard again the mysterious atonal sound that had preceded the arrival of the Amazons. He turned his head to observe his surroundings.

He was aboard some huge, metallic golden vessel. There were women warriors everywhere, perhaps a hundred of them. Hugh struggled to sit up, and Oolu helped him to accomplish this. The Vandorian searched for some sign of the nature of their propulsion. There were no sails, masts or booms. The ship's forward movement was so constant and rapid that there seemed to be no conclusion other than that they were being propelled by some unknown power source. Possibly it was this which emitted the unearthly singing tone. Hugh gazed up at the sky. The growing morning had cleared beautifully. He judged that he had not been unconscious for long; the sun was still low in the sky.

He looked at Oolu. The Gwarpy was waiting expectantly, but had remained silent. The little creature loved to converse, but seemed always to restrain himself until the other party was ready.

"What's happened to the others?" asked Hugh, and then—as he often did—asked a second question before getting an answer to the first: "How is it that you've remained without so much as a leash on you, while I'm decorated with these links of chain, practically from head to foot?"

Oolu turned, searched for a second, then pointed.

"There's the Prince!...and Erbin and Evrawk, too!" he exclaimed. Toward the bow of the ship stood the three, their hands bound behind their backs. "They seen that you were gonna be okay, so they let Oolu keep an eye on ya." Oolu looked back to Hugh and chuckled: "Women people kinda like Oolu. Long time ago... way, way long time ago, them Amazons and them Gwarpys usta live real close by—in the jungles along about the great river... Then the witch—and I think, mebbee some of them Gnome fellers—they started. warrin' with the women an' stuff, and the women all left the jungle..." Oolu suddenly dropped to the deck, as limply as would a cat, and lay comfortably on his back, his stubby fingers locked behind his head; his eyes followed a plumpish white cloud that floated above. "There's still," Oolu continued, "som'a Oolu's relatives livin' down there round the great river. Anyways, the Amazons that's here on ship know all about that stuff...an' they like ol' Oolu." He chuckled again. "They call him a 'Corola': 'the creature who speaks'..."

"Did Ailwon or the old wizard know about this?"

Oolu pondered the question for a moment: "Nope," he said, "I don't think so. Nope. There's lots'a stuff gone on in the jungle that even ol' Elgan or even ol' Shandar don't know about... Oolu heard about this from his mama one time..."

Hugh was incredulous: "And even though you were coming down here with Ailwon to meet these hostile women—even then you didn't tell anyone?"

"Well..." began the Gwarpy slowly, "I think mebbe Oolu forgot about it..." Then he was sure. "Yep. That's right. He forgot about it."

"And you don't feel a bit guilty, do you?"

Oolu looked a little puzzled and he stuck out his tongue while he pondered the question. "Guilty... guilty?... Oh!" he exclaimed. "That! Nope! Oolu ain't feelin' that." He chuckled again, and searched for another cloud. "Nope," he said.

An exclamation went up from among the three in the bow of the Amazon ship. They turned and began to walk toward Hugh and Oolu.

"We're almost upon it: Zan-Dura!" exclaimed Ail-won. The ocean air was whipping his long blond hair as he approached. His face showed excitement that did not quite disguise the fear that lay beneath it. "Hugh... " he said, "I'm happy to see that you're all right."

"We've a difference of opinion there," muttered the Vandorian, as Oolu helped him to his feet.

The Amazon commander approached. "Come with me," she said, "we are about to enter the crater of Zan-Dura." The five followed the woman to the ship's bow, climbing a short flight of steps to stand on the raised golden deck. Hugh made known his displeasure at the awkwardness of the movements which his bonds had imposed on him. But his disgruntlement was swept away by the sight before him: the home of the Amazon women lay just beyond a mile wide barrier of reefs, remnants of the volcanic birth of the island of Zan-Dura. The cones and funnels of this volcanic giant were bathed in the early morning sun appearing as golden as the metal of the vessel that approached it. The ship made its way through the inner reefs; straight ahead a huge wall extended from the island to the Sea of Kresna. This was the entranceway to the harbor of Zan-Dura. High above the entrance, chiseled into the volcanic rock of the crater, was a huge octagonal shape overlaying a great spread of intricately carved wings.

The ship passed through the high gateway, with towering structures on either side. Atop the towers embedded in the stone were two gigantic crystal beacons, which flashed in the sunlight. The Amazon vessel entered a dark cavern in the wall of the crater. The singing tone rose in intensity. Ahead, through the tunnel opening, could be seen a structure from which a ruby glow emanated. It was in the center of a blue-green lake which filled the interior of the crater. Beyond this structure was the city-nation of the women of Zan-Dura. Its buildings rose in tiers against the crater wall. Long flights of steps led upward

toward a central terrace, from which rose a shining
obelisk. At its top was another of the mysterious
crystal objects.

The ship passed by the structure which stood in the
center of the inner lake. The vessel's velocity de-
creased to a slow glide as the constant energy-tone
ceased; it seemed not to completely die but to be
blended by a sound that came from the central
building. The sound was that of a large number of
female voices, in perfect unison, repeating over and
over, one phrase:

"... Ki-est-oh-vel-oh..."

Then, from within the city, came the sound of a
giant gong. The voices rose in volume, as a procession moved outward from the central building along
a long white causeway leading to the city. Four
abreast they came: Amazon women in flowing blue
robes, chanting over and over: "...Ki-est-oh-vel-oh..."

The Amazon ship then turned toward a docking
area, gliding to an open place amidst twoscore other
ships. After being taken from the Amazon vessel the
prisoners stood for a moment, looking in amazement
at the beauty of Zan-Dura. But they were prodded
forward, and began to climb a long ascension of
steps, passing through a towering archway. All
around them was evidence of the Amazon's fierce
love for beauty and grandeur. There was an intricate
blend between the great pliant power of their archi-
tectural design and the use of nature: massive fa-
cades embellished with elaborate carvings and
sculpture were integrated at various levels, with exotic trees and gardens as a living part of the design.

All along the way, Hugh had protested his being
shackled, but his protests had gone unheeded. At the
same time Ailwon had sought information from the
Amazon commander, but had received none. Finally
they arrived before the throne room of the Queen of
Zan-Dura, and as they entered they were greeted by a
resonance of gongs. The five—flanked by lines of
warrior women—made the long approach to the

©HILDEBRANDT

throne of Queen Azira, which was elevated upon an
enormous dais. Behind the throne, carved into the
wall, was the great winged crystal.

At last they stood before the Queen, who studied
them silently. She was dressed in crimson and gold
and sat very straight. Her face, though beautiful,
appeared stern and humorless. Her hair was silver
and very long. Upon her head rested a ring of gold
centered by a red crystal with gold wings. Ailwon
swallowed hard; Gorta had appeared no more formidable. After a long moment she broke the silence:

"I have been told that you intrude upon our lands to
seek friendship and aid. It is also claimed that you are
a Prince of Alfandel, of the land of the twin lakes—do
not speak, yet... " she held up her hand as Ailwon
opened his mouth. "We shall determine if you are
truthful, and we'll find out the nature of your intrusion. You—" the Queen said pointing her finger at
Oolu, "you are the first of the Corolas that I have ever
seen... " She leaned forward slightly, "I must admit,"
she continued, "to being somewhat disarmed by your
presence in this group... but I am still wary of any
invasion of the sanctity of our homeland." She sat
back, and looked toward a group of elders.

"Senqua, what is keeping our new Princess? She
must be here to witness this event."

One of the older women answered: "She has been
informed. She is coming."

"Good," said Azira.

Another moment passed with no word being spoken. Hugh squirmed irritably. Queen Azira sat perfectly still. Then she turned quickly, and her face
showed her satisfaction. Through an archway that
entered onto the dais came the Princess Zyra.

Amazons, both young and old, are physically striking, but the woman who now entered the room was
exceptionally lovely. She was tall and statuesque. Her
hair was very long and raven-black, her face rich with
an exquisite, dark beauty, the skin deeply tanned and
sleek. Through the disciplined training as an athlete
and warrior, she had developed the cat-like litheness

that was true to her nature. As she approached she was studying the captive male beings with an attention at least as strong as they were according her.

"I apologize, Queen Mother, if I've held up the interrogation of these invaders," she said to Azira.

It was obvious that the Queen had a great affection and respect for the Princess.

"It is of no consequence, Zyra," she said, beckoning the young woman to stand beside her. "Now," said Azira, motioning to the elder called Senqua, "let us begin."

Senqua, who appeared to be older than any of the other women, walked to the center of the huge room, to a large carved circle in the stone floor. Within the circle was an inlay of the winged crystal. She turned, pointing toward Ailwon. "Unbind him," she commanded, "and bring him forward."

The Elfin youth was released from his shackles, and brought to stand at the center of the circle, facing Senqua. Ailwon appeared nervous as the old woman looked deep into his eyes. "Now," she said, "we shall learn the truth of this adventure." She looked up, raising her arms toward the arched ceiling. Ailwon's eyes traveled upward. There was a dark octagonal opening cut into the stone. Then, as Senqua started her chant and the clear voice drifted upward, the darkness began to recede, to be replaced by a crimson glow. This was accompanied by a repetition of the vibrant atonal sound they had first heard. Ailwon was bathed within a shaft of crimson light. He felt the pull of light and sound all around him and within him—a deep, sonorous vibrating luminescence that quivered through his whole body, drawing out words that spilled from his mouth with joy, for the truths that he was compelled to disclose were those that had prompted this entire quest to which he was so devoted.

Within the throne room there was no other voice than that of the Elfin Prince, and when he called out that the Witch of Zorak had been slain, Queen Azira stood straight up. Finally, Ailwon finished with an

impassioned plea that the warrior women of Zan-
Dura join in the quest for the freedom of Urshurak.
Senqua again raised her voice and pleading hands,
and slowly the light and the sound disappeared.

"Bring the youth forward," said Azira gently, "release the others... and you," she crooked her finger
toward Oolu, "come sit beside me." The Gwarpy
scampered up the steps, chuckling all the way, and
stood at the arm of the throne. He looked up and
grinned at Zyra, who observed him stoically.

Ailwon went forward. "Come up," said Azira. The
youth ascended the steps. The Queen began to
speak:

"You have just experienced the power of the crystal
of Kresna. You have felt the power of that which fell
from far beyond... that fell—ages ago—to the depths
of our ocean, and around which was formed our
crater of Zan-Dura." She paused, then asked: "Have
you before heard of this? Did you know of Kresna
before you came?"

"I had been told that you possessed a great power,
but knew no more than this... "

"It had been scarcely harnessed centuries ago
when the sorcerer Shandar came, and the rulers of
that time were reluctant to disclose our secrets. I have
no fear of doing so," Azira said, smiling with confidence. "It is from Kresna that we are able to draw
upon our powers to replenish our race. It is Kresna
that powers our ships. It is through this power that
our queens are selected... The procession you witnessed was the final ceremony of this event." She
glanced up at the new Princess, then went on:

"Now, as to this matter of our joining your quest..."
She stood, and looked down at the Prince, whose face
clearly showed his expectancy. Azira smiled. "It is
difficult to refuse such a look of hope... but, I am
afraid I must... " The tall, slender woman strode
slowly to the side of her throne, her hand running
lightly over the engraved arm. She timed her turn
toward Ailwon perfectly, for he was ready to utter a
protest. She stopped him with her raised hand. "You

have done Urshurak a great service...you have slain the hated Gorta. It was she who was the most feared enemy of the Amazons, and I will admit to some feeling of sympathy for Urshurak, and for Alfandel in particular: it is the great twin lakes of your land that feed the waters of the River Garnon, and it is from the Garnon that fresh water spreads to Zan-Dura. Without this it would be far more difficult for us to maintain our independence..." She paused, and Ailwon seized upon the opportunity:

"Then why will you not join us? Do you disbelieve the threat that the Death Lord makes? Do you not realize that in this quest to save ourselves—to free ourselves—that no one of us can succeed without the aid of all others? You must—"

"We *must* do nothing!" Queen Azira's voice had become resolute. "The Amazons of Zan-Dura have squelched every invader for centuries... When it was *we* who were threatened—when it was *we* who were being attacked by the forces of Gorta, and the forces of the Death Lord—" her eyes were afire, her voice echoed in the great throne room, "when it was the women of Zan-Dura who were being killed in the jungles, who were being dragged off into slavery— where then were our allies? Why was it that no one—absolutely no one—was willing to join our noble quest to throw back the oppressors? It was the Amazons alone who defeated all who would overcome us... And it will be so again. We will seek the aid of no one!" Her voice dropped, and her eyes searched out the eyes first of Ailwon, then Erbin, and Hugh, and Evrawk.

"And," she continued, "we will give aid to no one. We will not hinder you, we will see that you are fed and refreshed. Then you will be taken back to the mainland." Azira turned toward Oolu who was looking extremely sad. "I have done you a disservice... Your ancestors *did* help our people. They of course did not fight, but they administered to our wounded, and gave us shelter. To the gentle Corola we will always be grateful." She turned back to Ailwon. "This matter is finished."

"I'll be damned if it is!" It was the voice of Hugh Oxhine. He strode forward to face the Queen, ignoring Ailwon's pleading eyes. "I haven't fought the rot of the jungle, taken a rap on the skull, and been fettered in irons—only then to be snubbed by some snobbish women!...Not without speaking my mind!" The Amazon guard closed around the Vandorian.

Hugh's anger had been set afire. "You lay claim to such injustices," he said, "to such lonely valor and suffering. It seems to me that not one of you here is now in pain. It was those who preceded you by hundreds of years who bore the brunt of your battle." He looked toward Zyra. "Is *she*—with her glowing good health, her gold-trimmed luxury—is she caught within the trap of suffering?" Hugh's eyes were ablaze, and they locked with the cool gaze of the Amazon Princess. "Of course," sneered the Vandorian, "you would not see fit to leave the comfort of this golden splendor—this tropical paradise....You would not find it seemly to give aid to a bedraggled lad, such as this," looking toward Ailwon, "even though he dared to risk his life, dared to face Gorta, the terrible witch, beneath the swamp! Why should you align yourself with such insane beings, who dedicate themselves to freeing the suffering thousands chained in slavery beneath the bastard Torgon?"

He started up the steps toward Azira and the Princess, brushing aside Ailwon's restraining hand. "Understand me, *your highness*," he spoke with withering disdain, "I am not one of these insane beings, either. I accompany them for one reason only: revenge! My vision is considerably less noble than theirs. But I am willing to accompany this ragged band. And I will fight beside them, for, *unlike you*, I have known real pain! It was not some distant ancestors that I buried, with their throats torn out! It was my beloved wife and children... But you wouldn't know of such things..."

Zyra's dark eyes had not flinched before the burning stare of the archer's. Nor had her face disclosed

Opposite: Zan-Dura, The Amazon Isle

anything beyond icy calm. "It is apparent that you have suffered a great loss," she said. Her voice was level, displaying neither anger nor compassion, "But it is not in the service of your loved ones that you wear your loss as a decoration." She turned from his look of hate, to the Queen, "Does your decision hold, my mother?"

"Yes."

"Then," Zyra continued, turning to Ailwon, "you are all dismissed. You will be attended to as promised by our Queen Mother."

It was apparent that the matter would be discussed no further. The Amazon commander told the group to follow her. The Elfin Prince's head drooped dejectedly. "You did your level best, lad," said Evrawk. The five were led from the throne room. When they were gone Zyra turned to the Queen.

"I have only today been confirmed your successor and your spiritual daughter," she said. Her voice was soft, her eyes warm. "I hesitate to question any decision made by one of your great wisdom and

experience... "

"But," said Azira, smiling.

"But," replied Zyra, nodding her head, "I would point out that it is said that the chief power of the Amazon woman lies in her willingness to see clearly the possible consequences of her actions—to look at them with the aid of history and tradition, but without enslavement to either. And once looked at so clearly it is the power of the Amazon woman that she can act then on her deepest convictions... " Azira's eyes filled with pride for the wisdom and courage of her new daughter.

"And," said the Queen, "you might have added, that the love of freedom is the deepest of our convictions."

"I might have," returned Zyra, "but I knew that you would." She smiled, reaching down to the Queen. Azira grasped the young woman's hand and stood. And with hands clasped the two exited the throne room of the Queens of Zan-Dura.

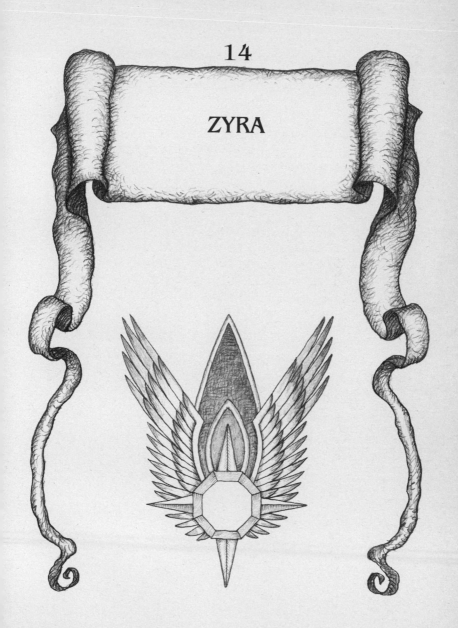

14

ZYRA

Hugh picked his way across the rocky shoreline along the western exposure of Zan-Dura. The sea stretched endlessly away, waves crashed against the sides of the crater, urged on by a raw wind that had grown with the passage of the day. The Vandorian shivered. His thick hair and beard were still wet from having bathed in the sea. He and his companions had been offered a luxurious bathhouse within the Amazon palace in which to remove the sweat and grime of their long journey. The others had accepted this hospitality gladly, but Hugh had declined. He felt uncomfortable within the confines of such places of splendor. He had thus been directed to a place, somewhat removed from the city, where his needs could be met within the waters of the ocean.

Now he climbed upward, pondering the implications of the Amazon refusal to join the quest. The accusations that he had hurled at the warrior women had given him cause to question his own dedication. Did *he* wish to continue? He realized the fervor of his own quest for revenge was almost dead, and suddenly he felt very tired. He thought again of the death of Gorta and again heard Ailwon's words. Their true meaning was becoming clear to Hugh, but to acknowledge them meant a change in his purpose, perhaps even a new direction in his life. Perhaps, he thought, the haughty Amazon Princess was right: he was using the loss of his family to give him purpose to continue—to even exist. He wondered at the feelings that arose each time he thought of the Princess Zyra. He detested what he considered to be her attitude of aloofness and superiority; yet he had been completely stunned by her beauty, and his curiosity had been piqued by unknown seductive qualities he detected beneath the regal cool of her exterior. And he felt terrible that he had experienced this arousal. His wife and children were dead for less than a moon cycle. What right had he to look upon this exotic creature, Zyra, with anything other than the eye of an impartial observer?

Hugh reached a level spot on the terrain. He was at a point which was higher than all but the tallest stone pinnacles that punctuated the elevated land. He could now look down upon the city that lay glittering within the crater. It was good to be by himself. He felt refreshed by the sting of the wind that came unhindered, blowing in across a thousand miles of ocean. He glanced toward a towering peak across the way, and reacted to what he saw with a startled gasp. A woman stood erect, poised upon the rimmed edge of the stone spire. She appeared to be ready to jump, and Hugh shouted to her. His voice carried to her, and she turned to look at him. Even at that distance the Vandorian could tell that it was the Amazon Princess, Zyra. She looked away, and without hesitation she leaped. Her arms were held back, her legs and feet perfectly placed, her long hair flowed as she arched outward high above the sea, the picture of disciplined power and grace. She extended her arms, straightening her body. Downward she fell, down, down...finally knifing into the churning waters. After a long moment she rose to the surface, and began to swim smoothly toward the rocky shore. Hugh's heart was beating wildly with sheer fright or admiration—he couldn't tell which. Perhaps it was both. "Damn," he breathed aloud, "what a beauty she is... what an incredible creature!"

"She is that," came a voice from directly behind

© HILDEBRANDT

him. The archer turned abruptly. Queen Azira stood
not more than a dozen feet away. She was garbed in a
hooded cloak of crimson, which whipped about in the
wind. "I did not desire to overhear you," she said. "I
was just about to speak when you let known your
feelings for my spiritual daughter." Hugh blushed.

"... I only expressed..." he stammered. "I have no
feelings as a man toward women such as she." He
looked directly at Azira. "I offer no offense to you—but
I believe women of great beauty are not to be
trusted." The Queen looked amused. He rushed on,
"They are so fussed over and pandered to that it
seems impossible for them to understand things of
reality...and she..." He turned to look down to where
Zyra had climbed from the ocean, and now stood
drying herself, the curved symmetry of her body
showing dark against the light of the descending sun.
Hugh felt a sudden churning in his stomach, and he
struggled to bring alive the old distrust and hurt to
combat his newly aroused passion. He continued,
"One such as she—this Princess Zyra—one who is
unique among beautiful women," he swallowed hard,
keeping his face turned from Azira, straining to
regroup his thoughts while his stammering words
came to a complete stop. Finally, he blurted angrily,
"How can one such as she feel anything but obvious
disdain for the rabble who mire themselves with the
struggles of the world?"

The Amazon Queen was studying Hugh closely.
With her silver hair covered, Azira appeared scarcely
older than the Princess, though she projected the
wisdom of her years. "Your philosophy regarding the
appearance of things seems quite strange to me,"
she said. "I would assume that in the lands beyond
Zan-Dura, you yourself would be considered an object of beauty. You are tall, handsome of face, muscular of body. Have *you* been so fussed over and
pandered to that you find it impossible to understand
things of reality? Can *you* exhibit naught but disdain
for those who are involved in the struggle to exist? I

suspect that you view yourself as being very mascu-
line. You are strong and aggressive, rational, brave,
hard, nonemotional. You claim that beautiful women
are none of these things. They can be only soft,
passive, irrational, fickle. Yet when one—such as my
spiritual daughter—cannot be viewed in this faulty
light, your only reaction is to condemn her to a
shallowness which, in truth, only reveals the pathetic
limits of your own vision. I will not defend Zyra further,
for she requires no defense from me." Azira looked
down upon the boulders, to where the Princess was
climbing upward. "I will say only this: my daughter
has the capacity for great and powerful love within
her." She turned, and began walking. "Come with
me," she said, over her shoulder, "I have something
you should see, and we haven't much time before the
journey begins." Hugh wondered about the choice of
words in regard to the departure of the allied band for
the mainland, but he followed her silently.

They followed a path which gradually descended
toward the northern sector of the city. But before they
reached it, they entered an exquisite garden, filled
with tropical foliage and flowers and birds of the most
exotic colors. A pure white building lay comfortably
nestled at the garden's center. Seated around the
garden were several women who appeared to Hugh
to be grotesque. Their bodies jerked and shifted and
they emitted disjointed sounds of moaning and
laughter. Azira stopped, and turned to Hugh. "These
are our sisters from whom we have learned much.
They are very much different from the rest of us, and
yet they are very much the same. They live here, in
this most beautiful of gardens, not because we desire
to set them aside, but because they find joy in this
place. Their sisters who are more physically able than
they take turns caring for them. We all jealously vie for
this honor, for we are taught much here. We learn of
the impartial regard that nature has for the distinc-
tions of physical structure, and we learn to become
more able to see beyond the veil of appearances. We

do not learn guilt or pity here, nor do we learn to disregard ourselves, nor the manner in which we appear." She paused. "But I am spoiling your experience. Come," she said, and they went forward.

Hugh stared at the people incredulously. There were a score of them within a circle before the house, and more sat in various parts of the garden. The Vandorian had been exposed to grotesque and deformed people in his own land, but he had always avoided them. And now to see such a large number of them gathered together, and to try to understand that they, too, were Amazons, of the same race as Zyra... Hugh deliberately stopped his thoughts. Then a familiar chuckle reached his ears. He spotted a brownish form beneath the shade of a fruit tree. "Oolu!" he called.

"Hey, Hugh!" cried the Gwarpy. He leaped to his feet, then leaned back to take the hand of the skeletal woman who had been sitting beside him. Still holding her hand, and grinning broadly, Oolu approached. The woman beside him moved with considerable difficulty, her arms and legs lacking strength. Nor did she seem to have any sense of direction. "Hey, Hugh," Oolu repeated, "this's Toola. She's a good friend o' Oolu's."

Queen Azira was more surprised than the archer by the Gwarpy's appearance. "How did you manage to find your way here?" she asked.

"Oolu has a way of discovering things," said Hugh. The Gwarpy beamed at him. This was the first time the tall archer had ever paid him a compliment. He helped Toola to a seat on the grass. "Watch," said the Gwarpy, "Toola knows how'ta do lots'a stuff." The young woman sat cross-legged, staring up. Her eyelids drooped, her mouth was agape, and it appeared as though she was totally unaware of her surroundings. Then, slowly, she lifted her hands, and began moving them in the air, and while her arms were raised awkwardly, the movements of her hands were graceful and rhythmic as if she were in concert with some unheard music. Hugh was staring at her, and it was then that he noticed the effect of the wind on her hair, and he became aware of the breezes moving across his own body. He followed the direction of Toola's gaze, and saw the sweep of the wind through a giant willow. He saw that all around him, the garden was alive with the gentle, singing power of the wind, and that the movement of Toola's hands perfectly matched the graceful undulation of the willow.

Oolu was chuckling delightedly. "See, Hugh, all the stuff ol' Toola knows—hey! Now watch!" he cried. Toola leaned over and scooped up a handful of earth, letting it run through her fingers, holding a small amount in the palm of her hand. This she examined closely, pushing it about with a delicate, probing finger, crooning to the earth, finally letting it slip back to the mother from which it came.

"Betcha hardly nobody nowhere does that even once," murmured Oolu. "Ol' Toola here does it all th' time, yep. Knows that's where we come from—that's where we'll go. Good place, yep."

The Vandorian looked away from Toola. He glanced quickly at Queen Azira and at Oolu, for he had discovered that his eyes were wet. But this had gone undetected, and Hugh blinked rapidly. He started to speak, but suddenly, from the city, came the resounding echo of three gongs, each from one of three great towers. "What," he demanded of Azira, "is *that* about?"

"That," she said, looking toward the lofty pinnacles, "is the war signal of the Amazons of Zan-Dura, a signal that has not been sounded for over three centuries. The signal which now tells us that we must set aside the security of our beloved land, and the distrust of the outside world which we have clung to. We must fight beside the Prince of the White Elves and his allies. We must go forth to Golgorath—to do fierce battle with the monster, Torgon. And not until he is overcome can we return to Zan-Dura." Her face broke into a smile of amusement. "I think, Hugh Oxhine,"

she said, "that with your mouth hanging open as it
now is, you are providing an irresistible target for all
manner of tropical insects that frequent this land.
Perhaps you had better make your way back to the
palace. My people will soon be assembled in the
Great Court, and as soon as I arrive, the announcement will be made, though I'm sure that by now—"

But Hugh heard no more. He was running at top
speed toward the city. He heard the excited voice of
Oolu shouting good-byes to the women of the Garden
of Beauty, and then the Gwarpy was in hot pursuit of
the Vandorian.

Hugh sensed that Oolu was only a few paces behind
as they entered the city on the run. The gongs
continued to sound. Amazon women, fully armed,
trotted in units through the winding streets and
across lofty causeways. The Gwarpy had caught up
with Hugh, and they raced side by side, Oolu chortling
with excitement. As they reached the palace, Erbin
and Evrawk were coming down the wide expanse of
steps. "What's happened?" called Evrawk, "what in the
name of the earth, moon and stars is going on here?"

They met at the base of the stairway. Warrior women
hurried past them at regular intervals. "I hope this
means what I'm hoping it means!" said Evrawk excitedly.

"It's got to mean what you're hoping it means!"
Erbin retorted. "I told you that!" He held an elabo-
rately carved mug in his thick hand. "Terrible wine,
these ladies make," he said, frowning, but taking a
long swallow nonetheless.

"They're going to fight for us!" Hugh shouted,
grinning broadly, then corrected himself. "*With* us, I
mean..."

The Dwarf twins let go a loud hoorah in unison.
Oolu jumped up and down. "I knew it! It just had to
be!" exclaimed Evrawk. "The old woman, Senqua—
she came and got Ailwon a couple of minutes before
those bloody gongs began...told us to wait..."

"We'd be damned if we'd waited any longer!" inter-

rupted Erbin. "Now let's find where everybody's headed."

An Amazon unit jogged by, and the four followed
them. Within minutes, they were running down an
arched tunnel. The gongs had ceased. They had been
replaced by the chanted phrase: "*Ki-est-oh-vel-oh*,"
which translated meant: "In sisterhood is the perfect
love." The unity of voice grew louder as Hugh, Erbin
and Evrawk, and Oolu neared the end of the tunnel.
The chant was not—as before—soft and lilting, but
strong, rhythmic, purposeful.

The four exited the dark of the tunnel into a broad
arena-like court, which was lit by six glowing crystals
atop tall, slender spires along the eastern wall of the
court. Beneath the soft light were a multitude of
Amazons, assembled in great curved rows, standing
erect on a descending structure of stairs.

Facing them at the apex of a carved, golden elevation were Ailwon, Princess Zyra, and old Senqua. The
chant continued for a moment, then a hush fell
across the court as Queen Azira entered, walking
slowly, ascending the stairs to stand between Zyra
and Ailwon. She lifted her arms toward the assemblage, and her voice carried clearly throughout the
court: "My sisters—my daughters! It has by now been
made known to you what lies before you—what lies
before us all. There is no need for me to speak at
length to you. I will tell you this: it is *my* decision that
we undertake this dangerous venture... Thus I have
decided to go with you, to face the forces of oppression beside my sisters." Azira continued, "As you
know, I at first refused to lend the weight of our
powers to those who have set upon this quest to free
the continent." She glanced at Ailwon. "But then," she
continued, turning to Zyra, "I was reminded of something of which I had lost sight, but which my spiritual
daughter—with the wisdom of her youth—had remembered." The Queen's arm encircled the young
woman's shoulders, and she spoke words heard only
by the two of them.

Zyra was smiling as she stepped forward. "My sisters!" she shouted, "we will prepare our provisions, armaments, and our ships. We will work through the night. We will set out toward the Great River Garnon at dawn."

Hugh was standing with his companions only a short distance away. He could see Zyra's face, could see the excitement in her eyes as she raised her voice again: "We will be the first—the first in three hundred years—to go off to battle. And we will be the first *ever* of the Amazons to go beyond the southern reaches of the continent! We shall be the ones, my sisters, who will be far to the north, in dark Golgorath, when the forces of oppression are driven into the sea!"

There was no cheer in response to this, but instead the resounding chant of thousands of unified voices: "*Ki-est-oh-vel-oh! Ki-est-oh-vel-oh!*"

Zyra stood, her arms outstretched, her raven hair flowing back, the dark beauty of her face intensified by the intoxication of dedicated purpose. Hugh stared at her, transfixed, his heart hammering, completely at one with the Amazon Princess.

15

THE TRAITOR

©HILDEBRANDT

Between the Black Mountains of Golgorath to the north and the Kolgar Mountain range to the south, lay the Plains of Kiberuk, the harshest and most severe of wastelands. In part pitilessly exposed to the sun, and in part perpetually in the shadow of the dark clouds that hung above Golgorath, it seemed that only the toughest and grisliest of life forms could survive. From out of this land had evolved that race of beings who were called Gnomes.

The Death Lord, Torgon, held the allegiance of these barbarians beneath the power of an iron hand. The Gnome tribes, hidebound with superstition reinforced with primitive ritual, were easily incited to carry out the work of the Death Lord. Though small of stature, the Gnomes were physically powerful and tenacious and when collected into large numbers and aroused to a feverish pitch, these barbarians had produced absolute terror among those of the allied nations who had experienced their blood-chilling attacks.

Midway through the sixteenth day of the quest, Gwynn and her companions approached the Retnor Pass through the Kolgar Mountains. They were understandably apprehensive, for it was here that many brave Elves had been lost to barbarian ambush. The band of Andeluvian fighters looked about for some sign of Deciedon and the promised escort, but could find no sign of them anywhere. Gwynn raised her hand, pulling her horse to a halt, and those behind her did likewise.

"I have no real fears that any danger exists up ahead," she called back to them, "but just to make sure, I'll ride on to give the area a closer inspection before we enter it."

"Allow me to do that, Gwynn."

The request came from Cordan, a soft-spoken Brown Elf, who was the oldest of her rebel fighters. He had been among the first to take a stand contrary to his past beliefs and to answer the challenge Gwynn had made when she had declared the absolute need for resistance to tyranny. He prodded his horse forward to a position beside her. Now he said quietly, "Against the remote possibility that a danger might exist, it seems sensible that you, having always led us into battle, be in a position to do so again...should this be necessary."

"Thank you, Cordan. What you say makes sense. Go ahead. We'll await your signal."

Cordan rode slowly into the pass between the cluster of rocks, the horseman carefully searching for signs of danger. Finally, he stopped, turned and started back, raising his arm and calling to them that all appeared clear.

"Let's go, "Gwynn said, and they began to move forward. They had entered the wide area bordered by the rock formation; Cordan rode slowly toward them. Suddenly he glanced to his right, shouted a warning, and kicked his horse into a gallop. Above the sound of horse and rider came the deadly whistle of an arrow, and Cordan fell from the saddle. His steed veered sharply off course, then reared up, frightened by the sudden loss of the weight of his master.

At the first instant of Cordan's warning shout, Gwynn reined back her mare, and her sword flashed in the sun in an almost simultaneous movement. Suddenly, the air was filled with barbaric screams and

war cries. On all sides of the Andeluvians, fierce
Gnomes sprang up from the earth where they had
hidden themselves in shallow depressions in the
sandy ground, and hundreds more swarmed down
from the rocks above. They came from every direction, screaming, brandishing weapons, converging
on the startled Brown Elves. A young man beside
Gwynn cried out in pain, a lance protruding from his
chest. Terrified horses reared and whinnied. Then the
barbarians were among them. Gwynn felt strong
hands pulling at her leg, trying to drag her from the
saddle. She kicked furiously, then wheeled her horse,
knocking away a lance that was shoved at her, sending a scrawny Gnome to the dirt. Clouds of dust rose
to mingle with the clash of arms and the battle
cries—and the anguished screams of the wounded
and dying.

Within seconds, Gwynn knew that she and her
rebels were doomed. Her mind flashed to her youthful cousins, and to her aunt and uncle. Then, above
the melee, she heard an enormous voice: "Surrender!
Surrender, and you will be spared!"

Looming through the dust, she saw a huge, dark
figure astride an enormous black horse. It was her
first view of the fabled gargoyles created by the Death
Lord: a Vilderone. "Surrender!" he bellowed again.
Gwynn recognized that certain death for herself and
her comrades was the only alternative to his command. She wheeled her horse, and charged into the
confusion of fighting Elves and Gnomes, shouting to
her companions to surrender. In a moment, the din of
the battle had died completely, and the Andeluvian
rebels quieted their horses, surrounded by their
barbaric captors. A full dozen of Gwynn's people had
been slain and a score wounded, but Ianen and
Glenden had come through the melee unscathed,
though badly shaken. Gwynn waited. She had raised
her arms to denote surrender, but she had not
relinquished her sword, and now held it aloft. The
Vilderone who was apparently the commander of the

attack sat motionless, watching the young Elfin woman. He had been joined by another half dozen hulking gargoyles. Their heads were protected by masked helmets. Gwynn wondered if there were any faces at all behind the ominous metal coverings.

Finally, the Vilderone general spoke in low tones to his henchmen, and three of them moved forward. They came straight toward Gwynn, one of them carrying loops of heavy rope while another held chains. Gwynn's sword was wrenched from her hand, and her horse was led a few paces away from her companions. Her arms were pulled behind her back, and her wrists bound.

"Stop!" cried Ianen. "What are you doing to her?" He started forward on his horse, as did his brother. Barbarian lances were raised, bows drawn taut and arrows leveled. "Get back!" Gwynn shouted. "At this point, we're still alive. Let's not change that without good cause." The youths checked their horses. When Gwynn was securely bound, she was led back to the Vilderone leader. The gargoyle turned in his saddle, leather creaking beneath his huge bulk. He raised his gloved hand, signaling back toward a cluster of boulders. Several other figures appeared from behind the rocks.

Gwynn watched as the group approached. At the rear were more gargoyles, perhaps a dozen, and in front of them several of the runty, large-headed Gnomes. At their center, and leading the grimly silent assemblage, was a figure clad in a hooded black cloak and a long white tunic. The brilliant sun glared in reflection from the silver that adorned his black weapon belt. Gwynn's eyes began to widen as the mysterious figure came closer. There was no mistaking it, the uniform was that of a horseman of the White Elf army, of a Lejentor, of a high-ranking officer of that legendary group. The approaching white and black clad figure moved with an easy, athletic grace, striding confidently, his shoulders square.

Gwynn drew in a deep breath, not feeling the bonds

tighten about her as she did so. It was true! There had been a traitor within their ranks as they feared! It had been one of their own who had slain the Sevenas twenty years before, and had somehow found out about Ailwon and sought to have him murdered too! She could see the blond of the Lejentor's hair, falling from beneath his hood. The figures behind him seemed to blur in her vision, but his stood out in vivid detail. Gwynn felt sudden nausea in the pit of her stomach. It was the hero, Deciedon, the living legend of the White Elves! He who was admired the most by all among the allied nations, the governor of Alfandel who had ruled so ably for twenty years! He raised his white-gloved hand to her, his handsome face splitting into a wide grin.

"I see by the expression on your lovely face that you are shocked to see me here, Gwynn," he said, as he arrived before her. His voice, as always, was deep and melodic. "Well, that's quite understandable, of course. I've taken great pains these many years to obscure my double identity." He looked up, studying her carefully. "You have certainly come full bloom, my dear. But even years ago—the first time I saw you at the Dwarf Kingdom—even then I thought you the most beautiful of creatures. Which brings to mind a point that might be of interest to you..." He reached up to her, taking her gently by the arm. "Why don't we sit for a few moments," he said, steadying her as he helped her to dismount. "I feel very badly that it has been necessary for you to be bound. But you are, of course, an extremely valuable asset so long as we have you captive. If you were to escape—well, I'm sure you can see that we can't allow that to happen."

Deciedon began to guide Gwynn toward a large boulder, but stopped. Turning back, toward the Vilderone leader, he said, "Oh, Sorkmun, I trust you won't mind my having a few moments with this young woman before you depart? I won't have another opportunity for quite some time." He half turned Gwynn toward the silent gargoyle general. "...How gauche of me to overlook the introduction. Gwynn, this is Sorkmun," he said to her. "He is the right hand of Torgon—the highest of all in Golgorath, save the Death Lord himself." Sorkmun grunted, and Deciedon turned both himself and Gwynn away from the Vilderones. He leaned close to her and whispered: "Actually, it's debatable whether or not it is he or Rogmun who is the highest ranking of Torgon's generals... and *nobody* is the Death Lord's right hand, even figuratively," he smiled, "but Sorkmun is not too fond of me, so it doesn't hurt to sweeten him occasionally."

They stopped before a large boulder, where he eased Gwynn to a sitting position. Deciedon remained standing, one foot on the rock, his right forearm resting across his thigh as he leaned confidentially over her. "Ah, your people have all been disarmed," he said, looking past Gwynn.

She turned. Her comrades' weapons and horses had been taken from them, and they had been grouped tightly together by the fierce Gnomes who surrounded them. "What will be done with my people?" she said.

"Don't worry, my lady," he answered, "they will be well taken care of." The reply was so casual, yet implied such thoughtfulness, that Gwynn felt immediate relief and was instantly guilty and astonished. Standing over her was the traitor to the quest to which she had dedicated her entire being, the one responsible for the deaths of many of her company. She and her people were his captives, helpless. She wondered desperately if he was, in fact, playing the role of spy for Alfandel. But after a studied moment, he began to speak:

"I believe that you will find this amusing... or at least ironic." He looked down at her. "You see, my dear, it is because of your beauty that I first learned that your Prince Ailwon existed. I'd had some suspicions that something was being kept from me by those two old enchanted gentlemen, Elgan and

Shandar..." He laughed. "I had no idea, however, that this secret was of such importance to the struggle. Once learned, of course, this knowledge completely altered my course of action, and thus the Death Lord's. Excuse my lack of humility. I've never considered it a desirable trait. I see that I'm confusing you. Forgive me. You see, Gwynn, on my last visit to Penderak to confer with those charming little people, I found myself in conversation with—what's his name?—Erbin, that's it! Erbin, as I'm sure you know, has a tendency to imbibe a bit too heavily." He glanced up toward the Vilderone officers, who were growling among themselves. "I'll have to make this brief... my friends are growing impatient. Anyway, in the midst of our friendly chat, I inquired—very subtly, of course—as to your availability. Well, poor Erbin let slip a couple of facts which completely caught my curiosity. And then it was just a matter of some very intricately designed questions, coupled with a very steady provision of spirits for the little fellow. Well, I'm sure that Erbin felt confident that he'd covered himself very well. I doubt that he even remembered much of the conversation. Such highly emotional beings as Erbin are prone to commit extremely foolish blunders..."

Gwynn felt a charge of anger stirring through her blood. Deciedon stood. "It certainly worked well for me, though. I'm sure that you can readily observe that. Soon, Torgon will have you as a hostage within his stronghold, and before too many days have passed, your young friend, Ailwon, will join you. I'm ready to embark now on the journey to meet this mysterious Sevena..." He leaned forward, reaching down to gently touch her cheek. "Would that I could accompany you to Golgorath. I made certain that Torgon understood you would be a part of my reward for our victory."

Gwynn could see now beneath the near-perfect facade. She could see clearly how cold and unfeeling was his greed. She turned her head sharply, biting viciously at the gloved hand that fondled her. Deciedon's reactions were as sharp as his mind, and her teeth missed him by a fraction.

He stepped back, appraising the hatred in her eyes. "I almost expected as much," he smiled, "and I'm not at all disappointed. In time, your fires will cool—but hopefully never die." He called to the Vilderone general that he was ready. Sorkmun grunted, and two of his henchmen came forward, pulling Gwynn to her feet.

Sorkmun prodded his horse, and the huge stallion carried him forward, stopping in clear view of the barbarians who were massed around the Brown Elf rebels. The Gnomes watched expectantly as the dark gargoyle raised his arm above his helmeted head. Gwynn felt sudden terror rip at her heart. Deciedon's smooth voice came from behind: "I hope, dear Gwynn, that you realize the revulsion I feel for this next act. This is completely the work of the Death Lord."

She lunged forward against the iron grips on her arms, screaming out just as the Vilderone general dropped his hand. Instantly the barbarians attacked. The Brown Elves were completely helpless. Gwynn thought that she would faint, wished that she could, but her eyes were held open with horror. Pain-filled cries rose into air that was bright with the reflections of the unrelenting sun. The Brown Elves fell. One after another, they fell: upon the ground, and across the bodies of their companions. Pleading voices cried out for mercy. The red blood spurted, drained, ran across the yellow earth. Gwynn was nearly blind with rage and with grief. Her sobbing screams were fraught with the vilest of curses, hurled at the murderers of her people. Through the cries of the dying, she heard the voice of Glenden, sounding much as he had years before when as a child he would run to her for comfort. Twice he screamed out, "Gwynn!" And she saw him, his hands clutching at this chest, at the arrow shaft protruding from it. Then he fell. It was the

last Gwynn saw or heard. Mercifully, she was struck
from behind by the butt of Deciedon's sword. She fell
unconscious into his arms. He carried her to her
horse, looking down at her.

"I am sorry this was necessary, dear Gwynn," he
said, and even though she was unconscious, he kept
his voice genuinely sincere, "but I do hope you will
have learned to be more amenable. It is necessary for
both our sakes. There has never been any doubt
about the victor in the coming battle. I intend both
you and I to be on the winning side." He lifted her into
the saddle, and she slumped forward. "Bind her to
her horse so she does not fall," he commanded a
Vilderone who stood beside him, "and see that no
harm or injury comes to her—from her own hand or
any other." He strode to his own pure white steed,
swinging effortlessly into his silver-studded black
saddle. "Remember, friend Sorkmun," he said to the
hulking general, "it is Torgon's wish that the woman
arrive before him completely unharmed."

Sorkmun nodded silently. Deciedon raised his
hand. "I will see you again at Golgorath," he said. The
Vilderone made no sound or movement, and Deciedon spurred his horse southward.

Sorkmun watched as the White Elf Lejentor rode
away. Then he turned toward the scene of the massacre. The tortured cries had ceased. Only the excited
voices of the Gnomes punctured the stillness of the
wasteland. The barbarians were busily searching the
silent forms of their victims for items of interest.
Sorkmun wheeled his horse suddenly, signaling to
his underlings. There was a hurried formation of
almost twoscore of the gargoyles. Their general
started forward at a canter, and the mounted Vilderone followed, the unconscious captive at the
center of their detachment.

The smell of death had drawn carrion birds to the
place of silence where the bodies of the Brown Elves
lay motionless. To the circling birds the only signs of
life were the few scattered horses that wandered in

search of scrub grass, some distance from the dead. Finally, the vultures began to land, cautiously approaching the lifeless beings. One hopped within the midst of the carnage, began to feed, and was followed by others. Suddenly two of the vultures flew up, then another and another. One of the bodies had moved. The creatures settled back to the ground, but at a distance. The being slowly rolled from his back to his stomach, moaning as he did so. It was the youth, Ianen. With great effort, he pulled himself to his knees. He was covered with blood, both his own and that of others whose bodies had hidden him. A scalp wound continued to ooze, dripping heavily to the sand beneath him. Only a half dozen feet from him lay his dead brother. Ianen crawled forward, taking the slain boy's face into his bloody hands. His shoulders shook with his sobs. Finally he lay still, his labored breathing punctuated by low, rasping moans. He sensed movement nearby, and lifted his head. A horse—his own—had moved within a few yards of him. The boy whispered a name and the horse responded, coming forward close enough for Ianen to reach out and grasp the dangling stirrup. With intense effort, he pulled himself to a near-standing position. He coughed violently, and retched bile onto the ground. After resting for a long moment, he whispered to the horse, and slowly, painfully, pulled himself onto the animal's back, slumping into the saddle. The animal moved forward, instinctively headed toward home, toward Andeluvia, toward the sinking sun. Behind, the carrion birds returned to carry out their ancient ritual of cleansing.

16

THE VALLEY
OF LIFE

The time of winter had been harsh. Sweeping across the bitter cold Sea of Balta, the frigid northeasterly winds had roared over Norbruk and Loamend with such relentlessness that well past the equinox the land of the Gwarpys still lay beneath a covering of snow. But with each passing day the sun had gained prominence and strength in its arc across the sky, warming the air, forcing a withdrawal of the frozen vestiges of winter. Soon the earth was black, yellow-green shoots were poking up among the dead grasses, and long before the Gwarpys' Rite of the Bobabo trees, the hills of Loamend had become rich with the sights and sounds of life.

The squat, ashen-barked, enormous-girthed Bobabos were the center of the Gwarpys' life system. Thus, the early ancestors of the furry creatures had established a springtime ritual to give tribute to the great trees, and this custom had been followed faithfully ever since. The celebration commenced with the first movement within the trees of their life-giving sap, and ended when the bloom of their bright yellow blossoms gave promise of summer fruit.

It was before dawn on the final day of the Rite of the Bobabos that the black sorcerer, Shandar, drew near to Evshimin, the place of his origin. With him was Elgan, the white wizard. Together they had come to secure the Crownhelm of the White Elves from where it lay within the secrecy of the Valley of Life.

With a score of Gwarpys, friends and relatives of Oolu, the two wizards made their way through the mountains bordering the southern portion of Loamend. It was within these tall mountains that the Valley of Life lay hidden. The silent group made their way along a half hidden path. Ahead of them was a narrow pass covered with a curtain of vines. Shandar walked straight to the entanglement and parted it, revealing the entranceway to the valley. The Gwarpys' awe for this place was such that they never entered here; they would wait for the wizard and sorcerer to return.

Shandar and Elgan entered. The dark passage was wide enough to permit only one at a time. The stone walls were moist and covered with moss, a dense growth of vines formed a living ceiling. As the two men proceeded, the passageway grew darker. Another curtain of vines was before them, marking the end of the pass. They parted it and emerged into the cool light of pre-dawn. There before them lay the Valley of Life.

At the center of the valley stood the Great White Bobabo Tree, Evshimin. All Gwarpys believed it to be the very center of Urshurak, and indeed, as Elgan and Shandar stood looking into the valley, it seemed that this was so. High mountains surrounded the valley and the slopes were covered with thick green moss, creating a soft carpet beneath their feet as they descended. They passed by squat, thick-based palm trees that seemed to be survivors of a time more ancient than either Elgan or Shandar. Great insects flew about, their wings shimmering in the pink light of dawn. Slowly the sky grew brighter and birds began to sing as Evshimin awoke in the golden glow.

Elgan and Shandar continued their descent through overgrowths of flowering vines and great swaying ferns. Fan-like leaves, the height of a man, grew all about them, and on the green spongy floor there rose mushrooms of all sizes. The wizard and sorcerer came to another curtain of flowering vines.

Shandar stepped forward. He parted the vines and there, towering above all, was the Great White Boba-bo Tree; the ancient guardian of the Valley of Life.

The sun broke over the range of mountains to the rear of the great tree and its brilliant golden light seemed to turn the leaves to flame. Streams of light flowed through the branches and touched the two beings. Shandar fell to his knees and bowed low, kissing the black earth. Elgan stood behind the sorcerer, his arms extended. The wizard's gaze was on the flowering vines clinging to the white skin of the ancient tree.

The colored thicket that had formed over thousands of years had an opening at its center, creating a living cavern. From this flowed a spring, bordered by soft mosses and gently swaying ferns. A score of paces beyond its source the spring had created a crystalline pool and just before the stream became the pool, it was bridged by a flat elliptical rock, half covered with thick, spongy moss.

Shandar stood; he and Elgan walked to the pool. A gentle breeze moved the surface of the pool and it shimmered in the risen sun. The sorcerer turned toward his companion of old, his lined black face asking the question, but Elgan shook his head, and Shandar moved toward the tree alone. He started through the ferns beside the stream, his movements creating no sounds. Then he was before the shadowy opening of the Great Bobabo, and entered into the primeval essence of Evshimin.

Elgan sat upon a rock to wait. For a moment he studied the rising morning sun. He tried to envision the ancient metallic Ark, within which the Crownhelm was kept. He imagined the Crownhelm as it would appear within the Great White Tree, unmoved for twenty years, since before the birth of Ailwon. And he thought of the power of the Crownhelm, a force that was a spiritual blend of the rawest of elements. They

© HILDEBRANDT

were welded together centuries ago by unknown arcane powers and made manifest in a helmeted crown for the White Elves to carry down through the ages to the titanic confrontation which would decide the fate of all Urshurak.

The old wizard was so caught up in his thoughts that he wasn't aware at first of the changes occurring around him. He didn't feel the sudden shift in the breeze, nor did he detect the increased power within the voice of the stream; he didn't feel the drop in the air's temperature, nor did he observe that the sun had been lost behind the darkness of clouds that had not been present just moments before. But then the sky became blue-black, the air cold with a shouting wind, the voice of the running waters roared, its song rising into the wind, singing aloud of beauty and violence.

Elgan stood, the wind whipping his white hair and beard. He looked across the pond that had suddenly become alive. Shandar stood watching him. Before the thin form of the sorcerer, lying on top of the flat rock slab, was the Ark of Crownhelm. The sky had grown exceedingly dark, yet the metallic surface of the Ark was brilliant, all of nature seemingly reflected from its beveled surfaces. Elgan traversed the curve of the pond to arrive beside Shandar. Neither spoke. The sorcerer passed a long silver staff through the handles of the Ark, and he and the wizard raised the precious burden to their shoulders. Shandar looked back. The wind had become almost violent, and his loose brown robe flapped wildly against his thin body. He stared at the place of mystery. The opening in the thicket had closed. Shandar turned back toward Elgan, eyes wet, and the tears appeared to be of both joy and sadness. The two started to climb just as large drops of rain began to slant through the wind. The Ark of Crownhelm swayed between the two old men as they climbed slowly out of the Valley of Life.

17

ABU-SAMBAR

The River Garnon drew its waters from the northern regions of Urshurak, the twin lakes of Cryslandon, and from its tributaries across the central portions of the land. By the time it entered the final third of its journey toward the Sea of Kresna, the river had gained in enormous volume and the dense growth of the Dagnar Jungle that bordered the southern portions of the Great River reflected the life-giving properties of the mighty water.

Those aboard the Amazon ships of Zan-Dura bore witness to the power of the Garnon, as they moved upriver, drawn northward by the power of the magnetic crystals. On both sides, along the banks of reddish clay, were masses of broad-leaved magnolia trees and leaning water oaks from which drooped thick strands of silvery moss to drag in the current. As well, there was a profusion of blooming vines and flowering plants, from which a heavy perfume hung on the air. Along the banks lay the huge, lazy alligators, and beyond them the more timid forest creatures that scampered away into dense undergrowths as the long golden ships moved upriver, emitting their strange singing tones, the glowing crimson lights preceding them.

Hugh Oxhine watched the passing jungle life as he leaned against the starboard rail of the Queen ship, the central vessel of the Amazon fleet of eighteen. He rested his forearms on the golden rail, his rolled sleeves exposing the heavy musculature of an archer's arms. To a casual observer he would have seemed relaxed. Actually, Hugh was in a turmoil such as he had not known in his lifetime. All his naturally solitary instincts were at war with his feelings—and his feelings were at war with his sense of decency. On a mission of vengeance for the murder of his family, he now found himself incontrovertibly in love—and with a wholly unattainable person. Zyra was always, and constantly, in his mind and unconsciously his eyes searched, as always, for her.

He found her standing on the platform over the control room at the bow of the huge vessel, talking to the Queen, Azira, and to the Elfin youth, Ailwon. Her dark hair was blowing, the sun highlighted her sleek figure. Hugh felt the exciting discomfort that he experienced each time he looked at her. Just then she turned and descended the ladder from the bridge. His heart began to pound and every muscle went taut. Then she turned again and went through the small door of the ship's control room. Hugh relaxed, not sure whether he felt disappointment or relief. Damn woman, he thought, she made him feel as if he were some lovesick boy. But he had little hope that his feelings would change within the near future, even though she exhibited nothing beyond politeness toward him. Now, with a conscious effort of will, he forced his thoughts into another channel although Zyra stayed stubbornly in the back of his mind. Hugh deliberately concentrated his gaze on Oolu who was examining the fascinating Fire Crystals for the dozenth time. The brilliant gold and blue Fire Crystals were completely unlike anything Hugh had ever seen before.

The archer remembered the first incident involving the Amazon weaponry. When the Fire Crystals had been loaded aboard the ships Erbin had demanded to know what manner of device they were. Ailwon, who had learned about them only a short time before, explained that these were extremely powerful weapons, capable of firing charges that roughly equated the effect of lightning bolts. Ailwon had been very excited at the prospect of the allied nations controlling such weaponry. There were only nine of the weapons, as opposed to the hundreds of gigantic machines of war that the forces of Golgorath possessed. But these Fire Crystals were so potent and mobile that they were certain to lend a great deal of weight to the allied nations' chances for victory.

"The Crystals were not designed as weapons," Zyra explained. "First of all they were used as tools in mining and in sculpture. Then one day some of my people faced death and saved themselves only by using the Crystals as weapons. They've been used only sparingly since, even though there were specific units of women kept constantly trained to employ them should they be needed. I myself have been trained in the art of the Fire Crystals. The Crystals are considerably more than a weapon or a tool."

"How d'you mean?" Erbin demanded.

Rising, Zyra replied, "The power is that of the Crystal of Kresna: the same spiritual power that gives the Amazon women life; the same that powers our ships and gives us light. Those who use these Crystals are given long and extensive training, and much of the training period is devoted to spiritual control, which is the means by which energy is released through this device."

Hugh remembered the pride in Zyra's voice as she explained that the power of the Crystals was an extension of the being of the women who fired them. Again he saw the intelligence of her dark eyes, the warmth of her smile... again he watched her reach forward and lay her hand on Erbin's shoulder....

"ABU-SAMBAR!" Hugh ceased his reflections as the shout came from the ship's bow. It was delivered in Evrawk's booming baritone.

The port city of Abu-Sambar was revealed as the fleet turned a bend of the river. Already the lead ships

were moving into the huge docking area. The long
wooden landing was virtually deserted. A few small,
weathered fishing boats were visible. Beyond them
Hugh could see a dozen large trading vessels docked
within a half-hidden alcove. These were ships of the
various cultures of Urshurak, and had once moved
actively through the waterways of the continent. But
since the growth of terrorism, since the rebirth of
distrust among the nations and the spread of despair,
there had been an almost complete cessation of
trade. Now the ships lay rotting in the harbor, and the
jungle slowly crept into the Azmurian city to reclaim it
from its creators.

The Mother Ship of the Amazons steered toward the
dock, its crimson glow and singing tone ceasing as
the golden vessel glided in. Standing on the wooden
wharf were soldiers of Azmuria and Norbruk.

"It's the Azmurian Shakín: Ali what's-his-nose... "
cried Erbin.

"Ali Ben Kara," corrected his brother.

"Right!" said Erbin, "And...gawl! The other one has
to be one of those Norsepeople! Bet it's Tark-Volmar
himself!"

To Oolu the names weren't of particular significance, but he delighted in the general excitement
that was being generated, and he was chuckling
almost nonstop.

A ramp was dropped to the wooden dock, and a
small group disembarked. The time requirements
were such that the Amazon army was to content
themselves with watching the brief activity from on-
board. Only Queen Azira and her successor, Zyra,
plus Ailwon and his companions left their ship. They
were approached by the princely Ben Kara, who was
smiling warmly, while the Norseman chieftain trailed
behind, staring up dumbfounded at the incredible
Amazon vessels—whose decks were lined with curious
warrior women.

"I am delighted!" exclaimed Ben Kara, his eyes
shifting from Ailwon to Queen Azira, and back again.

"And incredulous that finally I am face to face with the Sevena of the White Elves... I am overwhelmed!" He stepped forward to grasp Ailwon's hand. He shook his head. "Shandar and Elgan told me that I was to expect you to be successful... but this—" he said, looking again to Azira, and gesturing to the long line of huge Amazon vessels, "this is astounding!" He half turned to Tark-Volmar, "Is this not astounding, Volmar?" he asked.

"Hmmph," grunted the bulky Norseman who was clearly astounded.

"You are to be congratulated," Ben Kara said directly to the Elfin Prince, and his eyes and voice clearly denoted his sincerity. Ailwon did not attempt to hide his delight at winning the praise of this noted Azmurian leader, who had earned respect among all within the allied nations. But the Prince immediately, and gracefully, began to spread the credit for their accomplishments thus far by introducing each member of the group surrounding him, beginning with the Queen and her spiritual daughter. Ben Kara nodded warmly and politely to each, while he himself presented Tark-Volmar to the others. The Norseman repeated his gruff "Hmmph" with each introduction; he merely sighed and shook his head when he was presented to the grinning Gwarpy, Oolu.

Ali Ben Kara asked if he and Tark-Volmar might complete the journey to the White Elf capital aboard an Amazon ship. The request was gladly granted, and the two were invited to board the Queen Ship when the voyage resumed.

The Elfin Prince, the Amazon Queen and Princess, and the Shakín began to discuss strategy. Tark-Volmar stepped back, observing the strategists, particularly the slender youth, Ailwon. The Norse chieftain looked on for several moments, periodically shaking his huge head, mumbling phrases like, "skinny little magic boy," or "the damnable heat of this country." Hugh Oxhine wandered away, no longer able to stand the discomfort of being so close to Zyra, while Erbin hurried into the almost deserted city, in search of liquid refreshment. Oolu tagged along with the Dwarf.

Evrawk, after listening for a moment or two, also wandered away from the serious conversation. Deciding that there wasn't time to explore the city, he strolled toward the overgrown inlet where the deserted trading vessels sat mired in a green scum of stagnant waters. An old Azmurian man sat on the edge of the wooden dock. He held a long cane fishing pole, his line dropped through the thick green surface. The skinny old man nodded, and Evrawk returned the nod. The Dwarf strolled slowly on, examining the first vessel. "That is a Penderak ship," he murmured, noting the heavy construction and ornate carving of the wooden ship. After a few moments he started back, pausing as he passed behind the old man, who still sat almost motionless, pole in hand. "Excuse me, sir," said Evrawk, "are you hoping to catch something here?"

"Nope."

Evrawk thought for a minute. "Well, it really isn't any of my business," he said, "but if you don't expect to catch anything here...why are you fishing here?"

The old man looked up with sleepy eyes. "It is because I don't want to catch anything," he explained kindly. "When I sit—and dream—I feel more comfortable holding my fishing pole, for I love to fish. It is just that I do not always desire to catch anything. For the catching also requires the cleaning and cooking." He nodded, affirming the wisdom of his logic. "Now when I want to *catch* fish I go to the main wharf, or I go to my favorite place along the river bank... where a 'gator—as old as I—saves me a spot.... " His voice cackled with laughter, exposing the pink of a near-toothless mouth.

Evrawk laughed along with the old man, though he was not quite sure that he had grasped the entire drift of the fishing discourse. The Dwarf produced his large-bowled pipe, and began to pack it. The old

man's eyes grew wide. "Hey, I have never before seen a
pipe like that," he said. He laid aside his pole, and
struggled to his feet. Evrawk had personally carved
the object of admiration, and felt considerably flat-
tered. "Would you like to look it over?" he asked,
offering the pipe to the Azmurian.

"Not yet," replied the old man, and he began to fish
about amidst the mounds of dirty white clothing that
draped his skinny body. Finally he brought forth a
slender, black, exquisitely carved pipe—the stem of
which measured over a foot. He held it out, and each
examined the other's prized possession with much
appreciative comment.

Presently they fired the pipes, and started toward
the main docking area, the old man shuffling and
chatting constantly in his high-pitched rhythmic tone.
He talked of the almost one hundred years that he
had lived and worked at Abu-Sambar. He vividly
described its once thriving condition, when trade
flowed freely in and out of the port city. He told of the
raids that had begun to take place some fifty years
before, when the forces of the Swamp Witch and the
fierce Lord of the North savagely attacked the trading
vessels, murdering, maiming and taking slaves. Once
Abu-Sambar was burned nearly to the ground, and
then rebuilt.

"Now..." said the old man, "there's not much goes
on here. Pretty quiet. I like the quiet, too... quiet's
okay lots of times...." He gazed at the river, and at the
numerous colorful waterbirds that stood on the far
side. "When it's quiet," he continued, "I can hear the
voice of the Great River. It tells me lots, you know..."
He looked at the Dwarf, nodding his head and cack-
ling gently. "But you know," he added, "it would be
nice if more was to pass through. If there were more
people to talk to... the way it used to
be...."

Evrawk heard Hugh Oxhine's strong voice shouting
his name. "Hey!" cried the Dwarf. "You just watch what
comes past in a minute or two!" He pointed toward

the sharp bend of the wooden dock, where heavy foliage hid the Amazon fleet from sight. "I have to go!" he exclaimed, "but you just hold on there!" With that the Dwarf turned, and clattered across the wooden dock, disappearing around the bend. The old man shook his head, chewing on his gums, leaning on his fishing pole for support. He spat into the water, then cocked his head at the first sound of the singing tones. The sound grew in volume. Then into view came the first of the majestic golden vessels, gliding slowly. The aged man's watery eyes opened wide. He began to cackle as ship after ship passed, the mysterious tones rising, and he continued to cackle until the last of them had disappeared from sight, and the sound of their power could no longer be heard.

He stared upriver for a moment, expertly dispatching a mosquito that had lighted on his bony neck, and then looked down at the pipe that he had been fondling. He stuck the stem into his almost toothless mouth, puffing steadily until gray smoke poured upward from the large bowl. Then he started toward the main docking area, toward the jungle beyond, where the ancient alligator reserved his favortie place.

"Now today's the kind of day when you *want* to catch somethin'...." the old man said aloud, and he shuffled purposefully down the wooden dock.

18

DEATH AND REBIRTH

T he sun had disappeared an hour before, and within the throne room of the Andeluvian king and queen, only a solitary candle cast a flickering yellow light causing shadows to dance across the walls. The long room was empty, save for the King. Zarin had forsaken the late evening meal that he and his wife, Wanel, had made traditional throughout most of their marriage. Instead he had come here, bringing with him a large flask of wine. He seldom ate meals of late, spending the major portion of his waking hours within the throne room, where he sat brooding and drinking. His body was becoming rotund and puffy. The clarity of mind that he had enjoyed in previous years had succumbed to a depressed confusion.

He was slowly pacing the floor, fingering his goblet of wine. The days had run into weeks since his sons and his niece, Gwynn, had left for Cryslandon to join the White Elf Prince in the struggle against the Death Lord. He supposed they must have arrived by now. He took some comfort from having followed the advice of the White Elf governor, Deciedon. But this was small solace. War was imminent. Hated war! And now, not only his rebellious niece, but his young sons as well, would be involved in this dreaded event.

Zarin sighed as he lifted his heavy body into his

throne. He gulped at the wine, not tasting it. He stared
at the floor, rubbing his fingers against his forehead
and through his gray hair. And the question knifed
painfully through the thickness of his mind: Why?
Why? ...

Outside the royal hall, the silence was broken by a
staccato of hoofbeats. Then a cry went up, and the
sound of excited voices and of people running was
heard. Zarin frowned, pushing himself to his feet. He
heard the door of the chamber outside the throne
room being opened. The footsteps and voices grew
louder. A long, anguished scream—the voice of Queen
Wanel—preceded by an instant the bursting inward of
the entrance doors. Three men, Zarin's advisor, Elsep,
and two others, were carrying a limp form. Beside
them, moaning as if she were in great physical pain,
was Wanel. The body was laid gently down. Zarin
moved heavily toward his wife, whose face was covered by her hands. The King's eyes were fixed upon
the dark form, from which came barely audible
moans.

"What is it, Wanel? What has happened?" asked
Zarin. As he moved toward his wife he laid his hands
on her shoelders. Her body was quivering. She tried
to answer, but could not, and again buried her face in
her hands. The King looked toward Elsep, who stood
motionless, holding aloft a torch which clearly revealed the tears running freely down his face. Now
Zarin looked at the limp form. He dropped to his
knees beside the body, and Elsep stepped forward.
Torchlight fell across the blood-smeared face of
Ianen, whose eyes were wide with the brightness of
near-death. The King reached down, running his
hands across his son's face, across his forehead and
his eyes, across his lips. Zarin could not speak. Only
his hands moved in a desperate, gentle caress.
Ianen's head rolled slowly toward the King, his mouth
agape, his lips torn and swollen.

"Father..." the dying boy's voice was barely audible.

"...Yes..." answered Zarin, who was crying now.

"Glenden is dead... they are all dead... Only Gwynn—she has been taken...." He coughed; saliva ran from his mouth, across caked blood. Zarin's entire body was shaking as he watched his dying son.

"...The traitor... Deciedon is the traitor... He has betrayed us...." The voice was scarcely a whisper: "... You must hear me..."

Wanel was kneeling beside them. "We hear you," she said.

Ianen moaned. His head moved slowly, his eyes searched his mother's, then his father's. "I am not sorry... Do not grieve for me... Do not grieve for Glenden..." He drew a short, hard breath and his face had the look of ecstacy. He reached up to his father and his mother, grasping them, pulling himself upward. "...We are together now!" he cried out. But the cry was less than a whisper. His eyes closed, his jaw grew slack, his head fell back limply. Only the grip on his father's shoulder remained taut. Zarin leaned down, kissing his son on his torn and bloody mouth. Gently, he pulled the lifeless hand from his shoulder and stood as Wanel knelt, rocking and cradling the body of her son.

Zarin walked away, approached the throne. He stood before it, motionless. Slowly, he clenched his hand, drawing it back, smashing it into the palm of the other. Again. Again. Feeling pain. Again... Feeling the long-buried scream rising in anger, in sorrow. At last, he sprawled across the throne, the sobs heaving upward from his belly. Finally he was still. He rose, and turned.

Wanel was watching him. Neither could see the face of the other, but both felt the flow of love between them.

"I am going to support the nations in their struggle," said Zarin.

"And I am going with you," said the Queen. "We will go to Cryslandon together."

"There will be much suffering," said Zarin quietly. "Perhaps our people will go, to help us... to help us alleviate the suffering..."

"They will go with us," said Wanel. She reached her hand toward her husband. "We will bury our boy... then we will go...."

19

BLOCKADE

I t was early evening as Deciedon approached
the Place of Crossing over the River Garnon.
Nature had provided this monolithic arch
that spanned the river which divided Penderak from
Loamend. The Place of Crossing, where he was to
meet the Vilderone general Rogmun and his captive
Ailwon, had been within Deciedon's sight for almost
an hour. He sat his horse easily, holding the reins with
one gloved hand, while the other hung loosely by his
side. Horse hooves clicked across the rocky surface,
joined by the musical clink of roweled spurs. Deciedon was smiling as he contemplated past and
future successes, particularly his meeting with the
White Elf Sevena, the last threat to his power. His mind
had also turned to the forthcoming rendezvous with
the Vilderone. But he had the capacity to make rapid
mental preparations and at the same time consider
his own accomplishments and talents. He was seldom unaware of his own movements and actions,
and he was always aware of the reactions of others to
him. This acute awareness, however, was cloaked
beneath a totally convincing facade of carelessness
for his own well-being, coupled with well-feigned
concern for others. He had directed his entire life
toward perfecting capabilities that would make possible his acquisition of great power. As a child, he had

mastered ordinary skills with such ease as to remove almost any sense of challenge. Quite simply, he knew he needed skills—so he acquired them. The challenge remained only in his ability to manipulate those around him—and with the passing years, he had become a master at controlling others, delighting in the exercise of this particular talent.

He pulled his mount to a halt. The smoke from a campfire rose from a spot near the river. He reached down, patting the satiny neck of his pure white stallion. He took considerable pride in the beautiful animal, for it furthered the heroic image that he projected. Deciedon was capable of recognizing things of beauty, particularly within the scope of how they might make him appear to others. He urged his mount forward, down toward the Vilderone encampment. He thought of those hulking brutes, and he smiled again. He knew that they disliked him—as did the Death Lord—but it did not matter. He held their respect and that was all he needed. He remembered being a captive at Golgorath. While attempting to strike a deal with Torgon, he had been challenged by a huge Vilderone officer. The gargoyles and the Death Lord himself had gathered to watch the puny White Elf disemboweled. Deciedon laughed as he recalled the ease with which he had dispatched the Vilderone, separating his head from his brutish body.

He rode past the guards into the Vilderone encampment, greeting the general, Rogmun. Rogmun grunted in return.

"I see that the White Elf Prince had too great a lead for you to catch him," said Deciedon. He swung down from the saddle, handing the reins to a waiting Vilderone. Again, the huge general's reply was unintelligible.

"Well, no matter... " Deciedon said cheerfully, "we will soon take him. You will be happy to hear, Rogmun, that we captured the Brown Elf maiden, Gwynn. It has been she who has led those rebels who threw such chaos into your raiding parties during the past year or so. And she is, by way of coincidence, the love object of the White Elf brat."

Rogmun stared at the smiling Deciedon. The general's brutish features were stern, but he nodded in agreement. "That is good," he replied.

Deciedon slapped the gargoyle's armored back gently. "I knew that would please you," he said. "Even now, she is being taken to Golgorath, to go before Torgon, and she is being guarded carefully under the command of *Sorkmun*." He emphasized the name, studying the reaction of the Vilderone, who vied with his counterpart for the favor of the Death Lord.

"I see," continued Deciedon, "that you are prepared to initiate the blockade—excellent!" He was looking up toward the cliff on the opposite side of the river. The Place of Crossing arched two hundred feet above the water. Three Vilderones were climbing down the cliff side, away from the charges they had planted.

Without another word, Rogmun walked toward the river, and Deciedon followed. On the opposite bank, a dozen archers awaited their leader's signal. Each of them held a heavy, metal crossbow with an arrow which was constructed expressly for detonating the charges. Rogmun waited until his henchmen who

had planted the explosives had climbed down to safety, then he raised his arm. The archers stepped forward, raising their crossbows, and as the general dropped his arm, they fired in near perfect unison. The first explosion was closely followed by the others, resulting in a series of blasts that sent huge boulders skyward. The entire structure of the Place of Crossing crumbled, dropping tons of rock to the river below, sending clouds of dust and water vapor upward amid the roar of the falling boulders.

The spectacle, and the implications of it, were such that Deciedon was truly pleased. He laughed, congratulating Rogmun as the settling of the debris revealed the entire width of the River Garnon to be blockaded.

"This is marvelous—just marvelous!" he exclaimed. He and the gargoyle general started back toward their horses. "Now all we need do is position ourselves, and await the arrival of our friends. Ah, at last I will meet my leader: the Prince of Alfandel! I fear he will find the meeting less pleasurable than I..."

Smiling still, Deciedon paused and glanced back to where rivulets and little cascades of water found passage through small gaps in the great rock pile that blocked the normal flow of the Garnon.

20

CRYSLANDON

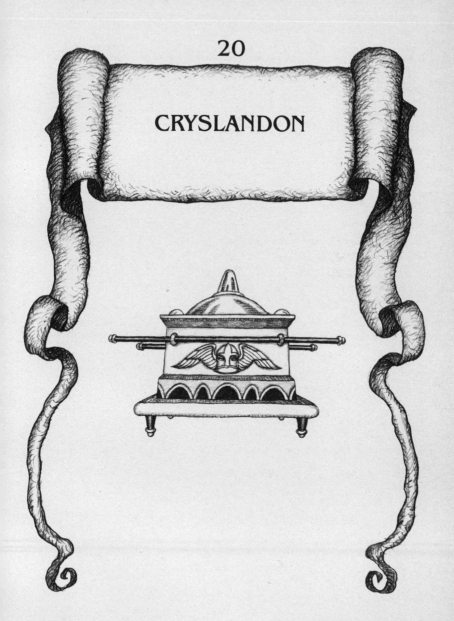

F ar to the south of Golgorath and the Plains of Kiberuk rose the emerald green of the Arbroic Hills, serving as a rampart between those dark northern lands and Cryslandon—the ancient citadel of the White Elf nation of Alfandel. The city rose in levels on a great hill between the twin lakes of Gorheim and Germaina. At the center of Cryslandon stood the Tower of Enlightenment, and spreading away from this were the city streets and the surrounding buildings. A great canal led inward from the River Garnon through the outer wall and circled the city completely. On a bright day—when light was reflected brilliantly from the great circular walls, golden domes and towers, Cryslandon appeared much like a radiating sun.

The Crownhelm of the White Elves was returned to the city when exactly one cycle of the moon had elapsed since the beginning of the quest to bring about the Fulfillment; this was in keeping with the Prophecy. Daybreak had just begun to fully reveal the surrounding land, as the Ark of Crownhelm was being carried down slopes of the southeastern approach to the city. Bearing the Ark were Gwarpys from Loamend, led by the ancient beings, Elgan and Shandar. Across the way, blue-gray clouds stretched above the northern horizon like great flying beasts. The pristine white shaft and golden dome of the Tower of Enlightenment were bathed in the golden glow of dawn. It was toward this that the Ark was carried; it was at the tower top that the Crownhelm would be kept until the arrival of the Sevena. The wizard and the sorcerer, with their companions, arrived at the southeast bridge just above the juncture of the twin lakes where the great river begins. Coming toward them were two young Elves. The two Elves reached the ancient beings. Their eyes were shining: they would bear the crown of their ancestors into the city, and carry it to the upper chamber of the Tower. The old men smiled at the two as they accepted the treasure from the Gwarpys. With the Ark between them, the bearers walked forward, recrossing the bridge. Following them were Elgan and Shandar and the small group of Gwarpys. Awaiting them was a score of mounted White Elf soldiers: the Lejentors, resplendent in their white and black uniforms.

The procession began into the city. It passed through the great outer wall, and across the broad, circular canal. The roadway, which led straight to the Tower, was lined with White Elves and with Dwarfs. There was no cheering, no shouting. Only a hushed silence, and the sound of many feet moving as the processioners walked forward between the onlookers. Then a solitary voice was heard. It came from the Tower, a pure, crystal-clear, wordless chant, drawing them forward.

The procession continued along the great avenue, through the gateway of the second circular wall, past tiered gardens and white-and-gold-domed buildings. The Tower of Enlightenment was directly before them. Those that lined the way joined the procession as the Ark passed by. The Crownhelm of the White Elves was carried up the wide, curved white steps which led into the vast circular hall surrounding the Tower. Outside, the congregation of White Elves and Dwarfs numbered into the thousands. A special guard of young Elves, wearing golden tunics over their white garb, awaited the arrival of the Ark, and they now replaced the Lejentors at the head of the procession into the Tower.

The Ark was within the cavernous hall; the single chanting voice was joined by hundreds of youthful voices which echoed throughout the great cylindrical chamber as the procession moved slowly across the floor of marble, inlaid with an intricate design in gold. The voices drifted and echoed:

Rise, oh rise! Brethren, all rise!
Our souls awake, our ancestors call.
We must now raise our sacred cry,
The purest question, to live or die.

Then the Ark of Crownhelm was carried beneath the arching portal that gave entrance to the steps leading up to the Tower of Enlightenment. And then it was gone from sight. No one but the White Elf guard and its bearers ascended to the upper room. The youthful chanters moved across the hall and slowly the building emptied. The clear young voices completed their chant:

Tis time for battles to be won!
All shall awaken ere we're done!

Elgan and Shandar were left alone within the hall. The wizard sighed. At last the Crownhelm was returned to its proper place. He looked about. He had not been here in quite some time. Shandar had moved noiselessly away, lost in the exquisite architecture of the great building. It had been years since the old sorcerer had visited Cryslandon. Early morning sunlight slanted through the lofty windows, highlighting the white and gold of the hall. Voices came from outside. Three Dwarfs entered the hall.

"Elgan! Hello!" the voice of the Dwarf patriarch, Esrund, boomed out the greeting. "The sight of you is balm for my tired old eyes, welcome!" As the white-bearded old Dwarf came forward, he was noticeably limping; the trip from Penderak had been difficult for him. Flanking him were the red-haired Wilda, and the black-patched, curly-haired Nolan.

The tall wizard bent down, embracing his old

friend, and exchanged warm greetings with the other Dwarfs. Suddenly Elgan exclaimed:

"You don't know about it—Ailwon was successful in the Marshes of Zorak...Gorta is dead!"

The three appeared less elated than Elgan had imagined they would be. "How'd you learn of this?" asked Esrund.

The wizard nodded toward Shandar, who had gone unnoticed by the Dwarfs, but who now approached them. The three were enthusiastic about seeing the sorcerer. Nolan and Wilda had never met him, but of course knew a great deal about him. Esrund had known Shandar for many years; while the Dwarf didn't pretend to understand the serene ancient being, he was still very fond of him, and respected him greatly.

Elgan had been studying the Dwarf leader, noting the poorly disguised concern on the old Dwarf's weather-worn face. "Esrund," said the wizard quietly, "where is Gwynn—the Brown Elves—what has happened?"

Esrund shook his head. His teeth were clenched and his heavy sigh was released loudly through his nostrils. "Damn. I don't know what to say," he said wearily. He looked at Elgan, and then at Shandar. "We don't know where she is. She of course came through Penderak, was going on to Andeluvia. But she should have been here long since. Three—maybe four—days ago."

"Could be her uncle wouldn't let her, or the lads and the others, join up... " Nolan said hopefully. "Everybody knows he's—"

Esrund turned quickly toward the Dwarf. "Damn, Nolan," the old man said irritably, "we've been all through that—Zarin could have kept the others there. But not *Gwynn*." He shook his head again. "He couldn't have kept Gwynn from joining us unless he had her roped to a tree... "

Elgan pondered this alarming fact for a moment. Shandar spoke: "I have not seen the governor, Deciedon. Hopefully he is not missing too... "

Opposite: Cryslandon, The Elf Citadel

"Not exactly... " replied Esrund. "He ran into us when we were headed here...'Course we told him the whole story. Deciedon sure got excited when he heard about there being a Sevena and all... He was just awful happy—nice fella, he is. But then, all of a sudden, he got a real scared look...said he'd have to reach the Prince before he got to Cryslandon...said it had to do with knowledge of the traitor. With that, he took off on that lightning-white horse of his, and headed to meet Ailwon."

Elgan was about to comment on this disturbing turn of events when a combined clattering of horses' hooves and excited shouting could be heard through the open doors. The group hurried outside.

There were still a large number of Elves and Dwarfs gathered around the Tower, and within their midst was the cause of the commotion, which was growing rapidly. A young White Elf, who appeared so frightened that he might faint, sat atop an equally nervous brown stallion. The horse, it appeared, had run a considerable distance; it snorted and blew, and its sides heaved.

"What's going on here, youngster?" Esrund shouted the question.

The young man turned toward the old Dwarf. His eyes were filled with terror. "They're coming! They'll be here within five days!" he cried.

"Who's coming? Who'll be here?"

"The barbarians! The Vilderone! The forces of the Death Lord are advancing on Cryslandon! They have war machines beyond description! *The hills are black with them...*"

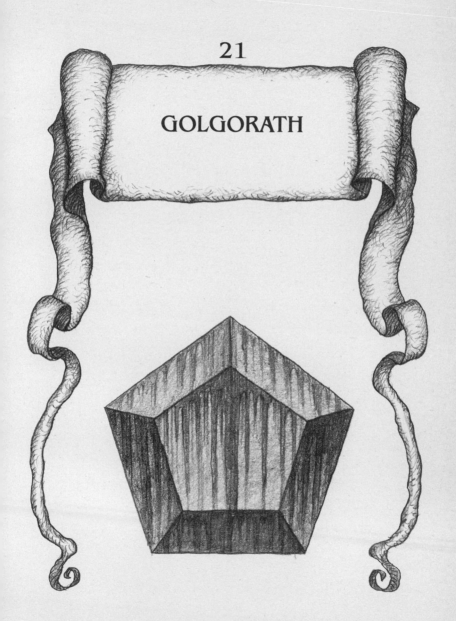

21

GOLGORATH

A flash of lightning ripped through the churning black clouds. The thunderclap that jolted Gwynn into awareness almost deafened her. She was sweating though the air was very cold. Yellow gases issuing from fissures in the crust nearly suffocated her. Gwynn and her Vilderone captors had been traveling in the Black Mountains surrounding Golgorath since the evening before. They were now making their way toward a pass which would lead downward to the plain below, while beyond the plain another range of mountains rose, outlined in a deep red glow. A thundering crash of lightening nearby blasted chunks from the meteoric rock. Gwynn's horse bolted, nearly throwing her to the ground, but one of the guards caught the reins, steadying the terrified animal.

For an unknown time she had been in shock at the brutal slaughter of her people. Then for days she had ridden, mourning and grieving, until her captors gagged her. Yet still she moaned, bound and swaying in the saddle. Throughout, the Vilderone exhibited no concern, except to see to it that she ate once a day. Except when eating, they kept her bound, even when she slept. She had no interest in their care for her or lack of it, but eventually realized she was alive only because Deciedon had ordered her safe arrival in Golgorath. Now she shuddered at the thought that he fully intended to keep her as his own prized possession once the allied nations were defeated. But she would never allow him to realize his desires, no matter what she had to do in order to deny them.

Somewhere in the horror of the past few days, Gwynn's courage, stripped bare, had hardened like a rock, and she had come to a grim decision. Fleetingly she wondered about Ailwon. But she no longer allowed herself the right to worry about him despite the fact that Deciedon had indicated that the Prince too would soon be a prisoner of the Death Lord. She was already a prisoner—and she was going to need all her energies to survive. Worrying about her lover would do neither of them any good now.

The redness in the clouds grew stronger. Rounding a towering outpost, Gwynn stared in horror. There below in the center of a vast plain lay the Crater of Death, stretching more than a mile wide from rim to rim. And from the center rose an immense iron tower. Out of an opening at its top raged a tornado of red flame. The glow lit the entire terrain revealing a totally lifeless landscape. Craters pocked the surface. Cracks in the ground miles long shot outward from the central crater. Violent electric storms raged in the black clouds that emanated from the monstrous tower. All the while a steady rumbling emitted from the bowels of the land. Gwynn could no longer make more than a guess at the time of day. The ceiling of black clouds that spread across Golgorath had continued to gain mass as they drew closer to the Crater of Death. Down toward this inferno of doom the Vilderone led Gwynn.

They had been descending the mountains for several hours. Finally they reached level ground and began to make their way along the side of an immense fissure. More of the foul gases belched upward to mingle with the black clouds above. The lightning continued in the distance as the terrible rumbling grew louder and louder. Now dead ahead rose the hideous black tower, its monstrous size growing more apparent.

Gwynn shuddered. As uncomfortable as it was, she knew what to expect from her captivity. But beyond was the Death Lord himself. Beyond was the legendary monster who had aroused such tales of horror that she dared not think of them. The past several years of her life had been directed toward this end, toward confronting Torgon. She had envisioned herself standing defiantly before him, beside Ailwon, the two of them at last facing this demon of death. But she had never imagined she would be brought before him as a helpless captive.

Closer rose the black mass of the Tower of Death. The fire at its peak erupted into the churning clouds. And then looming before them was the gateway into this domain of terror. Turrets of black iron jutted up from the mountains of the crater. A flash of lightning illuminated the scene for an instant. The entire structure was made of iron, streaked with age. Atop two towers which flanked the gate were giant weapons the likes of which Gwynn had never seen. The iron gate began to slide open, rumbling on its tracks. The Vilderones spurred their mounts onward into the black opening.

The gates closed behind them and they were immersed in total darkness. A feeling of suffocation and panic overcame Gwynn. Her captors shouted a command, and before them a crack of red light appeared. A gate directly ahead of them rumbled on its tracks and Gwynn found herself staring up at the Tower of Death itself, the center of the Death Lord's domain.

Surrounded by her captors, she started across a long causeway—one of four leading to the Death Tower. These causeways rose several hundred feet above the floor of the crater. The crater itself descended in three tiers with ramps connecting one tier to another. Gwynn stared about. None of the experience of her young life had in any way prepared her for the grinding oppression that filled this dark place. The cavernous crater was filled with thousands upon

thousands of moving forms, teeming across the causeways, crowding every level of the sweeping tiers, and covering the crater floor. Crowds of savage Gnomes shouted abusively and poked at Gwynn as she rode by, while huge Borgs stared at her with dulled eyes. The press of bodies was so close that the Vilderone had to continually kick and push the crowds. All around were the incredible war machines of the Death Lord, standing like gigantic, steel monsters. And all about the machines were the slaves: throngs of them—male and female; White Elves and Brown Elves, Dwarfs, Azmurians, Norsepeople.... They moved the ponderous machines up long ramps and across the enormous upper tier. Their bodies were filthy and covered with sweat, despite the cold of this place. And all the while they were beaten, whipped and cursed. Despite the abuse they moved sluggishly, slowly, barely able to extract anything further from their tortured, half-starved bodies, barely able to breathe the air, heavy with the reek of soot and sulphur.

Gwynn's mind was numbed by the cold and the crowding and the stench, overwhelmed by the constant screeching abrasion of metallic objects scraping against stone and steel; by the sharp cracks of the whips, the brutal commands, and the accompanying cries of pain.

And all of it—the frigid, stinking atmosphere, the cruelty, the strident, shrieking clangor—all moved in concert to a slow, continuous throbbing that dominated the great crater, that rose like some mammoth pulse beat from deep within the bowels of Golgorath...beneath the Tower of Death.

Having crossed the causeway to the tower Gwynn was pulled from her horse. Facing her was a gigantic pentagonal shape and at its base was the entrance to the Tower. Once again iron doors rumbled open. Surrounded by the gargoyles, the young woman entered the stronghold of Torgon.

She was led down a long corridor. The general,

Sorkmun, was in the lead, the jackboots of the
hulking Vilderones striking unified echoes through
the steel passageway. Countless passages twisted off
from the main corridor creating an enormous, dim
maze. A half-dozen times Gwynn was escorted
through opened triangular doors that reverberated
behind her as they clanged shut. Further and further
she was taken into the Tower of Death, until at last
they were confronted by an entranceway twice the size
of the others. The huge door rumbled open.

Gwynn stared into the darkness. The hall of the
Death Lord was enormous. At its center was a vast pit,
from which arose a pentagonal dias. Upon the dias
stood an iron throne, and on the throne was seated
Torgon, the Death Lord of Golgorath. A faint red glow
defined the massiveness of his head and shoulders.

Gwynn began to tremble as she was pushed forward. She was shoved to her knees by Sorkmun. She
stared up at Torgon, trying to penetrate the icy, silent
blackness. She could hear only the awful throb, see
only the white glow of his eyes coming from within the
somber hulk of his form. Gwynn felt as though she
could no longer breathe.

Now Sorkmun also fell to his knees, prostrating
himself before his master. Finally he raised his head,
and his deep-throated voice was almost pleading:

"My Lord, I bring to you a gift: this captive, this
sought-after enemy of the mighty Lord of Golgorath. I
bring to you this prized hostage, who will help to
insure your absolute success as you seek the destruction of those aliens who have denied you your
rightful place as the Lord of all of the continent...
Sorkmun presents this Elf, who is a gift to his master...."

Only dark silence came from the throne. Gwynn
continued to stare, trying to comprehend the reality
that once—a thousand years before—this awful presence had been a youthful White Elf Prince, a Sevena,
not unlike her beloved Ailwon. She had been so
overcome by the dread fear of all of this that she

scarcely heard the trembling homage that came from the gargoyle general. Then she grasped the implication of the Vilderone's words: she was being given away, handed over, a piece of property, to be handled however the Death Lord pleased....

"No!" she shouted. Sorkmun stared at her with disbelief. "I'm not some damned chattel to be given away! *No one owns me! No one!*" she screamed at Torgon. "Nor does *anyone own* anyone, you monstrous, cowardly bastard!"

Sorkmun struck her across the face, catching her before she fell, clamping her mouth closed with his huge, leathery hand. The chill of fear had gone from her body, and her face was flushed by the heat of her outrage. The Death Lord raised one great arm, pointing toward the door. She was forcibly picked up and carried from the Hall of Death by Sorkmun. She struggled to get free, for she had not had her full say.

It was late night when Gwynn was brought to the enormous compound of cells that held the slaves of Golgorath. The prison had been built near the southern gate of the fortress wall, on the second tier within

the crater. At the center of the compound was a huge barred area, which Gwynn would learn was called "the cage" and into which the slaves were often packed, to deny even the small degree of privacy provided by the cells. As she passed cell after cell, the Brown Elf maid could see the faces of the prisoners, pressed against the bars of the tiny grates, curious to see what new slave would command the accompaniment of the many gargoyles who were guarding her. They stopped before a cell.

Sorkmun had personally led Gwynn's escort of guards. "Thog!" he shouted. A giant Borg appeared from the shadows ahead, and approached. A grimy leather tunic covered his torso. He stared at Gwynn with pink-rimmed eyes. "Open this empty cell," commanded the Vilderone general. The hunched Borg secured a heavy metal device that hung from a chain attached to his belt. He inserted it into the cell door, the bolt released and the iron door was opened. One of Gwynn's captors removed the chains from her arms. Her wrists remained bound with rope. She looked up. Torchlight played across the faces within the cells. Sorkmun had turned to leave. Gwynn shouted out to the watching prisoners:

"Don't despair, my brothers and sisters! There is one who can face Torgon! There is a Sevena!" She heard Sorkmun curse, and wheel back toward her. "These bastards can't hold us... " she shouted, just before the Vilderone general struck her again. She was knocked against the open cell door, slamming it shut. Blood ran from a split in the skin above her eye.

"Throw the bitch in just as she is," was Sorkmun's command. Gwynn was grabbed, and shoved inside, her wrists still bound behind her. She skidded on the cold stone and fell to the floor as the door slid closed. Sorkmun's brutal face peered into the small grate at her. "One more word," he growled at her, "and you'll be gagged and tied until the traitor comes for you... Is that clear, Elf?"

Gwynn did not answer. She heard Sorkmun and the

others leave. She lay on her side; the wound above
her eye was throbbing. Then from somewhere within
the vast compound a voice called out after the
departing Vilderone:

"You bastards cannot hold us!"

Gwynn pulled herself to her feet. She moved about
the small room, finding it completely bare. With her
hands still tied and the cut above her eye running
fresh blood, this first night as a prisoner of the Death
Lord would be especially miserable.

She sat back down on the cold stone floor, her back
resting against the wall. Suddenly she felt a movement of a square of stone that she leaned against,
and she emitted a small cry of surprise. She pulled
away from the wall and watched as the rock slid from
its position into the next cell. The rock disappeared,
leaving an opening. Through it came a female voice,
raspy and middle-aged:

"Hey, dearie... " it was a Dwarf voice, Gwynn was
sure, "come on down here, where we kin see one
'nother."

Gwynn crouched on one knee, peering into the
opening. "Heh, heh," chuckled the voice, "sure enjoyed yer yellin' out there... That was ol' Din-Ganda
thet give ya th' vocal support... He's an Azmurian, 'o
course...Couldn't cuss worth a damn when he come
here, them people ain't good at it, ya know...but we
been learnin' him. He does it most ever' chance he
gets, now.... " She chuckled again. Then her voice
took on a more serious tone: "They kinda' roughed ya
up out there, didn't they, dearie?"

"Yes."

"Yeah...that's what they do real good. Ya hurt bad?"

"It's smarting quite a bit, but it's not a bad cut."

"We'll have a look in just a minute...I think I've got
this figgered. There's been plenty of slaves brought in
here since I come...an' I never seen such an escort as
you got. There's bin a rumor that that swinish traitor—that Deciedon—was blowin' off. One of our people
overheard 'im. He was out to git the hero gal from

Andeluvia. He was gonna' git her an keep her for hisself. Well, I could see from the torchlight, before that bastard walloped ya, how purty ya was... " A pause, then: "Yer her, ain't ya? Yer Gwynn of Andeluvia?"

"Yes... I am Gwynn."

"I knew it," the Dwarf said with satisfaction. "Gawl! We've heard lots about ya.... Hold on, I wanna look at yer cut.... "

Gwynn heard the Dwarf rustling about, apparently searching for something. Obviously her cell was not so completely bare. There was a chipping sound of striking stone objects. Then there was a soft glow of light, and in another instant the light was focused through the opening onto Gwynn. "Aw, ya poor thing," said the woman, "ya really got whacked good...Come up close.... " The young woman moved closer to the candlelight.

"Where did you get that?" she asked incredulously.

"Here. Lean real close, and I'll tell ya.... " Gwynn put her face next to the opening. Two plump, stubby-fingered hands reached past the candle. The hands held a wet cloth, and they began to bathe the dripping blood from the Elfin maiden's face. Then the raspy voice continued: "Made th' candle m'self... made all kindsa things...There's so much stuff used 'round here—tons an' tons of it...All that's needed is ta swipe it an' hide it, an' ya kin make damn near anythin'... " The Dwarf woman laughed. "I got so many rolls an' lumps underneath my clothes, them dumb guards kin never tell what's me or what's a hunk of somethin' else.... "

Gwynn's face was wiped clean of the blood. The Dwarf's hands were worn and calloused, but were extremely gentle. "Thank you," she whispered.

"Sure. Now turn 'round, an' back up ta me, an' I'll git yer hands loose."

"That'll be a tremendous relief," Gwynn sighed. "But, please, come close to the light, I want to see your face.... "

"Gawl! Never even thought of it." The woman bent down. Looking in at Gwynn through the opening was a rounded face, the top of which was covered with gray hair. The eyes were drawn into happy squints by the fullness of the rosy cheeks. The nose was wide, and centered by a small wart. The mouth was tiny, fitting neatly between the balloon cheeks and the double chin. Gwynn thought the face to be one of the most robust that she had ever seen and, all in all, the most unlikely visage to have encountered in the cells of Golgorath's prison. "What's your name?" she asked the Dwarf.

"Ferda," was the reply. "There's two others in here with me: Bethena, she's an Azmurian, and a White Elf woman, Therela—she's kinda sickly... We hafta cover fer her some of the work details... but that's okay. They're both sleepin' away right now... Ya learn to sleep thru just about anythin' after ya bin here awhile...." Ferda chuckled, then turned the soft light back toward Gwynn. "Now," she said, "turn 'round while I work them ropes loose." Gwynn turned her back to the wall, and the Dwarf woman began working at the knots that held her wrists. "Keep the rope handy," Ferda said, "we'll hafta tie ya back up 'fore they roust us out in the mornin'...I know it'll be tough fer ya ta do, but ya better hold yer tongue. Ya gotta learn not ta make it rough on yerself, else ya won't make it. There's plenty die here—every day... an' there's plenty that've gone mad. There, yer loose...."

"Thank you," said Gwynn, with a great sigh of relief. She rubbed her chafed wrists gingerly. Every muscle of her arms was aching. "How have you survived so well?" she asked, as the Dwarf woman blew out the candle.

"Well," Ferda said, speaking as softly as her rough voice would permit, "I hadda make a choice... Was I gonna stay alive er' wasn't I? This's a terrible damn place—you've seen that. They hate us here! They try ta take ever' damn thing away from ya... they try ta wipe out yer whole life... make ya feel like scum er' slime.

Opposite: Golgorath

It's a rotten place, that's fer sure. Ya git smacked fer doin' jist about anythin'." Gwynn had reached forward, touching the little woman's hand. Ferda continued: "So anyways, I made a choice. I decided that I'd make my way here... I'd git by, an' someday I'd be free...I knowed it, just knowed it....What you hollered tonight 'bout the White Elf Sevena...'bout somebody that could whup that damned Death Lord...well, that was music ta all our ears. But, deep down, I know'd all along that we wasn't doomed." She snorted and sniffed, and Gwynn thought that she might be crying. "Ya can't let these bastards git ya down," she continued. "They try to git ya ta turn on each other... but, Gawl!" she exulted, "how they've messed that up! All the feudin' an' mistrust that's gone on in Urshurak... for all these centuries...and it's *here,* here in the slimy hole of the Death Bastard, that the people've been brung together. It's here that we've found out about real lovin'...." She stopped, evidently a little embarrassed, then began to laugh gently. "Don't git me wrong, dearie, I'd trade the best day here fer the worst day in Penderak, I'd do that without thinkin' it over fer a second...It's just that there's things here that ya kin learn about...once ya make up yer mind ta do that...." Ferda stood up. "Now," she said, "it's time to get some shut-eye. Ya got anythin' over there ta sleep on?"

"Just the floor."

"That figgers. I'll git ya some beddin'...."

"Bedding?"

"Sure...got an extra hid underneath the floor, long with everythin' else. Ya make 'em outa swiped material. Be surprised how comfy you'll be—" She stopped, and bent back down to the opening, peering into Gwynn's cell.

They reached through the opening, exchanged the bedding and touched.

22

TREACHERY

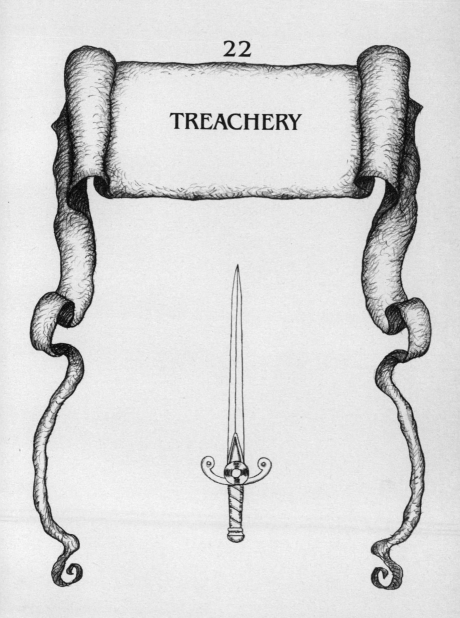

B y Gawl!" exclaimed Evrawk, "I've never seen anything like this!" He and Ailwon had been the first to examine the blockade of the River Garnon from close up. He pointed up to the cliff on the near side, and then to the one on the opposite side of the river. "You can see, lad," he said to the Elfin youth, "how deep the rock was that formed the Place of Crossing. I can't imagine how anything could have brought it down."

"It's baffling, for certain, Evrawk," replied the Prince, "and it does seem wise that Queen Azira has set out guards." He glanced back down the river, where a score of warrior women were moving into positions among the rocks in the area near the now motionless Amazon ships. The Queen approached; beside her was Ali Ben Kara, and trailing them, Tark-Volmar. The three stared at the huge pile-up of rocks that blocked their passage.

Tark-Volmar began a laugh from deep within his barrel chest. "Looks like some of those damn rock beavers have been out here!"

Ben Kara looked at him disgustedly. "You have a strange sense of humor, Volmar," he said, the irritation in his voice rising as his statement progressed. "Don't you realize the delay this will cause?"

"Of course, I realize it—I'm no ninny. But that doesn't make it less funny," shot back the Norseman,

scratching his belly beneath his fur vest. As the
voyage had progressed northward, there had been a
constant lifting of Volmar's spirits with the continual
decline in temperature of the environment.

Queen Azira was amused by the angry, little-boy
exchanges she had witnessed since the Azmurian
Shakín and the Norseman leader had joined them,
but right now she was more concerned with the
problem that confronted them. She turned to Ailwon.
"Even with the use of the Fire Crystals we will be
delayed by almost four days. As you've described the
dictates of the Prophecy to me, this will require some
extensive alterations in the plans leading to an attack
against the Death Lord."

"Yes," replied the youth, nodding his head resignedly, "although I must admit that foregoing a formal
celebration of my crowning is something of a relief.
But yes, you're right, this will require a considerable
alteration of our plans. I'm more concerned, right
now, about the very real possibility that this rock fall
was not due to any quirk of nature."

"I can't imagine how anything could have brought
it down," repeated Evrawk.

They traversed the rocky elevation back down to
the beach where a camp was being set up. The horses
had been taken off the ship. They were being attended to by Oolu—as usual—and by Zyra, who had never
before seen such creatures. She was completely
fascinated, both by the animals and by the communi-
cation between them and the cheerful Gwarpy. The
Amazon Princess was not prone to indulge in very
much frivolity, but Oolu's relentless friendliness and
his ability to find delight in just about everything
within his sphere had caused her to somewhat adjust
her guarded stance.

"I see, my daughter, that you have become completely captivated by the horse-beasts," the Queen
called to Zyra as she approached her.

"Yes," the girl replied, "and the 'Corola' is teaching
me much about these lovely animals." Oolu chuck-

led. He took great delight in the name attached to him by the Amazons. "I would dearly love to learn how to ride one, but this is hardly the time. I am at your disposal, my mother, to direct the operations of the Fire Crystals whenever you are ready."

"The Prince tells me we have no time to spare," said Azira, glancing toward Ailwon.

"That's true, Princess Zyra, we should begin as quickly as we can." The Prince smiled, pointing to his gray steed, to which Zyra had taken a special liking. "I'm afraid that wild Thelan, of whom you have grown so fond, would not be the horse for you to learn on. He seems quite docile beneath your gentle touch, but were you to mount him, he would suddenly be transformed into a veritable demon. I've ridden him for two years, and even now he—"

A challenging shout from an Amazon guard cut Ailwon short. Instantly there was movement throughout the encampment as women warriors made ready to act.

A pure white steed galloped down the beach. Its rider was garbed in a similar white, with a long black cloak flowing out. He held one arm raised in the air, but failed to slow his pace as he was challenged. "Queen Azira!" shouted the Dwarf, Evrawk, clutching the tall woman's arm, "that's a Lejentor...a White Elf! I believe—yes!—it's the governor—it's Deciedon!" He gave a joyous shout, as did Erbin, who had emerged from a group of tall pines that grew among the rocky inclines leading upward from the river. The command was given to allow the rider through, and Deciedon did not slow his pace until he had almost reached them, dismounting smoothly while his big horse was still in motion.

"Evrawk! And Erbin, my old drinking partner!" exclaimed the handsome man, clutching the hands of the twin Dwarfs who greeted him warmly. Then he looked up, his eyes fell on Ailwon, his face gained a look of awe and reverence. He slowly approached the youth, pulling back his hood as he walked, the soft

blond waves of his hair falling free. "You... you are
Ailwon, the Sevena..."the rich tones of his voice were
muted almost to a whisper. He stretched out his hand,
palm forward, as did the smiling youth. Their hands
rested on one another's shoulders for an instant, then
Deciedon fell to one knee. His voice was filled with
passion: "You are the one for whom I have waited—the
one who will fulfill the Prophecy...." His clear blue
eyes were shining. He shook his head slowly. "It is
hard to believe," he continued, "that you are the son
of my beloved King and Queen. After all these years
without knowledge of your existence, this is like a
marvelous dream come true..."

Ailwon was embarrassed. "Please, sir," he said,
reaching down to Deciedon, "it is I who should pay
homage to you. While I have yet to live among my
people, I know their entire history. And there is none
that stands so tall among them as the great hero,
Deciedon. Please rise."

Deciedon stood. He swept his gaze across the
gathered Amazon troops, and along the long row of
huge vessels. "This is truly an awesome sight," he
said, smiling. He nodded to Queen Azira. "I have long
heard of the great warrior women of Zan-Dura. But
the tales were so wondrous that I feared they might
only be legend. The reality is truly astounding!" He
frowned, pointing back toward the blockaded waters.
"However, I had hoped to encounter this great fleet
sailing full ahead. This barrier clearly presents a
serious problem." He turned back to Ailwon. "I have
some thoughts on a solution to this dilemma," he
said, "but first, my Prince, I have a great desire to
meet these people who have accompanied you."

Ailwon again looked embarrassed, feeling quite
subdued in the presence of this living legend. He
hurriedly began the introductions. As Deciedon was
introduced to Zyra, his eyes clung to her beauty for a
long instant, though he covered his inner arousal
with his perfected courtly manner. Remembering
Hugh, Ailwon's eyes searched for the archer, who had

removed himself from the main group soon after the
landing. He spotted the Vandorian seated a short
distance away beneath the shade of a pine. Hugh had
cut some shafts for arrows, and was in the process of
preparing them for the fitting of the arrowheads. He
had decided that morning that he would torture
himself no longer with the desire he felt for Zyra. He
would stay as clear of her as possible, devoting his
energies to the preparation for the upcoming battle.
He had been observing the interplay of this much
talked about White Elf hero and the group and,
unaccountably, he felt an immediate dislike and
distrust for the handsome Elf.

"Hugh," called Ailwon, "come and meet our noble
governor." The tall, broad-shouldered Vandorian
stood. He held an arrow shaft in one hand, and he
fingered the smoothness of it with the other. He
bowed toward Deciedon, but did not come forward.
The White Elf returned the perfunctory greeting, and
as their eyes met, Decideon felt an inner twinge of
fear for only the second time in his life; the first was
the moment that he had been brought before the
Death Lord, Torgon. He looked away quickly, returning his attention to the youth, Ailwon. "I'm sure you
are wondering about my unexpected arrival... " he
said. At the sound of his own voice, his fleeting loss of
confidence disappeared. "I have knowledge of a most
serious nature that I need to discuss with you, my
Prince... " He smiled and addressed himself to Erbin
and Evrawk as he continued, "I met your father and
your people not far from Cryslandon. Esrund informed me of the Sevena and the quest, so I rode day
and night to meet you. Your father, gentlemen, is
looking quite well. He had donned the Uxmun armor
for the journey to the capital city." The Dwarf twins
grinned, and Erbin nudged his brother in the ribs.

Zyra had moved close to Deciedon's muscular
stallion, and gingerly touched the satiny white of his
coat. Her interest did not go unnoticed by the White
Elf leader, and he stepped to her side. "I see that you

admire my steed. You need not be cautious in stroking him. He is a marvelous beast, a great and trustworthy companion. Both he and his sire have served me well in peace and in battle."

"I had never encountered these animals before," said Zyra, somewhat apologetically. "I fear I'm becoming completely entranced by them."

"There is no need for embarrassment, my dear," said Deciedon, smiling. "I myself have a deep affection for these fine creatures." He casually touched her arm, having just as casually removed his glove so as to feel the bareness of her flesh. Above them, Hugh Oxhine muttered beneath his breath, and spat onto the rocks.

"We must get started," said Queen Azira, who had been conferring quietly with Ali Ben Kara, with whom she was establishing a mutually respectful friendship. "Zyra," she said firmly, "make ready the Crystals."

"Yes," replied the Princess, and she moved quickly away, calling out crisp commands to her sisters who had been looking on.

Deciedon raised an eyebrow at the term 'Crystals' but turned back again to Ailwon. "I must speak to you, my Prince. Alone," he said earnestly, taking the youth by the elbow. Ailwon nodded, and excusing himself, he began to walk slowly away with the White Elf hero. Deciedon walked with hands clasped behind his back, holding the reins of his horse, who trailed behind. He spoke in a very guarded manner, referring to a knowledge of the long-feared traitor, dragging out the information so that before long, the sounds of the encampment came from some distance away. Deciedon led the Prince behind a group of enormous boulders which extended almost into the water. He had Ailwon's concentrated attention so that the youth was completely diverted from detecting the presence of the half dozen gargoyle archers, who—with their black steeds—were hidden behind the rocks. A little further on, another outcropping of rocks, thick with pine trees, extended from the slopes to within twenty yards of the river. As they passed beyond this point, the White Elf hero and the Prince were completely hidden from view from the Amazon encampment. Here Deciedon stopped, regarding Ailwon with his confident smile.

"I'm sorry it's so complicated," he said. "I'm sure you're confused by all that I've been telling you..." He moved casually away several paces, then stopped, his hand resting on the hilt of his sword, his face still lit by his smile, delighting in the troubled look on Ailwon's face. "The confusion you're experiencing is quite understandable. In fact, I've deliberately fostered it so that I could draw you away from the others...." He began to laugh quietly. "You see, my boy, this traitor of whom I speak, the one who killed your father, and the other Sevenas, the one who made possible the capture of your lovely Gwynn as she was en route to Cryslandon...." Ailwon's eyes went wide with horror. His tormentor had stopped laughing; his smile had disappeared, and the warmth was gone from his blue eyes. "This traitor, my Prince," he said, "is none other than," he bowed, "—myself."

Ailwon looked on in disbelief for another instant, then he pulled Elvgard free of its scabbard. "Ah," said Deciedon, admiringly, "...so that is the famous sword of the Sevenas. Quite a weapon, I understand. Works well against witches and monsters. But I am neither. I am, however, the finest swordsman on the continent, and were it to my advantage I would gladly give a brat such as yourself a lesson that you would neither forget nor remember. But this is not to my advantage, and so I've brought along some friends...." He waved toward the cluster of pines, where several hulking, armored brutes were moving toward Ailwon. The lad knew that they must be the Vilderones. He heard movement behind him, and looked back quickly. Three other Vilderones had closed off the escape route to the rear. On a growled command from the largest of them, they all rushed forward. Ailwon dodged away from one, who swung at him with a short club. He realized they were to take him alive, and knew this gave him a slight edge that would not otherwise be there. But he knew also that the chances of escape were remote. No shouts would reach the Amazon camp above the sound of the river. None could see him. He dodged again, kicking one of the brutes in the midsection. He shouted as he did so, hoping that someone might be near enough to hear. He whirled around, swinging Elvgard in a broad arc, slashing through breastplate and stomach flesh of a ponderous Vilderone. The brute grunted, and fell. But that was the last Ailwon saw or heard. He was struck hard on the head by the huge Vilderone general, Rogmun. The White Elf Prince sprawled forward on the loose shale.

Rogmun grunted another command, and horses were brought from their hiding places. Ailwon was slung over a saddle, and chained. Then the Vil-

derones, moving unconcernedly about their fallen
comrade, mounted their black steeds.

When Ailwon had fallen, Deciedon had retrieved the
sword, Elvgard. He studied the gleaming blade, then
pulled his own sword and tossed it into the undergrowth. Deciedon slid the sword of the Sevena into his
black sheath. He laughed quietly, and then, catching
the reins of his white horse, vaulted into the saddle.

Erbin was watching as Deciedon led Ailwon down
the beach. As the two White Elves walked off, Deciedon
had been speaking to the Prince in earnest tones.
Erbin experienced a sudden troubled feeling in the
pit of his stomach. As those around him went further
up the beach to watch the process of clearing the
blockade, the Dwarf remained—even though he had a
great curiosity in regard to the operation of the Fire
Crystals. He continued to watch the two figures as
they grew distant. Why did he feel so troubled? What
was it in Deciedon's face that had rung such a chilling
discord within Erbin's memory? As the Dwarf worried
at the problem, the Elves passed an outcropping of
rocks, then disappeared beyond another. Erbin
turned and started toward the others, still preoccu-
pied with whatever his memory was trying to tell him.
He walked a few paces toward the activity, to where
the clear voice of Zyra was directing the operations.
Suddenly he stopped. As recollection hit him, he felt
as though his short legs would give way beneath him.
Seeing Deciedon again had tripped something in his
mind which had lain dormant for these past several
months, obscured by the numbing effects of the
alcohol consumed on a certain fateful night. *It was
Deciedon who had maneuvered the secret of the
Sevena's existence out of him!*

Erbin cried out, and began running down the beach
toward the spot where Ailwon and Deciedon had
disappeared.

"Ailwon! Ailwon!" he shouted. "It's *him!* I told him!"
The Dwarf continued to shout at the top of his

lungs. He drew to within fifty yards of the first out-cropping. Suddenly Deciedon and the Vilderones, with Ailwon slumped across a gargoyle steed, galloped into view.

"No!" screamed the Dwarf. "No, you bastards!" From behind the rocks, the first arrow whizzed past his head. A second followed the first, this one almost dead center but a trifle low, and it tore through the fleshy part on the inside of the Dwarf's heavy thigh. The force of the steel arrow spun the Dwarf around, and he fell to his back on the sand, still shouting and cursing. He rolled over to his belly, shaking his fist at the departing horsemen. "Swine!" he screamed, as arrows thudded into the sand around him.

Several of the Amazons were running up the beach toward the Dwarf, but they were met by a fusillade of arrows from the rapid-fire crossbows of the Vilderone marksmen. Three of the women were dropped by the deadly fire, one falling into the water, where the blood from her death wound was drawn into the slow current of the river. The others were forced behind cover to await the reinforcements moving up rapidly behind them.

At the first sound of Erbin's excited hollering, Hugh Oxhine stood up. He laid aside the arrowhead and shaft that he had been working on and had watched the little man as he ran up the beach. Then the horsemen thundered out, and Hugh had been able to catch a glimpse—first of the white-and-black-clad Deciedon, and then of the blonde-haired Ailwon. The Vandorian had watched with horrified fascination as Erbin was dropped by the first of the arrows.

Hugh glanced behind him, cursing as he did so, for he had left his bow and his sword at the main encampment some distance away. When he looked back, two of the warrior women had been dropped by the flying arrows, and then a third fell. Though it was obvious that Erbin was in considerable danger, the steady outlet of screamed profanity gave evidence that he was far from dead.

Hugh began to run, staying within the shadows of the pine trees, running parallel to the beach where the one-sided battle was taking place. He came to were Erbin lay. Blood was running from the Dwarf's leg wound, but somehow he had escaped further damage from the flying arrows. Without breaking stride, Hugh raced into the open toward the prone Dwarf. An arrow sang past his back, another came short, burying half its length into the sand. Hugh bent, scooped up the Dwarf and raced back toward the cover of the trees. Erbin continued to curse but the cursing came now in the form of a defeated wail: "You swine," he sobbed, "you tricked me—you filthy swine!"

Hugh layed the Dwarf on the ground, propping him up against a tree. "Stay put!" he commanded, and he began to run again, staying within the safe confines of the trees. The fusillade of arrows had abated somewhat, and the Amazon women were slowly advancing. Hugh heard the sound of someone running several yards behind him, following the same route as he; but he did not pause to look back. He veered suddenly to the right, toward the beach, and could hear the snorting of horses, and the thudding of hooves on shale and sand. Through the trees he could see the dark figures of horses and riders in retreat, and as he neared the edge of the protective foliage, it appeared that only one of the gargoyles had not left. The bulky, armored figure had experienced some difficulty in mounting his excited animal, and was just getting into the saddle as Hugh emerged into the open on the run. The archer ran full tilt toward the gargoyle, and as he did so, he realized his error. From the corner of his eye, the Vandorian caught a glimpse of another dark figure, and felt the sudden chill of vulnerability. But it was too late to change course. Without slowing a half-stride, he leaped once, hitting the top of a yellow boulder, and springing from it into midair. The Vilderone had just put spurs to his steed, and the horse bolted forward

at the instant that Hugh's hurtling form made contact. The archer caught the armored brute about the
neck, sending them both into the water, as the horse
ran free. Hugh landed on top of the gargoyle within a
three-foot depth. He was unsure of his next course of
action. He had thought to take the brute alive in
hopes of extracting information as to the route along
which the captive Ailwon was being taken. But as he
struggled underwater with his foe, he knew that this
would be no easy task. The gargoyle clearly possessed tremendous strength, and furthermore, Hugh
did not know whether the other Vilderone had fled or
remained to aid his comrade. The gargoyle and the
tall man struggled to their feet. Hugh's back was
exposed to the shore, and he sensed that at any
moment, he might be struck down from behind. The
Vilderone's helmet had been torn loose with the
plunge into the river, exposing his fierce, brutish
features. His thick lips were drawn back in a snarl to
show his incisor teeth. Each powerful figure had his
hands about the other's throat, and each had tucked
his head between his shoulders as much as possible
to minimize the effectiveness of his foe. Suddenly, the
Vilderone released Hugh, striking at him with one
huge fist, grasping for his dagger with the other. The
Vandorian rolled his head as he was struck, reducing
the force of the blow which nevertheless tore flesh
from his scalp. He was knocked partially off balance,
looking up just as the Vilderone's arm thrust at him
with the dagger. Hugh twisted sideways, drawing his
own blade, dodging the gargoyle's thrusts, lunging
back, driving his knife into the brute's side, into the
open area between front and back armor. The Vilderone fell beneath the water, bubbles frothed to the
surface, mingled with the bright red of blood. The
gargoyle did not rise, and Hugh turned toward the
shore. The Amazon princess, Zyra, stood over the
slain form of the remaining Vilderone, her sword half
covered with blood. Hugh stared at her, and she
returned his stare, her eyes disclosing no emotion. He

Opposite: Zyra, The Amazon Princess

© HILDEBRANDT

saw blood running from her shoulder. "You're bleeding," he said.

She glanced at her wound, then back to Hugh.
"Yes," she replied, "and so are you." She turned,
running back toward the encampment, passing by Ali
Ben Kara, who was running toward Hugh, his short
black bow in hand. Ben Kara shouted—not at Hugh,
but at someone further down the beach. An enraged
bellow came in answer to Ben Kara's shout. The huge
Norseman, Tark-Volmar, was headed toward them,
astride a captured Vilderone steed.

Volmar pulled to a halt before the two standing
men.

"I found this beast standin' around chewin' on
scrub—hold still, you bastard!" he shouted, pulling
back on the reins. "I'm goin' after the magic boy," he
shouted, and wheeled his horse away from the other
men.

"Wait, Volmar!" commanded Ali Ben Kara. "We must
go as a unit!"

"Wait. I'll be damned if I do!" roared Tark-Volmar.
"They'll have the boy all the way to Golgorath before
you get goin'...I'm going *now!*" He dug his heels into
the horse's flanks, and they thundered off down the
beach, the Norseman's red braids flying out beneath
his helmet.

Ben Kara cursed, then looked quickly at Hugh. "I'd
better go after him," he said angrily. "Follow as
quickly as possible!" He ran for another Vilderone
steed, tearing loose the reins, swinging onto its
broad back. As he galloped by, he shouted to Hugh:
"Watch you don't bleed to death!"

Hugh raised his hand to his face. Blood was running from his scalp wound. He began running back
toward the encampment, passing the trio of slain
women, who had been laid side by side; the white-
robed Senqua bent over them, chanting. Erbin was
being hoisted into the saddle by his brother. The
wounded Dwarf's left thigh was heavily bandaged; his
pants leg had been torn away, exposing the short

bulging leg muscle, half covered with blood. Hugh started to question Erbin's joining the pursuit, but thought better of that. He had been able to tell by the Dwarf's rantings as he lay wounded that somehow Erbin felt responsible for the betrayal of Ailwon. There would be no holding back the Dwarf. It would be far less painful for him were he to die during the pursuit, than if he were to stay behind.

Oolu held the reins of Hugh's stallion and of his own pony. The Vandorian had never seen the Gwarpy look so troubled. Hugh's weapons were slung across Santor's saddle. He swung up into the saddle, his soggy clothes squishing as he did so. He glanced behind, where a mild commotion was in progress among a gathering of the Amazons, who were trying to hold Thelan, Alwon's wild gray horse. Nearby, Zyra was taking leave of the Queen. He saw the two women embrace. Then the archer's eyes grew wide with surprise. Zyra had moved over to mount the gray.

"Hey!" he shouted back at her. "You can't do that! That horse will throw and trample you in a minute! You've never even—"

"Attend to yourself, Vandorian," she snapped back at him. Then the Amazon Princess swung up, shooting a quick glance at Oolu. "I hope, Corola, that you have informed me properly..."

"Oolu tells Zyra the straight stuff, yep," replied the Gwarpy.

With that, Zyra snapped her heels against Thelan's sides. The gray stallion leaped forward, stopped short, bucked, reared, whirled about... and Zyra stayed astride, allowing the lithe power of her body to move in concert with the great power of the beast. The gray horse stopped dead still, and Zyra repeated the snap of her heels against his sides. Thelan galloped forward, his tail flying straight back. Hugh shouted to Santor, and the big stallion responded instantly. The Amazon, the Vandorian, the Dwarfs and the Gwarpy were hot in pursuit, following the tracks made by the horses of their comrades and of the abductors of

Ailwon. They passed the lifeless forms of the gargoyles and the place where the Elfin Prince had been
captured. They raced past a large group of boulders
rising abruptly from the beach and clattered on to a
bed of shale where tracks were still visible. The small
band pushed forward rapidly, unaware that they were
watched from behind the massive rock outcropping.
They were watched by the small, fierce eyes of the
Vilderone. They were watched, also, by the cool,
confident eyes of the traitor, Deciedon, holding his
own steed so that the animal would not whicker at the
pursuers.

Deciedon laughed lightly as the small band passed
in hot pursuit, following a false trail left by some of
the gargoyles. Now the traitor looked down at Ailwon
who was showing signs of gaining consciousness and
was being bound and gagged.

"Well, my young Prince, I must take my leave
again," he said to Ailwon, who had not gained his
senses enough to understand the words. "I have
further business to attend to," Deciedon continued,
"but I shall see you again when you reach your
destination, your permanent destination—in Golgorath." The traitor turned, and swung up onto his
beast. He turned to the Vilderone general, "Rogmun,
remember Torgon's order. The Elf must arrive alive."
Deciedon spurred his mount and rode off alone
toward Cryslandon.

23

DRUMBEATS

In Loamend there had been scant rainfall during the spring of the Year of Fulfillment. Following the final day of the Rite of the Bobabos, the rain clouds that had appeared briefly that day had disbanded, and had been replaced by high, feathery, white and silver formations that scattered themselves across the skies. The days of springtime advanced toward the heat of summer.

One full moon's cycle had passed since the beginning of the quest for Fulfillment when the rain clouds returned to Loamend. They appeared first as an ashen haze that dulled the bright sun, slowly building force and weight. By midday the clouds had thickened to a heavy murk, the sun had disappeared altogether, and the sky had grown gray. Then came the first big drops of rain, striking against the hard earth, smelling sweet as they dampened the collected dust. The rainfall began in earnest, became unrelenting, falling without letup for two days. Through this continuous curtain of water the small, allied band doggedly made their way along the false trail they believed would lead them to the White Elf Prince.

It was evening of the second day of rainfall. There was only a dim remainder of daylight when the Azmurian, Ali Ben Kara, drew his borrowed Vilderone stallion to a halt, and those behind him stopped also.

In Ailwon's absence the Shakín had assumed unoffi-
cial leadership of the group, despite the continued
disgruntlement of the Norseman, Tark-Volmar. The
horses stood with lowered heads beneath the continual drizzle; Ben Kara awaited the expected protest. He
was not to be disappointed.

"What are we stopping for, Ben Kara?" came the
bull-voiced question.

The Azmurian sighed, and turned toward the Norseman. "Because, Tark-Volmar," he answered with
exaggerated enunciation, "it is getting dark, and we
will soon no longer be able to see to follow the trail
that dictates our course. That is why I suggest that we
stop, while we still have enough light to establish a
campsite."

Volmar was unconvinced. He nudged his steed
forward, beside Ben Kara. "By thunder, I wish to get
out of this damned country," he growled. While the
Norseman was quite willing to adjust to almost any
situation when it was necessary, he was quite un-
willing to do it quietly—especially in the presence of
the princely mannered Ben Kara. "We've encountered
nothing but water and mud since the day the magic
boy was grabbed. And the little fella tells us that we're
not gettin' any closer to our quarry," he continued,
pointing back toward Erbin. "I say we push on...The
Dwarf's eyes seem sharp enough to follow a track as
obvious as this, even in the dead of night. By thunder,
I want to catch those bastards, before they skin the
White Elf."

"Perhaps the Norseman is right," said Zyra. "Perhaps we could catch them by morning if we were to
travel all night."

"Of course we could," said Volmar. He glanced back
at the Amazon woman, for whom he was gaining a
grudging respect—especially when her opinion coin-
cided with his.

Ali Ben Kara pondered this for a moment. He, too,
had learned to value the Amazon Princess' judgment,
even if, occasionally, it did seem to be a trifle rash.

Leaping astride Ailwon's gray stallion, for instance—
without ever having ridden before, and having been
forewarned of the horse's wild nature—had certainly
been a rash act. And yet she had made it work for her.
Now, two days later, she was riding as though she had
been doing it all her life. The Shakín looked toward
the Vandorian, Hugh Oxhine, for possible support.
But the archer was staring off the other way. Ben Kara
had noted that Hugh refused to enter any discussion
with which Zyra had involved herself. The Shakín had
quickly fathomed Hugh's problem. So much for that,
he thought. He would consult the expert as to the
feasibility of traveling all night.

"What do you feel we should do, Erbin?" he called
back to the Dwarf. "Can you determine if we have any
chance at all to catch them if we were to keep going?"

Erbin sat his pony between his brother and the
Gwarpy, Oolu. His eyes were shadowed beneath his
hood. Accumulated rain dripped from the protective
covering down onto his ample nose, to his reddish
mustache and beard beneath. Since Ailwon's abduc-
tion, the Dwarf's disposition had taken complete
leave of its usual good nature and positive outlook.
He blamed himself totally for the perilous situation of
the White Elf lad. There had been some attempts to
ease the Dwarf's torment, but these had been abandoned when it became apparent that all such attempts would be shunned. To add to this, the unrelenting chase had taxed Erbin's physical reserves,
severely weakened as he was from his leg wound. Now
he maneuvered through the others, pulling to a halt
several paces beyond the Azmurian and the Norseman. He leaned forward on his pony, then swung to
the ground, balancing on his good leg. He held to the
pommel of his saddle with one hand, studying the
muddy tracks carefully. Finally he raised up, and
turned to the others.

"They're not real far away—can't say just how much.
Mebbe only a half day."

But, at that same moment, the keen ears of Oolu

had detected a familiar sound. He jumped off his pony, scrambling through wet grass and wildflowers to the top of a rise off to the left of the group. Only Evrawk had noticed. He too left his small horse, climbing up to where the Gwarpy stood stark still, listening. It was then that Evrawk noticed that the sky had begun to clear.

"You hear it what Oolu hears, Evrawk?" was the whispered question.

"No. What is it, Oolu?"

"Drums. Gwarpy drums, is what...You'll hear quick soon in a minute er two...there!"

"Yes!... just barely... What're they saying?" asked Evrawk.

"Oolu hears 'em good. Shh... lemme listen." He stood still for another moment, his shoulders hunched, his bowed legs planted wide. Suddenly he began to jump up and down.

"What's going on up there?" Hugh had started up toward them.

"Hear them, Hugh? Hear them Gwarpy drums what's tellin' Oolu the great news? We ride on false trail." Oolu cupped his hands, shouting down the hill. "Erbin, Erbin! Don't be sad no more cuz Oolu jist heard the news that ol' Ailwon is still alive, but we ride in the wrong direction. He passed Oolu's home just a short time ago. An tho th' gargs still got 'im, the drums says that we kin catch up yet! Jist foller ol' Oolu! We be there in the morning." He was running down the hill as he shouted the final sentence. The squat muscularity of his furry body propelled him with a leap onto his pony's back. He caught the reins with almost the same motion, shouting gleefully to the little animal who responded instantly, galloping back up the rise that his rider had just descended. Evrawk and Hugh followed quickly, springing onto their own mounts.

"Quit standing there feeling sorry for yerself, you fathead!" Evrawk shouted at his twin brother. "Let's go!"

With a typical lightning change of mood Erbin let go with a loud, "Yahoo!" Then he hopped twice on his good leg, vaulted into the saddle without touching his stirrup and followed his brother and Oolu up the hill, disappearing beyond the crest.

Hugh had to hold Santor in tight rein; the big chestnut sensed the excitement and had the urge to stretch out and run. The archer looked back to the woman astride the now nervously prancing gray and the two men on the stolid black war-horses. The three stared back at the Vandorian in amazed disbelief at the sudden turn of events. "What are we waiting for?" Hugh shouted, and an inner smile flashed behind his stern look. He had acquired an ability to respond almost instantly to an abrupt change of circumstances.

"What's that crazy little beast blabberin' about?" shouted Volmar. "Drums? What drums?"

"*Those* drums!" Hugh shouted back. "Open your big ears, Volmar!" The rhythmic beat of the relayed

message was now heard, though still some distance
away. The archer wheeled Santor, yelling back to the
others, "If Oolu says that this is the direction that
takes us to the boy... then that's the direction I'm
headed! Come on, Volmar! You haven't even the rain
to grumble about anymore!" Hugh eased the reins
and the eager stallion sprang forward. He was grinning broadly as he rode hard after his three companions, in whom he had learned to put such trust.

Zyra and Ben Kara looked toward one another
quizzically, then without another word they galloped
up the rise in pursuit of the others. Only the huge
Norseman remained.

"Damn," he mumbled. He wished he could understand his mercurial companions. He looked up. It had
quit raining. A cool blue had entered the steely gray
of the sky, giving definition to the clouds as they
began to break and blow toward the southwest.
"Damn!" Volmar muttered again. "Get movin', you
stubborn bastard!" The Vilderone stallion thudded
up the hill, carrying the Norse leader out of sight. The
clouds continued to scatter, and the glow of the moon
appeared. The rhythmic beating of drums continued
across the rolling wet grasslands of the land of the
Gwarpys.

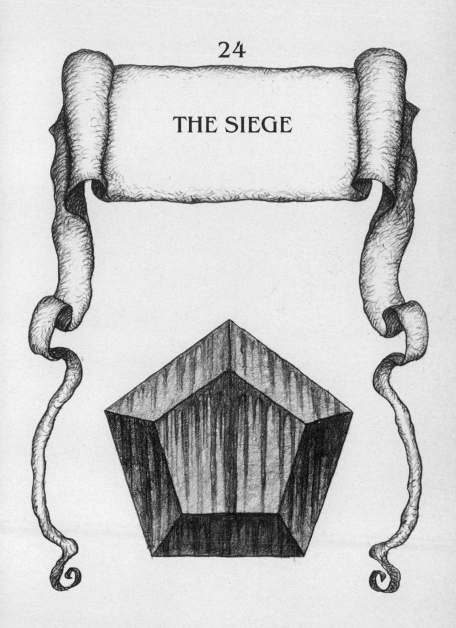

24

THE SIEGE

The King and Queen of Andeluvia had led their people from their homeland through the Retnor Pass, following the same route as the small rebel band of Brown Elves on their ill-fated journey toward Cryslandon. Before Zarin and Wanel reached the Lecune River they had encountered the remains of the slaughtered Elves. Fortunately there was no way to distinguish individuals among the scattered clean bones which was all the carrion birds and beasts of the wild had left. The Andeluvians hastily buried any remains they could find in the sandy earth that covered this harsh land. Having completed the painful chores, the Brown Elves then pushed onward toward the citadel of Alfandel.

The green of the hills facing Cryslandon was marked by the dark panorama of the army of the Death Lord. An unbroken line of barbarians and war machines stretched across the entire horizon, and at the first sight of it King Zarin felt the churn of sickness in his stomach. He turned toward his wife. His eyes were filled with horror, and when he reached toward her the Queen took his hand. She also was frightened. She knew the absolute loathing that had arisen within her husband, that resulted from his dread terror of warfare.

The Andeluvians had pulled their horses to a halt
atop a hillside overlooking the city of the White Elves.
The sky above Cryslandon was filled with heavy gray
clouds. The Brown Elves had approached from the
southwest. Below them a steady stream of people was
leaving, moving across the bridged waters that ran to
the rear of the city, connecting the twin lakes to the
River Garnon.

"It appears that they are evacuating," said Zarin.

"It appears so," replied his wife.

Zarin turned in his saddle. His young advisor, Elsep,
was directly behind him. In times past Elsep would
have been indignant had he not been asked to give
the command to ride forward. But the youth now
appeared confused and frightened, and had been so
since the night of the death of Ianen. Zarin motioned
with his arm, and they started down toward the city.

The road that they followed was narrow, and cut
through a broad field of tall wildflowers and grasses.
The Andeluvian horses trotted forward, raising dust
from the fine, dry earth. The heavy rains that had
drenched Loamend and the southern portions of
Alfandel had not reached Cryslandon, though dark
clouds had threatened daily. The long line of people
that continued out of the city had almost met the
approaching Andeluvians. Some rode in horse-drawn
carts, but most were walking, three and four abreast,
moving silently beneath the overcast sky. The somber
procession was composed mostly of small children
and the elderly. Coming toward Zarin and Wanel was
a middle-aged White Elf, riding a spotted mare. She
appeared to be a leader of the refugees.

"Where are you headed?" Zarin called to her.

"To Penderak," she answered. "All who are too
young or too old to defend our land are going—along
with those of us who will escort them." She had drawn
to a halt beside the Brown Elf King. She turned, and
looked back toward the great army of Golgorath.
"Though I cannot see," she said sadly, "how the city
can possibly hold against those hordes…unless help
arrives soon. The Dwarf army is here, and the skilled

soldiers of Azmuria. But no one else... Our hopes
were high!" A group of small White Elf children was
passing. They stared up at the mounted Brown Elves
with innocent, puzzled eyes. "Move along, children,"
coaxed the Elf, "you will hold up the rest." She turned
back to Zarin and Wanel. "But now," she continued, as
if there had been no interruption, "the situation—as
you can readily see—is dire. The promised Sevena has
not arrived, nor the powerful army of warrior women
that he was to bring. The Norsepeople have not
come...." Her voice trailed off. She looked at the
unarmed Brown Elves. "You are Andeluvians... Have
you come to fight?"

"No," replied Zarin, "we have come to help, but not
to fight."

"Then the heroine—Gwynn—she is not with you? Nor
her rebel band?"

"No. She has been—"

"No one has come that was supposed to," the Elf
interrupted. "Only the murderers have come...." A
shout came from another of the mounted White Elves.
"I must go...." she said hurriedly, and cantered off
down the ranks of refugees.

The Andeluvians pressed forward again, passing
through the entrance gate, crossing the bridge, entering the city. Zarin looked up at the Tower of
Enlightenment and at the surrounding white and
gold buildings. He had not been here in many years,
having chosen to withdraw from any role of leadership as the growing storms of warfare had drawn
nearer. He was struck with the thought that this great
city represented the focal point of the bloody struggle
about to begin. As the Brown Elves rode through the
streets, it seemed that every man and woman that
had remained was armed and ready for battle. But, as
the White Elf had asked: what chance did they have?
Surely the end to the long stalemate was to result in a
crushing victory by the legendary Torgon, and bloody
deaths or enslavement for those who had opposed
him.

"Will we seek out the wizard, Elgan, as we had

discussed?" asked Wanel, as they rode deeper into the city.

"Yes. It seems logical. The Sevena Prince has apparently not come," Zarin replied. He shook his head and shrugged. "We will offer our help...and the bad tidings that we bring."

"Do you wish to seek out this wizard alone?"

He turned to her. "No," he said, "let us no longer be separate. I want you to be with me—please come." She nodded affirmatively, and there was a trace of a smile on her lips. She called to a White Elf soldier—a Lejentor—who was hurrying past. She inquired as to where they would find the wizard, Elgan.

"He is at the northern gate," the Elf shouted above the noise of the city street, "he, the sorcerer Shandar, and the Dwarf leader." He started to pass, then stopped. "Do you know the way?"

"Yes, we've been there," called Wanel, and then as the White Elf started away again, she called, "The governor, Deciedon...where is he?"

"He left many days ago... he has not returned." Then the Lejentor was gone, and Zarin and Wanel looked at each other with relief. They had not relished the possibility of encountering Deciedon when they arrived. They continued on past the Tower of Enlightenment, traversing the length of the city, crossing the canal that encircled the buildings of Cryslandon, finally arriving before the enclosed northern gateway. The King and Queen left their people and entered the white building, climbing toward the top. As they made a turn of the stairwell they stopped suddenly.

"I'm sorry if I startled you. I saw you coming, and wished to greet you...." The voice was deep—though tinged with age—and rich, as the voices of nature are rich. It came from the ancient sorcerer, who was seated on an oval of white stone against a curve of the wall. His eyes were dark and serene, his lips were large and seemed to indicate a smile, though there was no smile formed by them. One long, wrinkled bony hand pulled slowly on the triangle of his beard,

while the other lay relaxed across his thigh. His bare
brown feet showed beneath the simple robe, resting
lightly on the cold of the stairs. "You are, I believe,
King Zarin and Queen Wanel," he said.

"Yes," replied Zarin, "...and you are Shandar."

The sorcerer nodded, and laughed softly, "And I
have been so for many, many years. It sometimes
seems that I have been Shandar...." he laughed
again, "forever." He rose, looking into both their
faces. "I am happy that you have come, despite the
danger into which you have entered." He stepped
down toward them, reaching both hands forward.
Each of them received one of the old man's hands,
feeling the warmth of peace that came from his
grasp. "I see pain in your eyes," he said, "that, I
suspect, extends backward from the terror that exists
in those hills beyond."

They both nodded. "There is pain..." said Wanel.
"We have come to relate sad events... but we come
also to offer you our peace."

The sorcerer smiled. "The last pleases me, very
much, as it will all who are assembled here. As for the
first, let us go up to the others. I'm sure you are not
interested in relating this sadness twice within so
short a time." They climbed to the top of the huge
gateway. There, the Andeluvian King and Queen were
greeted warmly by Elgan, Esrund and the Azmurian,
Kor-Dada, the longtime friend and aid of the Shakín,
Ali Ben Kara.

Zarin and Wanel, with much difficulty, told of the
tragic events that had brought them here; of the
slaughter of the rebel Brown Elves and their sons, the
capture of Gwynn, and the exposure of Deciedon as
the long-hidden traitor. The latter fact would have
been extremely shocking had there not been growing
suspicion over the governor's long absence. Now the
talk turned to their immediate plight. Gwynn was
now—assuming she'd been kept alive—a captive of
Torgon. The condition of Ailwon and his companions—beyond their success at the Marshes of Zorak—

was unknown. They were long overdue, and the traitor—his double identity still unrevealed to Ailwon—had gone in search of the Prince.

The six somber leaders went out atop the gatehouse walls. They looked upon the vast armies and siege equipment of the Death Lord which gave evidence of the harsh reality that all of their existences might soon be halted.

The wizard and the sorcerer stood next to one another, their aged hands resting atop the stone wall. Elgan looked up toward the shrouded sky. "Do you suppose, Shandar," he began, "that it will rain today?"

Shandar leaned forward against the stone. "You know *quite* well, Elgan," he said with mock seriousness, "that I have predicted rain for today."

"And for the last six days..." came the wizard's reply. He stroked his thick white beard.

The sorcerer continued to gaze toward the horizon. "It will rain *today*," he said, nodding his head sagely, without a trace of a smile on his face. The old man suddenly straightened. "He comes," he said quietly, "the traitor comes."

All looked toward the silent army of the Death Lord, but none—save Shandar—could detect any activity. Then Elgan saw it, and Esrund, who called out excitedly: "You're right! He's coming! The swine is headed right for us!"

Now Deciedon could be seen—a black and white figure atop a white horse, moving slowly through the ranks of Torgon's army, between the towering siege machines. He rode into the open, coming steadily forward, his cape flowing, his finely trained stallion high-stepping, its head held proudly.

The group stood silent, watching. The Lejentor slowly traversed the full distance of the ramp and stopped, directly before the gateway. He looked up at those assembled atop the wall. Now his face took the form of friendliness, and delighted surprise. "How marvelous," he called up, "to find you all gathered

here! I assume that you are somewhat taken aback to find me in the company of the barbarians." He gestured toward the army of the Death Lord and laughed. "I can safely refer to them as such; they cannot hear me from this distance."

"We are not surprised by your dramatic entrance, Deciedon," Engan called down. "We have been made aware of your deceit, of your responsibility for the massacre of the Brown Elves, and for Gwynn's capture."

Deciedon frowned. "Then I must hasten to say that I come as an ambassador, to offer terms. Torgon demands complete surrender...But I am disappointed," he went on flippantly. "I truly looked forward to seeing the shocked looks on your faces when I disclosed that it was I—your living legend—who betrayed you... but no matter. I do wish to disclaim taking credit for the murders of the rebel Elves. That was entirely Torgon's idea. I do not usually concern myself with such senseless activity.... The capture of Gwynn, however, was entirely my doing. And she shall remain my prized possession...."

Esrund cursed him, and Deciedon laughed. "I understand your anger," he said, "but you might reserve some of it—I have more to say. The women of Zan-Dura—the army in which you placed so much hope—will not be coming, I have made sure of that. You are doomed to failure. You cannot possibly stand against all of this...." He swept his hand toward the menacing army, looking up at the silent group: his face was now cold, his voice was slow and cruel, "Now. You will surrender to me. You will come forward unarmed. You will come to me, meekly and mildly, and you will present to me the Crownhelm of the Sevenas. Or, you will be annihilated."

"No, Deciedon," Elgan called, "we will not do what you demand. We—all who are within this city—have chosen our course. We shall not submit meekly to your tyranny, to your oppression. We shall not surrender."

Deciedon had expected as much. With a sudden, sweeping movement his white-gloved hand whipped across his body, thrusting Elvgard skyward. "Look!" he shouted. "Do you recognize *this*, you fools! The sword of the White Elves!" He laughed again. "I have captured your Prince Ailwon—your Sevena—your only hope! He is a prisoner of the Death Lord. There is nothing left for you but surrender, or death! Surrender to *me*."

"In a mule's rear we will," spat Esrund, who—with the others—looked down upon the mocking figure that paraded his stallion in a slow circle, all the while brandishing the Elfin sword.

"I am going down to him," said Shandar.

"You can't go down there!" Esrund exclaimed. "The bastard'll kill you!"

"Perhaps."

Elgan looked into the face of his ancient friend, and knew that he would not be deterred. "You feel this way is necessary?" asked the wizard.

"Yes. Even *he* must be given a choice... there *must* be a choice." Shandar looked down at the traitor. "It seems only a minute possibility that Deciedon would accept any diversion from this power-bent path. But should the possibility be realized, it could lead to the freedom of all.... And, beyond this," he concluded, "the Prophecy must be fulfilled." As he said these words he looked again to Elgan, then he turned and left, making no sound as he descended the stairs. The Brown Elves, the Azmurian and the Dwarf all looked at one another helplessly, and then toward the wizard.

Below, the sorcerer exited the gateway. A slow roll of thunder greeted him from the north. He started toward Deciedon, who now sat his horse quietly, watching as the old man approached. A breeze began to stir. Shandar felt the coolness of it against him, and he felt the coolness of the flagstone roadway against his bare feet. He looked past the waiting White Elf traitor to the green hills beyond, seeing beyond the army of the Death Lord, seeing beyond Kiberuk and

Golgorath, seeing across the ocean and beyond. The
thunder came again, louder. Shandar looked up. The
dark clouds were now in motion, and the sorcerer saw
beyond these deep into the yawning reaches of
space. He felt a sudden vibrance of joy. He had
reached the white-and-black-clad figure who sat so
confidently astride the great stallion. In the eyes of
the old man as he looked up, Deciedon looked small
and defenseless.

"Of all in the great city of Cryslandon, you have
been chosen, ancient one?" Deciedon asked. "It is
you who has been chosen to offer the surrender?" He
rested the long blade of Elvgard across his saddle.

"No. It was I who chose to come. There will be no
surrender. I have come to you, my son, to offer you a
gift...."

The traitor eyed Shandar suspiciously. "What kind
of foolishness do you speak, old man?"

"Perhaps you do not realize that it is not too late for
you to choose—perhaps you never realized that you
could choose your course—that your life need not be
corrupt and filled with destruction." The sorcerer
stepped closer to Deciedon. "There is a truth: the
choices that are offered to the sentient beings of the
world are far greater, far more varied, more difficult
and more wonderful than even the miracle of nature.
Choice. It is for this that we struggle with the oppressors. We do not seek revenge, nor justice. We seek—we
demand—the freedom to choose." Shandar's eyes
were filled with the offer of peace. "Deciedon, it is not
too late—"

Shandar's voice was lost to the loud laughter of the
traitor, and to the crash of thunder, which had come
closer. "Now I understand, ancient one," Deciedon
said, as his laughter subsided. "You are trying to *save*
me...that *is* amusing. Now...let me see. You desire for
me to make a choice, is that it?" He looked up,
running his hand across his jaw, "Hmmm... a
choice...Aha! I have it... *this*, old one, is my choice!"
The gleaming blade of Elvgard flashed up. Decie-

don's horse wheeled sideways so that his master
could strike the sorcerer. But the blade of the White
Elves would not come down. Lightning flashed all
around them, and the resonance of thunder followed.
The sword became a thing alive, and flew from the
traitor's grasp, spinning through the air, singing
within the gleam of its flight, ringing across the
surface of the ramp. Deciedon was seized with an
instant of terror. He stared down at Shandar, who had
not moved. The old man looked up at him sadly, then
he deliberately turned and started back toward the
city. Deciedon looked after him, cursed and spurred
his horse, drawing his long dagger. The sorcerer half
turned at the sound of the hoofbeats, catching the
downward thrust of the slashing steel across his chest
and stomach. There were cries of outrage and horror
from atop the walls. Shandar crumpled, holding his
wound. Two White Elf soldiers ran from the gateway
through a torrent of rain that suddenly poured down

from the heavy skies. Deciedon wheeled, and galloped toward the waiting army of Golgorath. A shower
of arrors was released from atop the walls, but sailed
harmlessly past the fleeing figure atop the white
stallion.

The guards ran forward. Shandar had risen to his
knees, and then to his feet. He stood swaying, clutching his wound, as first the guards, than Elgan reached
him. The rain mixed with the gush of blood that ran
from the slash in the old man's body. There was a
shocked silence among those surrounding the sorcerer. None seemed able to speak. He reached toward
Elgan. "Help to support me, old friend," he said, "and
I can walk. Make sure one of you rescues the sword."

They started toward the gate, Shandar leaning
against the white wizard, trailing blood into the road.
Lightning forked above them, followed by a tremendous clap of thunder. Shandar looked sideways at his
friend. Elgan's white hair was plastered to his forehead, he blinked against the downpour.

"As I told you," began the old sorcerer, "I seldom
miss on my predictions of rain." He attempted a
laugh, but blood rushed upward in his throat, running from his mouth and nose, causing him to cough
painfully. The Elfin guard retrieved Elvgard as they
reached the gate, and started inside. An earsplitting
shriek split the wet air, and the wall shook from the
force of a huge flaming sphere that shattered the top
of it, not a hundred feet from the main gateway.
Flames sprang up from both sides of the wall, amid
chunks and fragments of rock and the flow of burning
liquid. The siege of Cryslandon had begun.

25

GWARPY COMPOUND

The Gwarpy drums beat their message across the hills of Loamend: The White Elf Prince had been captured! Led by Oolu, the allied band approached the place of origin of the message. It became clear to the Gwarpy that it would turn out to be none other than the very compound within which he had been raised. He was going home. Without slowing the pace set by his galloping pony, he gleefully related this message to those behind him.

The rain clouds had all fled to the southwest during the night, and the early morning sky was clear when the group rode up to the Gwarpy compound of the family of Oolu. Outside the walls of the compound a Gwarpy beat upon an immense drum fashioned from a hollowed out log. He stopped as the group approached.

The mud walls encircled the compound, at the center of which stood a giant, ashen-barked Bobabo tree. Slender spires of smoke from a half dozen cooking fires extended upward, here and there were collected groups of earthen pots and bowls. Scattered everywhere amidst the cooking fires and pottery were Gwarpys of a variety of sizes and ages. As the allied band dismounted their weary horses, the Gwarpys scurried, scampered or hobbled to gather around them.

Oolu was so excited that he could scarcely contain
himself and made no real effort to do so. He jumped
up and down, and jabbered at a terrific rate; a good
many of his relatives reacted in a like manner. It was
only when Hugh reminded him of their mission that
Oolu quickly began to extract the information for
which they had come. The news was understood
rather poorly by all in the allied band other than
Oolu, for the sentences were so abbreviated, and
delivered so rapid-fire from so many individuals that
it took another Gwarpy to clearly decipher what was
being said. It was reestablished that Ailwon had been
observed yesterday less than a mile from the compound under heavy Vilderone guard, but apparently
in reasonably good physical condition. They learned
the direction of the abductors, learned in fact the
exact route they had taken. Communications had
been constant with those Gwarpys along the route,
and would be resumed within a short time. In the
meantime sabotage was being perpetrated upon the
gargoyles: a landslide (created by the Gwarpys) in the
Arbroic Hills forced the Vilderone forces to head east,
taking a route that would lead them into a blind
canyon.

The members of the allied band were delighted—
once they were able to decipher the meaning of all
the jabbering. The message had, finally, become
clear: they were less than a hard day's ride behind
Ailwon.

The horses were taken to be rubbed down, watered,
and given the usual magic treatment that Gwarpys
offered to horses. There would be a very brief rest for
everyone. Erbin was taken to have his injury administered to. The oldest and wisest within the compound
would perform the application of a medication made
from Bobabo leaves and bark. Erbin was introduced
to Great-Great-Grandma Thoonu. She sat beside a
cooking fire. She was gray and tiny, placid and
sleepy-eyed, and chewed constantly with her toothless mouth. She ordered the Dwarf to do as he was

told. The hot application would be painful. He was to chew on a leaf of the Bobabo—just as she was doing—while he was being taken care of. Erbin followed her instructions. Within a minute he was feeling far more mellow and happy than he ever had during his long career of imbibing. He became fast friends with Great-Great-Grandma Thoonu, and when he left the Gwarpy compound his pockets were stuffed full of Bobabo leaves.

Oolu had seized the brief respite from their pursuit to introduce his friends to his relatives. This was his old friend Evrawk, he began proudly, and this was his new friend, Hugh... and his new friend, Zyra... and his new friend, Tark-Volmar... and his new friend, Ali Ben Kara.... And this was his family: his grandpa, Angu; his grandma, Litu; his ma, Shooku; his pa, Sortu; his sister, Colootu; his brother, Cornu; his sister, Fritu.... The introductions seemed endless, despite Oolu's rapid, half-out-of-breath delivery. There were more sisters, more brothers; there were uncles and aunts, and there was a terrific number of nieces and nephews of a great many sizes—the majority of whom declined to stand still to be introduced, and scurried about the compound, scrambling amidst the huge Bobabo roots. The introductions had been given an added impetus of variety by the chatter, chuckles and chortles of those being introduced. Midway in the process, Tark-Volmar left the group, grumbling beneath his breath about the time wasted trying to converse with a gaggle of gibber-jabbering Gwarpys. He had been sipping at a bitter hot drink, which was made—naturally—from Bobabo leaves, and which would, he was told, fulfill his nourishment needs for the next several hours, along with providing a lift to his spirits. He was dubious, but continued to sip as he strode about the compound muttering, "Gaggle of gibber-jabbering Gwarpys." Suddenly he was struck by the remarkable wit of his own phrase. He began to chuckle, then paused and tried a variation, "Gibbering, gaggling jabber," a gem which sent him into a positive gale of laughter.

The horses were brought forward, ready for riding. The Gwarpys were thanked profusely. The members of the allied band began to mount their steeds. Ali Ben Kara stared in disbelief as Tark-Volmar came forward, in the midst of a nonstop fit of belly laughter. The Norseman vaulted into the saddle, patting the huge gargoyle stallion and speaking with sentimental affection to the same horse that had been referred to previously only as "a stubborn bastard." Volmar's thunderous laughter was joined by Erbin's, as the Dwarf came on the run, showing scarcely more than a limp. He climbed into his saddle, and when he and the Norseman looked at each other they began to laugh even harder. All were mounted, and amid shouted exhortations from Erbin and Tark-Volmar, the allied band galloped out of the Gwarpy compound with Oolu leading the way.

The Gwarpys stood about, watching the disappearing riders. All watched save Great-Great-Grandma Thoonu who sat quietly, moving the well-chewed wad within her mouth from side to side, as she carefully picked fleas from her gray fur.

Opposite: The Gwarpy Compound

26

FIRE CRYSTALS

The midnight sky above Cryslandon was turned bright by the awesome power of the war machines of Golgorath. Red clouds of smoke, rising high above the Elfin citadel, could be seen from miles away.

Thus, as the war vessels of Zan-Dura approached the besieged city, the Amazons were fully prepared to do battle. Aboard the mother ship, Queen Azira's gaze followed the fiery glow upward to where—high above—it met the deep blue of night. She stood atop the elevation in the bow of the ship, in the crimson battle attire of the warrior Queen. She had long ruled over Zan-Dura, yet shortly would come her first moment of warfare. But she had no doubts as to her abilities to lead her sisters in battle. The history of the Amazons had been filled with wars and skirmishes to ward off attackers, and the past two hundred years had seen no relaxation in preparedness, even though there had been no more than an occasional skirmish with raiding forces sent by the Witch of Zorak.

The powers derived from the Crystal of Kresna propelled the eighteen ships of the fleet at the maximum of speeds. They turned a wide bend of the River Garnon, and the great city came into full view. For two days it had been brutally pounded and battered by the war machines of the army of the

Death Lord. It was beset by dozens of fires, the air
about it was choked by the dark billowings of acrid
smoke. The northern walls had long since succumbed to the battering, allowing the huge catapults
to move close to the city. Now the final barriers were
near to crumbling in a number of places. Siege
towers had been rolled close to the inner walls,
powered by teams of Vilderone horses and the massive strength of the Borgs. Fierce fighting had ensued
at the tops of the walls, defended by White Elves,
Azmurians, Dwarfs, and the Norsemen who arrived
shortly after the siege began. They were desperately
fighting to hold back the seemingly endless throngs
of savage Gnomes that surged upward. Already some
of the barbarians had successfully scaled the walls,
and hand-to-hand combat was occurring at the outer
edges of the city.

The Amazon fleet reached the headwaters of the
River Garnon. As they approached, Azira had quickly
determined the outer layout of the city, and directed
their strategy. The first necessity was obvious: the war
machines must be destroyed. The lead warship, the
mother ship and six others entered directly into the
city, splitting their number, half moving eastward and
half west through the circular canal, headed toward
the northern wall that had borne the brunt of the
attack. The remainder of the ships also split their
number, heading both northeast and northwest,
against the flow of waters that came from the twin
lakes. Once into position they would attack from the
rear.

As the Queen ship moved through the canal, Azira
could see the furor of activity within the city. People
swarmed about the major fires, attempting to subdue
them, their faces reddened by the glow from the
flames. Others knelt beside the wounded, or carried
them toward places of safety. Despite such action,
many of them saw the Amazon vessels sailing swiftly
by. With scarcely a pause for reaction to the mys-
teriously powered ships they began to cheer lustily.

© HILDEBRANDT

The mother ship was fast approaching the northern entranceway. The huge gatehouse had been battered at during the entire siege, first with the catapulted explosives, then with huge battering rams, and now with both. It had become the focal point of the attack, for once it was broken the barbaric hordes could stream directly into the heart of the city, across the largest bridge of those that spanned the canal.

All during the encounter, the gatehouse had been bravely defended—despite the bombardment—by the deadly archers of Azmuria, and by the bowmen of Alfandel. But now the thick walls of the tower had been severely damaged, the huge doors had been blown and battered open, and the portcullis was being hammered at by an enormous battering ram powered by a hundred of the hulking Borgs. Exploding projectiles continued to crash against the sides of the wall, occasionally obliterating a half dozen or more of the Borgs, crushing their huge bodies with a barrage of fragmented, flaming rock. But others would move immediately to take their places, stoically stepping across the charred and broken bodies of

their fallen brothers. The portcullis would give way at any instant. The defenders were ordered to retreat.

The Amazon vessels moved quickly into the docking areas. Queen Azira left the mother ship, calling instructions to the other ship leaders: "Take the Fire Crystals to vantage points along the wall. Quickly!" Teams of six started from the ships with the great weapons of Zan-Dura. There were four of them with four more aboard the ships outside the city, and four bearers to carry each. One woman—the 'Tessalier'—directed the firing, while the one who would actually unleash its power was the 'Kovier.' The Fire Crystal from the mother ship was set up to aim directly at the gateway entrance, where—from behind—came the bludgeoning sounds of the battering rams and explosions against the white stone walls. A hissing of an enormous flaming meteor-like projectile passed above Queen Azira, to explode right above the canal. The shuddering force of it slammed her against the rail of the bridge. Burning fragments of metal showered all about her. Azira managed to keep her footing. She looked back. The waters of the canal still rocked with the force of the explosion. One of the ships of the Amazon fleet had disappeared, had been replaced by flame and smoke, by jagged slabs of metal, and by grim floating reminders of what an instant before had been the living flesh of Amazon women. Azira choked back tears of outrage, and turned to face the hordes of the Death Lord.

With a great crunching groan, the battering ram broke through the stout resistance of the portcullis, accompanied by triumphant screams from the Gnomes who were massed just beyond. Into the city of the White Elves poured the barbarians, emitting their terrible war screams; the first wave pouring through with thousands massed behind. Facing them, in the center of the bridge, were six warrior women and their Queen, standing in position behind the Fire Crystal. Azira gave the command to fire; there was no need to direct the Kovier toward a target. She leveled the point of her weapon toward the mass of shrieking barbarians rushing at her. Her mind erased all else but the target. Her mind and body became one with the power of the Crystal of Kresna which was projected at the enemy. As the Kovier released the power of the Fire Crystal her mind and soul were cleansed of every trace of malice or hate, and her target drew the charge toward itself. The power leaped outward with a blinding flash, the air was charged with the heat of a livid, white bolt of energy that forked and split and sought its target, striking with a crackling burst of white light, striking again, and again.... The barbaric shrieks for blood ceased as the bolt of the Fire Crystal bored through and encompassed the throng, leaving only charred remains. Those outside the wall fell back, their war cries having turned to screams of terror.

The remaining two Amazon weapons had been placed on top of the wall, the fourth having been destroyed along with the ship, while the war vessels bearing the other Fire Crystals had moved into position. And now began a colossal battle between the weapons of the warrior women, and the huge black war machines of the Death Lord. The people within the city—rejuvenated by the powers that had arrived from the far end of the continent—massed their forces beside the foot soldiers of Zan-Dura to await the outcome. The hordes of Golgorath retreated to the Arbroic hillsides, and they also waited....

The air became filled with the fiery flight of hurled, roaring meteors, and with the crackling of the forked charges of the Fire Crystals. The sky about the city was filled with the brightness of explosions that left craterous blots in the earth, that blasted great chunks from the walls, that sent geysers of flame and sparks skyward, and obliterated beings and weapons in an instant. Again and again, the living lightning charged the night air... striking the ponderous machines of the Death Lord, exploding against them, searing, burning... boring through the thickness of iron.... One by one the huge catapults and siege towers were bent and twisted by the power of the Crystals of Kresna. Finally, just as the first traces of dawn began to compete with the lurid light of warfare, the Death Lord's machines lay in smoking ruins. The Amazons had triumphed, though not without heavy losses. In all, six of their weapons—and those that had operated them—had been completely destroyed, and one other was inoperable. But every single major weapon of the Death Lord had been rendered useless. The thrust of the struggle for Cryslandon had been turned.

Behind the battered inner walls of the city, the cavalry of the White Elves—the Lejentors—sprang to their saddles, wheeling their mounts into formation, galloping across the bridge, through the shattered central gateway, charging toward the massed army of the invaders. Following them were the mounted swordsmen of Azmuria. Then came the Amazons—led by their Queen—and with them were the foot soldiers of the White Elves, the robust Norsemen from Norbruk, and the people's army of the Dwarfs of Penderak.

Atop a hill, Deciedon stood beside his horse. He watched as the allied armies approached in a disciplined phalanx across the narrow plain between the city and the foothills of the Arbroics. He then looked to the long stretch of Torgon's forces. He saw row after row of fierce Gnomes, the masses of huge Borgs, and thousands of the sullen, armored Vilderones. The allies were yet outnumbered. But these Amazon women had arrived long before he had planned, bringing with them the awesome, unprepared-for weapons. His plans had been dealt a severe setback. By this time he had been positive that he would be in possession of both the city and the Crownhelm.

He mounted the white stallion and spurred it to a fast canter. Behind a hill—out of sight of the approaching allies—stood a huge catapult, which had been held back for just such an unlikely eventuality.

The meteor-like projectile had already been set
ablaze, the chain that would project it was pulled taut
by the massive windlass. Deciedon rode to the top of
the hill which hid the catapult. The Lejentors—whom
he had led for so many years—were so close that he
could almost make out their faces. They were following the pattern of a maneuver he had himself devised,
their horses moving at a fast canter, the spearhead of
the leading troop bristling with lances, the sides
impregnably defended. Deciedon signaled, and the
catapult was fired. The flaming metal sphere roared
beyond the advancing horsemen, exploding above
and slightly to the side of the Amazon formation.
There were casualties but the steadily moving column quickly regrouped. Another signal was given,
this time by the Vilderone commanders, and the
armies of Golgorath surged forward to engulf the
puny force that dared oppose them.

Deciedon waited, still convinced that those he had
betrayed must certainly succumb to the superiority of
numbers. But the traitor had for so long occupied
himself with plots and schemes, and had so long
been concerned with nothing beyond the acquisition
of power, that he had forgotten what he had once
known. He had long since blinded himself to the
fighting quality of peoples in quest of freedom. He
had forgotten the fierce spirit that enabled them to
overcome overwhelming odds. Thus Deciedon's
mind—normally so agile and lightning quick—was
slow to grasp what was taking place before him.

Like a sword thrust into the heart of a great hulking
body, and just as deadly, the allied forces fought at
the heart of the great throngs from Golgorath. Accus-
tomed to easy victory, the hordes of barbarians fell
into confusion, those on the outskirts unable even to
reach their intended victims. Slowly the central core
began to retreat from the ferocity of the allied fighting that left scores of Gnomes and Borgs piled at the
center of the battlefield. Those who wanted to retreat
had to virtually fight their way through the press of

their fellows, only to encounter a grim circle of
Vilderones turning them back into the melee. Utter
chaos resulted. But it was not until the army of Torgon
had succumbed completely to fear, forsaking any
trace of discipline, battling furiously with one another,
it was not until then that Deciedon comprehended
that the superiority of numbers had been meaning-
less—had, in fact, contributed to what had now become a rout.

Skirting the battlefield, the traitor fled northward
toward the sea-girt, rockbound safety of Golgorath.

The Vilderones attempted to turn back the tide of
retreating barbarians, bellowing commands to stand
their ground, cursing and hacking with swords at the
terrified Gnomes and Borgs. But this only added to
the rampaging terror and confusion. The remaining
gargoyles reluctantly joined the full-scale retreat to
the north.

At last the fierce attack of the allied armies came to
a halt. Their foe had virtually disappeared, leaving
scores of dead and wounded. The allies had won the
day. They had won against overwhelming odds, had
turned away the army of Golgorath, had saved themselves and kept the Crownhelm from the hands of the
Death Lord. As they turned back toward Cryslandon
they saw that the Tower of Enlightenment was unscathed, stood yet as a citadel against the power of
oppression. But the northern section of the city had
been pounded to rubble, scorched and gouged to a
state beyond recognition. And, while buildings and
walls could be rebuilt, the lives that had been lost
could not be reclaimed.

All across the hills, and across the narrow plain, lay
the bodies of the wounded and maimed, the dying
and the dead.

The Andeluvians—those who were not administer-
ing aid within the city—went out into the battlefield,
even before the last of the fighting had ceased. They
began at once to give help to the wounded and

comfort to the dying. With them were their King and Queen, Zarin and Wanel.

The Brown Elves could see the complete impracticality of carrying the wounded back into the city, which was still beset by numerous fires. Aid would be given—to both the allies and enemy—right on the field of battle... and here the dead would be buried.

The Andeluvian King and Queen knelt beside the casualties, giving words of comfort to those who cried out for help, searching for signs of life within the silent forms. They touched the bodies, both the living and the dead, with tenderness and love. The dread terror and nausea that Zarin had expected to experience did not occur, and when it did not he gave it no further thought.

The allied armies were returning. Zarin and Wanel saw them approaching, but their attention was taken by a lone figure, fifty yards distant, kneeling over the

body of another. As they approached they saw that the kneeling figure was a young Amazon woman, apparently uninjured, but racked with frantic sobs. They reached her, and Wanel knelt beside her. The woman for whom she wept was dead. There was a gaping wound just below the older woman's throat, where a fragment of the exploded fireball had pierced her body. Her head was twisted to the side, her neck apparently broken. The warrior's helmet had been torn loose, and her silver hair spread outward on the grass. Her face was soft, calm, a strong face—even in death.

Wanel put her arm about the heaving shoulders of the young woman. "Was this your mother?" asked the Queen. The Amazon tried to speak, but was unable to do so. Zarin knelt down. He took the distraught woman's hand. "You are her daughter?" he asked gently.

"We are *all* her daughters," she managed to blurt out, "and her sisters... This was the Queen of Zan-Dura... Queen Azira is dead!"

27

DESPERATE DECISION

The elation at having turned back the hordes of the Death Lord had been extremely brief. Activity within the city had scarcely paused. The struggle to save the lives of the wounded and to quell raging fires continued at a desperate pace. Within war-torn Cryslandon, the people of the allied nations worked shoulder to shoulder. They would work to save the living now; those they could not save and those already gone they would mourn later.

Within the hall which surrounded the Tower of Enlightenment, Elgan paced slowly back and forth. The wounded Shandar sat, half leaning against the arm of a chair of white stone. His right hand and arm were held against the heavy bandage that bound his wound. His breathing had become extremely labored, yet his face showed little sign of the approaching death that he had spoken of so matter-of-factly during the time since he had been struck down. The rain that had fallen during the first day of the siege had not resumed, but the clouds remained heavy and there was little light within the cavernous hall. Elgan stopped his pacing opposite his old friend.

"You could be lying down," he declared for the half-dozenth time. "This heroic stance is not necessary."

Shandar shrugged, wincing slightly with pain.

"Heroism plays no part in my sitting up," said the old man. "I have little time left for sitting up. I shall spend considerable time lying down. When the time is right, I will do as you have so dutifully insisted I do." He smiled. "It is a pity you will be elsewhere..."

The wizard shook his head. "I'm not sure I approve of your levity in view of a situation that might mean the demise of all of us."

"It is from you, old friend," returned the sorcerer, "that I have learned to extract what humor might be garnered from a situation—no matter how dire. I believe we have both taken considerable comfort from such a sane philosophy. But I in no way wish to demean your sadness."

"I know."

Shandar stood, grimacing as he did so. He began to take up the pacing where Elgan had left off. The old wizard observed that the sorcerer actually seemed to have gained strength in the past several hours. But Elgan fostered no illusions. It would be heedless to question Shandar's claims of his impending death. He was about to speak, to assure the dying sorcerer that he perfectly understood that Shandar had in no way attempted to make light of his own troubled emotions. But at that moment, Esrund and the Azmurian, Kor-Dada, entered the hall. Both of them were bone-weary, their faces blotched with soot, their eyebrows and beards scorched. "The fires are pretty well under control," said the old Dwarf. "Have you decided?"

"Yes," said Elgan, stroking his long white beard, "we will not wait...not against a faint hope that Deciedon was lying. We—all who will come with me—must leave as quickly as possible. It is a hard five days to Golgorath. The Day of Fulfillment is almost upon us. We'll wait as long as possible—until the final moment...Then, Torgon must be faced."

"And who is to face him?"

"I shall."

Esrund looked down at the floor, slowly nodding

his head. "That makes sense, all right," he said, looking up quickly at the Azmurian. "If anybody can face that filthy swine, it is Elgan!"

"Yes," replied Kor-Dada, "this would be our only hope. It is better this way than to await another attack."

Esrund nodded again, more resolutely this time. But when he turned back to Elgan, his face looked very resigned and sad. "We'll go get things ready, then," he said, and he looked awkwardly toward Shandar, not knowing what to say to the dying man. The sorcerer stepped close to the Dwarf. Blood was oozing through the bindings, and Esrund stared at it. Shandar placed his hands on the Dwarf leader's wide shoulders. "There is nothing you need say to me, my friend," he said. "What is to take place is not a tragedy." Esrund stared hard into the dark eyes of the old sorcerer. He tried again to speak, but could not. He turned quickly, and limped toward the door.

Kor-Dada embraced Shandar, being careful not to cause the old man any additional pain. "I, too, do not know how to word my thoughts," he said, tearfully. "You have been with my people since before the beginning of our civilization. I did not believe you could ever die..."

"My time has been longer than long. Believe me, this body is glad to go. Good-bye, Kor-Dada...I wish you peace and love...Please tell this to all."

The Azmurian nodded, and strode quickly away.

Shandar sighed, coughing violently when he did so. He made his way back to the chair, easing himself into it. Elgan moved beside him. "I'm sorry," said the wizard, "that you cannot be at Evshimin."

"Yes," Shandar said, smiling at the thought, "but I knew when we took the Crown that this would not be possible." He looked at Elgan. "But I shall go there. This transition that we face is not so great. We both know this. It is just that we have gone on so long that we often lose sight of this knowing." The tears came suddenly to Shandar's eyes. He touched the weathered face of the wizard, feeling the texture of the skin, feeling the being that was Elgan...for the last time. "I am sad," he said,"I know we can never really be separated, but I am sad that I will never again see that which has become very dear." Softly he touched Elgan's cheek again. "I hope, now, that you will ignore my preachings about the philosophy of humor during times of stress...I hope you will leave quickly, my friend..."

Elgan dropped to his knees before the sorcerer. He reached slowly forward, touching the bloodied wound of Shandar. When he withdrew his hand, it was wet with blood, and he touched it to his lips. The friends of a thousand years looked at one another for the final time. Then Elgan stood, and without speaking he left the hall. The great gold door closed quietly in the corridor of the entranceway. The wizard was gone.

Shandar sat motionless.

He felt very alone. His mind traversed the long passageway of years, of the struggles upon the land, of rising hopes and of deadly despairs. And the journey's end now seemed so bleak. For this crestfallen moment, the old man lost his grasp of the serenity he had learned during the centuries of his years. During this bleak moment, his fears turned upon him, making him painfully human. It was a sudden spasm of physical pain that awakened Shandar from the long moment of his depression. His body stiffened, and he gasped. He stood upright, his hand clutching his chest. He looked about the shadowed hall, and from the darkness came the vision of a child. Shandar stretched forth his hand, and again he touched the birth-slickened skin of the babe, and again he heard his own words proclaiming the heir to the Crownhelm of Alfandel, proclaiming the Sevena, proclaiming Ailwon, the savior of Urshurak.

Resolution returned to him. He would do what he had told Elgan he would do—go to the upper room of the Tower of Enlightenment; he would climb to the Crown's keep. He would wait there. He would stay alive to wait against the overwhelming odds that the White Elf Prince would arrive to be given the Crown and the Sword. He crossed the wide expanse of the hall, passing beneath the arched entrance to the tower, and he started upward. The traitor had not lied, he knew this. But Ailwon *would* come; this, also, he knew. The climb up the long curves of the stairway was arduous and pain-filled. The old man's breathing came in tortured gasps. The life of his body was being slowly drawn from him. But there was a long flow of peace that entered him as he ascended...

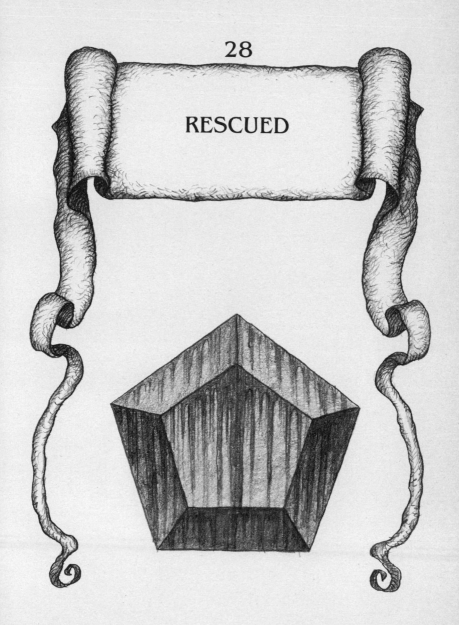

28

RESCUED

The creatures known as the Vilderones had been created by Torgon himself, during the second century of his reign of terror. These gargoyle beasts possessed the brute power of the Borgs and the savage instincts of the Gnomes. And although they had been provided, also, with an intelligence which had considerably greater depth than either of the barbarian races, it was limited, for their capacity to experience emotions was also limited. Only their need for savagery had been given no bounds.

Yet among such creatures, the laws of survival work even more strongly—and the fittest do indeed survive, adapting to the primal drive for life. The Vilderone general, Rogmun, had developed a capacity to think that considerably exceeded that of his fellows; thus he had risen to his high rank, and thus he had led the mission to capture the Elfin Prince. Unknown to Torgon, the gargoyle general had also experienced an emotion more acutely than most of those he commanded. The emotion was fear—a prime necessity in survival. Rogmun had carefully disguised this by his deliberately brutal manner and actions. This inner stirring had become especially pronounced since the night that he had broken into the domain of the wizard, and had encountered the ghostly vision.

He had, at the same time, experienced the mysterious sensation of the voice-like ringing within his inner hearing. None of his underlings had apparently heard the strange sounds; or if they had, they—like he—were too afraid to mention it. By the following morning, the sounds had disappeared, and there had been no reoccurrence—until they had captured the boy. Since then, the horrible sensation had plagued him often, especially when the Elfin lad was nearby, especially when the youth looked directly at him with his clear, undisguised gaze. Rogmun had protected himself in the only way he knew: he escalated the brutal treatment he would normally have dealt a prisoner. Such treatment had its limits. Torgon had absolutely demanded that the boy be brought to Golgorath alive. But no matter how often or how roughly Rogmun had abused Ailwon, the White Elf Prince had refused to display any feelings of hate. The Vilderone's actions would arouse the youth to anger, but never hate. This was evident, and Rogmun could not understand it. Brutal treatment provoked hate; it had always been apparent to him. Yet the attitude of this strange youth was unchanging: even in the midst of his anger, it seemed he understood Rogmun's confusion. And it was during such encounters with the Elf that Rogmun would detect the faint beginnings of the ringing voices. Then he would escape the presence of the lad, as quickly as he could.

It was shortly before daybreak, and Rogmun awoke in a particularly bad temper. They were camped within a low mountain range, having still not escaped the land of the Gwarpys. They found themselves confronted by the unscalable walls of the canyon. This misfortune had aroused as much suspicion as irritation, and two extra guards had been set out before the Vilderones had bedded down for the night.

Now Rogmun stood up, gathering his helmet and weapons. For a moment he stared, unseeing, at the pinkish fringe of light that blossomed up behind the mountains to the east. Then he started through the

encampment, growling at the sleeping gargoyles to
wake up. He approached the White Elf Prince, chained
to a Bobabo tree. He paused before the youth,
wondering how the lad could sleep so soundly sitting
upright, his arms spread outward and above him by
the manacles about his wrists. Rogmun gave the
youth a hard jab in the ribs with his heavy boot,
causing Ailwon to grunt and jerk his head up sharply.

"Wake up, Elf!" growled the Vilderone. He stared
down at the White Elf, and Ailwon stared back but did
not speak. Rogmun turned away, glancing at Ailwon's
guard to make sure the gargoyle appeared alert. He
strode to his horse. No ringing sounds, he thought,
with satisfaction; he saddled his black steed. He
checked each position of the lookouts, all of whom
were posted a considerable distance from the encampment, insuring that no one would be able to
sneak close before being detected. Each guard appeared to be awake and alert. Rogmun tramped back
toward the center of the camp to join the others in the
morning meal.

As he headed back to join his henchmen, the
Vilderone general glanced past the captive Elf, toward
the inclining boulders and rocks, among which grew
the spreading Bobabos. Rogmun neither heard nor
saw anything unusual.

Moving with the stealth of predators, the members
of the allied band crept closer and closer, bent low to
the ground, and in some cases crawling, staying
behind the cover of boulders or trees or undergrowth.
They crept to within only yards of the positions of the
guards on the near side of the encampment.

Ali Ben Kara motioned, and two figures slid forward, flat on their stomachs. Erbin and Oolu slithered
behind and between rocks and foliage, almost as
silently as snakes. Soon they had disappeared. Their
companions waited. The distant voices of the gargoyles drifted up to them.

Hugh lay flat, peering through heavy undergrowth.
To his right was a rounded boulder which he would

circle when the moment came. He looked to his left, and could see Zyra, crouched low, her sword already in her hand. Only a few days ago, he would have completely discounted the Amazon's chances of killing one of the hulking Vilderones—especially when the formidable task demanded that the gargoyle be killed in almost complete silence. But now he knew Zyra's chances of success to be at least as good as his own.

Beyond her was Ali Ben Kara, and beyond him was the Norseman, Tark-Volmar. But both had moved beyond the scope of Hugh's vision. Somewhere between them was Evrawk, who had finally been made to acknowledge that he could not single-handedly cope with a brute over three times his size, and would not act independently of the attack on the encampment.

Hugh worried a bit about Tark-Volmar's ability to attack in silence, though he entertained no doubts about the bulky Norseman's fighting ability. But thus far Volmar had moved as silently as the rest, and the Vandorian decided he had better tend to his own chores.

The Vilderone guard—little more than a score of paces away—stood up, turning slowly, looking directly at the spot where Hugh lay hidden. Every muscle in the archer's body grew taut, his fingers clenched the hilt of his dagger. The visor of the gargoyle's helmet was pushed back, and Hugh could clearly see the brutish features of his face. The creature stared blankly for a moment, then stretched his bulky physique, yawned, turned and sat back down holding a long javelin. The Vandorian detected a slight movement in the branches of the trees a half hundred yards beyond. There was a pause, then another movement—slightly closer to the encampment. The guard had taken no note of this, and Hugh allowed himself a quiet sigh. Oolu was in the Bobabos, moving through the network of branches toward the captive Ailwon. A moment passed. Then, from the

trees, came the short, chortling sound of some unknown bird of Loamend: the first signal from the
Gwarpy. More silence, then there was the sound of an
object striking the ground, then rolling. This would be
the work of Erbin. There was the distant sound of
Ailwon's guard, as he moved to investigate the noise.
Another silence. The bird of Loamend chortled again.
Hugh drew a deep breath, glancing toward Zyra's
place of hiding. The Amazon had disappeared from
sight, and was already creeping forward with her
sword at the ready. Hugh rose to a half-crouch, and
silently started around the boulder, toward the unsuspecting Vilderone guard...

Ailwon moved his body in an attempt to work out
the stiffness of the night. This was no easy chore,
confined as he was by the chains that bound him to
the tree. And he dared not appear as if he were trying
to free himself. The Vilderones—especially Rogmun—
needed far less excuse than this to administer a kick
or a blow. His face was bruised in a half dozen places,
and it seemed that every bone in his body ached from
the thumpings he had received so regularly.

At the beginning of his period of captivity, Ailwon
had acknowledged to himself that he was genuinely
frightened. Not only was he a prisoner of these
fearsome creatures, but—if the traitor was to be
believed—so was Gwynn. He had not let his fright be
known to the gargoyles, for he had guessed that
showing fear would only accentuate the brutality of
his treatment. And then the fear left him, replaced by
hopeless despondence. The entire quest—the entire
direction of his life—seemed doomed. For a period of
time, Ailwon felt extremely sorry for himself. Finally
he had accepted the reality of his circumstances...
despite their grim quality. He would live from moment
to moment, ever watchful of an opportunity to
escape.

Such alertness enabled Ailwon to distinguish the
unusual quality of the chortling sound that came

from the branches above him. During the time spent in Loamend, he had heard no such birdcalls before. He looked up, at first seeing nothing through the thick foliage of the Bobabo, then he discerned a brown form among the green. The form moved quietly—and then...yes! it was...Peering down at him, grinning from ear to ear, was the magnificent Gwarpy face of Oolu!

The White Elf almost forgot himself—almost cried out joyfully. But he checked himself and looked away from the branches. Ailwon waited. Then he heard—off to his left—the sound of an object striking a boulder, then rolling... Ailwon's guard stood, looked toward the direction of the noise, then moved to investigate. A couple of the Vilderones in the group gathered by the campfire had also looked up at the sound of the striking object. But when the guard took action, they returned to their morning meal.

Now Ailwon could detect movement from the opposite side of the tree, where the chain that bound him was fastened. Oolu, hanging head down from a low branch—discovered the chain was clasped by a metal rod. In another moment, a whisper came from behind Ailwon, telling him: "...only jist a twig's holdin' them chains now what yer kin bust quick soon, yep...Don't do nothin' til ol' Erbin hollers..." A pause, then a soft chuckle: "Ol' Oolu's sure glada see ol' Ailwon, yep." A soft rustle of leaves indicated the Gwarpy's departure. In another moment, Ailwon heard a second-chortling bird sound: this one had come from a tree further away. The Elfin lad was unaware at the time that this had signaled the approach of the four, who had crept silently toward the Vilderone lookouts.

He waited quietly, though it felt as if a dozen butterflies fluttered about within his stomach. Having discovered nothing strange, Ailwon's guard had returned. One of the gargoyles stood up from the campfire, a cup of the bitter Vilderone brew in his hand. He started toward Ailwon. This was a morning ritual. The Elf Prince would be released long enough

to drink the steaming brew. It would be discovered
that the chains had been tampered with. Unless
something happened quickly, Ailwon would have to
act on his own.

The Vilderone had almost reached him. He was
helmetless, and his close-set eyes appeared to be still
filled with sleep. He emitted a guttural cough, and
spat into the loose brown dirt. Just then the voice of
Erbin let loose a completely unintelligible, but very
loud war cry. Every Vilderone head jerked toward the
scream that came again just as a Vandorian arrow
was propelled from the foliage, puncturing the neck
of Ailwon's guard, who dropped instantly, the arrow
having run through the entire thickness of flesh and
sinew. Ailwon pulled hard against the tautness of the
chain. The twig snapped as the White Elf sprang to his
feet. Still holding the steaming cup of brew, the
gargoyle pulled free his sword, taking one step

toward Ailwon, and beginning—but never completing—another.

The youth swung hard, the chain came forward in a long, ringing arc, striking the Vilderone across the left side of his face, mashing his nose sideways. The hulking creature went over backward, steaming brew and all.

Ailwon leaped across his fallen enemy. Dust rose from the shuffling activity of hand-to-hand combat, along with the furious cursing of Vilderones and the oft-repeated war cry of the Dwarf, Erbin. He had joined Evrawk in a fierce attack upon a javelin-wielding gargoyle, who backed steadily away from the hacking battle-axes, his eyes showing clear astonishment at the ferocity of the brother Dwarfs.

Another gargoyle charged Ailwon, a mace held in his fist. The lad swung with both hands, and the length of chain snaked out, wrapping about the onrushing Vilderone's neck. Ailwon pulled, breaking the neck of the gargoyle. The lad pulled the chains free of the silent body. He glanced quickly about. Though the fighting seven of the allied band were still outnumbered, they were fast reducing this disproportion. The Amazon Princess, Zyra, ducked under the ponderous swipe of a Vilderone blade, lunging forward, driving her sword beneath the protective breastplate of her adversary, leaping to the side as the large figure fell toward her. She whirled about, in search of another to feel the bite of her steel. Just beyond her, Hugh Oxhine swung his long blade with both hands, while beside him Tark-Volmar powered his huge battle-ax in a like manner. Three of the Vilderones—Rogmun included—engaged them, unable to gain an advantage over the furiously attacking pair.

Ali Ben Kara crouched in the position of the Azmurian bowman. He let fly, and his arrow—deadly at more than a hundred yards—pierced the chest of a gargoyle sentry, who had come on the run from his position on the southern slope. The sentry fell, his

Opposite: Rogmun and Ailwon

death cry echoing back to the campsite. He slid
downward, carrying small rocks and shale with him,
finally coming to rest a few paces from the body of a
second guard, who had also met a deadly Azmurian
arrow. A third advancing sentry had halted in his
tracks, ducking behind cover, starting back up the
hillside. Ben Kara, bow in hand, started after him on
the run.

Ailwon detected movement behind him, and turned
quickly. The first gargoyle he had knocked down had
recovered, and was advancing on him again, blood
smearing his pale leathery face. Ailwon sprang
toward him, swinging the lethal chain lengths. The
Vilderone was better prepared this time, and had
secured a stout spear. But still he backed off from the
lashing chains.

Through the fray, Rogmun saw the Elfin Prince, his
unprotected back toward the Vilderone general. Rogmun took a final swing with his mace at his adversar-
ies, then left his henchmen to continue the battle with
the archer and the Norseman. He charged toward the
youth, the black bile of his hate filling his huge form.
At almost the same instant, Tark-Volmar muscled his
battle-ax through the defense of the gargoyle before
him, shattering the steel of his helmet and the hard
bone of his skull. The Norse chieftain whirled. He
looked up and saw Ailwon.

"Magic boy!" bellowed Volmar. "Behind you!"

The blond-haired youth twisted around, leaping
sideways in the same movement, as the heavy gargoyle mace swung harmlessly past. He leaped again.
Now his back was to the Bobabo where he had been
bound. He swung the long chains, warding off the
attacks of Rogmun.

"Hold the bastard for just another second, boy!"
Tark-Volmar shouted, running over and between fall-
en and still-fighting combatants. Rogmun turned
away from Ailwon, rushing to meet Volmar's charge.
The bulky figures met, just to the left of the smolder-
ing campfire, the dark Vilderone general spitting

words of hatred, the red-bearded Norse chieftain
bellowing and cursing. They circled, swinging
furiously, dust rising, mace and battle-axe clashing.
Then Tark-Volmar lunged, driving his weapon downward, splintering steel, flesh and bone, cleaving deep
into the chest of the gargoyle creature. Rogmun fell
backward, falling into the nearly spent fire. Ashes and
sparks burst upward from the force of the huge form.
The Vilderone moaned, rolling sideways from the
coals of the campfire. Then he lay face down, and did
not move.

The battle was over. Every one of the Vilderones had
fallen, and appeared to have expired. The one-sided-
ness of the outcome was almost overwhelming, and it
took the victorious allies an instant to comprehend it.
Then the jubilation burst forth. Ailwon was free! Their
elation exploded in shouts of joy, and in embraces.

There was one of the enemy who was in the throes
of dying, but had not yet expired. The Vilderone
general, Rogmun, opened his eyes. His gaze was
distorted by a red haze, and through it he saw the tall
Vandorian hesitate, then move toward the white-clad
Sevena. To the dying Rogmun, the movement of the
archer seemed to unfold with an extreme slowness...
He saw the tall man embrace the boy, saw him lift the
youth, saw the white glow of the aura that surrounded
them, and heard the beginnings of their laughter
which steadily lifted in pitch, becoming the mysterious ringing voices within Rogmun's inner hearing.
And there was no longer a fear of it, as the last breath
of his life escaped him...

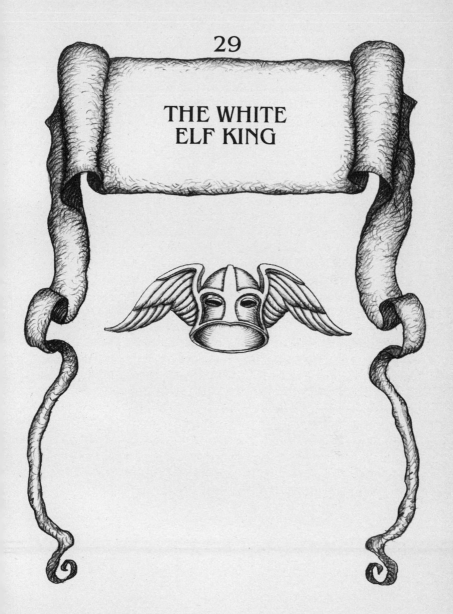

29

THE WHITE
ELF KING

It was midmorning of the second day since Ailwon's rescue as he and the allied band approached Cryslandon. Heavy clouds continued to fill the skies above the White Elf citadel, allowing only patches of light to fall across the distant hills. Ailwon had begun to experience a feeling of elation as they had drawn nearer and nearer. But the appearance of dark smoke, rising from the city's location beyond the hills, served as a damper on his excitement. An ominous sense of apprehension gripped them all and their already rapid pace increased.

But neither Ailwon nor his companions were prepared for the shock that confronted them as they topped a rise and the city came into full view. The land before them was pocked by craters and by still-smoldering skeletons of war machines. The collective moaning of the wounded and dying from many makeshift shelters drew their eyes to the multitudes that still lay across the battlefield. The city itself appeared one third destroyed, with crumbling walls and buildings, and smoke still rising in a dozen places.

The riders moved forward slowly, awestruck and horrified. There were hundreds of people working among the wounded. One of them started toward the approaching band. As he drew nearer, Evrawk declared: "That's Zarin, I believe... yes, that's him, all right." And to Ailwon: "That's Gwynn's uncle—the Brown Elf King."

Zarin appeared to be extremely tired, and yet he moved forward surely and resolutely. He was staring at Ailwon. "You have come," he said. "Wanel was positive you would..."

"Yes," said Ailwon, "but what has happened? What is this horror?"

"The forces of Golgorath laid siege to the city...and almost succeeded in destroying it. The Amazon forces arrived just in time to avert our complete annihilation." He glanced at Zyra as he continued: "Torgon's army was driven away. But, as you can see, the losses on both sides were enormous." He looked back to Ailwon. "We were told by the traitor—before the battle—that you had been captured. After the fighting was finished, it was decided that the armies could wait no longer. It was a desperate decision, but few believed that you would arrive in time, if at all. They have marched to Golgorath. Elgan leads them. The old sorcerer, Shandar, lies dying..."

"Where?" shouted Ailwon.

"In the upper room of the Tower of Enlightenment," Zarin pointed toward the tower. Ailwon dug his heels into the sides of his horse, galloping toward the city. "Is the lad aware," asked the King, looking after the fleeing Ailwon, "that Gwynn has become a captive of the Death Lord?"

"He knows," said Evrawk.

Zarin nodded. He looked at each of them. "I believe that some of you knew my sons, Ianen and Glenden. They were with Gwynn en route to Cryslandon...They were both killed." He looked away again, toward the figure of Ailwon, who had almost reached the battered gateway. "You are too late," he said, looking back toward them. "According to the Prophecy, it is less than three days until the Fulfillment. Yet it is a full four days' ride to Golgorath."

THE WHITE ELF KING

"Then there's hope," said Erbin. He turned to his brother. "Shandar's dying," he said, "let's go." Evrawk nodded, and the two galloped their ponies toward the city. Without a word, Ali Ben Kara rode after them.

Zyra nudged her mount forward, stopping beside Zarin. She looked down at him, hesitant to ask the question: "Among the women of Zan-Dura...she said finally, "...are there any casualties? Have many of my sisters been killed?"

"Yes, a considerable number. No one race was spared," he said, and he turned away from her, knowing that she was now the Queen of her people, dreading to tell her the circumstances that had caused this. He saw Wanel coming toward them, and his voice indicated the relief he felt at seeing her approach: "My wife comes...We will walk with you into the city."

The riders dismounted. Leading their horses, they started toward the city—all except Oolu. The Gwarpy had decided that he would not go to see the dying Shandar. He knew that the old man would need all his remaining energy to perform his last tasks. He would not again see the ancient Shandar, but now he wished to go into the battlefield, among the wounded. He walked away, his head down, his pony following slowly. Then Tark-Volmar questioned Zarin as to whether the majority of his people who had been struck down were within the city or on the field of battle. Most of the Norse wounded and dead were outside the city, he was told. His people had arrived during the latter part of the siege, and their major encounters had occurred in the combat on the field of battle. With that, the Norse chieftain hurried away to join Oolu.

Only Zyra and Hugh remained walking with the Brown Elf King and Queen. Zarin and Wanel walked on either side of the Amazon, both talking to her softly. Hugh was several paces behind. He could not determine the words, but he watched Zyra closely for a reaction. He sensed that the Andeluvians were

breaking news to her that would be especially painful.
Suddenly the Amazon stopped dead still. She half
turned toward Hugh. Her eyes were wide with terror.
The archer stepped toward her, but she turned back
and began to run toward the gateway, which was now
less than a hundred yards away. Zarin and Wanel
looked helplessly at the tall man. "Her Queen was
killed during the battle," Wanel said sadly. "She lies
now aboard the mother ship, in the canal beyond the
gateway... " She looked toward her husband. Zarin
was watching Hugh, closely. "I see great sadness on
your face," he said.

Hugh nodded silently. He watched as Zyra disappeared within the torn and charred gatehouse. In his
mind a clear picture of Queen Azira took shape: she
stood atop the rocks, overlooking the sea, her fine
crimson garment whipping in the ocean wind... and
he saw her standing within the Garden of Beauty,
watching him, the corners of her mouth turned
upward in a wry smile. Wanel's voice broke the vision:
"And the Princess feels such pangs of sorrow... Your
sadness is for her, also..."

"Yes."

Zarin reached out, touching the archer's arm gently. "I have long been one who has kept himself from
others. I have never seen you before, but I wish to
share your sorrow... my friend."

Hugh did not speak, but his eyes closed, his broad
shoulders sagged. He opened his eyes again, and
when he spoke the words, the voice sounded foreign
and far away. The words he now said aloud he had
never said even to himself:

"I love her. Zyra. She does not love me—does not
even care for me, particularly—but I deeply love her."

"This is a wonderful thing," said Wanel. "It is apparent how strongly you feel. It is a great mystery that
such wonders can arise amid the hideousness of
war." The Queen glanced toward her husband, her
eyes warm. She looked again to Hugh. "We must go
back to our work, now," she said. "Perhaps you are

wrong about Zyra. Perhaps she does love and care for you... or will soon." They turned, and left him.

Hugh watched them for a moment, feeling their warmth. Then he mounted Santor, and caught the reins of Thelan, the spirited gray that Zyra had left standing. Following his rescue, Ailwon had given the stallion to the Amazon as a gift.

The Vandorian entered through the gateway, emerging into the torn and seared city. He started across the stone bridge, the slow clicks of the horses' hooves loud in the silence. The wounded and dead had been removed, and there appeared to be no other beings about. Off to Hugh's right, the twisted and segmented remains of an Amazon vessel still floated atop the canal waters. He looked to the other side. The Amazon ships that had not been destroyed were docked there. Hugh completed the crossing, and rode toward the mother ship. He spoke to Santor, and the chestnut stallion stopped, as did the gray. The tired animals stood quietly; their heads drooped. Hugh dismounted, descending the steps that led to the dock. He walked close to the golden ship, from which a low chant could now be heard. On the deck of the ship lay the dead Queen. At her feet stood the old woman, Senqua, who had not left the slain Azira since she had been placed aboard. Senqua was chanting an incantation. Then she raised her eyes and hands toward the clouded sky, and chanted, in a voice cracked with age and emotion: *"Ki-est-oh-vel-oh..."*

Before the bier was Zyra. She knelt beside her spiritual mother. Her head was bowed low, her long black hair touched the floor, and her shoulders shook with gentle sobbing, which grew until her voice cried out her anguish.

Hugh turned and tied the reins of the gray stallion. He mounted his own steed, and began to make his way toward the Tower of Enlightenment.

The upper room of the tower was rounded and spacious. There were six great arched openings spanning its entire circumference, and on bright days

it was filled with light. But the clouded sky above
Cryslandon had eliminated the normal light of morning, casting a dark gloom about the room. At the
center was a huge, round stone slab, upon which
stood the Ark of the Crownhelm, the Sword Elvgard,
and the shield and armor of the White Elf Sevenas.
Seated crosslegged facing the Ark was the sorcerer,
Shandar. Kneeling next to him was Ali Ben Kara,
saying his final farewell to the sorcerer. Ailwon, Erbin
and Evrawk stood watching.

Ben Kara had said all but the final word, and this he
seemed unable to do. He stared down at the dying
Shandar, his eyes red, his cheeks and upper lip
glistening with moisture. He squeezed the hilt of his
sword rhythmically—his body tense and desperate. He
tried again to speak, but his voice caught in his
throat.

Shandar shook his head slowly. "I remember you
as a boy, Ali Ben Kara. You were never too adept at
these good-bye situations. It appears that you've not
changed, despite the addition of years." He smiled,
laying his hand upon the Azmurian's convulsing fist.
"This is not an altogether undesirable trait... " The
old man's body stiffened beneath a sudden spasm of
pain, his bony fingers tightened on Ben Kara's hand.
"You must go now, my son," he said quickly. His voice
was strained.

The Shakín stood. "I love you!" he blurted, and fled
from the room. Those remaining could hear the rapid
descent of his footsteps.

Shandar began to struggle to his feet. "Help me
up," he said, and his voice was firm. All three came
forward to assist him. The old man then stood
upright, supporting himself with one hand held firm
against the stone slab. He stared at each one of them,
and his dark eyes were almost fierce. "Now," he
began, "I have not much time remaining. I've kept my
body alive some number of days beyond its capacity.
It cries out to my being to release it. I have no more
time for tearful good-byes—dearly as I crave sympa-

thy right now... And *you* can afford to let moments slip away even less than I. It is four days—at least four days—to Golgorath. There remain only three days until the dawn of the Fulfillment..."

"Yes!" cried Ailwon, "how can I—"

"Stop!" commanded Shandar. "You will arrive in time. Now take the armor and tunic. Put them on." Ailwon stared at him. "Quickly!" said the sorcerer. The White Elf took the protective garments, and moved away from the center of the room. The old man coughed, shuddered, then stood straight again. He spat blood on the floor. The Dwarfs watched him, their eyes glistening. He looked down at the squat figures. "We—all three of us—are aware of the love that runs so powerfully between us. This awareness must replace my desire to have you near me as I die. Give me your hands—I can stand without support for a moment... good. Let me feel the rough texture of your honesty, old friends... good. This is all I can spare. Now, come to the stone. Open the Ark for me..."

The red-bearded Dwarfs did as they were told. Tears now ran freely down their ruddy cheeks. The Ark was

opened for the first time since before the birth of
Ailwon. A white radiance glowed upward from it.
Ailwon moved toward them from the shadows,
garbed in the glistening silver mail of his ancestors.

Shandar smiled. "Now, you who are Ailwon, kneel
before me..."

Ailwon knelt. Shandar first laid the Shield and then
Elvgard before him. Then he reached within the
glowing receptacle of the Ark. The sorcerer straightened, holding the glistening, winged Crownhelm of
the Sevenas. He stepped toward the kneeling youth,
who started up. The words came, and Shandar's voice
was not the voice of the dying:

"May the power of creation, that which made you
and all living things...give to you now the strength to
perform that which will liberate this land, to allow
freely the attainment of love..."

The Crown was placed upon the head of the youth,
and the King of the White Elves arose, holding his
shield and his enchanted sword, the power of tens of
centuries vibrating within the upper room, singing
through every cell of his body. The Dwarfs stared at
him in awe. This was not the same youth they had
tutored these past two decades. Ailwon looked at
them evenly through the visor which covered the
upper portion of his face. If he felt any wonder at the
transformation, he did not express it. It seemed as if
the boy had died. A stranger stood there, quietly
regarding them all. Shandar stretched his hand
forward, touching the armored shoulder. "Behold,"
he declared, "the child, born of the seed of Fulfillment... Behold, the savior of Urshurak." He stared at
the new King, and then at the Dwarfs. "You must arrive
by the sunset of the Fulfillment. Open your souls to
the powers that are all about you as you ride. And
when you arrive, it is my wish for you—my fervent
wish—that you combat the oppression that pours
outward from Golgorath with every part of your
beings... But do not hate those that—"

The old man gasped, and would have fallen, had Ailwon not caught him. "I have talked too long," he said weakly. The rattle of phlegm and blood was suddenly thick within his throat. "Help me to the north window, where I may watch you ride."

They did as he asked, laying him next to the opening of the arch. They looked down at him, seeing how weak he had become. The blood from his wound had begun to flow again, seeping through the binding, covering the front of his rough-textured robe.

"Shandar," began Erbin, his baritone voice quivering with emotion, "please touch me..."

"And me..." said Evrawk.

He reached up, touching the foreheads of both Dwarfs, and they felt the force of his spirit enter them. "Now," he said, "leave me...allow me to terminate this lingering." First Ailwon and then the brothers walked to the edge of the stairway, turning to look one more time upon the ancient figure of Shandar. His eyes were toward the open arch. The growing light of day edged the dark brown of his profile. "Good-bye, my friends," he said. His voice was almost a whisper.

The Dwarfs started down the stairway. Ailwon stood for a moment looking at Shandar, then followed them.

Ali Ben Kara sat within the shadowed silence of the tower hall, his face buried in his hands. Shandar would soon be dead. Ben Kara had envisioned a triumphant entry into shining Cryslandon, the regal coronation of the White Elf King, the great march to Golgorath of all the allied nations, and finally the mighty battle and eventual victory over the forces of oppression...

But none of this had occurred. Instead, there had been bloody skirmishes, rising hopes and bitter disappointments—and death, the deaths of many good comrades. And now it appeared that the unthinkable was to take place: they were to suffer crushing defeat and enslavement at the hands of the

Death Lord. Ben Kara sensed that the demise of the
legendary Shandar would signal the demise of the
free nations of Urshurak.

The Shakín rubbed his tired eyes. His body ached
with every long moment of the ordeal. Never had he
felt so tired or so filled with despair.

The opening and closing of the door within the
entranceway echoed softly through the hall, and then
footsteps started toward him. From the dimness,
Hugh Oxhine came into view.

"Is he still alive?" asked the Vandorian.

"Yes. But he will not remain so much longer."

"I'm sorry, Ben Kara," said Hugh. He sat down
beside the Azmurian. "I can only guess at your
feelings," he continued, "but it must be that losing
someone who has been with you and your people for
such an incredible span of time is a truly terrible loss.
Yes, I'm sorry. The Dwarfs and Oolu spoke of him so
often that I too felt as if I knew him." He looked about
the great arch of the hall, which even in half darkness
was awesome. "I've never been in such places as
these—not before I encountered the buildings in
Zan-Dura." He shook his head slowly, as he went on.
"It seems a hundred springtimes ago that I crossed
the Bolgads in search of the beasts that slaughtered
my family. I'm not sure, now, if it was them that I was
searching for. I believe that I've been in search of
something for a very long time—perhaps for myself—"
He sensed Ali Ben Kara's stare of wonder and shook
his head again, slightly astonished himself at what he
was saying. And he was not finished.

"You know," he said, "it used to be that when I saw
my own image in one of the ponds in the forests of
Vandor, I would feel a sadness. I did not understand it
then, but my sadness was there because I felt the
image was a stranger. But I am no longer sad. I know
now that I could not feel a sense of myself for two
reasons: I would not allow it, and I did not realize then
what I now know—that I am a part of all beings...
perhaps of all things." He turned, and looked square-
ly at Ben Kara.

"If we should reach Golgorath in time," he said,
"and then become engaged in battle, when we are in
the midst of the fighting to insure the final freedom,
when enemies fall beneath the force of my weapons,
portions of my being will fall with them."

The Azmurian was astounded at the change in the
steely, remote individual he had met a short time
before, and he had completely forgotten his own
feelings of hopelessness. They heard sounds beyond
the arched entranceway to the tower. Both stood.
Beyond the archway was almost complete darkness,
and the appearance of the Dwarf twins from the
shadows was very sudden. Neither spoke. Behind
them—appearing quite as suddenly as they—was Ailwon, garbed from head to foot in the white tunic and
glistening silver mail of the White Elf King. He seemed
to attract all the light in the dim hall, giving him a
height and dominance none of them had noticed
before. His surroundings appeared pitch-black in
contrast to the brilliance of the metallic Crownhelm
and his glinting armor and shield.

The youthful King looked from Ben Kara to Hugh.
He began to speak. In the great hall, his quiet voice
echoed with resonance and authority—the voice of
Ailwon, Sevena, King of the White Elves. "The long
quest is nearly at an end. It has been assured that we
will arrive in time. But we must ride as we have never
ridden before. The wind will be at our backs. Let us
go." He strode quickly toward the entranceway. The
others followed.

At the base of the long white stairway outside the
tower, the horses were tethered. At the center of them
stood a large golden stallion with flowing white mane
and tail. His bridle and saddle were of pure white.
Ailwon went straight to the great beast, vaulted into
the saddle and, turning, set off toward the northern
gateway. Hugh was the first to follow him, then Ali Ben
Kara. Erbin and Evrawk urged their ponies closely
behind.

Through the city they rode, past crumbled buildings with coal-black smoke still drifting from the

remains. They slowed their mounts as they approached the canal. Tark-Volmar sat astride his Vilderone stallion, and Oolu waited beside him on the shaggy pony. The Gwarpy held the reins of Thelan, the gray stallion, who pawed at the inlaid stones of the street. Ailwon and the others pulled their mounts to a halt, the animals danced nervously. Coming toward them, clad in the crimson armor of the Amazon Queen, was Zyra. She too went straight to her steed, taking the reins from Oolu, mounting smoothly. She looked at them without speaking. The beauty of her face was cold—frozen with the hardness of vengeance. Her eyes were filled with hate, and Hugh felt a shudder of fear run through him at the sight of the transformation in the woman he loved.

Ailwon spoke to his horse and the golden steed bolted forward, followed closely by the spirited gray of the Amazon. The allied band clattered across the long arch of the bridge, then through the gateway, onto the war-torn plain. On they rode toward the Arbroic Hills. On both sides of them were the figures of the wounded and the Andeluvians who worked among them. They rode into the Arbroics, toward the dark horizon, toward the Black Mountains of Golgorath, toward the fortress of the Death Lord...

Opposite: The Tower of the Death Lord

30

DEATH OF SHANDAR

Such was the height of the Tower of Enlightenment that from its upper room the surrounding countryside could be seen for miles on all sides. Shandar watched the small band of riders until they were well into the Arbroic Hills, then turned away from the arched opening. He looked beyond the stone, where the Ark of the Crownhelm remained—now empty. He felt extremely weak. The distance between himself and the window facing the southeast beyond which lay Evshimin, in the Valley of Life, now appeared to be considerable. Had he waited too long? He tried to stand. The pain of the deep wound increased, his mind began to float and the room grew suddenly dark. Shandar cried out, and slumped back to the floor.

He lay for a moment, breathing heavily, death rolling within him with each rise and fall of his chest. Now he grew cold with fear. After denying the inevitable for days, was he now to be struck so suddenly that the assurance he had given Ailwon would remain locked within, would rot with his body? He rested for a moment, then began to move forward on his belly. The southeast opening beckoned, and finally he lay beside it, his head buried within the crook of his elbow, his body tortured by the grueling effort.

He raised his head. He could see for miles toward the southeast, and toward the south, and toward the southwest—where the rays of the sun lay hidden behind the seemingly immovable gray clouds. Below him, beyond the city, the waters of the twin lakes met to form the enormous span of blue that was the beginning of the River Garnon. Across the way, along the western bank of the river, a final few of the great Trocalas emerged from the Forest of Delvinor to stand as silent sentinels. All of this was balm to Shandar. Now he was ready. Now he could hasten the end to the long centuries of his existence, after the one last effort he would make for the Sevena.

He stretched forth his gnarled brown hand, toward Evshimin. The vision of it was crystal clear before him. He saw the white Bobabo within the valley.

"Now my moment has come," he whispered.

The fire of pain seared through his body. "Now I offer the remains of my being!" he cried out. His body writhed, sweat pouring from his dark flesh, mingling with the blood that seeped from his wound. Then the pain was pouring from him as if the wound had become a yawning chasm, and he cried out: "Come now, O eternal!"

The vision of Evshimin became one with the reality of the vista that spread before him. Lightning flashed across the distant horizon, followed by a slow roll of thunder that rumbled toward him. Movement began within the foliage of the giant Trocalas below. Shandar heard the beginnings of the wind, saw the first rippling of the waters of the Garnon, and he felt the cool sweetness of the coming storm. Thunder crashed again, the clouds had become a churning blackness across the sky, the music of the wind had become violent with power. And the rain came within the force of the wind, blowing even into the tower room, striking the face and the skull of the ancient being. Thunder and lightning were all about, the waters of the twin lakes rose and plunged. Shandar saw and heard and felt the crystal reality that was the world, and yet he was detached from it. His sight and his knowing passed easily through the veil of time that disguised the eternal present, and he shouted joyfully, "I have crossed the barrier... Now touch me, O infinite love!"

The ancient sorcerer stretched forth his hand, his face in ecstasy. In his vision of Evshimin, the cavern of mystery reopened, while in the sky above him, the dark clouds parted and the brilliant light of day issued forth, racing across the rippling waters, toward the tower. As the golden warmth of the light fell across him, Shandar's outstretched arm fell lightly to the stone sill, and the old sorcerer died.

They could hear the raging storm behind them, but no one looked back. The wind began, steadily increasing until the horses of the allied band seemed to become refreshed by its power, seemed to gain strength from it. Only Ailwon had gained a fresh mount at Cryslandon, and the other steeds had been ridden for many days and miles with only infrequent rest. The wind blew even stronger, and scattered drops of rain slanted through it. They went up a rise, and just as they neared the crest they felt the sudden appearance of the sun as it struck their backs, as its light fell across the hills before them. Wild Thelan surged forward, the strength of his muscles renewed beneath the shining gray of his coat, his hooves but blurs upon the grassy hilltop. Zyra drew even with the White Elf King who had led the way. The band galloped down the hillside, splashing across a shallow brook, emerging onto a rolling stretch of land.

All about them and beneath them was the energy of power and joy. The land and the sky and the wind sang to them, urged them on. The riders bent low over their steeds exhorting them forward, and the horses stretched full out, galloping as they never had before. Scattered poplars flashed by on both sides, and the green distance of the Arbroics disappeared beneath the pounding hooves. And the challenge of Golgorath drew them onward...

31

TORGON,
THE DEATH LORD

The message had been passed from the Plains of Kiberuk to Golgorath—the allied armies were marching northward... The expected battle with the peoples who would march against Golgorath had produced a tumult of preparation for war within the Crater of Death. The always free-flowing hostility that would later be directed against the invaders was at this point expressed in massive discord among the multitudes of Torgon's forces. The Gnomes and Borgs, and the hostile Skelf clansmen from Norbruk, had indulged in a prebattle celebration involving much intoxicating liquid. The result was almost complete anarchy. Only the brutal and stolid Vilderones had kept the drunkenness, the quarreling and the fighting in check, so that some form of preparation could proceed amid the chaos.

The traitor Deciedon pushed his way through the squabbling, brawling thousands, on his way toward the slave compound. Despite their drunken state, the barbarians gave the fast-striding, immaculately clad figure ample room. It was widely known that he was not to be trifled with. During the past two decades, several of their fellows had fallen before his lightning blade—for no more than an offhand remark. Power and brutality were traits well understood by all who composed the ranks of the armies of the Death Lord, and one who could express both with such suddenness and indifference was feared and respected.

He had almost arrived at his destination. The bellowed curses of the gargoyles and the sharp cracks of their whips, coming from the tier above him, drew Deciedon's attention. He looked up. Amid the groaning and creaking of enormous wheels, the mechanisms of war were being slowly propelled into position behind the outer walls by throngs of slaves. Already a massive steel machine stood ready, rising more than a hundred feet into the air, bulking high against the dark red clouds. The traitor smiled with satisfaction. Even if they had the Sevena, the puny armies that would arrive from Cryslandon could not begin to cope with such awesome power. Nor did they have the White Elf Prince. He was a prisoner of the Vilderones, due to arrive at any moment. These facts were irrefutable, and he had assured the raging Torgon that this was so.

It had been no easy task for Deciedon to maintain his aplomb in the presence of the Death Lord. He was certain that no one else could have stood before that dark being, feeling the awful throb of his anger, and still have delivered an oration of such skill as to explain away the defeat at Cryslandon and the failure to deliver the Crownhelm. No one else could have constructed such convincing imagery of a complete and crushing triumph over the aliens... He had needed to draw upon his extensive knowledge of the history of Urshurak and the myth of the Prophecy. He had shown the Death Lord how these dual forces were being drawn inexorably together—something he himself gave absolutely no credence to, within the privacy of his own mind. But to Torgon he had carefully described the clear logic of it all. How could they not have seen it before? All of history had been slowly guided by the Prophecy toward this final Day of Fulfillment. How could they have ignored this? They had the Sevena... he would be brought before the Death Lord at any moment... and then the meager forces of final resistance would deliver themselves to be annihilated. They could do nothing else. The

Prophecy—all of history—had directed that it be thus. What could be more fitting? It would be at *Golgorath* that Torgan would at last achieve his ultimate triumph...

Finally, the Death Lord had agreed, and Deciedon had been allowed to leave. Had the traitor not been completely confident in his ability to convince Torgon, he would never have returned to Golgorath. Again Deciedon surveyed the battle preparation. His gaze traveled across the mile-wide span of the stronghold. He had underestimated the allied forces before, had been unsuspecting of the powerful weapons of the Amazon women. But he was sure that no more than one or two of the strange weapons had remained intact after the battle at Cryslandon. How could they even begin to cope with the awesome power that would confront them here? They could not hope to penetrate even the immense outer wall. What could they do but be brutally pounded by the dual power of the gargantuan war machines, guarding either side of the fortress gate? In addition they would be bombarded by the twoscore lesser machines, which were still almost twice the size of those they had had to cope with at Cryslandon. And then, when they had been pounded to a point of submission, the hordes of barbarians and Vilderones would swarm out of the fortress to murder or enslave those that remained. Deciedon smiled again. No longer, he thought, would he merely serve as a paltry governor to the White Elf nation. He would become Lord Chancellor of all Urshurak. Only Torgon, himself, would exceed him in power. And in the depths of his mind he entertained the idea that perhaps someday he could even arrange the demise of the Death Lord...

He arrived at the slave compound, and started toward the central area, where Gwynn was being held. He passed row after row of empty cells. Every slave but the Brown Elf maid was being put to service. It had been guaranteed to Deciedon that she would not be worked. He grimaced. Coming toward him was the stolid Vilderone general, Sorkmun, and the swaggering chieftain of the rebel Norsemen, Kolak the Black. The Vilderone growled at Deciedon as they met: "How did this happen? How was it that the aliens were not conquered within the White Elf city?"

"I'm certain," Deciedon replied, "that you have been informed of the events at Cryslandon...and," he continued, more caustically, "I'm certain that great warrior leaders, such as yourselves, will have no difficulty in squelching the insipid upstarts that march against us."

Sorkmun only grunted in return, but Kolak broke into raucous laughter. "I, for one," he bellowed, "am damned happy that the first attack failed. The Skelfs weren't involved with that one—I couldn't be more pleased over the opportunity to crush the life from the red-faced buffoon, Tark-Volmar!" The last statement ignited a cruel light in Kolak's green eyes.

"I am delighted," Deciedon said evenly, "that you view this opportunity with such positive regard..." He

directed the statement at the Norseman, deliberately ignoring the Vilderone's eyes. He strode past the two, resolving to eliminate Sorkmun, once he had gained power.

He stopped before Gwynn's cell. He peered through the small grate of the cell door. She sat on the floor of the bare room; her back was against a side wall. She stared straight ahead, and did not look toward him when he spoke to her.

"Well, dear Gwynn, they have provided you with quarters somewhat lacking in luxury...Ah, but before long you shall lounge in the most sumptuous of rooms..." He paused, watching her. Then he began again, in his deepest—most melodic—voice. "Even though this ordeal has cursed you with a tinge of haggardness, you are still the most radiant creature on the continent..." Even as he spoke his mind flashed to a vision of the Amazon Princess, Zyra. Already he had bargained with Torgon to obtain her, provided she was not slain in battle. The thought was delightful. He would have both a fair beauty and a dark one. "I have taken your Prince into captivity," he continued, "he is due to arrive at any moment. You know, my dear, that Torgon won't allow the Sevena to live. There will be no one to protect you—except the Lord High Chancellor of Urshurak."

Gwynn turned her head slowly to stare at him, unafraid. "Pity is not something to which I normally devote much energy," she said, "but I have enormous pity for you. Your entire being is driven toward grasping at those things that are only shadows of reality—that will always elude you. And it appears that when you realize this, it will be too late..." She turned away from him.

Deciedon was unperturbed. "It seems you've taken a turn toward philosophy. Quite out of place for one so young and beautiful," he said, and then laughed softly. "But no matter. You will not have to remain in this disgusting place much longer. I will soon have you brought to me."

His face disappeared from the grate, and as his footsteps faded Gwynn resolved to ask Ferda to give her the stolen dagger that the Dwarf woman kept stashed in her hiding place.

Torgon sat alone within the dark expanse of the great hall in the tower of the Death Lord. He sat motionless. Thoughts turned slowly and surely within the black void of his inner being. He *knew*. He would at last face the Sevena. And he had no illusions about this boy. The Sevena would not come to him as a prisoner. He knew that the traitor had not lied. That the boy had indeed been captured. But, as he had listened to the glittering veil of words from the deceitful one, he had known the truth. The boy would come—as the White Elf King. He would come wearing the Crownhelm and bearing the Sword and Shield of his ancestors. On the Day of Fulfillment, Torgon would face this last of the pretenders to the Crown, alone... and he would crush him. At long last, the gaping wound of his jealousy would be healed. At long last, the endless, gnawing hunger would be sated. At long last a thousand years of craving would be satisfied. He would *win* the Crown of the White Elves. The victory would be his alone. And then he would be master over all that was Urshurak. All would fall before him, all would worship him at his feet.

The boy-King would come to him. But Torgon would choose the place of meeting. Torgon would await the White Elf in the depths of the Crater of Death, far below this dark hall. He would go now to await the Sevena. He would descend to the place where—ten centuries before—he had succumbed to the gift of unlimited power, where he had been absorbed by a black void, an emptiness he could never satisfy—until the moment of this meeting.

32

DAY OF
FULFILLMENT

"...And lo, before the sun sets on the Day of Fulfillment the two of the same blood shall meet and both shall be fulfilled. But only one shall bear away the Crownhelm of the White Elves. And in that hour shall be decided the fate of the land of Urshurak."

The Day of Fulfillment had dawned much as did other days in the land of the Death Lord, dark and foreboding. The allied armies stood massed on the Plain of Golgorath, facing the immense fortress of the Death Lord. They had arrived the night before, with Elgan at their head. The wizard did not feel alone, for he was deeply imbued with the loving presence of the dead Shandar, and he felt greater power than at any time of his long existence. That this power would not be enough to overcome the monster that was Torgon, Elgan thoroughly realized. He had held to the hope that Ailwon would somehow arrive... but still there was no Ailwon. So it would be he, Elgan, who would face the adversary on the final day of the long struggle.

He marveled at the enormity of what lay before him, at the prodigious energy spent uselessly in the pursuit of destruction and oppression. He could see the gargantuan weapons on either side of the entrance. Beyond them was the tower of the Death Lord, exuding the blood-red gasses that belched angrily skyward. Now Elgan could hear the ponderous throbbing of the depths. He heaved a great sigh, staring ahead for a long moment. Then he turned, to look on his friends—as the first cheer went up from among the massed troops behind him.

Elgan stared beyond the long lines of the armies, toward the barren plain, where a small cluster of horsemen came steadily forward. Could it be? Elgan's heart leaped. The old wizard peered at the approaching figures that were rapidly gaining definition. Another shout went up... then another! The impossible had happened! It was he! Ailwon, the newly crowned King of the White Elves, was riding hard toward them, his radiant figure bright against the dark horizon.

And now the collected voices of thousands spoke the joyful message of the moment, echoing backward through the centuries of struggle, proclaiming bright hope for tomorrow:

...So cheer, you White Elves of Alfandel, for the final hour of the Day of Fulfillment, the savior of Urshurak has come!... And beside him rides the courageous archer, Hugh Oxhine!

...Cheer and embrace, you sisters of Zan-Dura, for coming toward you across the plain is your Queen, Zyra!

...Shout with joy, all you warriors of Azmuria! Your Shakín, the noble Ali Ben Kara, has arrived to lead you against the enemy!

...Cheer and shout, thrusting your fists to the sky, you Norsemen of Norbruk! Pounding toward you atop a huge black steed is your boisterous chieftain, Tark-Volmar!

...Cheer lustily, oh you faithful of Penderak, whooping with delight!... for yonder come the stalwart twins, Erbin and Evrawk, bent low over their galloping ponies!

...And smile, old Elgan, at the sight of the Gwarpy, Oolu, who brings joy to your heart.

...Cheer and shout and embrace, all you of the free

nations!... For now you are united with the shining
Sevena. Now you shall overcome a thousand years of
oppression!

Then, the small band had arrived, moving their
horses through the cheering throng. Elgan awaited
them, beside him old Esrund, beaming proudly at the
sight of his sons. Wizard and Dwarf alike stared at the
White Elf King, amazed at the transformation from
the boy. Ailwon reached down, touching the old
wizard's cheek, and the touch was gentle though his
face remained resolute behind the mask of the
Crownhelm.

He straightened, staring ahead toward the dark
mass of the fortress. "Our final obstacle is still to be
confronted," he said. He looked around quickly. "I see
neither of the Amazon weapons," he said, concerned.
"I understood that two of them had been brought?"

"They were brought," came the voice of Zyra. She
cantered the gray stallion toward them, having con-
ferred with her sisters. "But only one is functional,"
she continued. "The other was brought in the hope
that it might yet be repaired, but it could not. We have
but one... but it will be enough." Her face was hard
with the determination of one seeking vengeance.

Elgan stepped toward her. "I am grieved, my
daughter," he began, "at the terrible losses that you
have suffered. And I hope—"

"I appreciate your grieving," she interrupted, "but it
appears to me that there is a task at hand, is there
not?" Elgan nodded sadly, seeing that he could say
nothing that would deter that hatred so apparent in
her dark eyes. She turned the gray stallion toward the
fortress of the Death Lord. The horse whinnied,
dancing nervously; Zyra spoke soothingly to him,
rubbing the taut muscles of his neck. "It is obvious,"
she said, "that the only way in is through that great
door directly before us. The Fire Crystal can open it if
we can get it into position. Those monster weapons
on either side of the entrance appear to be extremely
formidable..."

"I can protect a very few of you," said Elgan, "for a very short time."

"That is all we will need." She turned to Ailwon. "The bearers will run the weapon into position. As soon as I begin to fire, you can begin your charge toward the gate... It will be open before you reach it." Ailwon nodded.

"And I will come closely behind," said Ali Ben Kara, who trotted forward on a sleek tan mare, having exchanged it for his tired Vilderone steed.

"Not without me, you won't," bellowed Tark-Volmar. He had stayed with his gargoyle horse, and the bulky steed carried the Norseman to a position beside Ben Kara.

"We'll all go together!" shouted Erbin from behind them, "all of us that have come this far!"

He and Evrawk came forward, leading their ponies, and beside them was their father, Esrund. Close behind were Hugh and Oolu, also leading their mounts. The Dwarfs had quickly—and proudly—introduced their friend, the Vandorian, to their people. Elgan walked toward them. He looked at the archer, and smiled. "I'm extremely glad to see you, Hugh. You look to be a considerably different person than the angry man I met at Mowdra."

Hugh nodded. "It is true," he said, and he returned the wizard's smile of warmth. He turned to his horse, swinging easily into the saddle. Erbin did likewise, and then Evrawk. Oolu chuckled, and scrambled atop the bare back of his long-haired pony, Carrot.

"You too are going, gentle Oolu?" asked the wizard.

"Yep, Ol' Elgan. Ol' Oolu wants ta be with all these here," he said, indicating his companions.

The Fire Crystal was carried to the front. Zyra sat her horse silently beside it. Ailwon moved his golden stallion to a position behind the Amazons, red light glinting from the silver of his war garb as he moved.

"Well," said Esrund to his sons, "it's finally come. Your people—and all the rest—we'll be right behind you." He grasped their thick hands with his own, then limped quickly away. The Dwarfs moved their mounts into line, beside their companions of the quest—Ben Kara, Volmar, Hugh and Oolu. They waited behind the White Elf King, their eyes upon the Amazons. Elgan had moved to a position parallel to the Amazons, climbing upon a huge rock. He glanced back, beyond the long line of allied troops, and his eyes swept across the horizon. A small band of light still showed beyond the mountains. He looked back, waiting, hearing the low moaning of the wind. He saw Zyra raise her arm, then bring it forward hard.

The Amazon bearers, and the Tresselier ran forward, across the empty plain. Violent explosions issued from the monster weapons and flaming metal spheres roared through the air. As he raised his arms, Elgan directed his every power toward the hurtling objects. One landed far to the right of the racing figures, while the other passed well beyond them. The explosions shot tons of earth and rock high into the air. But through the fire and smoke could be seen the Amazons, still running forward, their gold and blue weapon between them. Zyra slapped her horse, and he shot forward. Again the weapons fired the huge death spheres. Again they exploded off target.

Zyra galloped toward her sisters, urging Thelan on, holding his head straight forward—away from the explosions that tore the earth on both sides of them. The Amazons set down the Fire Crystal, and their Queen reached them just seconds after, dismounting before her gray steed had come to a complete halt. She handed the reins to the Tresselier, and ran to the Fire Crystal. Another sphere roared overhead, exploding behind them, and from the corner of her eye Zyra saw her frightened horse rear high in the air, pulling his reins free, galloping away. She shouted after him, but he raced away, and she watched helplessly as another projectile exploded, knocking the terrified animal heavily to the ground. She saw his head raise weakly, then drop, and he lay still. Zyra turned back to face the Crater of Death. They were now less than five hundred yards removed, and the fortress rose above them. The Amazon Queen closed her eyes, exerting every dimension of her will to erase the violence of her hatred, so that she could lend the force of her spirit to the force of the Fire Crystal. Amid the explosions that fell about her, she felt the calm of the Kovier settle upon her, and she aimed toward the apex of the great iron gate, engaging the mechanism of the weapon. A bolt of light leaped forward, searing the atmosphere, drawn forward by its target. It struck the machine to the left of the gate, exploding, biting out twisted chunks of steel with staccato precision, the metal seething white-hot, exploding again and again... sending off showers of brilliant sparks. Its brother to the right met with the same fate. Zyra then directed the fire of her weapon slowly downward, along the left side of the gate. She could sense the approaching White Elf King galloping up behind her. Ailwon flashed by as he rode full speed toward the fortress, the white tail of his golden steed blowing straight back, the blade of Elvgard held forward, shimmering. The power of the Fire Crystal seared, exploding—now against the opposite side of the gate, gouging out molten chunks, propelling them into the acrid air. With an enormous blast the entrance gave way. Ailwon galloped into the stronghold of the Death Lord without slowing his pace.

Zyra released her weapon. Her companions had galloped almost atop her, Tark-Volmar was reaching down without slowing the pace of his thundering steed. She caught the thick brawn of his arm, and he lifted her as if she were weightless. In the instant that she was lifted and placed behind him, she saw the grin of his admiration for her marksmanship, and the wild excitement of battle that shone from his eyes. To her left was Ali Ben Kara, and beyond him the Dwarf twins and Oolu. Clinging tightly to the broad back of the Norseman, she glanced to her right. The archer, Hugh Oxhine, was bent low over the big chestnut stallion, Santor. The Vandorian's sword was drawn, pointing skyward. Zyra stared at him for a second, then leaned out to look ahead... The enormous opening was directly before them, and Zyra could hear the screaming and tumult among the barbarians as they scrambled to escape the fury of the sword of the White Elf King...

Gwynn huddled in a dark corner of her cell. This was the Day of Fulfillment—the culmination of every event of the history of Urshurak. This day was to have brought about the titanic clash of opposing forces that would decide the fate of Urshurak. This was to be both the end and the beginning... and nothing had happened. This day—like the others—had passed slowly and drearily, accompanied by the methodical throbbing that sounded from the depths of the crater.

Then the monster weapons began to fire, vibrating the cell floor. The weapons fired over and over. Gwynn rushed to the grate. Within the narrow scope of her vision she could see hundreds of Gnomes, Borgs and Skelf Norsemen rushing along the tiers, climbing upward toward the fortress walls, and among them were the Vilderones, shouting orders. Gwynn strained to hear what was happening, but she could make out nothing in the tumult. She heard the sound of the great gate exploding, and felt the enormous vibration. Gwynn could hear confused shouting coming from above. Could it be? she thought... Could we have?... She hardly dared to think that it might be possible.

Torgon's forces had apparently all made their way upward to the southern gateway, and the area around the prison seemed to be empty. All Gwynn could do was to wait. She wished that Ferda was in her cell, but all the prisoners except Gwynn had been herded into the huge 'cage.' She heard the heavy tread of hobnailed boots. Vilderones were coming, and she peered toward the direction of their approach. There were two of them, and with them, the hulking Borg, Thog. She moved away from her door. Then the scowling face of one of the gargoyles appeared at the grate.

"Come, Elf," he growled, "you have been sent for."

Gwynn touched the handle of the dagger beneath her clothing, then moved toward the door as it was opened. She stepped outside. The noise above had increased. "What's happening up there?" she asked, not really expecting an answer—and receiving none. The Borg shuffled away.

"Shackle her wrists," said the Vilderone in charge, "and bring her along." He moved on ahead, obviously in a hurry. The other grasped Gwynn by the arm, turning her so that her back was toward him. A set of manacles dangled from his other fist. Gwynn reached beneath her garment, clutching the dagger handle, twisting her torso back toward the gargoyle.

The sweep of her blade sliced through one eye of the Vilderone, across the bridge of his nose, and ripped the delicate membrane of his other eye. He bellowed with agony, staggering back, clutching his eyes, blood spurting between his fingers. Gwynn stooped down, scooping up the manacles in the same motion. At the sound of his shout the other gargoyle had turned back, starting forward on the run. The young woman flung the heavy manacles... they twisted in flight, then struck the approaching Vilderone across his lowered helmet visor, dropping him in his tracks. Gwynn whirled, and her eyes grew wide with horror at the violent agony that gripped the wounded gargoyle. She lunged at him, her razor-sharp blade puncturing the leathery flesh of his throat, instantly ending his suffering. She bent over him and pulled loose his sword from its scabbard. Turning, she saw the other gargoyle staggering to his feet, charging at her, brandishing his own sword. She leaped forward to meet him, holding the huge Vilderone weapon with both hands. They met, their blades clashing. The gargoyle pressed forward, hacking at the Brown Elf, who dodged beneath his swipes or blocked them with her sword. Then she felt the prison wall against her back. She leaped sideways, just as her opponent's blade swished downward, ringing against the wall. Gwynn swung at the Vilderone, striking his helmet so hard with her blade that it dented inward. The gargoyle collapsed and did not move. She raced past him, down the stairs, toward the 'cage.' The slaves began cheering wildly as she came into view. As many as possible were pressed against the bars, reaching out their hands to touch her.

"Hey, dearie," shouted a rasping voice, "what's going on up atop?"

Ferda stood at the very end of the cage, her face pressed against the bars.

"Ailwon has arrived, Ferda!" shouted Gwynn. "He's here! I know it!" Her face was alive. "Now I've got to get

you out... I'll need plenty of help—I'm hardly the size
of a Borg..."

Gwynn grabbed hold of the lever that raised the
portcullis and pulled with all her strength. The prisoners gave a mighty cheer as the lever came to rest
and the gate began to rise.

Cracked and calloused hands gripped the bars,
hard muscles strained, muscles of the shoulders and
backs, triceps and forearms and thighs—straining,
sweat pouring... shoulder to shoulder they heaved,
Azmurians and Norse, Dwarfs, White Elves and Brown
Elves. The huge portcullis creaked upward. And then
they were free! At long last, the slaves of the Death
Lord were *free!* They poured out of the cage, cheering,
shouting... their hearts beating fiercely!

Gwynn was grabbed, hugged, embraced, shoved
forward to lead them. Brandishing her sword, she led
them upward. A contingent of Vilderones blocked
their way—for an instant. The gargoyles were swallowed up by the shouting thousands and left strewn
across the rampway. Onward and upward they swept,
having added steel weapons to the formidable arse-
nal that was their anger and the spirit of their
freedom. The din from the upper tier was enormous
as the former slaves reached the top of the rampway.
The allied armies had poured into the fortress, and
the hand-to-hand combat was fierce. The air was
filled with the war cries and shouts of fighting warriors, with the clash of arms, and with the screams of
the wounded and the dying. Already the upper tier
was becoming strewn with bodies and slickened with
blood. Into this charged the fierce mass of freed
peoples, led by Gwynn of Andeluvia.

As she fought, Gwynn's eyes searched right and
left... And then, in the center of the battle, the
brilliance of the sword Elvgard flashed in the air, and
she could see him. Atop the golden stallion, fighting
fiercely, garbed in the gleaming armor and the
masked Crownhelm of the White Elves... was the
Sevena... Ailwon... her love! She shouted to him

above the turmoil...and somehow he heard her. He fought toward her, and she toward him. They met, reaching toward one another, clasping hands, the power of their love running between them.

"You must go!" Gwynn shouted, "I'll join you as quickly as I can...He is there..." She pointed across the causeway to the tower. "Go straight to the center."

"I will find him." He leaned down, their lips met for but an instant, and then he was moving his steed through the fighting, gathering speed as he neared the ramp. Then he was galloping across the causeway, brushing aside attempts to waylay him, riding toward the tower of the Death Lord. Gwynn began fighting her way through.

Amid all the violence within the Crater of Death, the most vicious of the combatants was the Queen of Zan-Dura. Those of Torgon's forces who had survived the battle at Cryslandon had brought back tales to their comrades of the ferocity of the Amazon women. But none were prepared to face the fury that confronted them in the person of the crimson-clad warrior woman who attacked them relentlessly, tirelessly, felling one of their number with every rise and fall of her sword. Zyra had caught sight of Ailwon as he began to ride across the causeway toward the massive tower. He would lead her to this Death Lord, who was responsible for the murder of her Queen and of so many of her sisters. Frantically she looked around, spying an Azmurian horse with an empty saddle. She raced toward it, catching its reins, speaking soothingly as it reared in fright. She leaped astride, turning the horse toward the tower, forcing her way through the battle, then galloping onto the causeway. A half dozen gargoyles blocked her passage. They tried to pull her from the saddle, but found this to be a serious mistake. Zyra hacked at them with such ferocity that within a moment half of their number lay bleeding, while the remainder fell back from this furious woman warrior. She galloped on. But Ailwon had disappeared. She cursed her misfortune, and continued to ride on toward the great open doors of the tower, determined to find Torgon.

Meanwhile the Norse chieftain, Tark-Volmar, joyously vented his anger on the gargoyles, the Borgs—and especially on the rebels of his own race; while the Gnomes—whom Volmar considered more pesty than dangerous—were sent sprawling and tumbling by backward swipes of his huge fist. The red-bearded Norseman was having the time of his life. He remained in the near vicinity of his fellow members of the quest, taking great delight in their fighting abili-

ties. He admired the determined relentlessness of
Erbin and Evrawk. When paired, the Dwarf twins were
a match for the most formidable opponent. And the
fighting style of the archer Hugh, blending power and
agility into spirited swordsmanship, drew quick
glances of admiration from the Norse chieftain. He
admired the skill of his old adversary, Ali Ben Kara. As
the Shakín dispatched a mace-wielding Borg with a
powerful thrust of his curved sword, Volmar roared
his approval. His congratulatory backslap nearly sent
the princely Azmurian sprawling. "Damn it, Volmar!"
Ben Kara shouted. "I'm more likely to become a battle
casuality of your exhibitions of praise than from the
swipe of an enemy's weapon!"

The Norseman guffawed with delight, turning to
look for an opponent. And through the violent shifting of bodies, he spied the enemy he had been
searching for since the first moment he had thundered into the fortress. "Kolak!" he bellowed, and
began to bully his way toward his hated rival.

Ali Ben Kara watched with some concern as the
broad Norseman rushed through the throng. Then,
from the corner of his eye, he detected a blur of
movement, and he dodged not an instant too soon.
The blade of a broadsword, powered by a hulking
gargoyle, swished past his ear and shoulder. Ben
Kara squared to face the dark figure—knowing instinctively how extremely dangerous was this particular Vilderone—even without the knowledge that the
sullen gargoyle had already slain more than a dozen
of his allies during this pitched battle. Heeding his
instincts, the Shakín brought his every fighting skill
to the fore. The struggle was furious, but short...and
the Vilderone lay lifeless at his feet. The Azmurian
stared down at him for a brief moment, not knowing
that he had slain the feared gargoyle general, Sorkmun.

Tark-Volmar had rushed to within earshot of his
rival chieftain, and now he bellowed again, "Kolak
you traitor!... you bald-headed bastard!" Kolak

whirled to face him, his face livid from the insult.
When he spotted the source of the slur, he charged
forward, almost insane with hate, curses spewing...
They clashed, their battle-axes locked together above
them. With a violent thrust, the Skelf chieftain tore
Volmar's ax from his grasp, sent it crashing to the iron
floor. The death blow was raised above Tark-Volmar's
head, but he lunged forward, thwarting the downward thrust with his shoulders, clutching the bull
neck of his opponent in his mighty hands. He
squeezed, pressing the center of the throat inward
with the power of his thick thumbs. He heard the
useless battle-axe fall behind him, and squeezed ever
tighter. His teeth were clenched and he growled:
"Traitor!" Kolak's face was red-purple, his eyes
bulged. Then his pupils rolled back, and his body
became limp. Volmar released him. Kolak fell heavily,
his helmet, decorated gaudily with gold, rolled from
his head, exposing the shiny skull. Tark-Volmar stood
over him, breathing heavily. "So much for traitors," he
said. But there was no mockery in his voice, nor hate,
and he turned away and retrieved his axe.

The allied armies were outnumbered, but it hardly
seemed to be a disadvantage, and from the first
moment of the hand-to-hand fighting there seemed
little doubt as to the eventual outcome. Fortified by
the joyful arrival of their long-separated countrymen—the former slaves, the allies slowly but surely
gained control of the battle. The boisterous confidence enjoyed by Torgon's forces before the battle
soon dissolved beneath the fierce implacability of the
allied armies. They had not expected to encounter
such furious battle precision as was employed by the
warrior Amazons. Their attempts to cope with the
disciplined Azmurians—who wielded their curved
swords with such skill—seemed futile... Their numeri-
cal advantage became radically reduced, as they
succumbed to the flashing swords of the Lejentors
and to the spears of the White Elf foot soldiers. They
began to fall back before the ferocity of the lusty

Norsemen. And they began to flee before the Dwarf army, who wielded their pitchforks, scythes and axes, and who were led and inspired by the shouting white-haired Esrund in the ancient armor. Soon, the barbarians and the Skelfs—and even the Vilderones—were retreating by the thousands, forced downward into the Crater of Death, fighting for their lives, pursued relentlessly by the armies of the free nations.

Hugh and Oolu were inside the tower. The archer had seen Zyra ride away in pursuit of Ailwon, and he was certain of her intentions. Her mind was beset by the fever of vengeance, this he knew, and well understood. While he did not question her ability to defend herself, he was concerned that the absence of her usual cool judgment might render her vulnerable to a number of dangers. Beyond all of this, he was deeply in love with her, and if she was bent upon facing the Death Lord, then he was bent upon being at her side when she did so. Thus, he had followed her path into the tower as quickly as he could fight his way through. And Oolu had followed him. Hugh did not discover this until they were almost across the long causeway. The archer warned the Gwarpy about following him; Oolu would be defenseless if he were attacked. But the irrepressible Gwarpy was soon trotting beside his tall companion, as they entered the monstrous tower.

They had seen a young Elf enter, when they were still some distance away, and both were sure that it was Gwynn. But she was now nowhere in sight. A solid steel door denied them further progress down the main hallway, and they started through a passageway to their left. The corridor wound and twisted, and other passages branched away from it. They stayed with the first, trusting only in their instincts, and luck.

The pair came to another dark opening—an alternate passage—and out of it stepped a pair of fierce-looking Vilderones. They came forward menacingly, weapons in their hands. Hugh pushed Oolu behind him, drawing his sword as he did so. He had found

that the Vilderones—despite their formidable appearance—were not particularly adept swordsmen, and
not one of them had thus far been a match for the
quality of his fighting. But two of them at once—on
brute strength alone—would not be easy to handle.
Hugh quickly found himself being turned toward the
corridor wall, fending off blows from both left and
right. For an instant Oolu was forced out from behind
his protector, and in that same instant one of the
gargoyles decided the Gwarpy was far easier prey
than the archer, and he lunged toward him. Oolu
hesitated only a second, then scrambled away, with
the Vilderone in hot pursuit. Hugh started after them,
but his opponent blocked his path. The archer
cursed, and attacked violently. In a moment the
gargoyle lay face down, blood seeping from beneath
him. Hugh raced past him, running at full speed down
the dark, twisting corridor. He could not know yet that
despite his efforts he would not find Oolu.

The Gwarpy had fled for his life—and also to reduce
the odds against Hugh. The Vilderone ran behind,
cursing and brandishing his sword. Oolu knew that
he would have no trouble outdistancing the gargoyle,
no matter how relentlessly he was pursued. But he
was aware also that he was being chased farther and
farther away from Hugh.

Zyra was completely lost within the dark labyrinth
of the tower. The powers of her psyche had been finely
developed, and she normally would not have become
ensnared by the complications of this maze. But the
blaze of her hatred had dissipated the cool awareness that usually directed her movements. The further she traveled through the echoing passageways,
the closer she came to the deep, ever-present throbbing, and this gave rise to the slim hope that she
might yet meet Torgon.

When she had first realized that she was lost, she
had become all the more furious, and the occasional
Vilderone guard that she had met had felt the full

Opposite: Ailwon at Golgorath

impact of her outrage. Yet each encounter lessened
her fury, and as time passed in the dim corridors far
from the furor of the fighting, the high edge of her
anger became dulled. The longer she spent searching through the darkness, the less important became
her resolve to avenge the deaths of her Queen and
her sisters. She felt no lessening of her dedication to
their memories, but the passion to lash out, to kill
and kill again, had somehow lost its bitter hold over
her. Groping endlessly in the dimness, she wondered
if it had been this way for Hugh Oxhine. She knew his
story, knew that in the course of the quest, Hugh had
lost his original drive to seek out only the creatures
who had murdered his family. She wondered now if
his interest in her had had anything to do with the
change in him, for she was acutely aware—had been
from the beginning—that she fascinated the Vandorian. But she had originally felt little more than
tolerance toward him, having room for devotion only
to those of her own race. History had proven outsid-
ers to be untrustworthy. And beyond this, the rigid
nature of the Vandorian had made him unappealing,
despite his pleasing physical appearance. But in the
past several days she had sensed the startling
changes that were occurring within him. And in the
first instant of her shock on hearing of Azira's death,
she had come within a fraction of seeking his comfort—and had seen clearly how deep his concern for
her had become. Now, she freely admitted to herself,
Zyra wished Hugh could be with her. The imperturb-
able strength of the archer was exactly what was
needed to cope with this maze she had gotten into.
Zyra chided herself, aware that the freedom and
action of an Amazon's life made her more vulnerable
than most to the claustrophobic effect of these dim
passages.

She detected a slight movement within the shadows ahead, and her lithe muscularity became suddenly tense, her mind suddenly alert. Sword ready,
she moved cautiously, her eyes directed toward the

spot of potential danger, so that she did not see the hidden Vilderones until it was too late. They attacked her suddenly from the alcove she was passing. There were two of them, grabbing her before she had the opportunity to use her deadly abilities with her sword. The blade was wrenched from her grasp, falling to the floor, echoing within the long corridor. Her arms were pinned behind her by the iron grips of the gargoyles, and she was helpless. Then, a white-and-black-clad figure smoothly emerged into the dim light from the shadows.

"Deciedon!" exclaimed Zyra.

"Yes. We meet again. I'm astounded at my good fortune..." He moved closer to her. "I was in need of a hostage—having apparently lost the one I had counted on—but I never dreamed that I would come across one so beautiful." He reached out and dropped his hand on her shoulder. She shrugged it off, her eyes burning. Her stare was murderous. He shook his head quizzically. "I don't understand it. Women have always been fascinated by me," he said, and he laughed lightly. "Well, no matter. You will change later, after we are long removed from this place. I fear that the tide has been turned, and I must seek a safer abode. You shall be my assurance that I find one," he concluded, with a flashing smile. "She is not to be underestimated," he said to the gargoyles that held her. "Bind her tightly... then bring her along."

Zyra's wrists were secured behind her with leather cords, and she was then forced forward, held between her Vilderone captors. But they had gone only a few paces when Zyra tensed instinctively at the hushed singing of a propelled arrow. One of the gargoyles emitted a short, choking cough, before falling heavily, an arrow having pierced the entire thickness of his neck. The other jerked around, pulling at his sword... only to suffer a similar fate, as a second deadly shot pierced his chest, knocking him backward, killing him almost instantly. Only twenty paces removed,

Hugh Oxhine had notched a third arrow with incredible speed, but it would not find its mark within the body of the White Elf traitor. He had moved almost as swiftly as Hugh. Rushing forward as the second of his henchmen fell, he grabbed the Amazon from behind, pushing the point of his long dagger—the same that had slain Shandar—against her throat.

"Drop your weapons, archer!" he shouted, "lest I run my blade through her lovely throat... No. Better yet, drop them all down through the opening of one of those shafts... there, just beyond you... Marvelous," he laughed, as Hugh began to comply with his demands. "Throw them all away... every one," the traitor demanded.

"No!" shouted Zyra, to the archer, "you must not submit. If you have consideration for me... then run this traitor through... no matter what the consequences!"

Deciedon laughed. "He cannot do that, my dear," he said confidently. "I can see his concern for you—even from here. Probably he thinks he loves you."

"You're right," said Hugh, and he spoke quietly, but his voice carried easily to them, "I do love her... and it no longer matters what she feels toward me." The last of his weapons had disappeared, and he moved toward them slowly. "Deciedon," he said, "allow Zyra to go free. I will not follow you. I have no feelings of vengefulness toward you. I've killed many times today—only moments ago—" He pointed toward the still forms. "I feel no need to bring you to justice... Please," he pleaded, "allow her to go free."

"Either you are more· naive than I thought," laughed the traitor, "or you think that I am... Stop! Come no closer. I and my beautiful hostage are about to depart." He began backing away, his blade pressed so hard against Zyra as to almost puncture her flesh. He glanced back. The exit he sought was almost gained.

"Please!" shouted Hugh. "Please set her free!"

Zyra's eyes filled with tears. "Hugh... " she whispered, speaking his name for the first time...

Deciedon's voice was mocking, "How touching! I would like to, archer, but I cannot. Gaze upon your loved one for the final time." The door was within reach, and he began to pull his hostage to it.

From out of the shadows beside the doorway flew a squat furry creature, grabbing hold of Deciedon's right arm, pulling the threatening blade away from the woman's throat. At almost the same instant, Zyra pulled free of the traitor's grasp, diving away. Hugh darted forward, racing toward the White Elf and the Gwarpy. Hugh was an instant too late—Oolu was thrown to the floor, and the razor-sharp dagger slashed across his chest. Then the Vandorian crashed into Deciedon. They both went down heavily, Deciedon rolled to his feet. The dagger had been sent flying, but his sword was at hand, and he pulled it from its scabbard. Hugh had risen to one knee. The sword was raised, but never struck. Zyra had run full tilt from the side. Deciedon did not even see her. Both her feet left the floor in a high leap, to strike his body. Deciedon was sent sprawling. Then Hugh was standing astride the Elf, pulling the weaponless traitor to his feet. Deciedon was white with terror. The Vandorian's fist smashed into his face, jolting him against the wall, where he slid to the floor. Now Hugh raised Deciedon's sword, stepping to the side of the prone figure. He looked down. Deciedon was cowering beneath him. "There is no need," said the archer, staring at the sword he held. He turned away.

Zyra was already kneeling beside the silent body of Oolu. Her eyes were frightened as she looked up. "He is not dead," she said, "but I fear he is more dead than alive...We must hurry!" Hugh bent behind her, cutting her bonds, then lifted Oolu gently, staring at him, searching for signs of life. Zyra held the sword in her hand, leading the way as they started down the corridor.

This time she would follow her instincts; they would

find their way out. They ran through the twisting hallways.

Deciedon sat alone, slumped against the iron wall, his knees drawn to his chest, his face buried in his arms. He was weeping bitterly, the entire facade of his life swept away in one crushing moment. Lost in despair, he did not notice the six gargoyles who entered the passageway.

There wasn't a single Vilderone who did not know of the White Elf Lejentor and secretly fear him. When the gargoyles saw Deciedon in this state of weakness their fear suddenly gave way to hate. In their rage the Vilderones knew that this puny White Elf had failed their lord Torgon and Golgorath. They sensed, also, that the end, their end, was near.

They moved in unison toward the defeated Elf, slowly raising the massive broadswords clenched in their fists.

The ominous throbbing drew Ailwon steadily toward its heart. He left his golden stallion to make its way back across the causeway and fought his way into the tower.

Then from deep within his brain there grew a sound like a distant whisper, beckoning him down a flight of winding stairs. The whisper grew into an insistent, almost unbearable clamor as Ailwon descended into the depths of the tower. At the bottom of the stairs a vast corridor stretched before him. He crept down the hall, which ended in a massive pentagonal door. Slowly he raised the point of Elvgard; a thousand years of longing were concentrated in this moment. As the sword touched the iron surface of the door there was a brilliant flare of light; the din in his mind ceased, the great door rumbled open, and the White Elf King entered the heart of Golgorath.

The everpresent throbbing drew Ailwon forward; he fought the languor it created in his mind. The slow pulse of death drew him to the center of the hall, Elvgard clenched in his hand, ever closer to the

Fulfillment of the seed planted countless centuries before his birth...

As he reached the center of the room, Ailwon noted the iron floor was made of five sections; he was standing at the point where they converged.

Suddenly, the floor beneath him began to open. Ailwon leaped aside, as the aperture continued to grow, yawning wider and wider, finally taking up one third of the floor. The Elf stared into the seething blackness. At the top of the stairs doors rumbled open revealing the silhouetted figure of Torgon, Death Lord of Gorgorath. He stood silent, staring down at Ailwon with burning eyes. The White Elf could scarcely comprehend that the enormous figure looming above him was a reality... that at last a thousand year Prophecy had brought him to this instant in time to stand before the Death Lord.

Torgon spoke, and his voice seemed to come from some fathomless depth: "Finally it has come. And now, that which is rightfully mine, I will have. I will take that which was denied me—my crown and my sword. And Urshurak—shall belong to me!"

For a moment Ailwon thought of making one final appeal to reason, but his mind mocked him at the absurdity of even entertaining such an idea. The unwavering resolve that had marked his movements since leaving Cryslandon had begun to dissipate in the presence of this ancient being. There was movement beneath Torgon's cloak as he lifted his arm. He held a huge and hideous mace, and the Elfin King was certain that he himself would not even be able to lift it. The movement of Torgon's arm had parted his outer garment, revealing the shining black of what might be armor. Ailwon took a deep breath: "Since it must be, let us finish it," he said. He moved forward, skirting the pentagram, and Torgon started down toward him, white eyes glowing. The White Elf Sevena was partway up the tiered steps when Torgon attacked, and instantly Ailwon was caught in the dark terror of a nightmare.

The cavernous room echoed to the rasping snarl of Torgon's lust, the hiss and crash of his whirling mace spewed showers of sparks and fragments of metal with each crushing impact. At first, the Elf King was unable to attempt even a single offensive thrust with his sword. He was forced into constant retreat, dodging the terrible force of the Death Lord's weapon. His shield was battered from his grasp. Elvgard clanged against the Death Lord's armor, sending up a shower of sparks. But the blow was light and glancing. Then Ailwon was being forced backward along the edge of the yawning, throbbing, whispering pit. Suddenly he stumbled off balance, watching with horror as the dark blur of the mace sped downward. He rolled his head, the blow striking only the curve of the Crownhelm, splitting it even as its power warded off the complete devastation that would have crushed Ailwon's head like an eggshell.

Even so, he was knocked sideways a half dozen paces, falling heavily. Sparks of brilliant light danced wildly within his brain. He tried to rise, but could not. His scalp was split, and blood poured from the wound. The Crownhelm had fallen and rolled to the edge of the abyss. He heard the guttural sound of Torgon's laughter, which grew until it was raucous with mockery and with triumph.

Then—from deep within the White Elf King—came the clear voices of the sorcerer and the wizard, and the united voice of all whom he had loved and who loved him. The clarion call infused his being with a flow of power that would not be denied. The gleaming blade of Elvgard lay beside him, and he reached out, grasping its golden handle. Through the crimson haze of his blood, he saw the huge form of the Death Lord moving slowly toward him, and he struggled to his feet...

Crouched and steady, the Elf King watched his adversary, saw the great mace lifted for a death blow, and, holding Elvgard double-handed, Ailwon ran in under the whirling mace to strike. The great sword

struck hard and flared with lightning. The Death Lord
staggered. Ailwon was knocked spinning as Elvgard
arced high, hovered shimmering, and then plunged
into the abyss. Instantly the floor heaved, groaning,
and as the Death Lord tried to keep his balance, the
Crownhelm rolled and caught in his feet. With an
unearthly scream, Torgon fell into the whispering
blackness below and the Crownhelm went with him.

The Death Lord, Elvgard and the Crownhelm were
together at last—the Prophecy fulfilled.

For an endless moment, the White Elf King stood
staring into the emptiness below. The whispering
voices and throbbing ceased, and it grew deadly
quiet. Then from the depths of the pit a terrible roar
began to grow. The floor began to shake and a
column of flame exploded from the pit, throwing
Ailwon to the wall.

The first violent quake of the tower flung her hard
against the wall, pain searing through her shoulder. A
portion of wall burst inward, spewing flaming fragments across the floor, lighting the corridor. There
was a pause, then a quivering of the foundation
began, foretelling the impending eruptions. Ahead,
Gwynn could see the black pentagram of the open
entranceway, and she ran toward it, leaping across
the burning floor. As she approached she could hear
the growing sounds from within, like the sound of a
gathering storm. She felt a frigid draft, carrying the
pungent odor of sulphurous fumes from the dark. As
she reached the entrance, she could see the obscure
shape, moving toward her... parting the gloom with
the whiteness of its form... and then Ailwon stood
before her.

He leaned against the iron side of the entrance,
staring down at his blood-smeared hands, his chest
rising and falling heavily. Blood ran from a deep gash
beneath his blond hair, streaming down his face. His
armor and tunic were torn and ripped, his left
shoulder sagged limply. He looked at Gwynn, and his

eyes were childlike with disbelief:

"It is over."

He stepped toward her, and she caught him in her
arms, kissing the tears that ran down his blood-
smeared cheeks. "We must go," she said urgently.
"This terrible place is certain to claim us yet." He
nodded and they ran down the corridor to the twisting
stairwell, hearing the rising angry lament behind
them, feeling the increase of the shuddering movements beneath them...

They emerged into the upper hall of the Death Lord
only a moment before an enormous eruption from
below. They were knocked to the floor by the blast,
which shattered the throne of Torgon, dropping it to
the erupting pit below as the center of the floor caved
in.

Chunks of stone and iron were blasted into the
upper reaches of the cavernous room, then showered
across the floor. But fortunately, the prone figures of
the Elves were not struck by any of the larger fragments. They scrambled to their feet, running again—
now up the corridor. The entire structure shook from
the violence of another eruption. The length of the
corridor rose up before them, bending, splitting, a
nightmare iron snake with a life of its own. They
pulled themselves upward on their knees. They rose
and leaped, scarcely clearing the hissing abyss...
landing, scrambling again to their feet. On they ran,
nearing the open entrance. They could hear the
voices of the thousands, as friend and foe sought
frantically to escape the destruction of the Crater of
Death... Then the voices were lost to an enormous
groan and cracking of iron and stone... Gwynn and
Ailwon emerged from the tower just as the long
causeway collapsed, crumbling, roaring to the crater
floor two hundred feet below.

They stood staring, disbelieving. A quarter mile of
space denied them their escape. All around them, the
demise of Golgorath continued, dying with angry
bursts and eruptions, disgorging the excrement of its

hate in geysers of flaming gases. The great walls of the fortress began to crumble inward, and then the enormous circular tiers began to crack and slant, sending those slain in battle sliding and tumbling from the edges. Gwynn and Ailwon clung to one another, standing at the jagged edge of the remains of the causeway. All around them, the lightning was being drawn toward the dying power of Golgorath. A tremendous bolt forked downward. The tower behind them shuddered, cracked. An enormous section was severed, and fell into the erupting pit. Aliwon and Gwynn resigned themselves to their certain fate.

Then, through the clouds of smoke, through the sulphuric bursts and lurid glare, a pure white form drifted toward them, great wings moving gracefully, propelling the equestrian body: the Pegasus...Elgan! The two lovers cried out joyfully, as the flying horse glided down...

Zyra pleaded desperately with the Dwarfs: "There is nothing more that you can do. You must flee with us to safety! Discarding your own lives will not save them, and you don't know positively that they did not escape..."

"No!" shouted Erbin tearfully. "They are still there! I know it!"

The Dwarf contingent—Erbin and Evrawk and Esrund, Wilda and Nolan...and now Ferda—had fled with the others, out of the crater, beyond the crumbling outer walls. But there they had stopped, as the multitudes streamed past them across the plain, fleeing toward the safety of the rocky inclines that lay to the southeast. The Dwarfs had held firm, waiting, hoping that by some miracle Ailwon and Gwynn would emerge from the dying crater at the last instant. Here Zyra and Hugh—carrying the unconscious Oolu—had reached them, urging them to flee before it was too late.

"I can't wait any longer!" shouted the archer angrily, "your friend is dying...he needs help—quickly! He will need us all!" He looked at Zyra, and began to run toward safety. The Amazon gave the Dwarfs one last desperate look, imploring them to follow... then she, too, started across the plain.

The Dwarfs looked grief-stricken, from one to the other. Old Esrund asked the question: "Ailwon... Gwynn... Oolu... Shandar... the young lads... was it worth this?"

No one answered, and they turned sadly to seek the safety of higher ground—all except one. Nolan had spotted something emerging from the fiery bursts and billowing smoke. He rubbed his good eye, and blinked. It was no mirage, "Look!" he shrieked. "Look! It's a brown-eyed, bleeding miracle!"

"By Gawl!" shouted Evrawk.

"By Gawl!" shouted Erbin... and Esrund... and Wilda... and Ferda... and Nolan, who had spotted it first. They shouted and waved as the white Pegasus—bearing its precious riders—passed above them. A gigantic burst within the crater knocked them to the ground. The fissures in the ground cracked wider, tearing jagged wounds in the surrounding land. The Dwarfs ran for the safety of the hills.

Some distance ahead of them, Tark-Volmar and Ali Ben Kara struggled toward safety—the Norseman being supported by the Azmurian. "Couldn't you have avoided that falling chunk of iron, Volmar?" Ben Kara panted, "you weigh a veritable ton."

"If I could've avoided the damn thing, I'd have avoided the damn thing!" growled the Norseman. "I've gotta admit, though, that I could shed some of this poundage... I'm going to give up drinking!" he declared resolutely. At that moment, the flying horse passed over them, and Ben Kara looked up. His mouth fell open and he stopped dead in his tracks. Tark-Volmar followed the direction of his stare.

"By thunder!" the Norse chieftain bellowed, "I've been struck delirious by my wound... hurry up, Ben Kara—get me somewhere where I can find a good, stiff drink!"

Behind them dark clouds churned furiously. Lightning forked the sky, striking again and again at the crumbling tower. The ground heaved and in one final cataclysmic throe blew outward, revealing the very bowels of the earth. Churning clouds plunged into the abyss.

The allied armies were gathered in safety atop the Black Mountains, where they could see a great wave gathering force on the horizon. It roared over the flaming abyss and crashed against the rocks below.

It was many hours before the raging sea and sky subsided, until a single ray of light shone down on the calm waters which now covered Golgorath.

Elgan touched the closed eyes of the dying Gwarpy, calling forth his every remaining power...

33

CELEBRATION

Opposite: Hugh Departs Cryslandon

The intermittent falling of spring rain had failed to dampen a moment of the joy that now ran rampant throughout Cryslandon and the surrounding Arbroic Hills. Jubilant word of the Fulfillment had preceded the return of the allied armies, and by the time they reached the White Elf city, there were thousands to cheer them. The celebration had been going on for days... reaching its apex on this final evening.

It had drizzled throughout most of the day, but had stopped in late afternoon, and now the evening sky was startlingly clear and the stars were brilliant. The sound of festivities spread out for miles. It arose from the hills where the bright orange of small fires marked the campsites of revelers, it arose from nearly the entire area within the half-crumbled city walls, and it resounded from the great circular courtyard surrounding the Tower of Enlightenment. Musicians from all the nations of Urshurak played instruments brought from the four corners of the continent. It was a sound never before heard in all of Cryslandon! Dancers shuffled and stomped, jumped and skipped to the rhythms of the tireless musicians. With locked hands and laughing faces, they wove between long wooden dining tables and roaring cooking fires, urged on by boisterous onlookers. When the dancers became exhausted, they traded places with the onlookers, and the dancing went on. The great courtyard was a living tapestry of color and light and joyful sound.

None were more buoyant nor happier than the young lovers, Gwynn and Ailwon. Time and again, either he or she was urged to give a rousing speech or a stirring account of their ordeals. But each time, both refused—though with the best of humor. Ailwon—directed from birth toward the grimmest of tasks—was now diverting his every energy to the development of the fine art of merrymaking...while Gwynn was determined to influence her lover a step beyond merrymaking...

All present were, of course, hard-pressed to surpass the Dwarfs... Their sacred motto: "Freedom—Solidarity—Tomfoolery," gave hard evidence of how seriously they undertook the joyful task of having fun. Wherever a cluster of them were gathered, there was laughter and droll good humor, lively games and subtle pranks, dancing, debating and drinking. Black-patched Nolan, the red-haired Wilda and raspy-voiced Ferda indulged themselves in an endless series of toasts to good health and good fortune, and an endless draining and refilling of their beer mugs. Erbin seemed completely content to enjoy the revelry of his companions, while he himself sat smiling, expounding on the quieter pleasures of life, his feet propped up, his hands clasped behind his head—and his jaws working steadily on a wad of Bobabo leaves.

Several tables were occupied by throngs of Amazons, Azmurians and Norsepeople—a mixture of races that would previously have produced bickering and quarreling, at the least. But now the most severe conflicts were exchanges of good-natured ribbing. Ali Ben Kara stood, calling for the attention of those surrounding him. "I wish to make an announcement," he said, "in regard to what I believe to be a magnificent first step toward refinement, and perhaps the diluting of an often uncontrollable bad temper."

Tark-Volmar, who, along with his wife, Asar, was sitting beside Ben Kara, paused in the midst of the demolition of an enormous chunk of meat. He started up at the Azmurian Shakín suspiciously. Ben Kara continued: "This noble chieftain beside me, Tark-Volmar, in exchange for the gallant support of his people during the quest for Fulfillment, has secured from me the guarantee that I will teach him how to—" he paused "—paint pictures."

"Damn it, Ben Kara," thundered Volmar, in the midst of some subdued snickering and guffaws from his countrymen, "you swore you wouldn't tell!"

"That's true, my friend. But just how long did you intend to keep this a secret? And beyond this, I believe you are doomed to failure if you continue to regard your participation in art as a diminishing of your robust image." Volmar considered this for a minute, grunted and nodded in agreement.

His wife stared at him in astonishment at the disclosure of the secret, and continued to do so. The blustery Norseman stared back. "What's so surprising, Asar?" he demanded, "what's so amazing about me becoming a little cultured and refined?" He returned to his hunk of meat, tearing the final chunk of flesh away, and flipping the bone over his shoulder. He wiped the grease from his lips with the back of his thick hand, and took an enormous swig of ale, losing portions of it within the red-orange of his beard. He was aware of—but refused to acknowledge—the thinly disguised amusement of his Azmurian friend beside him.

The most subdued of the revelers were the Andeluvians, who were, nonetheless, enjoying themselves in a quiet way. Their King, Zarin, had discovered a new friend: the Dwarf, Esrund. The two were evidently deep in a philosophical discussion, in regard to the challenge of the reality of a reign of peace. Zarin, relaxed and serene, accompanied his conversation with gentle sips of a freshly discovered pleasure: a frothing mug of beer from Penderak... while

Esrund puffed contentedly on his long-stemmed
black pipe.

From the Tower of Enlightenment, unnoticed at first
by the happy throng, two figures approached the
festivities. One was tall and lean; the other short and
squat, and his bandy legs carried him somewhat
gingerly. Then the pair stepped into the light of a
cooking fire, and a roaring cheer went up from the
people. The wizard, Elgan, had arrived, and with him
was the heroic Gwarpy, Oolu! Now a throng was on
their feet, cheering wildly. Oolu, grinning a bit shyly,
was ushered to a place of honor. It was the first time
that he was able to join the celebration, and, most
importantly, it would be the first solid meal of his
convalescence, having been nursed for several days
on Elgan's herbal brew. Now a huge platter, heaped
high with steaming hot vegetables, roots and grain
was placed before him. The Gwarpy practically dived
into it. He ate and ate, chortling with extreme satisfaction. At last Elgan was asked to speak, on this last
night of celebration. The wizard rose and stood
quiet... while beside him the furry creature ate without pause, though he constrained his chortles in
deference to the old man's message. Elgan's voice
rang out across the court, and beyond, to the
hundreds of suddenly hushed revelers.

"Fortunately for all who are gathered," he began, "I
have but one thing that I wish to point out—and it is as
much a reminder to me as it is to you. The Fulfillment
of the Prophecy has promised that there will be no
more wars, and for this we may rejoice. A new day of
openness *has* dawned. But the brightness of this day,
and the length of its duration, is to be determined by
us. Now, it is up to us—*all* of us, my very dear
friends—to insure that the world that is Urshurak...
remains forever free." The old wizard sat down. The
throng was silent for only a moment, and then the
roar of their acclamation resounded into the night
air. The festivities resumed and Oolu continued eating... chortling... eating...

There was one last conflict to be resolved, and a crowd of Dwarfs had gathered to witness the drama. At the center of the onlookers, Esrund of the House of Uxmun and his wife, Maude, were again matched in the long running struggle to establish supremacy in arm wrestling. They had both agreed that this would be their final contest, as they were growing too old for a continuation of these shenanigans. The final match was fierce. Their short, thick arms bulged with the effort. Their faces grew redder and redder. Neither could budge the other. Suddenly Maude's eyes grew wide, shifting beyond the face of her husband. "Hey!" she shouted, "You can't take that beer...That belongs to Esrund!"

The old Dwarf leader jerked his head around, relaxing his dueling arm. Maude slammed his hand against the table. "There!" she exulted, "we're even up! And I...am the final champeen!" She stood, and began to limp away, chuckling loudly. Esrund limped after her, sputtering and fuming, and demanding a rematch to decide once and for all...

Very late, the Vandorian and the Amazon Queen left the festivities to spend their final moments together alone. They walked through the city, crossed the bridge and left through the southeast gatehouse, climbing a grassy hill to the top, where they could look down upon the city and upon the beginning of the River Garnon. They stood beneath a great cypress, saying very little, avoiding the inevitable. Finally, Hugh turned to look at Zyra. The clarity of the starlit night outlined the superb symmetry of her profile. The crisp breeze blew her dark hair, and her crimson cloak. The music of the city drifted up to them. Hugh spoke. "Is it still your decision that we must part tomorrow?"

"No, Hugh," she said quickly turning to him, "it is *our* decision. It is as difficult for me as it is for you. The facts have been clearly stated many times in the past few days—by *both* of us. Neither of us is prepared to sacrifice what lies immediately ahead for the sake of remaining together. My first commitment is to my sisters... and to myself. I am not ready to relinquish the challenge that destiny has placed in my path. I am not ready to forsake the leadership of my race. The feelings that I have for you are completely new to my experience. I am in no way prepared to forsake all that I have been to follow you about, as you go in search of the Urshurak that has opened before you. I say this, despite my enormous curiosity for all that I have not seen... and my deep love for you." She smiled as she said the last, reaching up, touching his cheek.

"I know," he said, resignedly, "none of this needs repeating. But somehow it seemed that if it were stated once more, perhaps the sadness of my heart could be reasoned away by the logic of my mind..." Tears shone in his eyes, "Once again, my heart has disdained my logic."

"Hugh," she whispered, "I was about to tell you of a decision I have come to... but you are starting to cry, I do not want to deny you it. How long has it been since you have cried?"

"I don't remember... not since I was a boy, I suppose..." he said softly, and Zyra held him. "Please," he said, "tell me what you were about to say..."

"I was going to say that Zan-Dura would never again be as it was before. It will no longer be cloistered—shut off from the rest of the continent. The traditions that we have clung to for centuries will be examined—all of them. I was going to tell you that I have decided to reword our sacred chant. It will now sound like this." Her voice was soft as she sang it:

"*Lorin-tor-est-oh-vel-oh.*" She looked up at him and her eyes were extremely dark and soft. "The meaning of this is: 'In the love of *all* there is the perfect love...'. Perhaps someday... perhaps..."

She did not have to finish the sentence. Hugh bent to kiss her, and together they sank to the cool dampness of the grass.

34

URSHURAK

Hugh was surprised and disappointed to learn that the wizard had already left the city. He'd been given assurances that Elgan would be with the others to exchange farewells before Hugh departed that morning. The archer had awakened and was dressed even before the first traces of dawn. He had eaten quickly, and had gone to secure Santor. After saddling the big stallion and tying his bedroll behind, he'd led the horse back to the courtyard of the Tower of Enlightenment.

Those who had become his fast friends during the time of the quest awaited him. Zyra was not with them. She had left the day after their parting, sealed in bittersweet joy on the little hilltop above Cryslandon. And now he found that Elgan was already gone.

"The wizard said to tell you that he'd see you again before very long," said Erbin.

"I don't know how that will come about," said Hugh, a bit sadly, "but he must have had his reasons for leaving without saying farewell. I suppose I might see him again...sometime." He looked at each of them. They were gathered in a half-circle about him. "...Well," he said awkwardly, "I guess there's no need to prolong this. I will say good-bye, now."

Tark-Volmar was the first to step forward. "I'd always heard," he said, "that Vandorians were grubbing mercenaries but if you're typical of your race, then what I'd heard was the worst pack of damn lies that was ever spread." He gripped Hugh's hand tightly. "I'll miss ya, Hugh."

"As I will you, Tark-Volmar. I'm pleased beyond words to know you as a friend."

Ali Ben Kara was next. "You are a tribute to the wisdom of the beloved Shandar," he said. "To witness the startling changes in you is to have understood the reality that all strive to exceed their present form—and sometimes one succeeds." The Azmurian and the Vandorian embraced.

"You shrugged off my first attempt at gratitude," said Ailwon, who stood beside Gwynn, "but I will offer it again... For without you, my friend, none of this would have been possible."

"And I want to add," said Gwynn, smiling, "that I think I can understand Queen Zyra's decision to return to Zan-Dura with her sisters—but I can't imagine a more difficult choice than the one she was faced with."

Hugh laughed lightly. "I thank you both for your generosity," he clasped hands with both, "and I wish you every happiness... until we all meet again." He turned to the Dwarfs. "It won't be long before we shall see one another, for I'm anxious to visit Penderak and share an evening with you at the Tavern-Meet that I've heard so much about."

"We'll sure be waiting for you, Hugh," declared Evrawk, "An', by Gawl," said Erbin. "I'm still waiting to hear the tales of the battles at the Pass of Camen, and of the heroics of Rolmar and Dunstan."

"An' ol' Hugh hadn't orta ferget that he's promised ol' Oolu," chimed in the Gwarpy, "thet he'll be visitin' ol' Oolu come nex' spring durin' the Rite of the Bobabos...yep."

Hugh laughed. "Well, by the great names of Rolmar and Dunstan, you'll find me in Penderak before long... and in Loamend, come next spring!" He bent down. The Dwarfs and the Gwarpy clung to the broad shoulders of the tall man, the spirit of their friendship coursing between them.

Hugh straightened. "Until I see you again," he said, "I will miss you all." He turned quickly, swinging into the saddle, and without looking back he urged Santor to a trot, disappearing from view beyond a battered structure—a reminder of the struggle against the oppression.

Hugh was now anxious to be on his way. He was soon crossing the blue waters that extended from Lake Gorheim. Daybreak danced across the rippling water. A cool breeze continued to hold back the heat of the first days of summer, and the morning was coming on, brisk and clear. Hugh trotted through fields rich with the life brought to them by the previous days of rain. An endless variety of insects already flitted through the wet green of tall grasses. Small birds chirped from the branches of scattered trees, fluttering back and forth among them. Dragonflies droned above him as the archer followed the winding dirt road toward the west. Slowing to a walk, he started into the hills, passing between campsites on both sides of the road. The camps were, for the most part, silent—after the days of revelry. But there was an occasional stirring among them, and the clear air carried rich smells of breakfast from isolated cooking fires.

The road led Hugh into a small wooded area of poplars and maples, into the soft shadows of early summer. The dirt road now became a path, climbing and descending as the wooded land slanted and rolled. The Vandorian had no quarrel with Santor's slow pace, as he drank in the serenity of the land. The path led into a small, active river, emerging again on the far side. Hugh allowed his horse to stop in the center, where the animal dipped his muzzle, drinking pleasurably. The archer listened to the music of the rapid water as it passed over the larger rocks and around the branches extending into the stream from a fallen tree.

"The stream seems pleased, doesn't it, that it has been fed so amply by the rains of recent days?"

The voice—set against the calm of the woodland—startled Hugh, though Santor appeared unaffected and continued his drinking. The wizard sat upon the moss-covered log on the opposite side, and the Vandorian wondered how he could possibly have missed seeing the old man.

Hugh recovered from his surprise, and smiled slightly. "I take it this is purely a chance meeting?" he asked.

"Well, not completely. I had a sense that you might be passing this way. There are other roads, but this just had the look of the one that you would choose. I, like you, had a need to be on my way, so I decided to say my good-byes to you out here."

Elgan chuckled. He stood, and stretched, then fetched up his walking staff. "Come," he said, "I can go with you a short distance if you wish."

Hugh urged his horse from the river, dismounted, and they proceeded down the path together, soon emerging from the wooded area into the light of the ascending sun. "Ah," sighed Elgan, "never has my body felt so light as today. I believe the reality of the Fulfillment has finally set in."

"I've heard," said the archer, "that you'll return to Mowdra. What will you do then? It seems that you are one who so enjoys the company of others. Will you get along all right by yourself?"

"Oh, I will get along nicely. There will be occasional visits from old friends... and when those occur I'll make the utmost of them." The old man chuckled before continuing, "You're right, Hugh: I *am* one who enjoys company immensely. But, like so many things, the opposite is equally true, and I shall also enjoy my solitude as I pass through my final years." He came to a stop, and Santor stopped behind them without any command from Hugh. Elgan pointed toward the south where, not too far away, the great forest began to gather its forces. "I am going to leave you in a moment or two..." he said. He looked directly at the tall man beside him. "I must say, also, that I do not feel that I will ever be completely alone again. And for an aged being such as myself, this is a most comforting feeling. At Mowdra I shall be able to experience the crisp awareness and serenity of solitude...and at the same time experience the loving presence of another." The wizard's eyes began to glisten, and his face reflected the joy of his words: "Shandar—my ancient friend—has bequeathed to me the greatest of gifts. He has left me his never-ending love. The touch of his hand is everywhere. He is more alive now than ever..." The wizard gestured toward the forest, where it merged with the open ground. "I can see his love as it emerges from the soft shadows into the sunlight. And I can feel it as warmth touches my skin. I can feel the love in the gentleness of this breeze. And when it storms, I will feel his love in the power of the wind. I will feel it in the moisture of the rain, in the crisp cold of snow..." The wizard pointed ahead. "Can you see, Hugh, how there is love and power in the way that road curves through the roll of the land? In the purple of the distant mountains, with the light of the rising sun upon them. In this is the love that is Shandar—all around us—in the incredible variety that together creates the marvelous unity of life and death—in this is the everlasting reality of the being who was my friend—and still is." He paused for a moment. "I know now that his entire life was both a fulfillment of his birth and a preparation for his death. And he could die so joyfully for he realized he was to be reborn into all of this." His old eyes swept the landscape. Then he sighed serenely, and began to fish within his worn robe for his pipe, finally producing and packing it.

Hugh watched the wizard as he took his time about firing the pipe. Then the archer felt a lift of joy as the significance of Elgan's words settled into him. "I can see," he said, "that you will get along extremely well. And, of course, you always have your workings of enchantment to entertain yourself—just in case boredom should ever confront you."

Elgan puffed away, smoke beginning to curl upward from the pipe bowl. "No," he said, shaking his
head, "my magic has left me. It was within me for a
purpose, and it is now gone—as the Crownhelm and
Elvgard are gone, and the necessity for armaments
and warfare are gone. My days of wizardry are over."
Despite himself, the old man sounded wistful. He
puffed energetically on the pipe, evidently to cover
some embarrassment at such an unseemly feeling.
The shapes became more fantastic: winged unicorns,
griffons and other creatures of legend. Now they were
huge, moving about in directions according to their
own inclinations, performing a stately pavane in the
clear stillness of the air. The Vandorian was laughing,
but Elgan watched them in utter amazement. "This,"
he said, "just bears out what a very wise being once
told me—'Despite all of our wisdom and knowledge
and the ability to figure things out and to make
logical choices, it is still a fact that at any given instant
in time, none of us has the slightest notion of what is
going on.'" He bent down, scooping up a handful of
black earth, crumbling it in his hand, then brushing
his hands together.

"I met a young woman—at Zan-Dura—" said Hugh,
"who spent a good deal of her time taking pleasure
from the feel of the earth, as you just now did."

"Yes. Oolu told me about her. She is apparently a
very wise and intuitive person. As for my doing it—"the
old man reflected, "I think I wanted you to feel that
part of me that is in the land—as we shake hands
before we part." Then the wizard turned away, walking
slowly toward the forest, planting his long staff deliberately, puffs of pipe smoke drifting along above him.
He paused, and turned. "Perhaps someday you'll visit
me… perhaps on your way to Zan-Dura." He turned
away again, chuckling with satisfaction. Hugh smiled
as he watched the wizard leave, watching until the tall
figure disappeared within the shadows of the forest.

The Vandorian mounted and spoke to Santor. The horse moved forward along the narrow road that curved toward the west. The land rolled bright green into the hills, and beyond was the soft blue of distant mountains. It was almost completely clear overhead where a hawk hung lazily in the morning sky, and above the mountains were great piles of white clouds. Hugh turned in the saddle. Behind him—to the east—was Cryslandon, the white and gold of the tower dazzling beneath the sun. The Vandorian turned back, flipping the reins against Santor's shoulder, and the big horse increased his gait. He gave the animal full rein. Santor stretched his muscles to a spirited gallop, and they rode into the immense openness of Urshurak.

AUTHORS' NOTE

Urshurak came into existence with the help of many people. It was originally conceived by us and developed further in a conversation with Ian Summers one day at the Society of Illustrators.

From the beginning, we conceived Urshurak as both a book and a film. We made about a thousand story board drawings telling the tale. With these drawings as a basis for our story, we contacted an old friend from Detroit, Jerry Nichols, and asked him to help us write the book. Jerry wrote six pages and sent them to us. They were perfect. The book was underway.

We continued to develop Urshurak as a film and involved three friends who are musical composers: Bill McGuire, Dominic Tombro and Dale Trimmer. Through their original compositions the story continued to grow.

It took two years from the point of conception to the printing of the first edition. During this time literally thousands of drawings were made. The visuals, in combination with the music and the words, formed the basis for the writing of many drafts of the manuscript. Civilizations were developed and destroyed—an entire continent was created.

Without the close collaboration of all involved, this book could never have come into being.

—THE BROTHERS HILDEBRANDT—